The Queen's Rival

"Made me fall in love with Diane Haeger's gift for storytelling all over again . . . an impeccably written piece of prose."

—Historically Obsessed (5/5)

"It's official—Diane Haeger is one of my favorite authors. I love her ongoing series about Henry VIII's court, and *The Queen's Rival* was no disappointment. I read it in less than twenty-four hours. . . . Four and a half stars to a well-written and very interesting book. *Definitely* recommended to all lovers of the Tudors and romantic historical fiction."

—Fresh Off the Shelf

"Brings to life one of the lesser-known but no less interesting figures in one of history's most dynamic and intriguing times. As a fan of English history, I have read tons of books surrounding this time period, and Diane Haeger promises to become one of my favorite authors."

—Night Owl Reviews (top pick)

"The author brought history to life with this story. The descriptions of court life, the beautiful gowns, and the intrigues were fantastic. In truth I did not want this story to end."   —To Read or Not to Read

"Bessie . . . [brings] freshness as a rarely used (if ever) character in engaging biographical fiction."   —*Midwest Book Review*

"Haeger plots swiftly and fills the court with a plausible cast of characters."   —*Publishers Weekly*

continued . .

The Queen's Mistake

"Haeger's characters, even her minor ones, have a certain depth that's often lacking in novels that trod this well-traveled ground, and she handles the love affair between Catherine and Thomas Culpeper skillfully and sympathetically." —*Historical Novels Review*

"Fans will enjoy Diane Haeger's take on sixteenth-century aristocratic permissiveness." —*Genre Go Round Reviews*

"Fans of tales of royalty will find Haeger's novel both historically accurate and sympathetically written." —*Fresh Fiction*

The Secret Bride

"Haeger delivers complexities of court and duty plausibly and with aplomb." —*Publishers Weekly*

"Haeger masterfully brings the past alive in her latest historical novel. A tale of thwarted desire and sacrifice, it is rich in court intrigue and lavishly detailed descriptions of court life during the early years of Henry VIII's reign. Both fans of Haeger and readers new to her novels will relish her insightful story about the one woman Henry truly loved: his sister." —*Booklist*

"An enjoyable, well-written book about one of history's true love stories." —*Romance Reviews Today*

Other Historical Novels
by Diane Haeger

"In Haeger's impressive Restoration romance, King Charles II and his mistress . . . leap off the page. . . . Charles and Nell are marvelously complex—jealous and petty, devoted yet fallible. Haeger perfectly balances the history with the trystery."   —*Publishers Weekly*

"Engagingly deep romantic historical fiction."   —*Midwest Book Review*

"Romantic . . . filled with intrigue and danger."   —*The Indianapolis Star*

"Set against the vivid descriptive detail of Rome and Trastevere, Haeger's tale of how the ring came to be obscured in the Raphael masterpiece resonates with the grandeur and intimacy of epic love stories. . . . This romance is first to be savored as the wonderful historical tale that it is."
                                                                —*BookPage*

"Lush . . . rich yet fast-paced story."   —*Historical Novels Review*

"Spectacular . . . Haeger explores the fascinating, rich, exciting, and tragic life of Henry II's beloved. . . . Lush in characterization and rich in historical detail, *Courtesan* will sweep readers up into its pages and carry them away."   —*Romantic Times*

"With her wealth of detail cleverly interwoven into a fabulous plot, Diane Haeger has written a triumphant tale that will provide much delight to fans of historical fiction and Regency romance."   —*Affaire de Coeur*

NEW AMERICAN LIBRARY NOVELS
BY DIANE HAEGER

The Queen's Rival
The Queen's Mistake
The Secret Bride

I, Jane

IN THE COURT OF HENRY VIII

DIANE HAEGER

NEW AMERICAN LIBRARY

New American Library
Published by New American Library,
a division of Penguin Group (USA) Inc.,
375 Hudson Street, New York, New York 10014, USA
Penguin Group (Canada), 90 Eglinton Avenue East, Suite 700, Toronto,
Ontario M4P 2Y3, Canada (a division of Pearson Penguin Canada Inc.)
Penguin Books Ltd., 80 Strand, London WC2R 0RL, England
Penguin Ireland, 25 St. Stephen's Green, Dublin 2,
Ireland (a division of Penguin Books Ltd.)
Penguin Group (Australia), 250 Camberwell Road, Camberwell,
Victoria 3124, Australia (a division of Pearson Australia Group Pty. Ltd.)
Penguin Books India Pvt. Ltd., 11 Community Centre,
Panchsheel Park, New Delhi - 110 017, India
Penguin Group (NZ), 67 Apollo Drive, Rosedale, Auckland 0632,
New Zealand (a division of Pearson New Zealand Ltd.)
Penguin Books (South Africa) (Pty.) Ltd., 24 Sturdee Avenue,
Rosebank, Johannesburg 2196, South Africa

Penguin Books Ltd., Registered Offices:
80 Strand, London WC2R 0RL, England

First published by New American Library,
a division of Penguin Group (USA) Inc.

First Printing, September 2012
1 3 5 7 9 10 8 6 4 2

NAL REGISTERED TRADEMARK—MARCA REGISTRADA
LIBRARY OF CONGRESS CATALOGING-IN-PUBLICATION DATA:
Haeger, Diane.
I, Jane : in the court of Henry VIII / Diane Haeger.
p. cm.
ISBN 978-0-451-23789-7
1. Jane Seymour, Queen, consort of Henry VIII, King of England, 1509–1537—Fiction.
2. Henry VIII, King of England, 1491–1547—Fiction.   3. Great Britain—History—
Henry VIII, 1509–1547—Fiction. I. Title.
PS3558.A32125I15 2012
813'.54—dc23
2012013251

Set in Simoncini Garamond   •   Designed by Elke Sigal

Printed in the United States of America

PUBLISHER'S NOTE

For my dear friend Karen Thorne Isé

Acknowledgments

This journey with Jane has been a true joy for me, and for helping me along that journey I have many people to thank:

Dr. Bill Creasy, for graciously clarifying issues regarding the religious themes and religious works during the Renaissance. Helen and Phlippe Tartavull, for their many years of generous assistance with all things French.

Jhanteigh Kupihea, my incredible and gifted editor, for patience and continued care with my words. Working with you is a true privilege.

Irene Goodman, my truly amazing literary agent, for so many years of encouragement, direction, and unfailing belief in me. Our shared love of France, travel, and the historical novel continue to be a great inspiration.

Kelly Stevens Costello. Your friendship and support are gifts for which I am thankful every single day.

Ken, Elizabeth, and Alex, my wonderful family. As always, you are my light, my purpose, and my anchor, without whom . . . ah, but then that would have been impossible!

According to historians, the details of Jane Seymour's childhood have been a mystery for ages. *The Oxford Dictionary of National Biography*, as well as Dr. Pamela Gross, associate professor of history at Adams State College—herself a descendant of Jane Seymour—and other scholars consulted for this work, find there is no record of the birth or baptism of Jane Seymour or her siblings. Dates given in historical works are based on scant evidence. Jane is thought by most to have been born between 1505 and 1509, and while I have consulted many sources, there is no absolute consensus. Thus, for the purposes of this work, I have chosen the year 1505. The few clues that history has left us about her early life, including her years at Wolf Hall and her brief engagement to William Dormer, were used as threads to weave this beautiful tale lost to time.

Accept the things to which fate binds you,
and love the people with whom fate brings you
together, but do so with all of your heart.

—MARCUS AURELIUS

I, Jane

Prologue

October 24, 1537
Hampton Court

"*Q*uickly, fetch pen and ink and some paper, Anne, for I will soon die."

Jane murmured the declaration to her brother's wife, already knowing the truth. Anne Seymour had been sitting vigil at her bedside, cloaked in the amber glow of a candle and the dark and shadows beyond the swagged bed curtain. Everyone else had gone to bed, so it was just the two of them now. They had been reminiscing as wind and cold English rain beat hard against the window glass.

"You'll not die; such a thing is unimaginable!" Anne replied a little too vehemently for the truth that lay before them.

"Yet there is much to life that happens, whether we can imagine it or not. And death still comes to each of us . . . So you must write it down, Anne, all that I am telling you. I know Hal well enough, and there shall be another queen soon after me—another mother for my son. I want my precious Edward to have this much of his real mother. I want him to know about my life. I fear this shall be the only way. I shall talk for as long as I can, and you shall write it all down."

Tears glistened in Anne Seymour's weary eyes. "It shall be done, Your Majesty."

"Every word of it, Anne, do you promise?"

". . . Even about William?"

"Especially about William," Jane said with a sigh as memories flooded her mind at the sound of his name. "Few know of him, especially in relation to me, so the words shall be William's legacy as well as my own."

"Will the king not be very angry with you if we do this?" the languid-looking blue-eyed woman dared to ask. She leaned forward into the light, revealing her stiff, embroidered white collar and pearl necklace, which hung over the tightly laced bodice of her gown, so she would not be overheard if there were spies about. Usually there were.

"In another day or so I think it shall matter very little who is angry with me but the wood and the worms."

Anne gasped. "Oh, sister, please speak not of such things, I bid you!"

Jane glanced over to the small cradle she insisted on having beside her, where her days-old infant son lay peacefully sleeping. "Now it only matters to me that he, whom I so dearly love, knows how little Jane Seymour of Wiltshire—who might have been Lady Dormer—came to be Jane, Queen of England, instead. The story shall be my legacy to him. That I lived a life much richer than people thought of me. So, pray, fetch that pen now. I can feel the heat of the fever rushing through me like a wildfire. Now we must begin. There'll not be much time."

PART I

Jane and Margery

Set me as a seal upon thine heart,
as a seal upon thine arm: for love is strong as death;
jealousy is cruel as the grave.

—SONG OF SOLOMON, 8:6

Chapter One

*S*he ran swiftly. They were faster. Brambles and thorns cut into her soft-soled shoes, but she could not stop. She need not turn around. They were upon her, near enough for her to hear them giggling as they chased her through the broad meadow carpeted with the waving wild bluebells of summer. They darted across the timbered estate of Wolf Hall, the big house nestled among rolling grassy hills, tall fragrant flowers, and endless fields, then down the gentle slope, ever nearer to Savernake Forest.

Jane was not to go into the forest. None of the Seymour children were permitted that folly. Not even Edward, the eldest. The favorite son. Their father had made that more than clear to them. Jane was a child of eight years old, and her little heart quaked at the thought of the repercussions of disobeying their father. But at this desperate moment there was no other option. They would catch her and torment her as only cruel, bored children could.

The broad beams of sunlight, like great silvery fingers through the arching boughs of trees, warmed her buttoned, velvet-clad back but gave way to heavy shadows as she darted between the tree trunks and low-lying ferns. As she ran, she felt perspiration drip from her neck down the length of her spine beneath the layers of cotton and heavy velvet. She was nearly out of breath, but deep within her, the instinct to survive flickered like a flame in the wind. She was so young, so untested, but she knew how to survive.

Deeper into the forest she was drawn, panic now guiding her. It was not an unfounded fear. She had been hotly pursued by this group before. *Just a bit of fun,* her brother always said as she wept afterward, her dress caked in mud, her face covered with dirt and tears. But this torment had nothing to do with fun. At least not for her. To Jane, the reason they singled her out was because she was common looking. With her broad forehead, weak receding chin, mousy hair, and pale blue eyes, she looked nothing like the other young girls who lived around the Wiltshire countryside that flanked her family's home. They had glowing, round, and ruddy cheeks, bright eyes, and shiny hair that reflected the sun like silk.

"'Tis settled, then. Little Mistress Seymour is going to be an old maid someday with dozens of cats, like the milkmaid round back of her house. No one else will want her with such a plain face as that," fat-faced Cecily Strathmore declared once they had caught her.

The cruel taunts predictably came as the collection of girls pulled off her headdress and began tossing it among themselves like a ball, giggling as they did. But it was Lucy Hill's blithe tone, full of delight at the taunting, that hit Jane like a physical blow. She once had thought they might become friends. In the next moment, as she stumbled and lost her balance, Jane felt the tight clasp of a firm hand on her shoulder. Then the heat of fingers through the velvet sleeve. It was not Lucy's hand but a male one, more certain in its grip. She was spun back around by that same hand and lost her footing with the force of it. Her dress billowed up around her and she stumbled back, tumbling with a little splash directly into a blue-black pond beside them.

"Forgive me, I meant to catch you!" the boy exclaimed, drawing her back up out of the mossy muck with the same awkward movement that had caused her to stumble. As the words left his lips, he pivoted back toward the others, shielding her.

"A wet rat. How appropriate," Lucy said.

"That is the end of it, Lucy!" he announced, with far more maturity than any ruddy-skinned, sandy-haired boy his age should have possessed. Through the fog of her tears and the water dripping from her hair, he appeared to Jane only slightly older than herself but possessed of a confidence that was striking.

"Meddler!" Lucy Hill whined, her thick lower lip turning out in a predictably childish pout. "You might save her from us, William, but you'll never save her from being ugly."

By any standard, Lucy was Jane's polar opposite. Lucy's hair, parted and showing at her forehead, was golden and shiny as it hung down behind her blue muffin cap, banded in red and white. Her brown eyes, fringed with dark lashes, were lively and full of mischief. Where Jane was thin, Lucy had a shapely body, one that amply filled out her gray clothing and bespoke her coming womanhood. Lucy's skin was like fresh cream, her features striking, compared to Jane's own pallid complexion. Jane's beauty, if there was a hint of it, was fragile. She was not a verdant, budding thing, as Lucy was. But there was beauty lying fallow beneath the awkward waiflike frailty, a consequence of neglect.

"Why on earth do you want to ruin our fun, Will?"

The question came from Cecily Strathmore. The voice was sharper, full of even more venom. Jane did not know her, but she was not as pretty as Lucy. Though Jane could see, as she pressed the wet hair away from her eyes with the dirty palm of her hand, that they shared the same air of entitlement.

"I owe her elder brother something of a favor. This shall be payment," the mop-haired boy replied with genial authority, having cleverly moved between Jane and the other girls with two impercep-tible steps.

Jane did not know this boy, whom Edward apparently did, but she could see, by the shiny gold buttons of his dove gray doublet and the gold braid at his cuffs, he clearly possessed the pedigree to which the three other girls aspired. It was odd she did not know him, when they all appeared to be acquainted with him. Then again, this fellowship of catty little country girls made it their business to know everyone in Wiltshire, including this elegant young boy. The four exchanged glances in the heavy silence that descended between the trees that sheltered them beside the forest pond.

Suddenly, and without ceremony, the girls all turned in a swirl of gray, blue, and green cloth skirts and began to walk away, as if bored by the entire escapade, which they had initiated.

"Are you coming, Will?" Lucy called playfully over her shoulder in the same entitled tone. But he did not reply, even as they broke into a run toward the meadow and out of the forest

Jane stood alone then, astonished by what had just happened. She faced the boy. There did not seem much honor in helping her, and yet he had done it. In spite of Jane's tumble, and her sodden appearance, she was grateful. She knew it could have been much worse. Jane looked at him more closely then, as she felt a chill prickle her skin beneath the wet gown.

He was a tall boy with long legs and a slim, regal neck, and he was clearly older than she was. Probably three or four years older. His face, on the brink of adolescence, projected a certain air of nobility in the set of his jaw and the slim line of his nose. It was Roman almost, Jane decided, like one of the statues lining the walls of the long gallery at home, and there was just a hint of arrogance in his wildly bright blue eyes that held a curious, youthful flicker of interest in her.

There was an odd, silent moment between them before Jane, like the girls before her, pivoted away from the boy and stepped back toward the meadow that lay, like a great flower blanket, beyond the bower of forest trees.

"Do you not mean to thank me?" he called after her in a voice slightly different from the commanding one he had used before.

"For pushing me into that pond? Thank you," Jane replied tersely.

"For trying to save you from Lucy," he called out.

"If that was saving me, seeing you angry would be rather unpleasant," she returned over her shoulder in a slightly louder voice.

The boy moved quickly until he was beside her. "You know perfectly well that was *not* my fault. I tried to help you." He extended a blue silk kerchief he had drawn from his doublet then and handed it to her. Jane dried her face hesitantly with the lovely slip of fabric. She was stunned by the rich elegance of it but did not let it show through her anger.

"And so you did. What were you doing in the forest anyway? Hoping to come upon someone to rescue?" She did not see his frown, yet she felt it. "You knew those girls meant to harm me, didn't you?"

"It seemed likely. My father says love is as strong as death, but jealousy is as cruel as the grave."

She tipped her head and looked at him more closely. "My father says the same thing; he says it is from scripture."

"My father agrees with yours, then."

"Your father?"

"Sir Robert Dormer."

"So, then, Will Dormer, son of Sir Robert, pray, what do those girls have to envy me about?" she asked as they began to walk in tandem. She continued to press the lovely fabric against her face and wet hair to dry them.

"You live at Wolf Hall; they live in the cottages surrounding it. In the case of Lucy, she is your groundskeeper's daughter. You knew that, did you not?"

Jane held up a length of her skirt and twisted the water from it as she slowed her step. The canopy of branches opened above them and the colorful meadow ahead broadened.

"Yes, I knew it, but I've not been permitted to play with girls beyond my sister, Elizabeth, so I know her very little."

"Can you not see how they might envy you?"

"You are William Dormer, son and heir of a great knight. I have heard of you. You live in that very grand Idsworth House. Why do they not envy you far more?" she pressed him as they began to trek through the open field of bluebells that moved with the late summer breeze.

"Because I am a boy, of course. My father is a gentleman of means, and their fathers want them well married when they grow up."

"You cannot be that much older than I am, though, and I won't be nine until October. You're a child just like me."

"I am thirteen," William said proudly. "And the father's burden is a heavy one to see his daughters well married."

"Something else your father says?"

"As a matter of fact, it is. Regularly."

"Why have I not seen you before?"

"We live mainly at Eythrope, our other property in Buckinghamshire. Idsworth House is our summer place, just over the rise."

"Well, your summer place is behind a grand gate and all of those trees, so I have never seen it, but my brother Edward says 'tis very grand."

"Quite large and drafty, actually. There's an awful echo in the wing in which I am commanded to sleep, and sometimes I think 'tis not the wind but a voice calling out."

"What sort of voice?" Jane asked him.

"An old man's voice. Angry. Telling me not to be there."

"That's dreadful."

"Especially when you are forced to sleep alone, as I am."

They walked now more tentatively together, her hair still dripping as Wolf Hall grew more loomingly large on the horizon beyond the fields.

As did the fate that awaited her there.

Jane was a child of only eight, but she knew better than to think she could escape punishment for falling into the pond.

"So what exactly did Edward do for you that you felt bound to defend me?"

"He told my steward that I was helping him with a new saddle when I wasn't. And because Edward is fifteen, and so nearly a man, they believed him."

"Would they have flogged you?" Jane asked, assuming the answer.

"Of course not," William said with a note of surprise, looking back at her. "My parents are quite fond of me. I am their only child, you see. They had another son after me, but he died, so now I have all of their attention and hopes."

"That must be nice."

"'Tis rather a lot of pressure, actually."

"I had a brother once who died, too. John was his name. After my father," Jane revealed.

Her revelation came on an awkward note of sadness, but in truth, the two had not been close. John had been older than Edward was when she was born. But still, he was her brother. And she always thought he might have loved her. The Seymour family did not value displays of affection, and so fantasy held more sway with Jane than it might have otherwise. Fortunately, she had Thomas. He was younger than Edward by two years, but he was sweet with her, and they liked to play the same games in the fields and meadows. More than Elizabeth, who was pretty. Too pretty. She hated to spoil her looks by frivolously running about. And Edward was too old to be much of anything to her. Seven years was an eternity, Jane thought. When she was Edward's age, she would be grown, and hopefully she would not fear returning home.

They were walking now up the wide gravel path, an avenue lined with bristling copper beech trees, the branches of which closed above them and which stood like a row of sentries leading back to the timber manor. Wolf Hall was modest in comparison with what she had heard of Idsworth House behind its massive black gates and bower of mulberry trees. Still, Wolf Hall was a commanding presence on the softly undulating landscape of Wiltshire farmland with its never-ending vista of meadows and fields. Jane had been born here, as had all her siblings. There was comfort to her in that shared history, with little else to count on for her future. She was too plain to hope she would ever find a grand marriage.

"Are you happy that I did defend you?" William Dormer suddenly asked, surprising Jane.

"Happier than my mother will be when she sees my dress," she replied, clinging to her sodden hood with one hand and his kerchief with the other.

"Shall I come with you and explain to your mother what happened? I think I learned how to do it fairly believably from your brother Edward," he said with an awkward yet boyish smile.

"Explain that I defied her?" Jane asked. "I think that shall be apparent."

They stopped in a small clearing. The shaft of sun between them was like a warming beacon, fingers of protection that she must move past, into the shadows beyond. Jane looked at the tall boy with the tousled hair, who seemed less of a stranger now. Yet he was still curious to her child's mind for how he had dropped so suddenly into her world when she scarcely knew anyone outside of her family here in the endless miles of Wiltshire. As she looked into William's warm eyes glittering in the sunlight, she held out the blue handkerchief he had loaned her.

"You keep it," he said as his smile widened. "I have others."

Unaccustomed to small kindnesses, Jane flushed and lowered her eyes. "Thank you," she managed to whisper before she turned and ran from him the rest of the way.

After William left, the steps to her house seemed to be many, fear making her heart beat furiously. The scent of her mother's rosewater perfume met her before Jane saw the imposing figure standing on the landing.

Her mother, slim and graceful, was still lovely after the births of all of her children. With wide blue eyes, direct and unyielding, sleek blond hair with only the smallest streak of gray tucked meticulously beneath a mesh caul, Margery Wentworth had been the classic ideal of beauty in the most vivid bloom of her youth.

Jane's father was also thirty-nine, but time had not been quite so forgiving to him. John Seymour wore his struggles to elevate himself and his family most prominently in the furrows etched deeply into his forehead. Even his warm smile brought out the web of lines at the corners of his deep blue eyes. When he was alone, Jane craved her father's embrace. There was a kindness there. When he was together with his wife, they were an impenetrable force that a little girl was meant to fear more than respect.

Compact and lean in his usual green tunic, nether hose, and white, full-sleeved shirt, her father watched her approach. She saw first his brows, thick and straight like her own, knit together in a slight, discerning frown. Then, with the next beat of her heart, she saw a comforting spark of amusement light up his expression.

But her heart began to race as her mother's discerning blue gaze settled on her from where she stood on the rise of the polished oak staircase landing, wiping away any sense of relief. Margery's lips became a slim, bloodless line, and Jane saw the shock in her eyes as the water dripped in a steady rhythm from her hair and sodden garments onto the bare wood floor beneath her slippered feet.

Jane could see her mother's body go rigid. She lifted her chin just slightly. Her father reacted instantly to his wife, almost as if they were two parts of the same creature. The action melted the amusement in his eyes, and his own expression turned to one of grave intensity. The next instant was very swift. Her mother descended the remaining stairs in what seemed like a powerful, ominous whirl of silk skirts, noxious rose water, and growing fury. She slapped her daughter across the cheek with such force that Jane's sodden headdress, hastily replaced a moment ago, fell to the floor in a wet thud. She staggered back.

"Brainless, fool child! You openly defy me, do you?"

"No, my lady mother, I—"

"And you have the hubris to speak as well?"

Jane's eyes were rooted in terror upon her mother so that she did not see her father. Rather, she felt his supportive approach from behind.

"Pray, Margery, do not be too harsh with the girl. Mayhap there was a circumstance."

"The *girl*?" she raged, her anger in full, dark bloom now. "Is that how she appears to you? To me, she looks like a cellar rat. Certainly she is no *girl* of my choosing!"

The harsh words hit Jane with the force of an axe, wounding her, and she felt deeply the pain of her mother's disapproval. There was no point in arguing. She, at least, was old enough to know that. There was no freedom allowed beyond the meadow, past the orchard, on the outlying edge of Wolf Hall. Yet her wet clothes proved she had crossed the boundary.

"You have defied me, knowing clearly how I value shy reserve!"

Jane lowered her eyes to calm her trembling chin and stop her tears from falling. "Forgive me."

"Have you only *that* to sputter as you stand there dripping on my polished floors and setting the worst possible example for your brothers and sisters? You went into the forest!"

She stared at her shoes. "Yes."

"You defy me wantonly and with clear disregard, as if you were the self-indulgent son of a Seymour, not a daughter! Do you suppose defiance was how I came to be so celebrated in my day? *Do you?* How I came to be written about and admired, when shy reserve is the only thing of value in a virtuous girl?"

"Margery, for the love of all the saints, you know perfectly well our Jane is no rat, but as quiet and gentle as a church mouse, just as you long have taught her to be."

"Well, at the moment she *looks* like a cellar rat. And I shall not tolerate disobedience from any daughter of mine! If you mean to behave like a boy, Jane, mayhap you should resemble one!"

"I bid you, do not take this too far, wife. Reprimand the child if you will, but be done with it."

Margery's eyes were wild now, glazed with fury. "Your daughter has no beauty, no obvious virtue, and clearly no regard for me, though she would do well to make me her role model! Yet you expect me to swat the back of her hand, then let go of this affair? Better to vanquish the folly bound up in the heart of a child, not soothe it," she declared crisply, her anger fading only slightly behind her iron resolve. "Children, obey your parents in the Lord, for this is right!"

Margery Wentworth Seymour was the true power behind the family, and she was fond of quoting scripture shortly before meting out some punishment or other to her children.

Jane studied the black braid on her shoes, pushing away the fear, but it flared hotly again when her mother gripped her arm, slowing the flow of blood through the soaking-wet fabric. She drew her forward toward the paneled library—a cold, forbidding room dominated by a portrait of the new young king. It was a copy, painted in Bruges, and not the best likeness. Yet John Seymour hung it prominently above the stone hearth anyway. It was his hope that he and Jane's mother might receive the king at Wolf Hall on his yearly progress someday. Then seeing it, King Henry might show favor on a faithful warrior and servant in the far reaches of Wiltshire—one who had shown loyalty to the Crown with every drawn breath, every hopeful court dance learned, every crossbow drawn or sonnet read in preparation for such a meeting. "Miracles do occasionally happen," Jane's father always said with his gentle, wry smile.

After all, his own distant cousin, Sir Francis Bryan, was at court, now a companion of the king. John Seymour had spent his life preparing for even one small opportunity of his own, like the one Francis had received, and of which he was now making the most. At least that was the way he explained it to his children every time he saw any of them gazing up at the king's image.

The scissors Margery had picked up and now clutched with vengeful determination were sharp, the handles etched silver. Her father had followed the two of them from the entry hall, but Jane could not see him. For a moment, she could only hear his labored breathing as her mother shoved Jane onto her knees with a force that lacked all maternal understanding. Jane fell before the fireplace hearth and the portrait of the king, her mother gazing down at her with what Jane always thought was a silly, mocking smile.

"From Colossians," her mother commanded. "What is it?"

On her order, their tutor, the family cleric, recently had made the children memorize a translated portion of the New Testament, which Erasmus was about to publish in Greek with a parallel Latin translation. He was said to be working on a full version, including the Old Testament, so while a few copies had been printed, the public awaited the full publication. But Margery did not see the value in waiting to mold young minds and souls.

"Children, obey your parents in all things: for this is well pleasing unto the Lord," Jane sputtered.

"Now Proverbs."

As her tears began to mingle with the water still dripping from her hair and into her eyes, she thought instead, *And be ye kind one to another, tenderhearted, forgiving one another, even as God for Christ's sake hath forgiven you*, but she dared not say that.

She drew a small breath to steady her trembling and to minimize the thin, horrifying trickle of urine she suddenly felt between her legs. "The eye that mocketh at his father, and despiseth to obey his mother, the ravens of the valley shall pick it out, and the young eagles shall eat it."

Margery favored that passage, Jane knew only too well, for the frightening imagery that terrified her children and thus kept them compliant. It was meant to make them all envision hell and the fiery pit there. It served to distance her heart, even at the age of eight, from a mother obsessed with rules and the projection of perfection, in herself and those around her, at all costs.

Jane did not feel the first snip; rather she heard the slice of the scissors. The clump of wet hair fell before her eyes like feathers from a Yuletide goose; brown, shapeless, damp. The second chunk was bigger, making it more difficult to cut. She could hear the blades of the scissors working back and forth, so close to her ear that it felt deafening. If, in her anger, her mother's hand should slip even an inch, she could cut off the tip of her ear. All that blood, Jane thought, and she really would be like a Christmas goose! Or one of the sheep out in the pasture being sheared for summer. Yes, that was what Jane felt like, held down now, powerless, her hair falling to the ground with each snip.

"Margery, 'tis madness!" her father shouted impotently.

"Or folly! Either way, a daughter who behaves like our sons shall resemble one of them, at least until she gains a grain of humility! Thanks be to our dear Lord that Elizabeth is nothing like you! You must remember in the future that you are a Seymour and a Wentworth. A small drop of royal blood flows through your veins. Yet it is enough of the honeyed elixir for me to do all that I can to train you up, if not in my image, then at least to revere it!"

The process lasted only a minute more, but it was a span of seconds that changed Jane's life. She focused on the tall clock near the library door, willing herself not to weep, nor run from the room until her punishment was complete. Jane could not imagine how spiteful girls like Lucy Hill or Cecily Strathmore would torment her if they knew she was being shorn of that single bit of feminine identity that set a plain little girl apart from her brothers.

She had never wanted to dislike her mother or to be different from the great beauty that was Margery Wentworth Seymour. A child's instinct to love her mother did battle with the urge to yell a defiant obscenity. Jane felt the two sensations roiling, fighting, wearing deeply within her as she glanced up then and saw Thomas and Elizabeth at the corner of the doorway, peeking inside. Jane saw their horrified expressions as the last wet clump of Jane's girlish identity hit the floor beside one of her father's dogs, who sat now beneath the trestle table watching her and wagging his tail.

Chapter Two

September 1514
Wiltshire, England

The first bit of good news from Sir Francis Bryan at the court of King Henry VIII came by courier, ushered in on the same warm September wind that blew golden leaves across the courtyard. It was a month since Jane's incident in Savernake Forest and two days since she had been let out of confinement in her chamber above the granary. Now the liveried messenger stood in the courtyard, his sleek face covered in a sheen of perspiration as the elegant green plume of his hat fluttered in the breeze. He removed his leather riding gloves while John read the newsy missive aloud.

Details were at last finalized. The king's younger sister, Mary, was to become the bride of France's aged sovereign, Louis XII. The match was a coup for England and France against their political enemies. A massive train was being assembled to escort the young beauty to the arms of her brother's rival-turned-friend, which would formally bond the two countries politically. Members of Henry's court, his royal guard, ladies-in-waiting, maids of honor, and pages of honor were being named by the dozen—all from the best families, according to Sir Francis. The country was alive with the gossip of who would be chosen. Also in the missive, Francis boasted that he had been selected to help the king's sister decide on the group who would have closest access to her, as his personal standing with the royal family had risen quite high. Excitement all across England had quickly reached a fever pitch.

The second bit of news to further improve Margery Seymour's disposition came later that same day. She and her husband had been invited to a banquet to be given by Sir Robert and Lady Dormer, held at the impressive Idsworth House. It was their first invitation. Guests were coming across rutted roads from as far away as Newbury, they were told, to celebrate the Dormers' thirteen-year-old son William's invitation to attend the Princess Mary as a young page of honor in the princess's train to France.

The honor for the family was massive, the scale of award beyond measure.

With envy for his own eldest son rising above his sense of dignity, John Seymour inquired of the Dormer groom if Edward might have the opportunity to reunite with his friend young William at the banquet.

He knew that pleading would be unseemly. But once the Dormer family returned to their even larger estates in Buckinghamshire, the opportunity would be lost to increase his own family's standing enough for Sir Francis Bryan to take notice. A friendship with the prominent Dormers was essential, so he had to cleverly seize the moment.

"Having once met the king myself on the battlefield at Tournai, and having been knighted personally by our previous sovereign," John said boastfully, rocking back on his heels, "mayhap I could offer young Master Dormer a word of advice on how to impress His Majesty's favorite sister with this most magnificent opportunity before him."

In truth, John Seymour's only actual meeting with Henry VIII had amounted to his anonymous presence among a battery of bloodied, mud-drenched, and weary soldiers on a sodden field in France. They had all bowed to a very tall, copper-haired man on the back of a great warrior bay riding at the head of a train of a dozen other elegantly armored soldiers. The young king had held up his hand to them in collective thanks as he rode off to the comfort of a massive tent, a hot meal, good French wine, and more than a few pretty girls from the town of Thérouanne as John slept in the mud with the others.

But those were details of no consequence, as far as he was concerned now, and John Seymour was not above a bit of prevarication to further elevate his family.

If it was the only way to keep content his Margery—a beautiful woman who might have married so much better—he resolved to do it.

Jane's father knew perfectly well the invitation for Edward that miraculously arrived the next day had been extended grudgingly. He had seen the subtly rolled eyes of the groom at the moment of its delivery. It was only slightly worse than the condescending look of the first groom when he had proposed it.

Unseemly, this second rather arrogant servant's expression seemed to be saying.

To the devil with you! John thought in response. *I shall see my family rise as you settle for service, if it must be with my final breath.*

Power was an elusive thing. In a time when knights and sheriffs were as plentiful and unimpressive as peddlers, John's former position as sheriff of Wiltshire never brought him anywhere near court. He had to do what he could to better life for his son. Edward deserved it. The boy was handsome and smart and he would have a brilliant future if John could only create a small foothold for him through their one connection to the court. What Edward did with it after that, by God's grace, would be up to him.

But Edward Seymour was the family's only real hope of advancement.

"She is quite a haughty woman, you know," Margery remarked, speaking from what she had heard of Lady Dormer's reputation. "While she is to be congratulated for her determination, I can only wonder how she managed to get that son of hers to attend the king's sister in France—and what great strings she had to pull."

"I suspect *you* will be the one to find out," John Seymour said blandly as he sat beside her in the room where they dressed. His groom, a tottering old man with coarse silver hair and a prominent wart on the tip of his chin, stood behind him, smelling of camphor and combing the master's hair with a wide-tooth tortoiseshell comb.

Margery sat beside him as her muffin-capped maid carefully wove a string of blue beads into the silk fall over her hair. He patted her arm with a hint of condescension so that she sniffed at him.

"Mayhap I shall."

"Oh, you shall, my dear. It has been a good many years since I have seen anyone get the better of you."

"I want Edward in that train to France."

"As do I," he agreed, both of them at last voicing what they had desired since hearing about the good fortune of Dormer's son.

"It could mean the world to the standing of this family if the boy were to go and make an impression."

"Agreed. But I cannot simply suggest to Sir Dormer that he find a way to see Edward invited along with his son."

"You saw him invited to the Dormers' banquet this evening. You are certainly resourceful when you put your mind to it." Margery's voice was rising and growing thin. It was a predictable precursor to one of her fits of anger. Like a weather instrument before a wind-storm, there was that little tremor that meant danger was not far off.

"A banquet and a royal invitation are two very different things, sweetheart," he tried with futility to remind her as she shot to her feet, stiffening her resolve along with her spine.

"Can you not call upon your cousin to aid us?"

"Francis Bryan is a *distant* cousin," he gently reminded her.

"Blood is blood. There is loyalty in it. Why else does he so regularly send us letters of what is going on at the court of our king?"

John rolled his eyes and swatted at the old man behind him to leave before he had a chance to apply the scented oil to his combed hair. "Sir Francis sends those to everyone, Margery. That young buck with whom I share only the faintest bit of blood is a braggart of the first order now that he has become one of the king's hunting companions. He likes to flaunt his alliances, not offer them up."

Undaunted, Margery Seymour, in a beaded mauve-colored dress, swept across the bare floorboards to a table beneath the window that held a looking glass and a large, heavily carved jewelry chest with a brass hinge and latch. The lid of the chest was engraved with the Wentworth family crest. Her own lineage was as impressive as her beauty, and she liked to keep the chest prominently displayed to remind herself, John, and their children that she bore royal blood through her mother's ancestral connection to King Edward III. It gave Margery the right, she believed, if not the relationships, to advocate for her son.

After their first child was named John for his father, Margery had insisted on naming her second son, Edward, after that king. It was a boastful reminder to everyone, especially in this provincial setting to which her parents had seen fit to consign her, that she had once, in the full bloom of her flaxen-haired, blue-eyed beauty, been important enough to be a muse for the celebrated poet John Skelton.

She now used the tale to guide her young daughters in her expectations for them, comparing them, prodding them, nagging them. Even Elizabeth, who had only just turned six, was already a victim of her mother's ambition.

It was obvious that even at the tender age of eight, Jane was sorely lacking in the refinement necessary to obtain an important suitor. That was going to change if Margery Seymour had anything to say about it. Her flawless face hid a steel core. She had taught little Jane a lesson last month. And the child's hair would grow back. Well before she needed it anyway. Jane was clearly meant to be plain, with lovely hair or without it. Poor girl had gotten John's looks—his receding chin, thick brows, and lifeless blue eyes. Ah, if only her beauty, which had won a master of words like Skelton, had taken Margery to court and not to Wiltshire.

Skelton's words flowed through her. *Ye be, as I divine, / the pretty primrose, / the goodly columbine.*

With a discreet nod, Margery excused her maid, then prepared to try another tack. She drew near her husband, more handsome now in his dress doublet of green grosgrain and silver braid. He was not a tall man, but he stood very straight, which made him seem impressive. The brawny physicality that had won him a knighthood from Henry VII at the Battle of Blackheath nearly two decades earlier had softened with time. The winning smile that had once charmed his wife now hid beneath sagging jowls, but she did not find his nightly gropings completely objectionable. After so many years, she knew how to seduce him to her purposes, quickly and efficiently.

With that in mind, Margery ran a hand skillfully down the

length of his doublet, across the folds of fabric accented by an ivory hem. As always, her touch aroused him instantly.

"We haven't time for that now, sweetheart," he murmured, his voice threaded with desire.

"I do not ask you for a great deal, John, you know that. But I must have you to do this for me. Write to Sir Francis on behalf of our son. Find us a way to match the opportunity the Dormers have been given. Edward is already fifteen years old. Their son is two years younger. 'Tis Edward's time."

"And your time as well, my dear?" he asked as she pressed a kiss along the vein that was pulsing wildly now in the thick column of his neck.

Jane stood in the alcove beneath the staircase as her parents and brother departed for the evening. Jane loved her elder brother more than anyone in the world, she thought, and she admired him for how handsome and self-assured he seemed. Yet he was something of a mythical figure to her and rarely spoke to her. She watched their mother smile up at him now with a light in her eyes that Jane only ever saw when their mother looked at Edward. The three of them were collected closely, speaking in low tones while they waited for the horses and drawn litter to be brought up from the thatch-roofed stables down the long gravel drive near their gate. Jane looked enviously at her mother's rose-colored satin evening dress with puffed sleeves and embroidered edges and rope of pearls. It was a new dress, ordered for the occasion. The hood had been made to match.

Jane knew she was nothing like her glamorous mother, nor would she ever be. She reached up and touched the front of her own hair, remembering then. The repercussions from that day in Savernake Forest never left her mind for very long. Defeated, she sank more deeply into the shadows beneath the stairwell, feeling set apart more than usual in a family where everyone else seemed golden and full of promise. Even her six-year-old sister, Elizabeth, held tightly to their mother's loveliness. Jane tried not to take that out on the little girl, who followed her around Wolf Hall as much as she followed Edward.

Remembering her hair again, Jane fingered the tendrils at the back where the jagged pieces touched the nape of her neck. It had become a habit this past month as the warm air whispered over her bare skin, which not long ago had been warmed by a full, reassuring mane like that of every other little girl in Wiltshire.

But she was nothing like any of them, and now there was not the faintest resemblance to hide behind.

She watched her family leave and waited for the jangle of the horses' harnesses out in the courtyard before she dared peek around the corner. Finally she cautiously emerged from the stairwell, the scent of her mother's rose-water perfume still lingering threateningly.

They were going to Idsworth House. The thought filled her with envy.

They would see that boy who had tried to help her. William. She had heard her mother say he was going to France to see the Princess Mary become queen there. Everyone in England was talking about the marriage.

Jane could not quite imagine such a thing herself—a voyage across the Narrow Sea among actual royalty, or being surrounded by such power and elegance. There could not possibly be anything more exciting or unfathomable.

"'Tis a good thing Mother did not catch you lurking there, or you might well have lost *all* of your hair." Thomas stood before Jane wearing a serious expression. His coloring was fair and his hair was light auburn. He was a strikingly beautiful boy with the same brilliant Wentworth eyes as their mother. He was loyal to Jane above all others, and he had actually wept with shock when he first saw what their mother had done in her fit of fury the month before.

"I would so have liked to go with them tonight," she wistfully confessed to her brother as they walked together toward the long gallery that faced the timbered inner courtyard of their house. The Seymour children spent hours strolling the gallery along a well-worn path, forward and back again, especially when the weather was poor. The household staff often set up games there to keep them from boredom.

"We all would have liked that," Thomas said. "But none of us are Edward."

"I met him, you know. Their son, William."

"Edward said he is a bit uncertain for someone with such an impressive fortune."

"He was quite certain with me," Jane countered, remembering how he had saved her from Lucy. "I envy him being allowed to attend the king's sister to France. That cousin of father's, Sir Bryan, with a place at court, always writes that the princess is very beautiful."

"Everyone at court is beautiful . . . and *rich*," Thomas countered, making an astute connection for someone so young as they moved to a carved oak bench beneath a bank of leaded windows.

"Did it hurt when she cut it off?" he asked suddenly.

Jane tipped her head. "It was only hair."

"I know. But there was just . . . so much of it. Are you still angry?"

"I try not to be. There is really no purpose in it. She is our mother, after all. We must love her."

"I don't always," Thomas confessed, glancing through the

diamond-shaped leaded panes onto a small garden. Two butterflies fluttered over a small fountain surrounded by a neatly trimmed hedge. "Perhaps I would if I were Edward, but I shall never be him."

"With John and Henry both dead, you are the second eldest now. You know how determined Mother is about everything. She will see Father make a brilliant life for both of you. She means to find a way to get Edward to court. Perhaps you shall go with him one day."

Thomas laughed at the absurdity of her statement, but then as usual his expression fell more serious. His smile faded and his blue eyes dimmed slightly. "I fear there is as much chance of that as of horses flying."

As Margery had suspected, Idsworth House, which loomed across a stone bridge and mossy moat, was enormous. It was heavily gabled, wrought of red brick, and ornamented with a great blanket of emerald-colored ivy. Many of the manor's mullioned windows were filled with colored glass and inset with mottos and the Dormer family coat of arms—a shield with a plumed silver helmet.

Margery felt her heart quicken at the grandeur as she watched a gathering of other well-dressed guests, none of whom she knew, move confidently toward the entrance. Two servants as still as carved statues dressed in gold and blue livery flanked the door, holding flaming torches. In that moment, in spite of the costly and heavily embroidered fabric she had whined and coaxed her way into obtaining, she felt underdressed. She could not let John know it, however, for the protest she had made to look her best. Insecurity was beneath the dignity of a Wentworth and the small but undeniable bit of royal blood that ran through her veins.

Determinedly, she tipped up her chin, as she so often did when she felt challenged, fending off her own demons of inadequacy as she prepared to advance into the fire. In the first blush of excitement over the invitation, Margery had not counted on the massive size of the crowd or what a challenge it might be to make her mark with Lady Dormer. Ushered into the hall filled with glowing candle lamps and flanked with massive tapestries on heavy rods over freshly lime-washed walls, Margery realized with a sensation of panic that she would not recognize the woman even if she were standing right beside her. She drew in a breath, then sought out a servant. Anyone would do.

John reached for a glass of Rhenish wine offered from a silver tray and cast a wary half glance at his wife as they stood beneath the entrance, penned in like sheep, with all the other guests. A trio of musicians, on dulcimer, pipes, and lute, played too rousingly for the space, and there was far too much undignified chatter going on around them.

Pressing forward anyway, she queried the servant.

"By your leave, where is your mistress? I should like to commend myself to her before the banquet begins."

He was a tall, thin man, slightly stooped, and quite preoccupied. "I am afraid I have not ever seen her myself, my lady." Margery could hardly imagine such a thing—to be rich enough to have servants so far removed that they had never actually seen the mistress.

"That makes two of you," John blandly quipped as he drank his wine in two quick swallows.

Margery shot him an angry glare as she felt the rise of panic. An obstacle that she must surmount lay before her. If only her husband were half so ambitious as she, they would be a formidable team. She might at last see the inside of a royal palace, sip the wine there, and hear the young king himself play one of his own famous tunes. Then she might sleep beneath palace eaves on the finest Holland linens on swan feathers meant for a queen. If Skelton had made more of an attempt than a lovely, trifling poem, she would not have had to wait so long.

Ah, those days when she had touched the edge of grandeur!

Her heart quickened along with her ambition. She would do this by herself.

Margery scanned the room for another servant. It would not do at all for the other guests to sense her ambition or her fear. John and Edward followed her too much like ducklings; silently, compliantly, padding across the floor as she waded slowly through the velvet-clad press of bodies, the yards of fabric, silk, velvet, the lengths of pearls, the flashing medallions, and the rich, wine-scented laughter.

"My pardon, but," she pressed a different, younger steward who was serving another guest, "pray, where might I find our hostess?"

It was not the servant who answered.

"'Tis my wife you seek?" the man beside them suddenly asked.

Margery felt her face go very hot. She was flushed as the man with hooded, deep-set, dark eyes turned to look at her. She felt her husband's impatience and her son's embarrassment as they came up beside her.

She heard Edward's quick intake of breath as she blithely replied, "I wished to inquire of her about those magnificent musicians. I've a mind to hire them for a party we are going to have at Wolf Hall."

His demeanor changed swiftly, closing off. She saw him assessing her in the way his black eyes narrowed and in the way his open smile faded to only a reserved upturn of the lips. "Our musicians, my lady, gain their employment from my family exclusively, as we find regular enough opportunities to entertain here and at our other homes."

She cast him a forced smile, trying casually to respond. "Still, I should like to commend myself to your wife for her discerning ear. Their music is really quite remarkable and jolly."

Like a door opening into a forbidden room, his smile deepened and a hint of kindness returned to his face at her flattery. He leaned nearer, as if he were about to tell her some little secret or other.

"If there is anything Lady Dormer enjoys, 'tis praise," he responded with an unexpected little chuckle.

In a pearl-dotted swirl of silk and a whisper of essence of oranges, a woman near them turned at Dormer's words. She faced Margery with a bright, somewhat false smile. She was an attractive woman, Margery thought as she quickly assessed her in the way that one beautiful woman often does to another. She rivaled Margery with her classic and vivid beauty, wide blue eyes, and fair, flawless skin, and Margery felt disarmed.

It was not often that anyone could match her looks.

"Oh, there you are, my dear," Dormer said, turning to Lady Dormer. "May I present Sir John and Lady Seymour," he said perfunctorily, already beginning to scan the crowd, no doubt for more important connections to reaffirm.

Margery made a small nod and slight curtsy to their hostess. In spite of her own superior lineage, it seemed in the moment the right thing to do if she wished to ingratiate herself. With the noise and activity swirling around them, Margery knew she would not have much time for so sizable a task.

"Seymour, is it?"

"My husband, Sir John, was sheriff of Wiltshire for a time. We are presently the owners of Wolf Hall," Margery said with a note of pride coloring her voice for the lovely old property they owned.

"Wolf Hall?" Lady Dormer made a little sniffing sound as she said it, as though there was something foul in the air. "That timbered old place beside the forest?"

Margery saw they had been assessed unfavorably. Their hostess was unimpressed.

"And sheriff of Southampton before that."

She might as well have said village butcher or candle maker, Margery thought, feeling the rise of desperation at the perceived disparity between them.

"He was also for a time sheriff of Somerset and Dorset." She heard the pleading tone in her own voice and forced, with great strength, a carefree smile.

"Indeed." Lady Dormer made the same little sniffing sound of superiority and began to scan the crowd, as if she could not wait for a reason to be taken away from this pointless introduction. "Well, welcome to you both."

As Lady Dormer turned away, some odd power she had never felt before forced Margery to reach out and clutch the woman's arm. Tension flooded the moment, quickly snuffing out any pretense of hospitality Lady Dormer had shown before. As she gazed down at her own arm, becoming ever more aware of the untoward connection, Margery forced a little nervous chuckle.

"I wished to commend your musicians," she said frantically enough that she felt John take a step forward. Lady Dormer lifted her arched blond brows disdainfully.

With unexpected determination, Margery turned to her son, hearing the frantic tone in her own voice but ignoring it.

"Your son and ours here—our Edward—have met, you see. I actually believe Edward, being a bit older, was able to help acquaint your son, William, with our little corner of Wiltshire on your last stay here. And I dare say they have forged something of a friendship."

She was prattling on and she knew it, but as with everything else in the last few minutes, it was absolutely beyond her control to stop it. She was a boulder of commitment rolling downhill, gaining more speed with each thump of her heart.

"I would not really say we are friends, Mother, but we *have* met," Edward spoke up with surprising ease for an adolescent as he bowed. Margery released her hand from the bell sleeve of Lady Dormer's arm. "'Tis an honor to be here this evening, Lady Dormer. Like my parents, I am very much enjoying the music."

To Margery's relief, something akin to a smile brightened Lady Dormer's face. The back-and-forth was all very unsettling amid so much noise and music. "Ah, yes. Edward. My son has spoken well of you."

"I am glad." He nodded to her, as he had been taught well to do. But there again was the expression of superiority from Lady Dormer, and a spark of condescension. "Perhaps he might come to Wolf Hall one day and we might practice French together. I am frightfully slow at the conjugations, I am afraid, but he has told me he is even slower."

Lady Dormer and her husband exchanged a quick glance, followed by a slight rolling of their eyes, which said that was never going to happen.

"Why, certainly," Lady Dormer lied with a smile so chilly Margery actually felt a shiver. "Although his French is passable enough for the king's court." Margery felt the pointed barb. "When he has returned we shall make a plan of it. Now pray, do excuse us. We must see to the banquet before our guests start fighting one another for food. But truly, 'twas lovely to have met you all."

And with that, they slipped back into the same cloud of entitlement from which they had emerged.

"That went well," Edward said drily.

"Well indeed, if you fancy catastrophe as a first course," John said sarcastically, feeding off his son's tone.

"Do be silent, the pair of you. I've got a dreadful headache and I must think how we can mend this!"

"We?" John asked. "Has this family not made quite enough of an impression for one evening?"

"Certainly not the impression I wished to make, for Edward's sake," Margery snapped, feeling entirely frantic now and losing the control she so obstinately maintained over her life. She glanced around, wide-eyed, her cheeks flushed. "I *must* get Edward and the boy together. Edward, you must remind him how agreeable your company is and—"

"And then what, Mother? His gentrified parents will move heaven and earth to have a lad from the country he barely knows join him on the voyage to France in the company of the king's sister?"

It had sounded so much better in her mind.

"There must be a way. We are certainly close now."

"We are no closer now than that steward over there is to the throne of England," John said coolly.

"She thought herself better than us," Margery grumbled of their hostess.

"Clearly," John agreed.

"Loutish boors," said Edward.

"No better," John said, biting back the same smile his eldest son tried to hide from his mother.

"We are gentry as well! By my heaven, you were knighted!" Margery exclaimed heatedly as other guests swirled around them.

"But they are wealthy, and that does make all the difference."

"Well, I am the one between us who bears the blood of royalty, not her!" Margery countered indignantly.

"For all of the good that trickle of crimson has done us," John remarked.

"Edward deserves to be in that party to France as a page of honor far more than the son of some wool merchant!"

She spoke the words harshly, but her envy could not be masked. Just then, a trumpet fanfare announced dinner, just as it was done at court banquets. Her resolve hardened along with her expression.

"How must you feel to see your son demeaned in this way?"

John rolled his eyes. "I know not if that was the intention."

"Well, it most certainly was the result. She believes me to be no better than one of her servants. I could see it clearly on her face, and therefore our son is no better. That shall not stand! I have been immortalized by poets. Not her! Anyone who is anyone has read *Garland of Laurel* and knows I am the subject," she whispered heatedly.

Now she wanted to spite Lady Dormer as much as to elevate her son.

They began the slow shuffle along with the other guests toward the elegant dining hall. "Will you write to your cousin at court now, or shall I?" Margery asked.

It was clear she meant to see it done . . . no matter what her husband said in response.

As angry talk of the incident in Savernake Forest finally began to fade at Wolf Hall, Jane was allowed back into the gardens to play with the other children. She had not, however, minded being sequestered at first because of her jaggedly shorn hair, which itched madly when tucked beneath her tight-fitting gabled hood.

She did not mind solitude. Jane liked to read on her own. Anything she secretly took from her father's library was a welcome challenge, and she preferred it over the Psalter that Father James, their village priest and tutor, forced each of the children to read from every day.

She might be young, but Jane craved escape with spirit and excitement. Stories of kings and queens, daring knights, and beautiful princesses captured her. Granted, there was not much of that to be had in John Seymour's musty library, but she had secretly come upon a small volume of *The Canterbury Tales*, which she kept like spoils beneath her mattress. Theft made the reading of the verses all the more sweet.

She was not a swift reader, and many things she did not understand, so it seemed to take an eternity to move through the bawdy stories, but when she could capture a moment by candlelight when she was meant to be asleep, she easily lost herself in the smart, humorous vignettes, like "The Prioress's Tale."

The stories reminded her of William Dormer. That boy was actually going to meet the king! He was going to wear incredible costumes and wait on a queen. It was as if he had leapt out of the pages of her book.

One late afternoon, when she was covertly reading, she was so lost in her fantasies that she did not hear the frantic knock at her door. A moment later, Thomas dashed inside, his face alive with excitement.

"Sister, you must come at once!" he said urgently. "Downstairs! You'll not believe what they are saying!"

Jane slipped the book back beneath her mattress, then picked up her hood and reluctantly fitted it back onto her head.

"What is it, Tom?"

"Father received a letter just this morning from court, from that cousin of his, Sir Francis Bryan, and now Mother is in an absolute state!"

"Mother is always in a state," she countered, as yet unimpressed. "So then you were eavesdropping?"

"As *you* taught me to do. And you should be happy I did, since I heard your name. Truly, sister, you really must come!"

"I am involved?"

Jane felt the blood rise hotly in her face, remembering with fear the last time she had displeased her mother. Her hair was still recovering from that experience. Reluctantly, she left the room behind her brother, who scrambled out the door.

The stairwell was as efficient a place to eavesdrop now as always, and as children who had spent their whole lives in these chambers and corridors, Jane and Thomas knew how to slip unnoticed from place to place if they so desired.

Margery and John were standing near the door. There was an open letter dangling from her father's hand. His other hand was on the massive open door, a messenger having just departed. There was a fresh wisteria-scented breeze blowing in from the courtyard.

"This cannot be serious!" Margery shrieked, panic lighting her eyes, making them shine as blue as water in the shaft of sunlight through the door. "We cannot possibly afford to send them *both*! Think of the money for her wardrobe alone to keep up with the other invited girls there—if such a thing were even possible to imagine! Gowns are far more costly than boys' costumes!"

"Be that as it may, they'll not take one without the other. Read it yourself. They have enough pages of honor as it is, so my cousin would be doing us an enormous courtesy just finding a place for Edward on the journey."

"But Jane? Saints above, John, can we not at least send our *pretty* daughter?"

"Margery, the girl is not yet six and does not take direction well. We could not risk proposing that."

Jane heard her name and tried to process what they were saying. It has got to be Jane for *what*? What wrong had she committed now? It was like trying to translate the Latin Vulgate of the Bible, never quite getting past the words to the actual meaning of the text.

"Pray, how will we possibly afford it, John? Our Jane cannot go to the French court looking like someone's poor relation or we shall be the laughingstock of England, and Edward's opportunities shall come to an end."

Her mother could not seem to speak without shrieking, Jane thought.

"Perhaps I can ask Sir Francis for a loan."

Margery slapped her forehead with her palm and rolled her eyes with incredulity. The shrieks grew louder. "You cannot be serious! You wish us to ask a great lord to do us a family kindness and then ask him to foot the bill as well?"

"A loan, Margery."

"'Twill not stand. No. There must be another way. Both of the children will need new costumes, shoes, costly beadwork, and lace to make certain they are fashionable enough."

"There *is* your grandmother's brooch."

Margery clutched at the large pearl framed by a jeweled halo pinned prominently to her dress. She looked as though she had been wounded with a dagger by the mere suggestion. Their bickering fell to an abrupt halt as she held fast to the gem. "Out of the question. 'Tis my birthright," she said with a snarl.

"It really is the only thing we have of substantial value, Margery, something to provide ready money on the scale required. It is that, I fear, or humiliate ourselves when we ask Sir Francis for aid."

From the hidden stairwell, Jane saw the sheer panic bloom on her mother's expression, like the unfolding of some grotesque flower, changing her face into something wild. *"Jane's hair!"* she gasped, adding it then to the litany of reasons not to send their daughter to France.

"That, I'm afraid, my dear, was your doing," John said blandly.

"'Tis pointless to assign blame now."

"Pointless was doing it in the first place."

"You know perfectly well I was angry, John, and besides, it was meant to teach the girl a lesson."

"The only lesson learned is to avoid impulsivity."

"Oh, do silence yourself!" she spat, rolling her eyes again. "And help me work this out."

A shift of weight on the floorboards caused a creaking sound, and both parents turned toward the stairwell. Reluctantly, Jane and Thomas both emerged, hands behind their backs, a sense of fear rising in both of them.

"So then. The two of you were listening," their father said, linking his hands behind his back and gazing down discerningly at them.

Knowing that at times silence was the best response, neither child replied as he looked back and forth at each of them.

"Since you have obviously heard the news, what do you think, Jane?" he suddenly asked his daughter as Margery moaned.

"It seems I must go if you wish Edward to go," she meekly replied.

"Petulant girl!" her mother screeched. "This is an impossible situation! You are bound to ruin this for all of us once people realize whose sister you are!"

The taste of this new cruel barb was bitter on Jane's tongue as she tried not to react, watching her own mother serve it up to her, full of disappointment. Still, Jane looked back and forth to each of her parents and waited silently, stifling the urge to burst into tears before a pronouncement was given or a decision made.

"I must sell it, then, mustn't I?" Margery resolved. "'Tis the only thing of value I have in this world, the only tangible memory of the life I used to have. But I must surrender it now."

"Give an inch to take a mile," John countered with his customary calm. "Think of what we might gain through Edward."

"Or what we might lose through Jane."

The next silence was long and awkward, stretching out for what felt like an eternity. Jane squeezed her linked hands, determined still to push back the hurt along with the press of tears at the corners of her eyes.

"Oh, very well, John," her mother finally groaned in concession. "Go up to London. Sell the thing if you can. But pray, make certain you do it quietly. 'Tis bad enough that the Seymours of Wiltshire must stoop so low. But for Edward I believe I would do anything— even sell the only thing of measure I have in this world," Margery proclaimed as Thomas and Jane stood motionless before her.

The two were quickly dismissed, and Thomas, Jane, and Elizabeth went to the apple orchard to watch the villagers who had been hired to pick the last of the ripe fruit from the trees. "I cannot believe you are going to France in the train of the king's sister. 'Tis a miracle," Thomas whispered to Jane.

Elizabeth, who was too young to be interested at all in this latest turn of events, was noisily eating an apple as she watched, happily biting and chewing and swinging her short legs back and forth from a wooden bench placed at one end of the orchard.

"I do not wish to go," Jane replied with a glimmer of anguish in her overly wide blue eyes.

"Why on earth not? There will be music and dancing and elegant food. You shall have new dresses and new shoes, and you shall make new friends!"

"In case you've not noticed, Tom, I make enemies far more quickly than friends," she countered. "I am not quite good at being with people."

"You are good with me," Thomas countered loyally.

"You've got to like me; you're my brother."

"'Tis not true at all. I don't like Elizabeth nearly so much as you."

Their younger sister looked at them with a small pout before she lost interest in their debate and went back to the remains of her apple.

"I'm frightened, Tom. What if I make a mistake? What if they realize I am not like them, not a nobleman's daughter? I'll not dare to open my mouth or someone might discover the truth about me. Then Mother would be more angry with me than she is now!"

"She is only jealous you get to meet the princess and she does not. I always hear her telling father how she was meant for better things than a life out here in the countryside, and about the poet who nearly married her."

Realizing that was probably true, Jane did not argue the point. "I shall needs be very quiet, though, remain in the background as much as I can, just as she has spent my whole life telling me to do."

"'Twould be a good idea. And I am certain Edward will help you."

Jane grimaced. "I shall feel fortunate if he even acknowledges me at all. Edward is like Mother, meant for better things."

"Perhaps you are as well," Thomas offered. In spite of herself, Jane smiled. *Better things.* Impossible as that was, it was a pleasant thing for a little girl to dream about. Although she really could not imagine what sort of future might be better than her quiet and secure life here at Wolf Hall.

It took eight days, with not a moment to spare, for Jane's and Edward's wardrobes to be cobbled together; everything was cut, sewed, hemmed, ornamented, and beaded swiftly once their father sold the brooch for a goodly enough sum. Their mother, in a sullen, serious state, went about the task of organizing everything, finding and paying seamstresses, tailors, and jewelers nearby. She did not laugh or smile and there was not a single expression of excitement shown for what her children were about to embark upon.

For Jane, the days before their departure for France were filled with fear, sleeplessness, and endless trepidation. She was nothing like these girls into whose midst she was about to be thrown. She would be with girls who could certainly only be worse than those who had chased her into Savernake Forest. Young ladies in Princess Mary's retinue would be educated, well versed in how to wound her. The only saving grace was that somewhere nearby, her rescuer, William Dormer, would be there. As the days had gone on, she could not quite remember what he looked like, since they had met only that once, but she felt certain that if she ever saw him again, she would remember him. Beyond that, Jane could not think of much else positive about going to France.

When the day came to depart for Dover, where Jane and Edward would join the other attendants, Jane did not want to get out of bed. She could hear the commotion downstairs; shoe heels, heavy footfalls, trunks and bags hitting the floor, irritated sighs, huffing, and whispers. There were no sounds of joy or excitement. She put her pillow over her head to stave it all off, but the low muffled sounds broke through the feathers anyway. It was the drumbeat of her future coming for her, loud, relentless, frightening.

When the door to her bedchamber was thrown open suddenly, she gave up, tossed the pillow aside, and swung her legs over the edge of the bed. She ran her hands through her newly growing hair, which she could still feel sticking out in the places where her mother had cut it. Jane stifled an urge not to burst into tears yet again. A moment later, her mother threw open the heavy draperies, and morning sunlight poured like water into the dark paneled room.

"Very well, Jane, so it is your turn. Edward is dressing and his last few articles are packed up. Now to you. Since everyone in this house has been enlisted to a task to see Edward prepared, I have engaged our groundskeeper's daughter today to see you dressed and ready in time to join him," Margery announced matter-of-factly to her daughter. "Lucy, this is my daughter Jane. Help her with a minimum of fuss. Is that clear?"

Jane felt the blood drain from her face as she looked directly into the eyes of one of the girls who had caused the travesty she faced every morning in the looking glass. It was a horrifying moment. To her surprise, Lucy's expression now was not its usual one of arrogance. Slightly older, certainly prettier, she stood in the doorway, her young face blanched and full of dread that the tables had turned. Jane quickly realized it was Lucy who feared *her*. It was clearly not her idea to have come here. Would Jane say anything to reveal Lucy's guilt? That question was sharply written beneath the freckles on her two rosy cheeks.

Retribution was a fast friend, Jane thought as she planted her feet on the cold wood floor, trying not to feel a small bit of satisfaction at the girl's expression of discomfort. Both of them knew in that moment that Jane now had the power. Jane knew Lucy was looking at her chopped hair—the incriminating evidence of her crime in the forest—and Jane's realization of it was like a silent punctuation mark between them.

Quiet power was a new and heady sensation to Jane.

Both girls waited to make a move until Lady Seymour had left the room. Jane was sorry to see her mother go for the first time in a long time, wishing she could have silently taunted Lucy a bit longer with the uncertainty of what she might reveal to the mistress of the manor. It was Lucy who advanced first. Her steps were as tentative as her other movements were careful.

"You might have told your lady mother," Lucy spoke softly.

"I considered it."

"She could well have relieved my father of his duty. My family desperately needs the income."

"I suppose," she deferred, waiting a moment to continue. "But then why did you mean to frighten me and chase me like that into the forest as you did? You have always been spiteful to me."

Lucy lowered her eyes with uncharacteristic humility and what looked like a tiny flash of fear. It was suddenly awkward for both of them in the tense silence, with all of the commotion beyond the door as the two young girls continued to regard each other, knowing what they both knew, neither of them saying it outright.

"I suppose it is that I have nothing, and I was angry that you have everything," Lucy replied with cutting simplicity.

"Everything except my hair," Jane answered, still unable to imagine the ridicule with which she would be greeted in France once she was seen without her hood.

"Was it because of me that they did that to you?"

"I was not to go into the forest," Jane answered flatly.

Another silence fell between the two of them. Lucy glanced

around nervously, her gaze landing on the collection of headdresses and gowns folded and tucked inside the open wooden traveling chest beneath the leaded windows. "And yet look at that fine silk hood with the tiny pearls. What a beautiful thing. If such a thing belonged to me, I would never take it off, so no one would see my hair anyway."

Jane glanced over at the chest herself and saw the hood to which Lucy had referred. She hadn't even noticed it before now, for all of her fears. At that moment, Jane was not interested in dresses or shoes or headdresses or dancing or banquets. Right now, all she wanted in the world was to remain safely home with Thomas and her other siblings, where there was no chance to be made sport of; go on playing in the fields beneath the broad blue canvas of sky; and fall asleep to the chirp of the crickets, sheltered from the darker side of the world by her brothers and sisters, who loved her as she was. Even Mother's predictable criticism seemed preferable to the unknowns in France that lay so frighteningly before her. It was then that she noticed the slightly frayed hem and the tea-colored stain on the bodice of Lucy's dress. Suddenly, as they faced each other, the resentment Jane had felt gentled itself into a small surge of compassion. She understood about envy because she felt that with Edward, who would always be their mother's favorite child.

"Would you like to try it on?" Jane surprised herself by asking as she pointed to the delicate pearl-dotted hood.

Lucy's pretty freckled face paled. "'Twould not be proper. Someone might see."

"You heard my mother. She is very busy preparing my brother Edward for our journey. 'Twas why she brought you to me. So she would not need to be bothered about it."

Lucy glanced down at the open traveling chest and the blue silk and pearl headdress placed temptingly on top. She took a step forward, then stopped. "You wouldn't tell?"

"I didn't tell about the forest."

"I fear I should not be able to take it off if I did."

Jane went to the trunk and pulled out the coveted article herself, then handed it to Lucy, who wore her hair swept into a plain beige-colored knit caul. She did so with total sincerity, an offering of peace from one child to another.

"I am to help you dress, not help myself to your things," Lucy reminded her with a declining gesture.

"'Twould only be for a little while," Jane encouraged with a slight smile, feeling far more empathy now than anger, knowing she was about to leave Wiltshire on a grand adventure and Lucy would still be here back in her plain dress and caul. Jane had never had a friend beyond the bounds of Wolf Hall. She was certain that William Dormer did not count because he was a boy, but perhaps Lucy might be her first.

"What will you wear when you leave here today? This?" Lucy asked as her eyes settled on a dress of robin's egg blue silk ornamented with lace and edged with tiny pearls to match the headdress. "Oh, 'tis very grand," Lucy said.

"The dress is too tight and the lacing pinches."

Lucy began to glance around the room, first for the undergarments, the embroidered cambric chemise, petticoats, and stockings. Beside them sat a neat new pair of beige slippers with blue beadwork across the tops.

"'Tis all of it fit for a princess," said Lucy, moving cautiously toward the collection.

"No matter what I wear, 'tis bound to be dreadful. I really do not want to go."

"I believe I would happily die to take your place!"

"Then I wish you could."

"Your brother will be there to watch over you, though. Master Dormer as well."

"You fancy him, don't you?" Jane asked of their neighbor as Lucy helped her slip the chemise over her head.

"He's the handsomest boy I've ever seen. Do you not agree?"

"I have really only ever seen my brothers, so I don't suppose I really know what I think of other boys," said Jane, suddenly realizing the truth.

After the petticoats were on and fitted, Jane went to the blue silk hood, drew it up a second time, and placed it onto Lucy's head over the plain mesh caul. Lucy made a little gasping sound as she went to see herself in the looking glass. She was smiling at her reflection, but Jane saw tears shining brightly in her eyes. Then, after a moment, with the matching gown still lying between them, Lucy said in a voice that was uncharacteristically fragile, "I am sorry for how the girls and I sported with you those times. I knew not how nice you were."

There were a great many things neither of them knew about the world, Jane thought, looking at her own elegant silk hood, which was like nothing even she had ever worn. It was meant to be worn at court, but now it lay on the head of the groundskeeper's daughter, whom, up until yesterday, Jane was quite certain she hated. Life certainly seemed full of surprises.

Chapter Three

October 1514
Dover, England

*T*he mighty ship *Henry Grace à Dieu* might have been a rowboat for how it bobbed and dipped across the choppy waters of the channel called the Narrow Sea, slicing through foamy waves on the journey to France. Jane hung her head over the railing beside one of the great bronze cannons and retched again, certain she had never been more miserable in her life. All of the introductions onshore had been a blur of bowing, curtsying, and total anxiety that she not embarrass herself or her brother. She had done her best to shrink behind the throng of other elegant young girls, none of whom even acknowledged her, as they clamored to be spoken to by the Princess Mary as she boarded the royal ship.

Jane had not seen Edward since they arrived in Dover from Wiltshire, when he had been whisked off by an elegantly dressed man who introduced himself perfunctorily as Sir Francis, their father's cousin. In that moment, as she watched Edward abandon her, she had longed to cry out and cling to him, sobbing with all of the fear she felt. She had never been made to understand how she had even been a necessary part of the bargain for Edward to come to France.

When the seasickness seemed for a moment to have subsided again, Jane turned around and sank, weak kneed and trembling, down onto the deck of the ship, wiping her mouth with a shaking hand and the lace edge of her sleeve. She thought then of jumping overboard, having decided that drowning would surely be preferable to everything about this day so far.

"Are you not meant to be with the other little girls?"

The deep male voice came to her on the cool breeze off the waves. She heard it before she saw the two sturdy legs in fawn-colored nether hose and brown ankle boots planted on the deck before her. Jane looked up, but the voice's owner was standing in a harsh ray of sunlight so that she could see no higher than the silk sash at his waist. She recognized nothing about him, only the elegant cadence of his words, which defined him absolutely as an aristocrat.

As she struggled to her feet, he reached out a large, firm hand to help her up. There were two jeweled rings on his fingers. One was a ruby the size of an almond set in tooled silver. The other set in gold bore what looked like a family crest.

"There, now, my girl," he said smoothly. "'Twill not do at all if you cannot speak when spoken to. I was reassured by your father that you were quite conversant."

The man she saw then as he moved to block the sun from her eyes with his broad back was startlingly handsome. He had thick auburn hair, widely set deep brown eyes, and a strong jaw.

"Sir Francis?" she asked weakly, suddenly recognizing him from that morning.

"At your service," he replied with a formal nod. "But John said nothing about you being so dreadfully prone to seasickness. You're white as a sheet just now."

"I have never been at sea, my lord."

"Ah, yes. How old are you again?"

"Nine years old this month, sir."

He grimaced. "A bit younger than I had hoped, but I suppose you shall fill the bill sufficiently. You are attired well enough for her service, *if* you manage to keep yourself clean," he added unkindly, indicating with his eyes the railing over which she had been sick.

"Am I to know what bill I am to fill, sir?" she asked, feeling another wave of nausea build as the boat rose and dove again into another sharp series of waves.

"Her Highness, the Princess Mary, favors the company of lovely English girls, since she has been told she has much competition in France. It makes her feel more secure to be surrounded by familiarity. You are not front-row material, but you shall do well enough to fill in the background."

It did not even surprise Jane to be told so boldly that she was plain. It was simply a fact that she had already learned to accept. And he hadn't said it cruelly anyway. He had stated it as a matter of fact, as if he were remarking on nothing of more consequence than the color of her eyes.

"Have you eaten at all today, young Mistress Seymour?"

Jane shook her head that she had not. She had been far too nervous, having arrived late to the shore with Edward, who had been angry and shouting that he would not be made to miss this opportunity for anything, even if he had to leave her and their suddenly lame horse behind at Maidstone.

"Let us at least fetch you a draught of ale below, then, shall we? Good for whatever ails a belly. And there are windows to be opened down there. You can sit near one and catch the breeze. Something has got to bring a bit of color to those pale cheeks of yours, after all. 'Tis my hope, at least."

Sir Francis seemed a kind enough man, in a formal sort of way, Jane thought as she joined him, and she desperately needed someone she could trust in this frightening new world. Even if he was a stranger, he was still Father's cousin, so she made up her mind to join him.

The swaying rhythm of the drawn litter, in which she rode toward Abbeville with five other young maids of honor, was so steady that Jane fought to keep her heavy eyes open in the mellow light of the setting French sun. It was late when the ship docked at Calais because the farewells between the princess and her brother King Henry had been so prolonged at Dover and everything had been set back from there. From her place in the back of the enormous crowd, Jane had caught only a glimpse of the royal siblings, but it was clear they were both young and fit and elegant beyond measure. As Princess Mary had moved quickly past the crowd, Jane had seen so much glittering beadwork on her gown that, as it caught the sun, Jane was reminded of the shooting stars in the night sky out behind Wolf Hall. How far she was from there, she thought, pushing away the deep longing for home. Even if these two places did share the same sky, they could not be farther apart in her mind.

After he had brought her the ale and her stomach had settled, Sir Francis had disappeared, as mysteriously as he had come, back into the crowd milling about the massive ship. She had not seen him again. Jane thought now, as she fought hard to stay awake, how entirely different he was from her father. Sir Francis had a sense of grandeur and an air of mystery about him, which she was sure life at court had cultivated. Her father had said Francis Bryan was a dear friend of the king. To Jane, that was almost like being friends with Almighty God himself, since no one was actually friends with a king.

For some reason, plain Jane from Wiltshire had been invited to accompany this god's sister to the mysterious land of France.

She looked then at the young red-haired girl perched on the bench beside her. She was a few years older than Jane and silently clutched an embroidered handkerchief and continually pressed it to her cheek in a self-soothing way. There were tears in her eyes. Jane was not certain why that surprised her, but it did. That any other girl should feel the same fear or hesitation she did was an odd comfort to her.

"I am Jane Seymour of Wiltshire," she hesitantly offered.

"Mary Boleyn of Kent," the girl said, sniffling in return and drying her eyes on the handkerchief, then wiping her nose, as a much younger child would do. "I have not seen my family in such a long time. My father will say I have grown quite fat when he sees me."

"You're not," Jane assured her sweetly.

The girl with full cheeks and a pink nose turned her small mouth down in a sad expression. "He shall think it. He can be terribly partial when it comes to his daughters, as he believes his fortunes are tied up with ours. My younger sister is actually quite remarkably pretty."

"Mine as well," Jane revealed sympathetically, remembering Elizabeth.

"Anne is young like you, but people already say she has the dark-eyed beauty of Cleopatra. At least they were saying that the last time I saw her. She has been educated in Antwerp this past year, since our father has great hopes for her at court one day."

"Are you to see them both here in France?"

"My father is a diplomat in Paris. He saw to it through his connections that Anne and I both were named maids of honor here. Although my mother is convinced I shall be sent home once Father sees how I have changed. Believe me, Jane, I am not the girl I was a year ago. Their worst fear is that a Boleyn daughter should be mocked."

"Nor am I the same, honestly. If you could see what is beneath this hood right now, everyone would have a good laugh at me," Jane revealed, feeling less self-pity than she had since her own mother had taken the pair of scissors to her hair.

Mary tipped her head. "Have you an injury under there?"

"Only to my dignity, as my brother said before we left."

"You've a sibling here with us?"

"My brother Edward. Like your sister, Anne, he is my family's great hope."

Suddenly, and for the first time, Mary Boleyn smiled as the horse litter began to slow as it rocked over the smooth cobbled stones, arriving finally at the great stone palace at Abbeville.

Everything was different here in France. Jane felt that the moment she stepped out of the litter and into the buzz and hum of a new and lyrical language swirling around her. Jane had tried to study French at Wolf Hall, but she realized now that books were a very different thing from hearing French spoken in a conversational way. She pressed back the growing sense of panic that was threatening to seize her again.

As the massive English assemblage gathered in the courtyard, Jane, as usual, was pushed steadily to the back of the group. It quickly became a crushing wave, as the girls and women subtly vied for a place near enough to witness the Princess Mary's entrance onto French soil for her first meeting with her new husband, France's aged king.

"He doesn't look so old and awful as they are saying," Jane murmured to Mary, who was beside her, pushed and pulled as well.

She was speaking of the tall, broad-shouldered, athletically built man who emerged regally from the grand chateau, elegantly draped in crimson velvet bordered with ermine. He had a kind of insolent grace that was both attractive, Jane thought, and a little frightening.

"That is the king's cousin, the Duke of Valois, and if Louis has no son, he shall be the next king."

Just then, a beautiful woman came within sight, and Jane knew it was the king's sister. She was elegantly clothed in a gold gown, and an egg-shaped ruby framed in diamonds glittered at her throat, with matching earrings dangling from her lobes. Jane thought the princess was the most exquisite person she had ever seen. With brief glimpses between the fashionable bell-shaped sleeves and intricate head-dresses blocking the path before her, Jane took in the princess's beauty. Spurring Jane's youthful sense of fantasy, the princess glided as if on a cloud toward a magnificent destiny that Jane could not quite fathom at her young age.

"There he is! There is the king!" Mary Boleyn exclaimed with youthful excitement.

Jane stood on her toes, straining to see, but others were still pushing her back and pressing forward at the same time. It felt like the sea between England and France that had battered her about. Suddenly, there was a break between padded shoulders and head-dresses and Jane caught a glimpse of a diminutive man, elderly and fragile, descending the same flight of stairs down which the dashing young duke had so effortlessly stepped moments before. This man's hair was thin and patchy, the color of a springtime snow after the first thaw. His face was drawn and bloodless, the color of parchment. As he moved forward toward the magically beautiful English princess, who was legally already his bride, Jane saw a shimmer of spittle drip from the corner of his mouth, a punctuation mark to a thought that seemed almost incomprehensible in her mind—that these two unlikely souls were joined before God as man and wife.

Her child's stomach rejected the vision faster than her heart did, and Jane placed a finger across her lips to push back a little spark of nausea at the disagreeable thought. The princess held her head up as the two at last came face-to-face. A woman in front of Jane with a wide, pearl-lined, gabled hood moved again so she had to strain to see, but the moment of the royal meeting ended quickly and was lost to her.

"I would rather die than marry an old man like that," declared Mary Boleyn, who was still standing beside her, her rosy face now mottled red with shock. "We were told he was not a young man, but I do not recall 'ancient' being part of the description."

"Our princess really is quite beautiful, though," Jane said as they were ushered forward.

"She is already a queen, you know. There would have been no turning back for her no matter what he looked like after their proxy marriage back in England."

Jane knew nothing about that, but Mary spoke with such authority, being older and potentially wiser, that she automatically believed the Boleyn girl.

The palace at Abbeville was different from anything Jane had ever seen. The tall walls were lime washed and bare of ornamentation, the floor cool marble. There were no carpets to warm them, so there was the constant echo of shoe heels as courtiers crossed the halls. Jane shivered as much from the newness as from the cold. She had been gone from Wolf Hall for only a few days and already she was dreadfully homesick. To make matters worse, it seemed the pages of honor, of which Edward was one, were sequestered from the girls, so that she still had not seen her brother since before they boarded the massive English ship. When Jane felt her lower lip begin to quiver at the thought, she bit it.

She must not disappoint her family.

The tears of a child would most certainly do that.

Jane and Mary Boleyn were pressed along with the others up a wide, curved stone staircase with a wrought-iron railing. When they arrived at what seemed like the front of a long line of silk-and-velvet-clad girls, they came to a round-faced woman with a steely, determined gaze. She was dressed in a forest green gabled hood and heavily embroidered dress with a pearl and gold chain at her waist. When Mary curtsied to the woman, Jane did the same.

"Mother Guildford," Mary said in deferential greeting.

The woman arched a thick, graying brow. "Why, Mistress Boleyn, I see you were included after all. Your father must have pulled a great many strings to see both you and your younger sister among Her Majesty's new train here in France."

"Is Anne already here, then?"

"I am told young Mistress Anne was brought from Antwerp last week. I know not what favors are called in to bring about these postings, but 'tis not mine to question."

Jane took in the kaleidoscope of velvet, silk, pearls, beads, and elegant, full, bell-shaped sleeves around them.

"Who have we here, then?" Mother Guildford said as her appraising gaze fell upon Jane.

"This is Mistress Jane Seymour."

"Ah, so you are Jane," Mother Guildford remarked with an indecipherable, thin-lipped smile. "You are Sir Francis's choice."

"I am honored to be so."

"You are awfully young. Too young, 'twould seem." She touched Jane's chin with a discerning pinch.

"I am nearly nine years old, mistress," Jane tried to respond with a note of pride, but it dissolved almost before it left her lips. They began to quiver again in the face of such a bold-looking woman with so deep and steady a voice.

"Yes, well, all of these other girls you see are at least twelve. Mary here is fourteen. Aren't you, Mary?"

Mary Boleyn nodded. "Yes, Mother Guildford."

"So what, then, I wonder, did Sir Francis have in mind in bringing you here?"

"I was told only to accompany my brother Edward to France, mistress, not why I was to do so."

"First of all, child, you must address me as Mother Guildford, as the French queen herself does. I was in Her Majesty's service before she was old enough to speak, and I am in charge of her girls. I am to organize you all and keep you in line. You would do well not to question authority, particularly the sort here at court, English or French. You shall go much further that way. Or at least have fewer problems. Mistress Seymour, you shall be in the dormitory with Mistress Boleyn and her sister, who is closer in age to you. That might be some comfort to you, at least in a strange land. This is your first time away from home, I gather?"

Jane bit her lip even harder now and lowered her eyes to force away the tears pressing forward. "It is, Mother Guildford."

"Then you would do well to make friends. Mary here is a respectable start."

The older woman bobbed her head like a punctuation mark at the end of a sentence, then turned her attention to the two giggling girls behind them. The encounter was over. But not Jane's fear and longing. No matter how they dressed her up, or what she managed to endure without weeping, she was still a little girl in a faraway place.

"She does look a bit young," remarked Sir Thomas Boleyn, standing in the shadows of the second-floor landing as the fresh crop of English girls presented themselves to Mother Guildford in the room just beyond him.

Boleyn was a slim, dark-haired, elegant man, accustomed to court ways. He had a slightly crooked nose and eyes a little too deeply set, but his thick glossy waves of ebony-colored hair, along with a slightly wicked smile, helped label him one of the most desirable English courtiers.

"She was the best I could do on short notice, and for the price," Francis Bryan responded on a note of irritation. "And Jane shall do quite handsomely to make your two daughters appear old enough for your purposes, as you requested. Perhaps Mary and Anne will even look worldly now."

"That might be stretching it," Boleyn replied snidely.

One of the English king's diplomats, Thomas had been posted this past year, by order of Henry VIII, to the Netherlands, where he had taken his younger daughter, Anne. His elder daughter, Mary, had grown a bit fat before they departed from Hever Castle in Kent, Francis recalled, so it was decided Anne would be the daughter capable of more quickly ingratiating herself, and to eventually move up the court ladder. The ultimate good would be to make an important enough marriage that it would benefit the entire Boleyn family. So far, little Anne Boleyn had not disappointed her father. Thomas was eventually able to bring her successfully into the house of Archduchess Margaret of Austria, where Anne was invited to remain with him until the invitation to France had come.

It was in that heady and prideful moment that he had decided to bring both of his daughters to the court of France and to see if either of them could find a more permanent post. Anne was young, so placing someone young like Jane Seymour beside her was a calculation to enhance his daughter's place.

Fortunately, Francis Bryan had never been above bribery.

Thomas Boleyn drew the small coin-stuffed black velvet pouch from his doublet and handed it to Francis, who tucked it away in the same fluid movement as both men glanced around, ensuring the exchange had not been witnessed.

"You might have found one a bit prettier, though," Thomas Boleyn could not resist saying. "In addition to being so young, your little charge there is really quite stunningly common about the face."

"Perhaps she will grow into her looks," Francis weakly defended.

"'Twould be more likely for a camel to go through the eye of a needle," Thomas Boleyn said unkindly, before he turned and melted back into the swirling crowd, leaving Francis Bryan wondering if he had not just made a very grand error in judgment by bringing his cousin's plain little daughter to France.

The bed was cold but the dormitory room was colder, filled with an icy draft, shadows, and the whispering voices of strange girls.

"Quiet, or she shall hear you!" Mary bid her younger sister in the darkness infused with pale moonlight streaming through the bank of uncurtained leaded windows. Jane, Mary, and Anne were in small beds next to one another beneath the windows.

"I understand not why you talk to her, or what she is even doing here. She is not like any of the rest of us. And she is as awkward as she is homely," Anne whispered back.

"Shh! She is bound to hear you, and she has been very nice to me."

"Well, I am not going to be nice to her," Anne pronounced cruelly from beneath her downy bedcovers. "There is far too much at stake here for both of us. Father said so."

Jane might be young, but she knew well enough that she was the present topic of conversation. She pressed the pillow over her head, trying to drown out the voices as another wave of homesickness descended on her.

There was no going back. This was her reality now, and she must somehow rise to the occasion and make a place for herself. At least she tried to tell herself that without bursting into tears so that the others would hear.

That whole week after Mary Tudor's wedding to the King of France, Edward Seymour avoided his little sister. At first, Jane told herself it was a coincidence when he walked the other way whenever he saw her. There were so many banquets, pageants, revels, and even a fireworks display, so many people to meet, that he could not be expected to come and reassure her, or to introduce her to the other pages of honor.

That was the story her heart allowed her to believe.

But as time went on, Edward's intentional avoidance of her became clear. Jane struggled not to feel hurt, but that had become unavoidable. As Mary Boleyn spent much of her time now with her sister, Anne, with whom she had been reunited, Jane was set adrift in a sea of other young women who knew precisely how to be seen and heard in the busy, high-stakes French court. Jane did not. She tried to stay quiet, to watch and learn, but the pace was heady and mistakes were likely. More than one of the well-heeled young girls was reduced to tears each day by Mother Guildford's condemnation of something said or a step taken out of turn. With her experiences at Wolf Hall as her primer, Jane vowed to avoid that indignity if she could.

As Sir Francis had predicted, she was made for the background, in order to add dimension, not distinction, to the English ensemble supporting the new young French queen. At large events, Jane receded into the crowd, never attracting the least bit of attention.

The same could not be said for Mary and her sister, Anne.

The Boleyn girls were always prominently placed in the front, always full of confidence, and in the case of Anne, she always found subtle ways to draw attention to herself.

But today there were no revels, no jousts, and no banquets. It was Sunday, and the old king and his new bride were having an argument in plain view of all of her ladies, with nothing to mask it. While his English was poor and heavily accented, the sentiment and the emotion behind it were clear to everyone.

"The English girls must go back," he repeated in his thick, rheumy baritone marked by his Gallic accent. "You are a French queen now."

"But they are my support and encouragement here."

The girls and women sat around the queen like a wall of defense, pretending to sew or play card games.

"There are many French women here who can be the same for you, but you must give them, and my country, a chance."

"Am I to keep none of my friends about me, then?" the beautiful young queen asked in a defiant tone.

"You may retain a small group without complaint, but only that, so I suggest you choose wisely," he replied coldly.

Jane, who was sitting a few feet away at a card table along with Mary Boleyn and two older, more established attendants—the Countess of Oxford and Lady Mary Norris—tried her best not to stare once she saw tears begin to glisten in the young queen's eyes. So this homesickness and loneliness did not become easier to bear with time and experience, apparently, she thought. Even a beautiful royal was susceptible to it.

A moment later, the old king, dressed this morning in a pale blue surcoat lined with ermine, leaned over to kiss his new wife on top of her head as though she were a petulant child in need of patience. The move brought a fit of rheumy coughing, and for a moment he seemed to lose his balance with the exertion. The young queen took a step nearer to him, concern suddenly darkening her flawless expression. As he continued to cough, he waved her away and two of his stewards approached, one providing a cloth for him to place over his mouth as they helped him to leave the room.

"That was wretched."

Jane heard the catty whispered voice from the table beside her and realized it was Mary's sister, Anne, who she had not noticed was nearby until now.

Knowing enough not to implicate herself in gossip, Jane kept her gaze impassive and faced forward, trained on the queen as Mother Guildford bent down by her side to speak privately. Jane watched the young queen's pretty eyes fill with tears before she surrendered her face to her hands and shook her head.

Mother Guildford put a maternal hand on the queen's shoulder, which at the moment was racked by sobs. Mother Guildford then looked across the room at the large collection of English ladies and girls, who sat in stunned silence.

"Her Majesty requires some fresh air. A selection of you shall attend her."

The aide began to scan the sea of suddenly hopeful expressions. "Lady Norris, Lady Oxford, Mistress Mary Boleyn, and . . . Mistress Seymour."

Jane heard Anne Boleyn huff angrily behind her.

It was Jane's first opportunity since she had come here to be in such close proximity to the queen. She felt the excitement even as her fear flared. This was a pivotal moment for her. She could not say or do anything wrong right now. But she was still so proud to have finally, after ten days, found this moment when she might actually make an impression with the queen.

Jane heard indecipherable grumblings behind her as Mary stood. Jane drew in a breath, straightened her skirts, and moved to rise, too. But as she did, she felt a firm tug on the linen fall of her headdress. As she turned to see if it had perhaps caught on the chair, she felt another tug just before her beaded hood clattered to the floor, leaving her head and her chopped hair exposed to everyone, including the young queen.

Jane heard her own horrified gasp, but it felt as if it had come from some other place, as if she was not quite connected to the moment or the sound. She knew what she must look like to them. She could see it on their faces, a sea of cruelly competitive little smiles, as she stood there, exposed and humiliated. When she glanced back, she saw Anne smiling innocently, her fingers steepled.

"Shall I go in Jane's place while she collects herself, Mother Guildford?" Anne asked so sweetly that Jane felt too utterly humiliated to counter the question.

Anne Boleyn was a force with which to be reckoned.

Jane readied herself to walk from the room in a dignified manner, at least to escape before the tears came. But then she felt a foot slyly move forward and catch on her toe, causing her to stumble and nearly lose her balance. Only then did Jane abandon all decorum and break into an ungainly sprint, feeling a first sob rush its way up her throat.

"My, what an awkward little girl," she heard Anne murmur cruelly as Jane brushed past her.

Out in the corridor, safe from view, Jane clung to a pillar, the choking sobs and the stress taking over as she folded in on herself and wept. A little girl lost. Alone, far from home. Humiliated. She was relieved that Mother Guildford had not come after her, since she was certain to face criticism for her unladylike exit; just now she could not bear another bit of harshness.

"I want to go home," she whispered to herself in a futile sob, holding her headdress in her trembling hand.

"'Twill do you no good. You must be strengthened by it, not undone, if you are to survive here."

To her surprise, the voice behind her belonged to William Dormer. She had seen him only at a distance since they had arrived in France, and yet now, as in Savernake Forest, he simply appeared before her.

"I do not *want* to survive here. I want to go *home*!" Jane countered through quivering lips as she brushed tears away with the back of her hand, trying vainly to steady herself. "People here are ruthless and cold and not at all what they seem."

"Then learn from that. While you must be here, why not make it count for something?"

He was older and probably a little wiser, but what he was saying made no sense to her. It was then that she saw him staring at her butchered hair, still free from her hood. "What happened?" he gasped.

Jane tried to flatten the chopped strands with her hands and tuck them behind her ears, as if she could make the reality of her appearance disappear with so futile a gesture. It was a nervous, pointless attempt. "It matters not."

"It matters to me," he said.

"Why?"

"Because we come from the same place. We are bound by that."

"You only visit one of your homes in Wiltshire. One of the smaller ones, from what I hear. Your life is nothing like mine."

"Our parents will stop at nothing to inch into the world of the English court, and we are both here because of that. We do have that in common."

Jane had not thought of it like that. She tipped her head and considered. There was something engagingly sincere about him. Something she felt she could almost trust. If she were not so afraid to trust anyone. She told him of what happened after that day in Savernake Forest and watched him cringe with compassion.

"I do not like that Boleyn girl. She is dangerous," she angrily admitted after her story.

"More dangerous than Lucy Hill?"

"Lucy is not so bad, actually," Jane replied, remembering their conversation and the vulnerability she had seen in Lucy's eyes before she left Wiltshire. Anne Boleyn did not have any softness at all. Her heart seemed as hard as her dark, fathomless eyes, and Jane vowed to stay as far away from her as she could for as long as they were in France. Soon enough she would go home, and the name Anne Boleyn would fade from her life and eventually her memories. Jane was counting on that, even as she was distracted by the pierce-your-soul blue eyes that she was sure were the deepest, most beautiful eyes in the world.

It was an odd feeling, caring for another person. It was a feeling to which William Dormer was certainly unaccustomed at the age of thirteen. He had recently come to realize that he was the only son of parents who had put everything into him except their emotions. Thus, he had grown to feel more important than loved, more needed than wanted. Caring for people had never seemed worth the risk.

Whatever it was he was feeling for the young Seymour girl, it was certainly different. It must be a protective instinct, he told himself.

Jane's life certainly seemed similar to his. As he walked, just having left her to return to her duties, William cringed again at her explanation of what had happened to her hair after that day he had met her in the forest. She seemed vulnerable. Life was going to be difficult for her. Plain faced, pale, soft-spoken. The confidence of the other girls made it worse for her. He was old enough to see that.

And yet, he thought, there was still a spark, the promise of something more that made her different, though what it was exactly, he could not tell. As he watched her a moment ago, rubbing at the jagged ends of her shorn hair as if the movement could undo the past, something awakened in his blood. It made him want to protect her, and it was powerful. He had never felt like that in his life.

"Ho, what are you doing there, lad?"

The man who seemed suddenly to appear like an apparition before William was imposing—a grand and dark, sweeping tower of a man dressed in black velvet edged in luxurious fur. William jumped and the man reacted with a restrained smile as if he enjoyed frightening people.

"So out with it. Why were you loitering around the queen's apartments? The French king needs no more reasons to rid himself of our train of attendants. You are obviously an English lad. I can tell by the rough cut of your tow-headed hair."

"Yes, I am English, my lord. I am William Dormer."

"I know not that name." The big man sniffed unpleasantly, then rolled his dark eyes. "Another position bought and paid for, no doubt."

William would have defended his family then if it had not been the truth. He knew perfectly well the strings his ambitious mother had pulled, the endless stream of costly gifts she had sent to court. Silver plate, a jeweled goblet, brandied cherries, a barrel of costly Spanish wine, a case of quail, and another filled with doves. But the bribery had certainly worked, since he was here, after all.

"Mind, next time stay where you are meant to, Master Dormer," the imposing man ordered as he went unceremoniously around a corner and disappeared in the same sweep of black velvet in which he had appeared.

Another voice came from behind. "You are a fortunate lad, indeed, that he did not see you straight out of France before you could make your mark. Do you know who that was? I see by your expression that you do not."

William turned to find a handsome, auburn-haired young man with wide-set brown eyes and an impressively strong jaw. His puffed satin sleeves were full of pearls that shimmered.

"Forgive me, my lord, but I know not who anyone here is, save the French queen herself, and the girl I was just speaking to, who is my neighbor at home in Wiltshire."

"Well, be aware that I am Francis Bryan and that was Sir Thomas Howard, the most powerful Lord High Admiral, son of the Duke of

Norfolk, a great politician at court and the man who heads this entire delegation here. I trust you know the name, if not the face."

"I do of course, my lord Bryan." William bowed awkwardly then, seeing the expression of expectation before him.

"That at least is something." Francis Bryan shrugged in a manner that said he found William of no consequence beyond this moment. "You shall be gone in a day or two anyway, so no matter, really. What did you say your name was?"

"Dormer, my lord. William Dormer."

"Forgettable." Francis sniffed unkindly, glancing around. "See if you can do something to change that."

As he walked away, William thought how right Sir Francis Bryan was. He was out of place at the court of France, able to utter barely a few words in French. At home in England, he felt confident and driven toward a life of comfortable local prominence.

William did not like it here, but he did feel somewhat protective of the awkward little Seymour girl from Wiltshire. It was a new sensation, having come from a world where his mother was the only female he truly knew. The domineering Lady Dormer certainly did not need to depend on anyone. Or at least that was the impression he'd had in his life so far.

Jane lurched forward toward the king. Anne had pushed her. She had not even had time to fully dress. She wore only her cambric shift and beige stockings. She stumbled onto the polished wood floor. The sense of humiliation pushed past the shock as the other ladies attending King Louis and his new English queen began to whisper and chuckle at her. Anne Boleyn cruelly snickered.

"She hasn't any dress!" the young queen gasped in broken French, fingers touching her lips to press back the sound of shock.

Jane felt blood flood her face in a hot rush. Pulsing. Horrifying. She wanted to run. As fast as she had run into Savernake Forest, she wanted to do so again. She glanced quickly around the vast room, desperate for a safe haven. The laughter rose as all eyes turned judgmentally upon her.

"Elle n'a pas une robe!" someone else echoed in French with a chuckle as Jane felt the heavy press of bodies behind her, an impenetrable wall.

Jane looked back at the new queen sitting on a raised dais beside the king. Suddenly it was not Mary Tudor's face but Lucy Hill who looked at her with that odd mocking smile that had first frightened her. Lucy with her freckles and wide mouth and huge blue eyes. *Oh, those eyes!*

"Jane! Jane! Do wake up. You've overslept! We shall be late!"

It was not Anne Boleyn pushing at her now but rather Anne's sister, Mary. "There's the masque to rehearse in ten minutes' time! Pray, do not make us late or Mother Guildford shall have both our heads!"

The fog of her horrifying dream began to fade behind Mary's frantic plea. Praise God, she had not embarrassed herself in public without her dress, nor become the shame of her family. Not yet anyway. She now remembered lying down for only a moment, giving in to the fatigue of another day spent standing motionless for endless hours while the king and queen dined, enjoyed the revels, strolled, and then challenged each other at the lute or primero. Such activities defined her month here in France.

Jane scrambled to her feet, having only a cursory understanding of the workings of a court masque, or what her small place in it would be. Participation in the rehearsal, however, was not optional. Jane and Mary dashed down the tiled corridor then, skirts flying, and Jane investing all of her trust in the hope that Mary knew where they were going.

The vast room into which they scurried, then drew to a halt, skirts flying up, was already full of milling courtiers. The hum of activity was everywhere, massive props on wheels were being moved into place, men were shouting directions, a collection of musicians was practicing a discordant tune in the corner, and ladies of various ages were holding up costumes to compare sizes and styles.

As usual, Jane recognized very few people. They were a sea of lovely but unknown faces moving before her, their titles and positions a mystery, as anonymous to her as she was to them. Some continued to look askance at her after the embarrassing scene when she had lost her headdress and had run tearfully from the room.

As she looked out, however, there was a single face she did recognize. A small perfect oval with wide dark eyes and strikingly long lashes met hers. The girl was gazing up at the tall, powerful Duc d'Orléans. She was smiling with an expression of such innocent adoration that it struck Jane with the force of a blow. This girl seemed entirely changed from the cruel one who had pulled off her headdress and tripped her a fortnight ago. How could anyone so young be two such different people? This girl, little Anne Boleyn, flirting with the grown heir to the French Crown? Yet she saw the absolute picture of childlike innocence. What an odd and frustrating little girl, thought Jane, relieved that soon their paths would never have to cross again. She was going to return home to England with the other unnecessary attendants from the queen's retinue, as the king wished it.

Jane was actually relieved to feel the cloying nausea of seasickness rise inside her again just over a month after she had come to France.

Even as she slumped, weak and trembling, against the polished ship's railing, she knew it meant that she was going home to Wolf Hall and to the comfort of obscurity there.

True to his word, after a bit of negotiating with the queen, the King of France permitted only a small contingent of English courtiers to remain with the country's new queen. Jane's brother Edward was among those chosen. Once the decision was made, Jane and a dozen other children were thrust into litters and herded unceremoniously back to Calais for the return voyage to England.

It was a reminder to her just how insignificant her presence had been in France. Certainly no one would even remember her, or her brief visit. But Jane would remember everything; the court, the infighting, and that nasty-tempered little dark-haired girl named Anne Boleyn, of whom Jane was enormously glad to be free.

"You acquitted yourself well in France," said William, coming up beside her and gripping fast to the railing as the sea wind battered her hair and cheeks, flushing them.

"It could not be that well, since I am returning to England."

"As am I. We were never actually meant to remain. And I, for one, am glad of it. I miss home."

Jane looked into his face and those eyes that stopped her from thinking every time she looked into them, as if they had a power all their own. "I no longer miss it at all."

"Your family, then?"

"Less than that."

William pushed out his lower lip, as though he were considering the statement. "Me either, actually." Then he smiled. "'Twas nice to be free of the structure for a while, though."

"English structure anyway."

"Yes," he agreed. "Your parents shall be glad you were there at least. 'Twas quite an honor we both were given."

"My parents are proud of Edward."

"I wish I could say that I understand, but I fear I have yet a great deal to learn about the world," William said.

"After this, I am not certain there is much more I want to know beyond the pages of my books. It seems to me now a rather confounding world."

"To me as well," he agreed. "But we are young."

"I certainly am."

"I still hope that I see you again after this. I would quite like us to be friends."

"That does not seem likely, since it took nearly nine years for us to meet the first time."

"The next time my family is in Wiltshire, I shall make certain of it."

Jane turned to gaze out at the sea again, her hands tightening on the railing as a wave crested and splashed them, but she did not say anything else because she knew how unlikely that was to ever happen.

Chapter Four

The glory of the Seymours lasted only so long as the King of France did. By January 1515, Louis XII was dead of consumption, and his young English queen was pregnant by her secret lover, Charles Brandon, her brother Henry VIII's most trusted companion. Everyone who had been left in France had returned to England shortly after Jane and the others had left.

Forgotten in the uproar of Mary Tudor's great scandal, Jane settled back into life in Wiltshire. William Dormer, she was told, returned to his parents, who were installed at their primary estate in Buckinghamshire. Edward, however, had made enough of an impression on his benefactor, the young and well-placed Sir Francis Bryan, that he returned to the English court, not Wolf Hall. Edward's advancement had been the family goal all along anyway, and to have helped her older brother in some small fashion made Jane glad.

It had been a defining journey for a girl who had only just turned nine. Jane was glad to be back home with Thomas and Elizabeth, and even with Lucy Hill, who made every attempt to make amends now by coming around and offering herself up as a personal servant as soon as Jane had returned. To her ministrations, friendless Jane quickly softened.

By midsummer after her return, her trip to France seemed all but a fading dream to Jane. Over the next two years, the Seymour family rallied around a single goal, watching from a distance Edward's steady progress at the increasingly grand and powerful court of the young, dynamic King Henry VIII. Two more children, a boy and a girl, were born to Margery Seymour.

Most of the damage her mother's temper had wrought had now been repaired. Jane's hair had long since grown back, and she had never told her mother what had actually happened in Savernake Forest. She never told anyone. The only one who knew was William, and she seemed destined never to see him again.

"Read it again," Thomas bid her as they sat together with Lucy and Elizabeth in their favorite spot in the orchard with their little brother and sister, Anthony and Margery, tottering between them. It was 1517, and their brother's most recent letter from court had arrived. Jane's reading skills were the best of any of the children left behind in Wiltshire. In spite of the fact that their tutor was their family chaplain, Jane had managed to wrest volumes by Ovid and Petrarch from Father James, which she devoured. She grew more fluent in both French and Latin. Reading was her passion, no matter the language.

"He says he has been befriended by the king's brother-in-law, Charles Brandon, the Duke of Suffolk, and that they spend much time at war games."

"No, read it as he wrote it," Thomas persisted. "That way, it's as if he's here with us!"

Her brother's expression was bereft. Jane knew how much

Thomas idolized their elder brother, how much they all did. Edward had risen and flown away to something very magical and grand.

"Great heavens, he hasn't died!" Jane said with a smile.

"By your leave, please do read it word for word."

"Oh, very well . . ."

>*Dearest family,*
>
>*It is already warm here. Richmond Palace is so vast that I continue to lose my way to meals, which has brought me much embarrassment, as I have turned up in the larder more than once. I have been in the company of the king on several occasions, but still have not been presented formally to him. Our sovereign seems a spirited man, although I have seen enough of his temper at a distance to know how unwise it would be to cross him, if he ever came to know who I was.*
>
>*I am told by my lord of Suffolk that His Grace knows I excel at the hunt, so I am always included in hunting and sporting events, although as a bystander. Pray, one day soon I shall be able to show him what the Seymours of Wiltshire are capable of . . .*

"Tell us again what it was like," Thomas pressed her.

"Awful, really. So many grandly dressed people, all shoving, pushing like sheep in a pen, trying to be nearest the queen. She had people to brush her hair, put on her shoes, clean her commode, flatter her every move . . ."

"But how grand." Lucy sighed at the description. She smoothed the skirts of the pretty blue dress she wore, which Jane had given to her.

They sat in rapt attention as if this were the first time they had heard it and not the tenth. Or perhaps it was the hundredth time that Jane had recounted the old, somewhat fading story.

She had lost track. And interest.

"I shall go to court one day, like Edward," Thomas proudly announced. "Just you see if I don't."

"You shall be bored and lonely," Jane declared sagely. "Better to make your life here in Wiltshire with me and Elizabeth."

Their younger sister yawned with distraction.

"I shall have Edward," Thomas countered, his expression full of ambition.

"Edward only loves himself. And adventure."

Thomas stiffened. "You're only jealous because you were not clever enough to be retained at court. But I shall certainly be clever enough and more ambitious than Edward by half."

Thomas puffed out his adolescent chest. His sibling rivalry was as clear as the new bit of hair growing above his lips, which he had refused to shave.

The rejection stung Jane because she loved Thomas more than anyone in the world now that Edward was gone. Sometimes, late at night, when she'd had a bad dream or could not sleep, it was Thomas's room into which she crept. Beside him, she could at last feel safe enough to fall asleep in the grand old house with all of its ancient and frightening creaks and shadows.

"Fine. At least I have Elizabeth."

"Oh, no, not me. I am going to marry and have my own house when I grow up, and dozens of servants like Lucy to attend me."

"Elizabeth!" Jane gasped as Lucy's cheeks reddened. "That was unkind."

"'Tis true just the same."

"I would serve any of you, happily," Lucy replied in that new, servile manner that Jane was still unaccustomed to, even after more than two years, from the girl who had once chased her into the forest and had marked her for constant ridicule. Something sharp in her own sister's tone suddenly reminded Jane of Anne Boleyn and her sister, Mary. Jane was becoming all the more aware of how different she and Elizabeth were, just as Anne and Mary had been at the French court.

She guessed that Anne was still in France, which Jane thought was the proper place for her. As far from England as possible.

But she did wonder about Mary. Even after Anne had humiliated her, Mary had continued in her kindness toward her. Jane was certain she and Mary Boleyn would have become the best of friends.

At first, she did not register a change in the boy nestled beside her, but then she felt his small body slump against her, like a heavy weight. She had forgotten her youngest brother, over whom she was to keep watch. Anthony Seymour was only two, and his usually bright smile was gone in an instant, masked with a blank stare, his face awash with perspiration. Instinctively, Jane pressed her lips to the child's wide, freckled cheek. She tasted the fire that spelled fever and potentially the sweating sickness, less feared outside of London, yet still a threat to guard against, like the violent merchant of death it could so quickly become.

Without losing a moment, Jane scooped her brother up and carried him in her outstretched arms, dashing toward the house, stumbling and straining, her small frame bearing the weight with difficulty.

"Bring the others!" she called frantically to Thomas over her shoulder. Dutifully, he scooped up one-year-old Margery in one arm and gripped Elizabeth's hand in the other.

Jane did not feel herself even breathe as Lucy turned the large brass handle on the massive carved front door moments later. Jane shoved it open with a thrust of her shoulder, panic pushing past the shock.

"Mother! Father! . . . *Someone!*" she cried out.

Her father, who had been reading in the library beside the entrance hall, came to the door, clutching an open book. His expression was one of mild irritation at the disruption. But one glance at Anthony's blank stare and sweat-drenched face and the book in his hands fell to the wood plank floor with a soft thud.

"Margery," he called to his wife, and the sound was more plaintive than beckoning. *"Margery!"* he repeated more strongly, his expression frozen in terror.

Then the little girl in Thomas's arms coughed, and the sound echoed across the silent hall. Margery Seymour descended the last step of the grand staircase in a shuffle of petticoats and heavy gray velvet skirt.

John, Jane's deceased eldest brother, had suffered these same symptoms. The same sickness. No one spoke of it after he passed. If he had not existed, Jane thought, neither did the threat.

"Lucy, take the boy upstairs," Margery flatly commanded the groundskeeper's daughter, and for a moment Jane held Anthony more tightly, unwilling to surrender him, unwilling to allow this brother to disappear as well. "Elizabeth, call for Father James. John, go to the kitchen and have Mistress Allen make a physic for them both," she instructed her husband with a dispassionate tone that stunned them all.

"Good Lord, Margery, a physic is not going to change this course!"

"Easier to prepare the crypt again than a physic?"

Her tone had switched very swiftly to a low growl. Accusatory.

Cruel. Jane rested her lips on top of Anthony's head, pressing into the mass of pale copper curls there, desperately breathing in the child's scent. As if, somehow, imprinting his scent on her memory would make it impossible for him to be stolen from her.

"You well know I did not mean that," said her father. "He is my son as well!"

Jane thought her mother might cry, but her eyes were dry and clear with resolve, the exact color of an August sky. "Lucy, I said take the boy from Jane. Get him upstairs at once."

Margery coughed again. "Give her to me," she directed Thomas, her flat tone brittle now, holding nothing of the maternal tone Jane had often heard her use with Edward when they were younger. This was compulsory behavior, like that of a lioness who operated by instinct, not feeling. "Thomas, go. John, get the boy away from here until we know for certain what this is, or until it passes."

Jane felt Elizabeth looking up at her. The implication was a clear and harsh reminder: daughters were not the same concern as sons. Thomas was quick, handsome, and essential to their mother's ambitions should anything befall Edward. Jane was not. Elizabeth, she thought, could at least lay claim to the family beauty and hold on to that for the future. Jane's only purpose was the care of her siblings, a responsibility that had been taken from her that very instant.

They were likely the only children she would ever have.

"I shall go fetch Father James," she said shakily of the young country chaplain who made his home with them as tutor to the Seymour children.

Margery Seymour did not respond. She simply took her youngest child into her arms and followed Lucy back up the stairs. Jane blinked back tears, helplessly watching them go, her life and her memories indelibly marked forever by each footfall.

Little Margery Seymour died first. Anthony died the next evening. Jane and Elizabeth were firmly directed by their mother that there were to be no tears. There was no point in them. As men were the least expendable members of a family, John and Thomas had gone to Kent and would remain there until the summer passed and the chance of catching the sweating sickness had abated.

Margery kept her teeth clenched as she spoke the directive dispassionately, only her lips moving. There was no sign that she felt anything at all for the third and fourth children she had surrendered back to God. Until Jane saw that she was digging her fingernails into her palms as she spoke. She could see small, bloody gouges in her mother's flesh. Mother was trying to feel something without anyone seeing, Jane thought, or stop herself from feeling something. Jane was not certain which. Her mother was an enigma.

The night that Anthony died, Jane tried to read from *The Imitation of Christ* instead of one of the more daring volumes she usually chose. The book was a great comfort. Father James had told them when they were very young that the king's grandmother, Lady Margaret Beaufort, had personally translated the fourth book into English from a French edition. Jane reread the words now, trying to make each directive mean something.

Some weeks later, when the threat of contagion had passed, Jane's mother insisted on a Mass. While she said it was for the souls of her two lost children, Jane knew that she was using the tragic circumstances as a social occasion. Edward would be home from court soon with Sir Francis Bryan and his influential—and unmarried—friend Lord Anthony Ughtred, so the timing could not be a coincidence.

As she tried to focus on the verses, Jane could hear her mother and father arguing in the next room. The debate concerned whether or not to extend an invitation to Sir Robert and Lady Dormer, who had recently returned to their local estate.

"We could host a small private supper afterward," Margery proposed.

Jane read the same passage again, but the argument continued, distracting her.

"I do understand, Margery, but we have not seen them for years, and I do not see this as the kind of occasion Sir Robert and Lady Dormer would relish. It is rather a more somber circumstance than that."

"And I do not detect the awkwardness in inviting them. I attempt only to be neighborly in it, John."

"I warn you, your ambition will show through as clearly to them as it does now to me."

"You dare to insult a woman who has so recently buried two of her own children at once?"

"They were my children as well. Do not use them to deflect my scrutiny," John countered.

There was a slight pause in the discourse, the creak of someone outside on the stairs, before Margery said, "Well, what precisely is wrong with getting on with our lives, since nothing will bring the children back to us?"

"I have loved you for many years, Margery, but I do not believe there is a woman in all this world with less maternal instinct and more ambition than you," her father growled.

"Insult me if you will, but we have living daughters, John, one with real prospects, and I do not regret my determination to pull something decent for Elizabeth from the ash heap of this tragedy. And if I can do it because of my tie, however distant, to our king, then I shall pay whatever the cost—even if it is my pride!"

"I suspect it does not dampen your desire that Lord Ughtred was knighted by the king and serves him now as friend to my own cousin Sir Francis Bryan. You have always wished to rival the Dormer family, and having them as our guests would achieve just that."

Jane had heard her parents arguing many times before. She knew her mother had never quite gotten over the rejection of her request for assistance from her own powerful relation at court, her first cousin the great Earl of Surrey, when she was seeking to place Edward in the French court. The rejection had only strengthened Margery's resolve. Clearly, she was not above using tragedy to achieve her goals.

"What would you have me do out here in the country where influence is as difficult to find as French wine? Marry Elizabeth to a pauper? A butcher, perhaps? Our widowed groundskeeper is in need of a wife!" she snarled sarcastically.

"Our children are barely cold in their coffins, Margery!"

"Yet life does go on for the rest of us!"

Stunned, Jane had risen from her reading chair and was standing now in the doorway of the chamber in which her parents were arguing. Elizabeth had been eavesdropping on the staircase landing and was standing beside her now. At just ten years old, Elizabeth Seymour was already showing the promise of her beauty, with wide blue eyes and exquisite apricot-colored skin. Jane saw the contrast between them more starkly every time she looked at her sister.

"May I have a new dress if I am to be trotted out?" Elizabeth asked sourly.

Both Margery and John looked up then, unaware, until now, that they had an audience.

"Of course, sweetheart, I've a new bolt of silk just arrived yesterday from Antwerp to make a dress for myself, but this does seem a much better use of the fabric. 'Tis robin's-egg blue and shall complement your eyes perfectly. I have already sent to London for a pearl-dotted hood to match."

Their mother was smiling and her cheeks were flushed with excitement as if she were planning a May Day celebration and not a funeral Mass for her children. Jane watched the scene silently and with a detached calm. The wound of rejection no longer stung as it once had. She looked from parent to parent then. Her mother's mouth held a smile, but her father's was a flat, unrevealing line that bore the stress he could not verbally reveal at his wife's insistence on proposing their very young daughter to a much older man.

In that moment, she could not recall why she had wished so desperately to return from France to Wolf Hall, for now she saw it as a prison she would probably never leave. She might be plain faced, but she was smart enough to know her future ended here as the caretaker of her aging parents. Dormer and Sir Anthony would be given an opportunity at the funeral Mass to reserve Elizabeth's hand—Sir Anthony for himself, Sir Robert for his young son. Jane's would not be given or offered to anyone.

"Of course we are not going, and that is that." It was not merely a statement by Lady Dormer, but a decree. "Such an invitation is unsavory, to say the least."

Lady Jane Dormer, with her stiff, beaded collar, commanded her dinner table of three as if she were the captain of a ship. She insisted that her husband and son sit at the far end of the grand polished table, while she sat at the head. It was a weighty, symbolic gesture not lost on any of them.

"But my lady mother can scarcely refuse a funeral Mass for departed children, can you?" William pressed as he took a small sip of

84

Gascony wine from a crystal goblet emblazoned with the Dormer coat of arms. Candles glowed between them.

William was taller now but still slim, with the same tousled, wheat-colored hair, darkened a shade since his childhood, but it was his magnificent eyes that had gained a weighty depth since his childhood.

"The woman is shamelessly ambitious. Everyone from here back to Buckinghamshire knows it," his mother scoffed.

"And yet the village priest did make it clear that the Seymour family is aware that we are back in residence here at Idsworth House. We lost too many of our own babies on our way to William not to find some compassion for their family," Dormer said.

Sir Robert was a pious man with a round little paunch, a slow-eyed gaze, and the unlimited patience of a saint. A Dormer family steward leaned in then and placed a large platter of stewed partridge beside the roast stag, dates, figs, oranges, and sugared almonds between them, and another came forward to serve it.

"I would like to go," William dared to admit, carefully watching his mother's eyes for the telltale narrowing, followed by the tightening in her jaw, both warning signs of an impending outburst.

Ever since he had heard about the funeral Mass, William had been reminded of the little girl he had first met in Savernake Forest, and their last conversation on the choppy waters of the Narrow Sea on the voyage back from France. Jane . . .

He had wondered about her from time to time when news or gossip of court was brought into the conversation. He'd heard that Jane's elder brother, Edward Seymour, had begun to make something of a name for himself in royal circles and that he was currently in the employ of the king's much favored little bastard son, Lord Henry Fitzroy, as Master of the Horse. Why that impressive elevation did not matter more to his mother, William was not certain. The Seymour family obviously had the court ties for which she so desperately longed. His mother liked to say it was because the Seymours had no great patrimony, not enough to make them suitable to advance a friendship. But William had come to believe that it was her envy rather than her sense of superiority that prevented her from associating with them. In France, he had heard Sir Francis boast that Jane's mother was a relation of the Lord High Admiral himself, so that connection must have been what secured Jane's place in the French delegation.

Had his mother not forced him to keep his distance from Wolf Hall, through the years when his family came to Wiltshire to visit, he might have seen little Jane again, and not just the village children who circled as flies to honey around him. Like that overly flirtatious Lucy Hill, with whom he had nothing in common, and for whom he had certainly no interest.

He had never forgotten Jane, and the memory of her awkward sweetness haunted him. He may be nearing seventeen, but William still lacked real friends.

"I am old enough to go on my own to the Mass," William calmly persisted, although he felt his heart beneath the elegant doublet beat very fast at his defiance. "I shall represent the family well."

As his mother's eyes narrowed, they carried a potent mix of surprise and fury. He knew very well that she did not like being defied. But like a captive trying to negotiate his own release, William felt compelled to press through the danger.

"Do not be impertinent, William. You are not to attend," Lady Dormer declared, her fork clattering onto her plate dramatically.

"Bollocks! Jane, you cannot keep the boy captive forever! 'Tis a funeral Mass after all, not a spritely dance around the Maypole."

"If it means steering our only child from the wrong sorts of influences, I certainly can keep him here forever," she growled with an almost masculine determination.

"The Seymours desire nothing from me, Mother. I wish only to make a show of honoring them as our neighbors in their time of great grief. 'Tis the proper thing to do."

"The boy is right, Jane."

"Lady Seymour is a dangerously competitive woman, William. I can smell that across the clover. Do you not recall what she did in order to see her son included in the royal entourage to France?"

"And now that son is at court making quite an impression, and ours is not," Dormer grumbled and lowered his head to his stew.

Lady Dormer's face flushed with anger. "She clearly has gifts of manipulation!"

"Or perhaps young Master Seymour simply acquitted himself better than I did."

"Mind your tongue, William. I do not require you making excuses for them in my own dining hall."

"Yet is it not you who always says God will put each of us precisely where we can do our best work? The good Lord must have something in mind for Edward," William muttered.

She slapped down her napkin and bolted from her chair. Robert Dormer held his fork in midair. His mouth, already open to receive it, closed again.

That was at the heart of the matter, and all three of them knew it. Families know the soft underbelly of each member as no one else does. The truth was that Lady Dormer had spent immeasurable hours, and massive resources from their sizable fortune, bribing anyone she could in order to find a way back to court for her son. But the effort had been to no avail, while their lowly neighbors saw their son hunting, dancing, dining, and thriving in the company of the king himself! The disparity between the two families was repugnant to a woman who had invested her entire existence in success.

William stood slowly, meeting his mother's gaze as he did. The bank of clouds outside the long dining hall windows broke, and a strong, silvery ray of sun shone through. William could feel it warm and sharp, heavy almost, on the back of his neck above his braided collar. Just then, he felt that it was God's hand pressing him forward—giving him strength against his overbearing mother.

"I am going to the Mass," he announced, careful not to expose a hint of disrespect.

"From impertinence to insolence all in one meal, William? I believe I have raised you better than that."

"I have no wish to disappoint you, Mother. I am simply attempting to follow the example of personal conviction which you so unfailingly set for me all of my life."

A quick sideways glance just then revealed his father's slight, bitten-back smile, and William knew that he had cleverly maneuvered his mother into a corner. His father's expression said he wished he had thought of it himself.

The little parish church of gray stone sat starkly beneath a heavy and equally gray sky on the cold and wet morning of the Mass. William arrived with a groom from Idsworth House as companion, although he directed the slim, ebony-haired servant to wait for him outside with the drawn litters and saddled horses. One litter in particular was ornate and very costly. On the side, it bore a crest emblazoned in gold. It was very clearly the conveyance of someone important. What would his mother have made of that? William thought smugly.

The family had already gathered inside at the front of the church as William drew off his gloves and entered. A few of them who were dressed in shades of gray and black were near the altar speaking with the village priest, so William hung back. Quietly, he slipped into a pew. There were fewer mourners than he had expected for a family of such prominence in the region as the Seymours. Perhaps it was due to the nature of the deaths, he thought, since the specter of the sweating sickness continued to terrify everyone even once it had passed.

William had never had the opportunity to grieve the loss of his own siblings, as they were stillborn or had died before he was born. It would have been nice to have had a brother, he thought as he watched a pale, ginger-haired adolescent boy sling his arms support- ively around the shoulders of two girls and walk with them into the first pew. He had known the Seymours had several children, and those must be some of them. He was not near enough to see whether one of those girls might be Jane. Would he even recognize her after all these years? William wondered then, feeling foolish for insisting on coming here to pay homage to a faded childhood memory. Even if he did, would she remember him? Such a quiet girl. Not quite shy, but one who, back then, kept her thoughts and feelings well guarded.

As the Mass began and the nave filled with the pungent aroma of incense and the low sound of a mournful dirge, William saw Sir Francis Bryan, whom he had met in France. Then he noticed two men behind Bryan dressed more brightly than the other guests. One wore russet-colored velvet slashed with brown, and the other was garbed in azure satin. Their caps were ornate, one dotted with beads, the other plumed with an ostrich feather. As the Mass progressed, William could see that they were whispering to each other. Their attention was clearly not focused on the sad circumstances that had brought them here. It was disrespectful, but they were not like any two men he had ever seen. At least not since he had been at the French court. His curiosity was piqued.

Everyone gathered outside afterward as a low-lying fog swirled around their ankles. Once again William hung back, trying to take in the scene without feeling awkward for being here. As she emerged from the church, he easily recognized Lady Seymour. A strikingly attractive woman with few of the ordinary marks of age for a woman with grown children, she had changed little. The man beside her, against whom she leaned heavily, was less notable, with his thinning gray hair, high, shining forehead and kind blue eyes.

Then he recognized Edward Seymour as one of the two well-dressed young men from the front of the church. The one wearing azure and the ostrich plumed cap. His companion was older than the Seymour heir, with thick hair that had begun to gray at the temples. His eyes were deep, hooded, and slightly brooding. William linked his hands behind his back to give himself courage and moved forward as he knew he must do.

"My lady Seymour," he said sincerely with a proper bow to her. "I know not if you will remember, but I am the son of your neighbor to the north, the Dormers, come to pay respects to your family at this time of great sorrow."

Her blue eyes lit magically with recognition like the flare of a sudden fire. "Of course I remember. Sir Robert's eldest son."

"Their only son, my lady. I am William, charged with conveying to you and your family our deepest sympathy."

She drew in a discerning breath before she tipped her head and focused her eyes on him. "Your parents were unable to accompany you?"

"I regret to say that is the case, yet both send their sympathies for your loss."

He could tell she knew he was not telling the truth by the way the corners of her mouth twitched just slightly, then lengthened into a cautious, knowing smile. He was not old enough yet to have become an accomplished liar.

"Well, you must join us at the manor now in their place. There shall be food and wine to sustain you for your ride home. I insist. It really is the least I can do for your show of kindness. And you remember my daughters, who can, no doubt, keep you better company than I," she said, eagerly glancing around for them. A moment later, she drew them both over with a firm tug.

They turned at the same time. William was surprised that he knew Jane at once—her pale, smooth skin, close-set eyes, and still slightly round face. The girl next to her must be her younger sister. Her eyes, like their mother's, were vivid, like blue glass reflecting the sun, he thought. They weren't as deep as Jane's searching eyes, yet still, he felt himself stir at the way her dress flared out at her hips and came to a tight pointed V at the bottom of her plastron. William swallowed and looked away, embarrassed at the effect of this ripening adolescent girl's body on his own.

"Master Dormer, allow me to present my daughter Elizabeth," Lady Seymour declared proudly. "She has just mastered her lessons on the virginal. Perhaps while you are in residence here in Wiltshire, we can prevail upon you to come and hear her play."

"'Twould be my pleasure." William nodded to the younger Seymour sister, yet fully aware of Jane still standing beside her, unannounced. He realized then that there would be no introduction.

"Hello, Jane," he said anyway, surprising himself, drawing her eyes and holding her gaze with his own. "Do you remember me?"

"How could I ever forget you, Master Dormer?" she coyly replied.

She did not quite blush as she spoke his name, yet William saw a sudden shade of rose. The blush defined the soft bones of her cheeks before fading.

Lady Seymour looked back and forth between them discerningly. "Ah, yes. Indeed. Jane. The two of you would have met in France. That's right." Her bland tone made the sentence sound like an afterthought and not a particularly pleasant one. "Since Elizabeth did not go to France, perhaps, Master Dormer, you shall be kind enough to tell her all about it while we dine," Jane's mother suggested, stepping between him and Elizabeth.

"'Twould of course be my pleasure as well," he said with well-schooled grace and a perfunctory nod.

Then Lady Seymour's eyes lit again. It reminded him of a wildcat seizing prey. "Oh, there he is. Come along, Elizabeth; there is someone else to whom you must be introduced." She quite suddenly and firmly clutched her daughter's arm above the wrist and twisted it, drawing her forward just before they disappeared into the crowd of guests waiting for their horses or litters in front of the little stone church.

When William glanced back, Jane had turned and stepped away from him as well.

"Wait!" He heard the desperation in his own voice as he reached out to grab her arm. He did not quite catch her, but his fingers brushed her arm and he felt her warm, pliant skin beneath the thin layer of her satin sleeve. She looked at him with slight surprise, eyes wide and, as always, impossible to decipher. "I was hoping to see you here," he confessed awkwardly, surprising himself.

"You have not been back in Wiltshire for a long time," she said suddenly, studying him.

"We've spent most of our time at Eythrope. But when I have been here it seems you are not, at least not at any of the celebrations, like May Day or New Year in the village. I confess, I have looked for you."

"I am always here. I have not left Wolf Hall since I returned from France."

"You sound as if you like it that way."

"I believed that I did. For a while."

He tipped his head. "And now?"

"Well, there were the children to look after before. But now—"

"Ah, there you are!" The female voice coming between them then was sudden but familiar. It was Lucy Hill, her face and smile as bright as if she had just come from running through a field. William had seen her from time to time since the incident in the forest when they were younger, so he knew her well enough. She always seemed to appear out of nowhere, as she had done just now, always smiling, always wanting to stay by his side. Her ruddy-cheeked expression held an open invitation, although to what, William was never quite certain.

"May I ride with you back to Wolf Hall?" Lucy asked him flirtatiously. "'Tis a rather long walk this time of day, so I would be grateful for the courtesy of a companion."

"Well, I have my horse . . ."

"Thank you, Master Dormer," she said without skipping a beat. "A ride with you on the back of your horse would be a grand adventure. I saw him when you arrived. He *is* a beauty."

William glanced at Jane, but she had looked away, the moment between them extinguished. They could not be more different from one another, he thought. Jane, Elizabeth, and Lucy, these three girls from Wiltshire. But only one of them made him wonder what was going on behind the deep pools of her indecipherable eyes. And to William Dormer, that made all the difference in the world.

He was just as she remembered.

Jane had few things of her own, but the childhood memory of the golden-haired boy and those startling eyes belonged only to her.

After dinner, Jane watched how her mother honed in with razor-sharp precision on the guest who had accompanied their brother from court. Elegant Sir Anthony Ughtred had been the impressively important captain of the king's ship *Mary James* and Marshall of Tournai. He also looked as old as their father. He had a neat graying triangular beard and dark rings beneath his eyes, probably from too much war. His teeth were yellow and there was hair in his nostrils, but he was distinguished beyond measure. A wealthy man, with no wife, Ughtred had met Edward during a skirmish with the Scottish at the border town of Berwick, and they had become fast friends, particularly when Ughtred discovered his new friend had a beautiful and very young sister. By the time the marzipan and hippocras were served, Jane saw that all thought of William Dormer had vanished from Margery Seymour's mind in favor of a bigger, more rare fish that had suddenly landed on her little Wiltshire shore.

"Will she be forced to marry someone so old, do you think?" William asked Jane, who was standing near the fire as two boys from Marlborough played a gentle duet on a flute and recorder to entertain them. The afternoon had turned chilly in spite of the fire, and Jane held her hands up to the glow from the warming flames.

"There shall be little choice when she comes of age, if Mother decides. Which is how it is for nearly everything."

He bit back a smile. As the musicians played, Sir Anthony was regaling the collected guests with the story of how he had once been forced by orders to refuse the king's own pregnant sister, Margaret, safe passage to Berwick back from Scotland. The power of it, he told them pompously, was as enormous as the burden on his conscience. The guests sat in rapt attention, no one noticing William and Jane, especially not Elizabeth, who was gazing up at Sir Ughtred with what looked like childish adoration.

"I fear our mothers are no different," William said quietly. "Mine fancies the king's own daughter, the little princess Mary, is going to be brought to me like a Christmas goose one day. Rather like your very young sister has been paraded out for Sir Anthony."

Jane could not help it. The image made her smile. She felt her cheeks warm as he looked at her, smiling, too. "If I did not find the humor in it, it would all be awfully intolerable. I have never found much humor here. Safety, yes, but not much to make me smile."

He tipped his head. "*I* made you smile."

"I suppose you did."

"Do you know what you told me the last time I saw you?"

"Do *you*?" She was surprised. "That was an awfully long time ago."

"Three years, and every word of it, actually. You said you fancied village life, surrounded by your books, to the complications you saw at court. You said the world confounded you."

"Impressive. I had forgotten about that."

"Everything about you was memorable to a lonely boy of thirteen with no brothers or sisters."

"Now your recall has turned to flattery."

"'Tis only the truth, Jane. All I wanted back then was someone to talk with who actually listened to me. I remember the sensation quite vividly, in fact. You had this extraordinarily soothing way about you, even then, that made you seem safe and interesting as well."

"I was frightened of the world back then. Certainly I was frightened of Lucy and then afterward of the dark-haired Mistress Boleyn."

"I saw you as eminently dignified, not affected by whatever peril Lucy Hill or Mistress Boleyn had in mind for you." He smiled encouragingly, remembering some of the cruel laughter of the other pages in France over the embarrassing blunder with Jane's head-dress. But to him she had never seemed to lose her pride. "Even as a forlorn little girl on that day in Savernake Forest, your dignity seemed to prevent you from capitulation. You appeared equally confident in France."

"Curious, how one is perceived," she said with a sigh.

"Do you suppose we might speak again sometime?" he asked her.

Jane thought a moment. She was not certain what she would have to talk about with a handsome and worldly older boy, or why anyone who looked like William Dormer would want to hear it. But there was a powerful connection when their eyes met. A silent invitation to something more.

It seemed dangerous, wildly spontaneous, certainly wrong, and thus, truly perfect.

"Without a proper chaperone, I see not how we could meet."

"Perhaps," he conceded, glancing around at the chattering guests. "I think your mother approves of me, though."

"She approves of Sir Anthony more."

"True," William chuckled. "Perhaps if she knew not that we were meeting?"

Jane felt herself smile in surprise. No one in the room even knew they were speaking to each other, nor did they care, for all of the attention focused on Elizabeth and Edward—the great hopes of the Seymour family. For the first time in her life, Jane was actually happy to feel invisible.

"Yes, perhaps if she knew it not."

"Might she not know tomorrow, say, around noon?"

Jane fought back a complicit smile, realizing more fully then how handsome he was in his walnut-colored satin doublet with shimmering gold braid.

"At two o'clock she always lies down for a nap, and I always read."

"What do you always read?" She heard in his voice that he truly did want to know.

"These days I mostly read from *The Imitation of Christ.* It has always made me feel hopeful."

"Verily, you have every reason to hope, Jane," William said, and in spite of being young and knowing nothing of men or boys, she knew that he meant far more than he was saying.

Across the room, with a full glass of wine in his hand, Francis Bryan took in the scene beside his cousin Edward Seymour.

"My, my, has our young Jane hooked a fish, do you think?"

Edward had not been watching his sister, a girl he had barely noticed when they were children. She had never been of any consequence to him, nor was she now. He was at Wolf Hall only because his mother had written to him several times over the past year, imploring him to look for an important match for his more comely sister, Elizabeth, and a means of introducing them. Tragic as death was, it had provided his mother with what she craved, so he had come home. Next, he would need to find a way to bring Thomas to court with him. They were his tasks as the eldest son. But all in good time, Edward reminded himself. Rome was not built in a day, nor would his own empire be.

"Jane has not enough bait to catch *that* fish." Edward chuckled. "The Dormers are very prosperous indeed, and he is the sole heir."

"Perhaps the bait tastes sweeter than it looks." Francis Bryan snickered unkindly.

"Do be realistic, cousin. There is no honey on those lips, only prayer."

"Still." Francis shrugged. "The boy seems rather drawn to her. 'Tis often the quiet ones who surprise the most. Untouched virtue doesn't hurt."

"Not at King Henry's court. Predictability seems to win the day there."

"Perhaps. I only mean you must keep an open mind and show a bit of creativity. You must be more like your brother, Thomas, in that regard."

"Little Tom?" Edward sniffed uncharitably.

"I have been at court a long time, my boy, and I have learned what to look for. I can spot cunning at a mile's distance, which I see every time I am here in the way he deals with your mother and father, getting what he pleases from both. Remember, I learned at the hand of our noble king himself. Do not be so drawn in by the head of the serpent that you forget the power of the tail, Edward."

Edward did not understand at all. And he was more than a little irritated that he was suddenly being condescended to. He saw little potential in his younger brother, albeit his very handsome younger brother, and even less in a sister whose best feature was her hands. But he must not let that show for all his father's cousin had so generously provided for him. Edward was not certain why he should bother with pretending that Jane had a future with anyone. She certainly was not going to make an important match, or probably ever leave Wolf Hall. That a neighbor boy was chatting with her to pass the time meant absolutely nothing at all. Edward was most certain of that.

The next morning Jane woke before dawn. She lit a candle and held her book up to the light until she could read the words. She had been too nervous to sleep much at all, scenes playing over and over in her head. She had been plagued all night by what she might say later to make herself sound even remotely interesting to a boy like William Dormer. He was probably just being charitable in asking her to meet him. That, and nostalgic for the voyage they had once shared together. Yes, of course that was all it was.

When Lucy came to help her dress, as she always did now, styling herself as something of a lady's maid to the two Seymour daughters, Jane longed to tell her for what occasion she was dressing. How wonderful it might be to have a true friend! She could not quite imagine it. Nor did she entirely trust Lucy just yet.

As Lucy carefully brushed out Jane's long, flax-colored hair and captured it in a delicate mesh caul, Jane wondered if Lucy could sense her secret plan. She felt her own pale face flush with guilty pleasure at the mere thought of William; how handsome he was, how tall, with a dazzling smile that held so much behind it. And yet her thoughts were her own, a treasure to be guarded when everyone around her assumed there was nothing behind her eyes or her compliant smile. That smile was her mother's legacy to her. She knew what people thought of her, and she had no intention of changing their impressions. Not just yet.

There was too much freedom for her in their misperceptions.

At the appointed time, she tried to walk calmly downstairs, to escape through the front door. That was a daunting goal when so many things might stop her. Her ruse prepared, she clutched a small, tooled, red leather prayer book in one hand and alabaster rosary beads in the other, gripping both tightly so she would not lose her courage. She had never done anything intentionally daring in her life, and this was as exhilarating as it was terrifying. She had meticulously thought through the plan in her sleepless hours the night before. Jane would not have long, she told herself, but in truth, beyond the explanation of a garden walk, no one would care.

Besides, everyone in the house was consumed with the presence of two such noble and important guests as Sir Anthony and Sir Francis. They were to remain at Wolf Hall for one more day. What key connections Lady Seymour could make before they left was her all-consuming and sole occupation.

Jane moved down the stairs onto the landing, pausing when she realized she had only a few minutes to make her way to the edge of the broad meadow and the stand of mulberry trees where they were to meet, or William would think she was not coming. If there never came another such time in her life, at least she would have today to do something dangerous. She reached the end of the steps, moved across the plank floor of the entrance hall, drew in a breath, turned the door handle, and . . .

"And where might you be off to, young miss?"

Her mother's strident voice resonated like a bell in the vast, cool hollow of the pitched ceiling in the entrance hall. Jane cautiously exhaled.

"I was on my way to the garden to read, Mother," she answered so sweetly that she surprised even herself.

"Well, I would like you to come brush out my hair first before I lie down."

She had never once asked such a task of Jane. Lady Seymour had her own lady's maid for such things. Jane looked up at her mother's preoccupied expression, seeing there would be no dissuading her. Her heart sank.

"Might I beg my lady's kind indulgence and offer up Mistress Hill to the task instead?"

To Jane's surprise, it was Francis Bryan who suddenly stood in the open doorway at that moment, wearing a pleasant, unassuming smile, his elbow propped nonchalantly on the doorjamb. "I leave, as you know, on the morrow, and I had earlier bid my young kinswoman here to read to me and offer her thoughts on *The Imitation of Christ* so that I might share them at court. I am, you see, rather dismally lacking in scholarly knowledge, and the king would surely be impressed if I could converse about something for which his own grandmother felt a true passion."

Margery studied him for a mark of sincerity. Jane knew the look well, and her heart began to race. She knew nothing about any such request, nor could she fathom why he was interceding on her behalf now.

"Truly, 'twould not be a kindness I would easily forget," he casually pressed.

Jane waited silently, afraid to move or speak for fear of swaying her mother against the idea.

"Then by all means, good cousin, take her," Margery finally said with a smile, "but do not think I shall forget the kindness you owe me in return."

Francis smiled slyly. "I would never underestimate your memory, my lady."

While well-placed and favored at court, Francis was something of a scoundrel, a man who favored personal enjoyment above all else, and he knew that the Seymours knew it. He had already been ejected from court once by the devious and jealous Cardinal Wolsey several years earlier for untoward behavior. Yet he had won his way back to his post as Chief Gentleman of the Chamber by knowing how to play the game better than the calculating cardinal. Jane had heard her noble cousin never did anything without motive.

She wondered what his motive was now.

They walked together out into the warm summer sun then, and Jane squinted in the glare of the harsh, full daylight. But the warmth on her face and neck was soothing as she heard the soft trill of birds in the trees beside the stable and the hum of a circle of bees.

"Are you actually interested in my opinions on *The Imitation of Christ*?" she asked him when they were safely away from earshot.

"Not at all. But how else could you meet with young Master Dormer unless I pretended to be?" he asked with a wry smile.

Jane felt a burst of panic mixed with surprise. "How did you know?"

"Deductive reasoning, naturally. In all my years at court, I have become a student of human nature, observation being the most keen teacher. I am twenty-seven now, so I have had a bit of practice. You might say there are few subtleties lost upon me."

"We only wanted to talk. He leaves for his estate in Bucking-hamshire on the morrow."

"So he does." Francis was smiling more good-naturedly now, looking straight ahead, hands linked behind his back as they walked steadily from Wolf Hall.

"No one suspects I would ever do something daring."

"And yet your dear mother seems always nearby enough so that you won't."

"She wanted only to disrupt me, not detain me. 'Tis a little game of hers. Out here, there is little else to entertain her. My sister tolerates her not at all and has the beauty to win her way as well as her little freedoms."

"I cannot give you much time, but I confess I have a devilishly strong fondness for a good game of deception. Besides, you have fire behind those deep blue eyes of yours that cannot go entirely unaided. Doubtless it is what captivates young Dormer."

Jane pressed down the swelling excitement she felt, not wanting to look too anxious or to rush headlong into something that was foolhardy with someone older and beyond her station. "I'll not disappoint your trust in me, Sir Francis," she said anyway.

"Oh, I know you'll not. I am counting on an ample return on my investment one day. Fortunately for you, I have always been something of a gambler."

In addition to a libertine? She longed to parry, but she chose to hug him very quickly instead and then dash across the field spotted with wild poppies toward the trees, where William was waiting.

"I thought you might have given up on me," Jane said, sinking into the tall grass and the pretty red flowers that swallowed them up and hid them both from view as the breeze blew the greenery and the blossoms back and forth in a gentle rhythm like the waves of the ocean.

"No such luck, I'm afraid," he said with half a laugh. His long, wheat blond lashes fluttered over eyes that mesmerized her. "I know you are younger than I, but I am quite fond of you, Jane."

"Are you?" She looked at him lying there, gazing up at her, hidden from the world by the grass, the wildflowers, and the fullness of her own gown. She almost thought this was some ghastly joke Lucy had put him up to when they had ridden back together on his horse yesterday, for why else would a boy, nearly a man now, look at her with such interest?

She saw that Lucy liked him. But Jane couldn't blame her at all for that. If anything, she understood it completely.

"You're just easy to be with, to talk to. I've told you that." He reached up to touch her cheek very gently. The connection was magnetic, as his eyes glittered in the sunlight. "You don't look at me with ambition, just simple sincerity, Jane. You did when we were children, and you do now."

Bees droned in the poppies nearby as she tried very hard not to look too deeply into his gaze. She tried to ignore the growing allure of the forbidden delights she found there. "That certainly describes me, plain and simple Jane."

"'Tis not at all what I meant." William propped himself on his elbows and was quiet for a moment, but the connection—a kind of kinship between them—lingered as he refused to draw his eyes from hers. Jane felt herself growing very warm beneath his steady gaze.

"Read to me," he bid her suddenly, breaking the intensity of the moment. He looked then at the volume still in her hand that she had used as a prop to escape her house.

"'Tis not poetry. If it's beauty you're after, you had better look elsewhere."

"From your lips, it shall surely sound like it."

Jane bit back a smile, then nudged his knee playfully with her own over the clumsy compliment. It was subtle, but the connection between them flared hotly. Jane watched the rise and fall of his chest as he lay back in the grass looking up at her with an expression that said she was lovely in his eyes. For a moment, she could not read the words on the open page before her.

"My mother is bound to be impressed that one of the king's own gentlemen came here for the Mass," he said, feeding the windswept silence and the stirring between them.

Hearing his hopeful tone, Jane looked up at him. "Your mother?"

"I hope this will not startle you, Jane, but I am going to speak to my parents about you. You must know that I should like you to be my wife one day when you are a bit older. At least I hope that it is obvious. I shall never be a man from King Henry's court like the one intent on courting your sister, but I can give you a tolerably comfortable life." William sat up now, his cheeks flushed, his eyes wide with the kind of devotion she had not known existed. ". . . And, of course, my love."

Although William spoke it as an afterthought, Jane felt the power of it down to her soul. "You love me? But you barely know me."

Her words were a whisper made shallow by disbelief.

"Do you not care for me even a little, then? I have known you for years, and I have thought about you constantly in all that time."

"You speak brazenly, sir," Jane countered, feeling an odd stirring between her legs, as though he were touching her there with his gaze, and with the slightly suggestive tone in his voice.

To break the power of it, she lay back in the tall grass beside him and looked up into the broad crystalline sky, feeling as though someone had just struck her. She was unable to catch her breath, but she was not entirely certain she wanted to. "You know this is absolute folly," she warned him. "I'll not be able to marry for two years more."

In response, William reached over, then tenderly kissed her cheek, very near her lips. He hovered there for a moment, looking into her eyes, capturing her gaze, and her heart, a little more with each breath. "You are young, surely, but I am old enough to know that I want to be betrothed to you, Jane. I crave nothing else so much in this world."

It was a declaration with such simple purpose that she knew, strangely, that it would happen. William gave her a level look again then. It seemed to Jane that he was staring right through to her soul.

"I do feel affection for you. I suppose I have since you saved me from Lucy," she finally admitted, still forcing herself to hold back because the expression of desire was so bright in his eyes.

"See there? Some good always comes from bad," he said. They both began to laugh, but soon the laughter fell away. After a moment's silence, William bent to kiss her again. She felt his breath on her face just as he very tenderly brushed her mouth with his own soft, slightly trembling lips. She could taste his hesitation and inexperience matching hers, which made the moment all the more sweet.

"Will you tell your parents?" he murmured against her mouth.

"Not until I know there is even one small glimmer of a chance yours will approve of me," she replied in a whisper as she tried very hard to keep her voice from shaking. "You must know that is never going to happen, even two years hence."

"I'll not give up. Not ever," William declared. "I know what I want, Jane, and who. Perhaps it is odd to be fated to one from such an early age, but I knew our destiny even in France."

Then, as if he could ensure the future by branding her as his own, William's mouth came down possessively on hers, and he moved his hands to anchor her hips beneath his. She could feel his heart hammering against hers and how solid and hard he was beneath his trunk hose, an invitation her own body urged her to accept. This must be a sin—surely it was primal—but that only made it that much more darkly exciting when she lived every day bound tightly by the strict confines of a proper life.

Jane felt her body ignite as his warm tongue swept into her mouth. As their kissing deepened and became sensual, his hands molded her more tightly to him and he began to move his hips in a rhythm so intimate that she felt as if there were no fabric barriers between them anymore. Their connection felt as if it went on forever. He moved and she moved with him. She tasted his groan in the moist hollow of her small throat as he ground himself harder against her, as if he could not stop. Then very suddenly he slackened with a gasp.

As she trembled beneath him, the realization of what had happened came to her. Or at least, what she believed had just happened, because Thomas had only ever told her the very basic details. "Pray God, tell me I am not with child now!" she bid him in a shattered whisper, still clinging to his shoulders.

"Forgive me," he said raggedly against her cheek. "I took far too much liberty just now, but you are not with child, nor shall you be until you are my wife."

"That is still your wish?"

"Is it not yours? Or have I offended you too greatly?"

Jane looked up at him as he sat up and drew his knees to his chest, both of them still buried deep within the tall, moving grass. She heard the broken tone in his voice. "We should not have sinned so boldly," she said, not entirely certain what she was hoping for him to say.

"Have you changed your mind about marriage to me?" he asked.

"My mother has always told me that a girl who allows a man to take liberties with her body will never become a proper wife, no matter what he says at first."

Before he could respond again, both of them heard Francis Bryan's call from across the field. Swiftly, he drew her to her feet and helped her straighten her dress. She tried not to look at the little stain on his codpiece, but it was even worse looking into the guilty expression in his eyes. It had been a few precious moments that had felt like a lifetime. Though she felt guilty as well, she was changed by them. Changed by William Dormer, because she was in love with him.

As she knew in her heart he would, William left Wiltshire the next morning for Buckinghamshire without a word, and Edward and Anthony Ughtred left as well to rejoin the king at Greenwich.

The air turned cold with the close of summer and the beginning of autumn. In the months that followed the deaths of Anthony and Margery, Jane's life returned to the mundane routine she had always followed at Wolf Hall. With no young siblings to care for, she now spent her time praying, sewing, reading, and waiting for some message to come from William to confirm what she already had trouble believing had ever happened.

But it never came, as somehow she knew it would not. Clearly Margery Seymour had been right with her warning, and that was simply that.

Chapter Five

1525
Wolf Hall

*N*early eight years after the funeral Mass, Sir Anthony Ughtred formally requested the honor of Elizabeth Seymour's hand in marriage. The gentleman had corresponded with Jane's father for those long and frustrating years and, apparently finding no one else to his liking, at last put forward the request. The house was filled with excitement from Lady Seymour to the servants. At last there was to be a marriage, and an important one.

"Perhaps the king will come for the wedding! They are to be married up north in Marlborough, which is close enough to His Majesty's palace at Ampthill," Margery dreamily mused as they gathered near the drawing room fire and a cold rain blew heavily against the drapery-covered windows.

"That is as unlikely a fantasy to come true as our dear Jane finding herself a husband," John Seymour sniped once his elder daughter had left the room. "What are we to do about her? She will soon be twenty and has no prospects at all. 'Tis something of an embarrassment to the family."

"I have put in as many hints in my letters to Sir Francis as I dare, but he proposes no one for her. He has already agreed to take Thomas on, which is of far greater benefit to us than a husband for Jane."

"I suppose having our two sons at court and one of our daughters well married is more than we dared hope anyway," John conceded.

Outside the dining hall, Jane turned away from the scene and leaned against the paneling as though she were a fly on the wall, taking in the mindless insults without reaction. She was an embarrassment. A failure. Yet her parents only gave voice to what she already believed of herself. Her dalliance that afternoon with William only underscored what she lacked. She was an unmarried girl of an advanced age with no suitors and no future.

As the years had passed, Jane forced herself to think of William less and less and to forgive herself by degrees for having, in that one adolescent moment, given in to pleasure. She had been foolish, but no one knew what she had done. That at least was a blessing from which to learn. There would always be that corner of her soul that no one really knew—the part of herself she would guard now even more fiercely—particularly from her parents.

"If I must listen to another word about our dear Elizabeth and her wonderful future, I do believe I shall climb the stairs and hurl myself off the roof!"

Jane heard her brother's declaration and turned to see him enshrined in the shadows of a little alcove nearby. Just then, she saw Lucy's plump face, eyes half closed in pleasure, lips parted, hovering near Thomas's face. Jane quickly turned the corner into the hallway before they could see her, and peered around the corner. Her brother's slim torso was pressed up against Lucy's, and her hands were in his hair. When she realized what they were doing, a little gasp escaped Jane's lips and she turned back to the cool hall, where her parents' conversation surrounded her once again, drowning out the sounds of her brother's passion.

By the time Thomas came out of the alcove, straightening his doublet, her parents were debating what kind of flowers Elizabeth should weave into her hair on her wedding day.

"Do you love her?" Jane asked her brother. From the corner of her eye she could see Lucy slip away back into the kitchen, straightening her hood.

"She helps pass the time; 'tis only that," he answered unapologetically. "Until I can be on my way to something better."

"I had no idea you were interested in girls."

"Let us just say that I am not so interested as my body is. Lucy is willing to overlook the distinction."

The comment, flippantly spoken, felt like a small, sharp weapon digging into a corner of her heart. Jane's mind wound very quickly, like silk thread leading back to its spool, to a memory with William. Clearly she had been for him what Lucy was for her brother now. He might not have taken her maidenhead that day, but she had never stopped feeling that she had given him her virtue, which made her feel oddly defensive now of the poor groundskeeper's daughter.

"Even so, do you speak tenderly to her sometimes? Tell her things she wants to hear?"

Thomas shifted his weight, and a floorboard creaked beneath his shoes, but their parents continued to prattle on unaware in the dining hall nearby. Thomas scanned her face, then gave up and simply shrugged.

"'Tis nasty business, sister, our animal needs. A blessing, perhaps, that you are not to be faced with any of that."

A blessing that she was ordinary looking, he meant. A gift from God that she would find no husband and not know the great burden of a man's powerful arousal or the full weight of his passion. Her humiliation flared, but she pressed it back. This must be exactly how William felt about her. Hers had been a childish fantasy. His had been a man's need, precisely as Mother had warned. She was angry with herself and humiliated, even after eight years.

"When do you leave to join Sir Francis?" she asked her brother, needing to change the subject from the thing that could not be changed.

"Just after the wedding. He will be attending and we shall leave together for Richmond Palace straight afterward."

They had not seen Sir Francis for more than a year, but he still wrote to the family regularly of his grand adventures with the king, and all the rousing gossip from court. King Henry had tired now of poor Mary Boleyn, who had grown up after her time in France only to find her way to the royal bed in the days after Jane had gone back to Wolf Hall. Mary's well-known tryst with the king was still a surprise. She had seemed so innocent, far too simple for a king with a reputation like Henry's.

Although didn't the English proverb say that still waters run deep? Jane tried to remember. Had Sir Francis not said the same of her? Was Jane still water, with her secret passion for a lost love about which no one even knew?

Court was like that, a magical, exciting world, full of such grand secrets.

"I envy you, you know," Jane said.

The taste of the confession on her lips was a bitter one.

Thomas smiled at her, which helped a little. He always helped. While she admired Edward from afar, and the pedestal on which she put him remained intact, he was a virtual stranger, and there really was no one in the world she loved now more than Thomas.

"You told me once you wanted nothing so much as to be home here at Wolf Hall, not a place like King Henry's court."

"I was a child then," she countered.

"When I was a child, I spake as a child," he replied, as though finishing her thought by recounting the verse from Corinthians. It was one their priest had them recite so often as children that it came quickly to them both. So many things bound them—their blood, their history, their parents' ambition. And now, like Edward, Anthony, Margery . . . Elizabeth, Thomas was going away, and she could not bear it.

"Look here," he said, chucking her fondly beneath the chin as her eyes filled with tears she rarely let anyone else see. "What's that face? There is something more going on in that head of yours than sorrow at my leaving, is there not?"

Oh, if there were anyone in the world she could tell, it would be Thomas, Jane thought. But stubbornly, defensively, once again, she pushed away her thoughts of disappointment over William, which had begun to darken with time. That day had never happened, she told herself now. She was no longer a child and she must put away childish things. She would live at Wolf Hall under the care of her parents, then would eventually become their caretaker. William would be at Eythrope. It was the end of her story—and the end of theirs. But resigning herself to that future seemed almost as difficult as pretending she had never cared for William Dormer at all.

In the little stone groundskeeper's cottage, across the pathways beyond the pond and beside the gate, Lucy began the ritual by drawing the small wooden box from beneath her bed. Her father would be gone for hours yet, out mending a pastureland fence, and the Seymour girls did not need her, so she was free with her time. *And her secrets.*

Lucy liked the guilty pleasure knowing the letter was here. It was like a potent elixir, running her eager fingers over the neatly penned words, feeling him inside of them. Even all these years later, the process filled her with a kind of excitement that had no equal. Long ago, Lucy had stopped surrendering to the guilt of stealing it . . . or simply not delivering it.

She opened the letter once again. As she did, she thought about William's firm hand touching the same slip of paper as if it were the column of her own neck, fingers catching on the vein that pulsed hot with her desire for him. *William* . . . It had always been him, since they were children. How envious she had been of his concern for Jane that day in Savernake Forest. She remembered the feeling even now.

At first the letter smelled of musk, or so she had thought. She had taken to pressing the page to her nose so often that her mind convinced her it still did.

Of course I shall deliver it to Mistress Seymour. No one shall know about it. You can trust me. We are friends now. I promise we are.

She could hear herself—her promise, the spoken lie—even now.

Greedily, she had read it, taking each nauseatingly pleading word for Jane's heart into her own. The words wounded her, each one like a drop of life's blood flowing out of her veins because he cared for someone else. He probably did not even know that she cared.

Please know, dearest Jane, that I meant every word I
said. The promise I made is carved upon my heart. It
may take some time to win my parents over because
they are sending me this morrow to Eythrope to handle

*our family's affairs there, but they both know I am
firmly committed to our betrothal. I pray that as the sun
rose, you woke with no misgivings over the liberties we
took with each other yesterday, as, at least on my part,
they were an act of total commitment to you, my
sweetheart. You are what I want, you are all that I
want. I know it now as I write this, and I shall know it
forever. You are different, special, wonderful. Please
write back to me to assure me I did not offend you with
my touch yesterday. If I am given no reply it can only
mean you have changed your mind over my forward
advances. I know not how my heart will survive, but I
trust the things we said to each other, and the kisses
between us forged a union that will last forever. I must
believe that. So write swiftly; we can trust Lucy to bring
me your response . . .*

Trust. Not *love*. Tears fell. They always did.

The ritual had become as natural as eating or sleeping.

She took some comfort in knowing that William had not written
again after that, at least not through her. *Tell me, Lucy, has she said
nothing? Sent nothing?* Upon his return to Wiltshire a fortnight later,
he had sought her out to ask. Then again a month after that. *Shall I
take her another letter for you anon, sir? Thank you, Lucy, but no. I've
been given my answer . . .*

Perhaps, like a change of the season, his interest in Jane was a
phase he had passed through as a young man, Lucy reasoned. She
had seen him just last month at Idsworth House, a grown man now,
when she had gone there to help with some extra mending. The

Dormers did not maintain a full staff of servants at their summer home, so help from the village was occasionally sought. William would never know how Lucy had pleaded with her father, threatening suicide if he did not comply and find some way to place her among the temporary staff.

"I must serve them, Father, please, *I must...*" She could still hear her own pleading, feel through her fingers the tears she had so dramatically called up to win her way. And in the end he had done her bidding because his daughter was all he had left in the world, his wife having died giving her life. She knew the tale well and she used it skillfully, just as she had decided years ago to use Jane, rather than attack her again.

How gullible are people of means, Lucy thought ruefully, *how willing to believe the best in others.* When they were children, Lucy had made amends with Jane because she had seen the concern William had displayed for her. She could never become William's wife, but if somehow she could win even a small piece of him, that would be enough. The Dormers were set to return to Wiltshire in July, and at last she would find a way to bed him. Hopefully, it was not too late to be his first.

That way, he would surely never forget her.

In preparation, Lucy had honed her skills on an eager Thomas Seymour. How willing he had been! She had not meant for Jane to see them that afternoon, or to suspect what was truly a part of her plan. For now, she meant to kill Jane with kindness. Figuratively, or otherwise, if it came to that.

The journey to Marlborough for Elizabeth's wedding was a grueling affair. The roads were rutted and muddy from a pelting June rain. Jane was particularly out of sorts to begin with, having to endure a younger sister's wedding before her own. Whatever she had with William years ago, it was long over, she reminded herself frequently. Jane tried very hard to put on the brave face of a young and content spinster now, one settled into her life.

Sir Anthony's renown was such that the Lord Treasurer, the famous Earl of Surrey, had agreed to attend the wedding in St. Peter's Church—the very place where Thomas Wolsey was first ordained. For all of her pleading and bribery through the years, it was this singular event that at last was to bring Margery's own important and powerful cousin from his vaunted place at court to mingle briefly with his poor Seymour relations.

Jane stepped from the drawn litter at last and drew in a breath of air, glad to be out of the muck and mire of traveling. The rain had stopped and the clouds had parted. She straightened her gray velvet dress and straightened the bell sleeves as the swirling activity behind her reached a fever pitch and the church bells tolled from the tower high above her. Ladies in their much more elegant silks and brocades were chatting and laughing and admiring the bride's dress as Elizabeth stood with her friends on the wide stone steps in front of the church door. All of the attention was on Elizabeth, with her sleek blond hair long beneath her jewel-dotted headdress. Jane pressed back the envy. It was a matter of course for her, a movement as common now as breathing. This was not her life. Not her fate.

And then there was Margery, standing in the center of it all, arms crossed over her chest, surveying the scene with such pride that it was a palpable thing.

"Sheer perfection," she declared of her younger daughter.

Jane saw tears actually shining in her mother's eyes. She was quite certain that it was the first tear her mother had ever shed. Certainly the first one she had ever seen. At that, the knife of disappointment twisted a little more deeply in Jane's heart as she forced a smile she did not feel.

Edward had found success. Soon, Thomas. Now, Elizabeth. Jane might as well have been Lucy Hill for her own lackluster life. No one noticed her. No one knew what she was feeling. *The great invisible Jane,* she thought, feeling incredibly sorry for herself.

"Don't just stand there looking envious!" her mother suddenly barked, bringing Jane back to the moment. "Do come over here and help me with your sister's train! 'Tis nearly time to go inside!"

Time heals all wounds . . . Time waits for no man . . . Time is the wisest counselor of all. The platitudes rolled around in her head like marbles. She moved forward, managing that same grim, forced smile. She realized at that moment how good she had become at showing the world the person they believed her to be. Deception was every bit as much an art form as were the talents of those who sold them—or their bodies.

Everyone has their own skill, she thought bitterly. Masquerading was hers.

The ceremony was grand by any standard, a mix of pomp and ostentation to rival any court wedding that Jane could have imagined. She sat on the slickly oiled wooden pew beside Edward and his new wife, Catherine, a girl he had married at court and whom Jane did not know. The pew smelled strongly of polishing wax as Jane trained her eyes on the dozens of flickering candles in their heavily carved holders, then on the crucifix of a suffering Jesus at the altar. She looked at anything to avoid looking again at the naked adoration on the slightly grizzled face of her sister's wealthy older groom.

Let it be over, Jane thought as they exchanged their solemn vows and her mother raised a handkerchief to her eye. Her brother clutched his new wife's hand as the couple at the altar knelt. They pledged their troth. *Just let the sounds of the vows and the music end, and lead me to a tall cup of ale,* Jane silently pleaded as they kissed and turned to meet the world, married now, joined forever.

As the guests took turns half an hour later toasting the couple, Jane busied herself by feeding scraps to the hunting hounds that rested beneath her feet under the table. Sir Anthony had a dozen dogs, who were free to roam the great dining hall of his manor. They were a great distraction. She thought how they might be the most interesting guests in attendance on this day, when she could not possibly have felt more pathetic or alone.

Francis Bryan set down his goblet and took up her hand to stop her from feeding the hounds. Until then, she had not even cared who was sitting beside her, or noticed.

"That dog is eating better than am I, which I confess is saying quite a lot," he chuckled.

Jane looked at his face and those kind eyes. He had a sage way about him, which she loved and trusted.

"'Tis just disappointing to be last at home. Thomas is going off with you to court, and Edward is in the employ of the king's son, Lord Fitzroy, now Duke of Richmond."

"It came to nothing, then, with that boy, I presume?"

"There was never anything there," Jane answered, knowing he meant William.

His cavalier expression quickly gave way to his customary wry smile. "Never mind that, then. I see she has not told you yet about the far more interesting circumstance that awaits you than life alone with your parents at Wolf Hall."

"I've no idea what you mean."

"Your mother was to speak to you of it on this morrow, but I can see she has not done so, or spared you a moment's time to prepare."

He shook his head, then picked his goblet back up as the music floated around them and several couples began to dance a branle. "'Tis a shame, since you could do with a bit of preparation, certainly some color on your lips and a new dress or two."

"Pray, why on earth would I require such things?"

"You certainly cannot serve the Queen of England in a dress like that, Jane."

"The queen?" Although foreign and exciting, it seemed a strange term to pass across her lips, especially in relation to herself.

He must have seen the shock on her face, because he continued.

"Several of Her Highness's ladies have gone from court recently. Like rats from a sinking ship, if you will pardon me, since the king has begun more actively to question the validity of their marriage and is casting his interest elsewhere, yet again. You are smart, Jane, and sly, but there is a loyal quality to you. The queen can use those attributes right now. I have behaved rather badly of late, spending too much time in the company of the king and a new lady love." He grinned devilishly. "Still, our queen is fond of me. I must make amends, so I have spoken your praises and arranged an appointment for you within her retinue."

"I am to go to court, then?"

He nodded and smiled. "If she favors you, it can only increase my standing, so do not look upon me too gratefully yet."

"Of course." She nodded, thinking perhaps this was some horrendous joke. "I mean you no offense, sir, truly, but why would you do this for me? Surely there are young women far more deserving."

His smile was twisted then, and pleased. "Oh, Jane, you are a smart little one, aren't you? So delightfully unassuming." He scratched his small, pointed beard, glanced around, and lowered his voice. "Very well. The truth is not just that I have thrown too much of my attention to the queen's rival; Her Grace suspects me of being led to all manner of dark pleasures by the king's new mistress."

"Are you not?" Though she did not know who this mistress was, Jane was certain that Francis would never pass up a temptation.

"Of course I am." He chuckled devilishly. "That is hardly the point."

"What is the point, precisely?"

"Truth is, I need a little mouse in the queen's corner since I can no longer be there myself. I must remain apprised of what is going on, and who better for the job than my sweet cousin Jane?"

"I can see how I would suit your purpose," she cautiously conceded.

"Perhaps you can put in a good word for me now and again and tell me if my standing with her is in any real danger."

"That'll not do either of us any good, shall it, if he replaces his queen? Thomas says there is a new girl who just might have that sort of influence over him."

"Oh," Francis scoffed. "Katherine of Aragon will never be unseated," he said with the greatest authority. "There is no female living who is powerful enough to unseat the daughter of Spain's Queen Isabella. Not even Anne Boleyn."

"Mary Boleyn's sister?" Jane gasped as her mind reeled with the memories of their childhood encounter.

"The very same. She was with us in France; do you recall?"

"I recall her only too well."

"I can imagine that you would. She really is quite bewitching now that she is grown, and there is a huge battle brewing. She may no longer be a great beauty, but Her Highness is a smart woman. You actually have many of her same qualities."

Jane had realized long ago that beauty was not one of her God-given attributes, but she had decided she was better off cultivating her other assets anyway. No one seemed to suspect that she was more than a plain face. But beauty was overrated . . . and hidden talents were always useful. Especially if she were to come face-to-face with her old rival, Mistress Anne.

PART II

Jane and Katherine

So my conscience chide me not,
I am ready for Fortune as she wills.

—DANTE ALIGHIERI

Chapter Six

March 1526
Richmond Palace

*W*ith all of their other children now gone from Wolf Hall, John and Margery Seymour were free to escort their eldest daughter to Richmond Palace in hopes of having an audience with the king.

As the court was busy preparing for the Lenten rituals, Jane walked between her parents, her heavy skirts swishing with each stride, and her heart moving to the rhythm of a steady drumbeat as they passed beneath a brightly gilded doorway. The echo of her shoe heels matched the thump of her heart as she traversed a vast tiled corridor with arched windows that faced the river. Jane was to be presented to the queen, and then, if Her Highness did not object, Jane would begin her service in Katherine's massive household. It would be a while, she was told, before she would be styled an actual lady-in-waiting to the queen. That was an honor given only if she acquitted herself well in the initial period. It was a comforting notion, Jane thought, still able to recall the incident in France, how she had tripped in front of the queen, and the horror of her embarrassment.

Through the grand presence chamber, past a massive series of tapestries depicting the triumphs of the gods, the trio silently strode. Heads turned as they moved toward the second set of heavily carved oak doors, flanked by stiff liveried guards, each bearing a dauntingly heavy metal halberd. Jane was surprised to feel her mother reach down and clutch her hand. She did not recall ever touching her mother's hand. It was small and very cold now. Jane felt herself tremble.

The second room, the more important privy chamber, was more richly appointed than the first. A long walnut sideboard stood against the wall full of gleaming Spanish silver, all of it glinting in the light cast from the bank of diamond-shaped leaded-glass windows on the opposite wall. Outside, she heard the sound of gardeners constantly clipping bushes and shrubs. At the end of the vast room, flanked by tapestries depicting two gruesome scenes of the Crucifixion, sat a heavily carved throne with a long crimson and gold tester behind it. The stout, dark-haired woman seated beneath it was not at all what Jane had expected. She seemed much older and more starkly unattractive than Jane had imagined when she thought of the grandeur of court. Her full, sallow face looked like rising dough beneath her ornate, gabled black hood. Her black dress was ornamented only by a large silver crucifix that hung over her chest.

Jane and Margery drew forward, then dropped into low, reverent curtsies. Her father bowed deeply. The silence around them was palpable.

"Lady Seymour, it has been many years," the queen said without benefit of introduction. Her soft voice was heavily accented. "Time has been kind to you, I see."

Jane knew that many years ago, her mother once had a place in the household of her powerful aunt, the Countess of Surrey, where she had met John Skelton.

"Thank you, Your Highness."

"And this girl, she is yours?"

Jane felt herself blanch at the implied insult of the queen's disbelieving tone.

"She is indeed, Your Highness. May I present my eldest daughter, Jane Seymour."

"Edward's sister. *Sí*, the resemblance is very clear. They look like their father." She smiled condescendingly. What might she have been like in her youth, able to capture not one, but two princes of England? It seemed unfathomable now.

Amid the tension and silence, Jane saw Francis Bryan. He was standing to the queen's left with a small collection of very dignified young men garbed in costly slashed-velvet doublets, heavy gold chains, and plumed caps. The man next to him was noticeably older, though fit and trim, and his hair was the same color as the silver gleaming on the sideboard. It swept back from a widow's peak at his forehead in a great wave to match his neat silver beard and mustache. He looked like a wax figure, lean and stiff, Jane thought, like someone not quite real. He was certainly a bit menacing. She straightened her back then, remembering her mother's constant remonstrations to always stand with dignity.

The women around the queen's throne—some standing, some seated in tall tapestry-covered chairs—were like petals on a rose; elegant and regal. Jane detected scents of cinnabar, vanilla, and rose water, the combination of which made her a little dizzy.

She was most definitely a thorn among roses.

"My lord Norfolk," said the queen, turning just slightly to the silver-haired man, her tone a little cooler and more formal, "you recall your good cousin Lady Seymour, I assume?"

His nod to Margery was tepid, as though he had seen her the day before, not decades earlier. "'Tis my pleasure, Lady Seymour," he said in a perfunctory tone.

"And my honor, Your Grace." Jane's mother was squeezing her hand so tightly that it began to hurt.

Her expression did not reveal the slightest hint of anxiety.

"I am reminded that you are to counsel with the king on the hour, Thomas. Pray, do make haste," the queen said to the duke suddenly.

Norfolk nodded to her. "Indeed I shall, Your Highness. Many thanks for the gracious reminder."

He had stiffened at the mention of the king, Jane noticed. At Elizabeth's wedding, Edward had told them that Mother's cousin, Thomas Howard, was now the powerful Duke of Norfolk, rivaling Wolsey for power and influence. Things were changing swiftly between the royal couple, and many of the most intimate courtiers had begun to choose sides. Jane was not yet certain on whose side she would find Norfolk, so she must take care not to insult him until she did.

"Very well, walk with me, then, Mistress Seymour," the queen suddenly bid her. Jane could hear the whispers rise as Katherine was helped down from the dais and Jane advanced.

The third room in the chain of rooms into which they moved was smaller and far more intimate than the other two. It was a grand bedchamber, and the smell of incense was very strong. A Spanish woman approached the queen, and there was a hushed exchange between them before Katherine lifted a censuring hand, indicating that she wanted no assistance. She wished to speak privately with

Jane. The walls and ceiling to which Jane cast her gaze were fully paneled in an intricate block design. At the opposite end was a large canopy bed dressed in crimson sarcenet and a grand fireplace. Above each were the king and queen's seal, an *H* and *K* surrounded by a Tudor rose.

The queen went to the window and Jane stood behind her, waiting for her to speak.

"Tell me, do you know what it means to be loyal, Jane?" she finally asked as she gazed wistfully past the massive courtyard to the great, glimmering, barge-dotted Thames beyond.

"I hope that I do, Your Highness, since there is little of greater value than loyalty."

"You betray your youth and inexperience, Mistress Seymour, both of which ring hollow in these halls. Many have left me for *her* apartments these past months. Can you imagine that harridan has her own suite of rooms now, more elegantly appointed than these? They are directly beside my husband's official apartments. Everyone still smiles at me and flatters me as they must, but privately they have cast their lot with her, paying court to *her* now, as if they believe she will vanquish me."

Jane still could not believe that the king's new paramour was that dreadful child she had met in France, grown to womanhood now, Mary Boleyn's dark-haired sister, Anne.

"I must have loyalty, Jane, some paltry bit of it left, as I try to do battle with this. Of course I have my precious Maria here. But the others are like the great Duke of Norfolk, who comes here and bows to me, but who follows his niece, Mistress Boleyn, boldly behind my back. His betrayal is as regular as day and night. You are fortunate to have a benefactor like Francis Bryan, who tells me not just of your loyalty, but of your clever mind." The queen turned back from the windows, then settled her eyes, glistening with unshed tears, on Jane. "I find that I could use someone with your assets when so many around me seem to be losing sight of theirs—a plain girl who, like myself, understands how cruel it is to be outshone."

In the awkwardness of such a personal moment, Jane curtsied again. The queen's words seemed to be meant as something of a compliment.

"But I warn you, Mistress Seymour, I shall not suffer betrayal. I know perfectly well that you are a second cousin to that she-devil, bound by Norfolk on your mother's side. Pray God you share only her determination and not her blind ambition."

"I met Mistress Boleyn once when we were children in France, Your Highness," Jane surprised herself by confessing. "She stuck her foot out so that I would trip and look like a fool right in front of the king's sister. I did not like her then and I would not like her now, no matter what blood we might share."

The queen's plum-colored mouth lengthened into an oddly malevolent smile, and she reached up to clutch the heavy silver cross at her breast. "Praise to my Almighty God," she muttered, and then began to whisper something in Spanish as she lifted the cross to her lips and kissed it.

Edward held his mother in a prolonged embrace beneath an archway in the corridor outside the queen's apartments, pretending to feel the loyalty he was meant to feel. He had been away from her influence for so long that he felt little emotional attachment. She was the woman of his childhood but not of his heart. That part of himself had been irrevocably broken by his cheating wife, Catherine, who had taken the last bit of his true compassion with her infidelity. But no one at court would have known that. He had become too experienced to let it show.

Still a good and seasoned courtier, Edward made a convincing display of it now that his mother was here.

"I cannot believe Jane's good fortune," she whispered with a smile. "Who would have ever thought of *her*?"

"Now, don't be too proud, Mother. You know part of the reason the queen has her here is to counteract *my* influence with the king's little bastard, the Duke of Richmond, and Norfolk schemes for his niece."

"Whatever her reasons," Margery said, kissing his bearded cheek, "Jane is here now, and I thank God for our king's penchant for infidelity."

Edward tried not to laugh at that, but he could not help himself. What promise she might have shown at court if she had not been married off to his father, that grizzled old cur.

Father or not, the devil take him. He had flirted with Catherine right before Edward's eyes at Elizabeth's wedding. He had seen it, and no matter how vehemently the old man denied it, he believed his father later bedded his wife. When confronted with his suspicions, Catherine had not offered up the same denial his father had. His wife had certainly seemed more concerned about her own pleasurable conquests and less concerned about hurting him, and so she had.

Because of her alluring beauty, Edward had refused to acknowledge how promiscuous she was, both before their marriage and after. He had thought himself skillful and handsome enough to tame her, but he had been painfully wrong. Elizabeth's wedding had been the end of things for them, almost before they had begun. But the world would never know the gaping wound left to bleed right beneath the layer of rich Italian velvet covering his proud, slightly puffed-up chest.

Now, once again, ambition, not love, was the thing.

Margery pulled away, and her eyes glittered brightly with all of her own hope and ambition. Edward knew she was thinking how much like his father he was, something she had often told him as a child, and he tried very hard not to shrink from the sensation of revulsion it brought.

His mother instantly understood his thoughts, but he knew she did not realize the full extent of his father's betrayal. No one did, as Edward had never made his accusations public. She had only sensed the growing divide between them. "Pray, will you not cease this quarrel between you and speak to him before we depart?"

"You would be better served asking me to drive the dagger at my hilt right into his heart, as he has already plunged one into mine."

"Will you not give him a chance to explain whatever dreadful misunderstanding has occurred between you?"

Edward tensed and took a step back from her, his taut body a ramrod of self-defense.

"He is your father, Edward. He is an old man now who cannot harm you."

"The damage is done."

"You are a Seymour, product of his own loins. I despair at the division among us. Have you no loyalty?" she asked him angrily.

"No, Mother, there is no loyalty between us," Edward coldly countered. He did not want to fight with his own mother or hurt her with the revelation. He favored his emotional neutrality with her as much as the geographical distance between them when he was here and she was at home in Wiltshire. "I am hardened now, Mother, grown and changed into someone you do not know beyond what you see. Go back to Wolf Hall with him, and I shall keep a watchful eye on Thomas and Jane as much as I am able. Perhaps one day you and I will have cause for a merry reunion. But by my troth, it shall not involve John Seymour."

Then he walked away from her. That really was the best that he could do.

"Ungrateful hound," Thomas thought ruefully as he watched his elder brother leave the room. Having witnessed the whole scene between Margery and Edward, he saw that she had been petitioning him to rejoin the family. Clearly that was not going to happen. Thomas suspected that the divide between Edward and their father had something to do with Edward's former wife. He shook his head disdainfully.

He did not know Edward or understand him. The gap in their experiences was too great. The blood tie that bound them was now frayed by years of separation. On the few occasions of Edward's visits to Wolf Hall through the years, they had rarely spoken. Edward had no time for his fair little brother with his smattering of freckles and pale Wentworth eyes.

As Thomas came into his own, there seemed to be an element of fraternal envy added to the mix. Thomas was as put off by his brother as Edward seemed to be by him. Thomas stood now in the presence chamber with Francis Bryan, his new benefactor, waiting awkwardly with everyone else as the queen took Jane away to speak privately.

For the moment, he chose to take in all the characters and ingratiate himself where he could, before Francis hauled him off to some horribly forsaken outpost to earn his keep. As if he could read Thomas's mind, Francis Bryan looked across the room at Norfolk.

"Intimidating, is he not?" Francis asked Thomas of the silver-haired, bold-looking man who had been stopped by the imperial ambassador on his way out the door to see the king. "You would do well to find him so. That is the Duke of Norfolk. He and Wolsey fight like mad dogs for the king's favor. Wolsey is more pious, but Norfolk is more quietly clever. Who knows how it will end between them."

"From the looks of it, I would wager that Norfolk will emerge victorious," said Thomas with an air of cool detachment, trying to make it appear as if he belonged here as much as anyone else. Inside, however, he was full of heady sensations, as if he had drunk too much Rhenish wine. All these powerful players, all the elegance. The beauty! The danger!

"People to avoid certainly include the stone-faced Spaniard across from Norfolk, not that a sane man would ever be moved to approach her anyway, other than her husband, Lord Willoughby. That is Maria de Salinas, and she guards the queen with an eagle's eye. Very little gets by her, so do not try unless your wish is for a quick expulsion from court or a swift death. Whichever she decides. The queen's influence may be somewhat diminished with the king because of his bastard son, but believe me, Maria knows how to protect her."

Francis described several others of the court for Thomas and pointed them out. He felt as if he were standing at the edge of a private garden, with all the great temptations of the world laid out before him. They were like vivid flowers drawing him in with their beauty and fragrance, and he was lured by the riches, power, and glory. He must be masterful about gaining access to this garden. And humble. Yes, an outward show of humility while one was bent on absolute success seemed essential here. Thomas could see that for himself now. No one, not even his dear Jane, must ever know the magnitude of his ambition. Or his ability to masquerade. Surely she would never understand how much deeper his ability went than her own.

Chapter Seven

*P*reparing for the May Day celebrations after the Lenten and Easter season kept the queen's household buzzing with activity. Jane was now in the very center of it all, still working hard to learn as much as she could about the important players, to honor the proper ones and to avoid the dangerous others.

The queen sat reading several dispatches brought to her by the Spanish ambassador, Don Luis Caroz, as Jane helped her pretty new acquaintances, Margaret Shelton and Anne Stanhope, arrange one of the table displays in the Great Hall. The vast hall was crowded with jabbering court ladies in brilliant silks and satins, hands pointing and directives flying. Workmen were busily hanging great sheets of richly decorated gold arras on the walls, and others were hooking torches into dozens of new braziers in an already overheated room on the unseasonably warm spring day.

The queen's court was to set the scene for the evening's entertainment in an obvious attempt to please the king. But everyone whispered what an increasingly futile task that had become. The setting for the court masque, Chateau Vert, the fictional castle of a great chivalric tale, had been under construction for several days, complete with brightly painted castle towers and red royal banners. The queen had insisted on organizing everything, including the play itself, which was set to follow the banquet. For the performance, court ladies were chosen to dress as the physical embodiment of the virtues Kindness, Mercy, Pity, Beauty, and Perseverance. Jane knew that all of the queen's most favored ladies had been vying for the chosen parts for the attention it would attract from the king and his friends. When the king himself sent back amendments to the performance, personally recasting each of the roles, and signing the sheet in his own hand authoritatively—Henricus Rex—disappointed tears filled Katherine's dark eyes. But they were unshed tears that she efficiently pressed away, returning to her duties in hopes of rekindling their partnership through entertainment first, if not romance.

The queen of twenty years had been given a secondary role by her own husband. She was simply to be one of the eight women who guarded the more glamorous virtues. Her name in Henry's own hand was linked with the character Disdain. The part of Perseverance, which she had hoped to meaningfully portray, as she felt her life particularly defined that term, was to go to someone else.

"'Tis all in good fun, Your Highness. I am certain the king means you no offense in this," Jane had heard Sir Henry Guildford try impotently to explain as Katherine planned to retire for the evening. As the king's Master of the Revels, Guildford was in charge of the entire celebration, the lavish banquet, the uniquely creative masque, the dancing and the music. Guildford did not, however, control the casting.

"I had meant to play the dignified part myself," she later told Maria de Salinas, as Lady Margaret Bryan, Francis's mother, brushed out the queen's thick rope of dark hair.

Margaret Shelton knelt to moisten the queen's feet with scented cream beside the glowing amber light of a blazing fire that cracked and sparked in the dark, vaulted room. Jane dutifully folded back the queen's counterpane, trying not to make it obvious that she was listening.

"That had certainly seemed the most obvious role for me to play, considering my current circumstances. I know the king's sister is to play the part of Beauty, and the Countess of Devon is Honor, which seems nearly as appropriate as me portraying Perseverance."

Her voice went very thin. She gazed back at the bed, which Jane had been told the king no longer visited. "I suppose it is fitting, though," Katherine said with a heavy sigh, "that Perseverance should be played by the girl who has worked so hard to steal my husband's attention and corrupt his heart this past year."

Jane knew whom she meant. They all did.

"But even though he wishes it to save his own reputation with his friends, I shall not play another role," the queen declared as Maria tied the white Spanish silk nightcap loosely beneath the gently sagging flesh of Katherine's proud Castellón chin. Lady Bryan, who had been with the queen for many years, began to snuff out the candle lamps across the room. "I have been a fool for love, certainly, but I cannot bear to let the entire court see it. Someone else must take the lowly role he intends for me. God save me, I cannot endure so great an insult as he would put upon me!"

"Then, Mistress Seymour, you must play the part for her," Maria calmly directed as she helped the queen toward the bed. "No one knows or yet cares who you are, so Disdain shall go unnoticed."

For a moment, Jane could not find her voice. In the silence, Francis's mother frowned at her. "Go on, then, child," she urged in a whisper. "Speak up."

The sensation Jane had at the thought of being cast as something so disagreeable, under any circumstance, reminded her of her embarrassment in France. And being taunted at Savernake before that. She swallowed hard, trying not to allow panic to overwhelm her.

"Humbly, Your Highness, I do th-thank y-you for the honor. But I know nothing of the p-part," she heard herself stutter, each of the words catching in the back of her throat before she pushed it forward across her tongue.

"Nay," Lady Bryan scoffed, waving a jewel-dotted hand. "'Tis only a little play and a little part. 'Twill do you no good to hesitate or equivocate. Her Highness has offered you a great honor tomorrow evening."

Jane glanced at the queen, who at that moment was climbing into her great canopied bed and being covered like a little child by two of her Spanish women—the only ones allowed the most intimate duties in her bedchamber. "But respectfully, will the king not be expecting to see the queen in that role?"

"He will not be told, of course, who played it until afterward. It has been quite a long time since he has expected anything of me. I am told quite often how I disappoint him too greatly for that," said the weary queen.

Jane could feel the tension wend its way through the dressing room like a living thing as she let two younger maids of honor fasten her gray satin costume for the part of a guard, with the word Disdain emblazoned on the long, flat stomacher of her dress. All around her, the other guard characters were dressing as well: Mary Roos Denys, Anne Percy, Margaret Shelton, and Elizabeth Carew. Jane heard the lethal whispers of disapproval and knew they resented her participation. The more important virtues were dressing elsewhere,

Jane was told, too elevated to share this ritual with such minor characters—both in the masque and in the reality of court life.

Jane was still an oddity, even in this more lowly group. She was a country girl to be scorned for her lack of title. Knowing that the Duke of Norfolk had avoided an association with Jane's mother during her visit only served to strengthen their catty and silent case against her.

It might have helped if, like Anne Stanhope or Elizabeth Carew, Jane were at least beautiful, or voluptuous like Margaret Shelton. But they seemed a judgmental group who had knitted themselves together with time and experience, showing little tolerance for newcomers.

"It was one of her little tests for the king," someone said suddenly, pulling Jane from her thoughts, although she could not identify who it was. The voice was high and willowy. Jane strained to hear without showing she was listening as a young girl carefully fitted the hood onto her head.

"By my lord, 'tis witchcraft, not wiles. Her beauty is far from the usual sort," said another attendant to the queen whom Jane did not know.

"'Tis only a court game between them so far, my husband says," the first attendant said. "The same one she plays with the king's poet, Thomas Wyatt. She plays at being a virtuous woman since she is not keen to end up like her sister."

Mary Boleyn, Jane remembered again sadly. The word "witchcraft" did not entirely surprise her when she remembered the little dark-eyed child who had so frightened her in France. *Curious,* she thought then, *where roads do lead.* How much she had changed and how much strength she had gained since then. Anne Boleyn had most likely changed as well.

Only time would tell who had changed the more.

They went in great procession then, the dozen ladies in beaded gray silk, their chests emblazoned in gold thread, each spelling out a different term. Each one flashed brightly as she moved down the lamp-lit corridor. Next they moved down a flight of polished oak stairs, each step creaking heavily as the women descended in a great train, following three liveried guardsmen, who were meant to lead the way. The sound of music from the Great Hall grew strong as they neared it. On the second landing, they merged with a different collection of women, all in gleaming white satin, the fabric more sumptuous, the design more daring. They wore full bell sleeves lined with sapphire blue silk, their hair swept up in matching fashion in diamond-studded sparkling mesh cauls. Jane caught sight of the king's sister, Mary, the former French queen, among them. The great beauty had changed little with the years, even after the scandal of her marriage to Charles Brandon. She still had the same extraordinary green eyes, long lashes, and luminous skin she had possessed in France. She looked to Jane then, as now, like human perfection. It was still easy to imagine why a man like Brandon had risked his standing with the king for her.

The Great Hall into which they all swept in a sparkling mass had been fully transformed into a great theater with tiered seating, a stage at one end, and a gilded proscenium arch at the other, decorated with little niches filled with marble busts. Directly opposite the stage was a single great carved throne. Above it, a massive transparent cloth painted in gold depicted not only the signs of the zodiac but also the stars, the planets, and even the constellations that fascinated the king.

Jane was stunned by the enormity and grandeur of the place.

Her legs began to shake as she moved forward with the others, seeing how many courtiers were collected in the audience. The fat-faced director motioned for the girls in gray to begin gently twirling and dipping as they neared the steps that led up to the stage.

Just as the splendidly dressed crowd began to cheer, the fife and drums broke in with the fanfare that Jane knew was the prelude to the trumpeting of the king's approach. The director held up his hand then to halt their entrance in anticipation of the king's. Jane felt anxious, as the king had been away on a hunting trip since her arrival and she had yet to catch a glimpse of him. Like a great wave, everyone pivoted toward the door and the blare of trumpets. Two heavy velvet drapes were pulled back to make way for His Majesty, and for the first time . . . Jane saw the King of England.

He was a massive man. Clothed in rich purple Florentine velvet trimmed in gold with a great baldric of jewels across his broad chest, he was an unbelievably tall, fit, and barrel-chested sovereign. Henry VIII moved forward commandingly, hands on his hips, a bit like a rooster. The ends of his copper hair were shining beneath his wide plumed cap as he smiled and nodded to the crowd.

"By my lord, that is him, isn't it?" she asked foolishly of Margaret Shelton, who stood beside her. Jane knew her tone sounded silly, but she was nervous, and she could not quite believe she was actually in the company of the King of England after having heard about him for so many years.

Margaret, a sensually attractive girl with a small nose and compelling sapphire eyes, cast a quick glance at her. "Best lose that doe-eyed look. This court is no place for any kind of innocence but the feigned sort."

"I shall try to remember," Jane replied compliantly because

she still could not afford to alienate anyone, and few had be-friended her.

Then she watched as servants scurried to set up a second throne beside the king, which had not been part of the original plan. She watched Katherine enter past the curtains a moment later wearing a conservative cranberry-colored velvet gown and a tight gabled hood. True to her word, she had declined to play a guard. But she seemed to bear the slight the king had put upon her with dignity, smiling and nodding to the assembled group. Before Jane had time to feel much pity, however, the king and queen took their seats and the di-rector clapped his hands briskly for the performance to commence.

As the girls with leading roles twirled onto the stage to raucous applause, Jane recognized Anne Boleyn immediately at the center of the group. While she had grown into the enormous coal black eyes that had always dominated her face, the essence of her remained unchanged. She wore her long black hair scandalously full, unbound, and ornamented with only a silk ribbon of sparkling jewels and a great peacock feather at the back. It was not just her dark hair and how she wore it that separated her from the other girls who took the stage with her, who were mostly fair; it was also the size and color of the huge blue and green emeralds and the rubies ornamenting her white gown.

As the allegory progressed, Jane watched in amazement as the king stood and removed the ornamental baldric from his own chest, then his doublet. As he took a burning torch handed to him by a waiting page, his own costume beneath was revealed. To everyone's surprise, he and his friends meant to be part of the performance. The words "Ardent Desire" embroidered in gold on his chest glittered and flared. As Henry descended the steps from his throne to the stage, everyone could see that William Compton, Thomas Wyatt, Nicholas Carew, William Brereton, and Charles Brandon were joining him now as Amorousness, Loyalty, Pleasure, Gentleness, and Liberty. All of the men gathered around the Chateau Vert on the stage and made a great dramatic show of asking the noble ladies to come down. Anne Boleyn, as Perseverance, boldly spoke her lines, imploring someone to rescue her from imprisonment. With great theatrical projection, Thomas Wyatt, dressed as Pleasure, asked if he might be the one to rescue her. Jane saw the king tense and his jolly smile fade as Anne delivered her lines to the handsome Wyatt to great hollers and rousing calls from the crowd.

Jane caught a glimpse then of the poor, proud queen sitting helplessly alone beside an empty throne. Her husband was clearly focused on a girl whose bold and open solicitation of him was apparent to everyone. It was a fascinating thing to watch, albeit a pitiful one, Jane decided, as the end of the performance brought the crowd of royal guests to their feet with boisterous applause.

As Anne Boleyn took her bow, so did the king, as though they were a great performing duo. Jane cringed for the queen's silent humiliation. Her gentle expression made it all the more heartbreaking. He certainly was handsome. That much was true. But King Henry did not seem a good or kind man at all to have allowed an injustice like that—whether it was his right as sovereign of the realm or not. She knew that a ruler believed himself and his desires above reproach, but she had not expected such a self-indulgent, hurtful display. For the first time she could recall, Jane was relieved to be plain. The last thing in the world she could ever imagine herself wanting was what Anne Boleyn was so clearly and boldly seeking to capture. Magnificent as he appeared, Henry VIII quite scared Jane Seymour to death.

A few moments later, the king took the willing arm of Anne Boleyn, her face bright with a self-satisfied smile. He then led her, in steps timed to the music, from the Great Hall. The rest of the cast followed into the banquet hall down the vast window-lined corridor. She had not realized until he spoke that Nicholas Carew was partnered beside her for the length of the procession.

"I believe you are new at court."

"Did the sheer terror in my eyes give it away?" she joked, only then feeling her heart slow enough to cast a crossways glance at the man she had heard several of the other girls whispering about as they strolled in the gardens yesterday.

He was handsome in an almost pretty sort of way, with the desired thick flaxen hair, high cheekbones, and piercing gray eyes. She knew from Edward that his reputation was as notorious as Francis Bryan's. They played at love and at dice as though they were the same thing, not caring which was which, even though Carew was married to Francis Bryan's own younger sister, Elizabeth. Jane pitied the poor girl who had been forced to marry him, because she was quite certain she would not know a moment's peace for the rest of her life as lady to such a handsome lord. Perhaps her own personal challenges explained why Elizabeth had yet to be pleasant or welcoming to Jane.

Carew chuckled affably as he led her to the table. "You did have a bit of that hunted look about you. But it is endearing."

"Would that were true," Jane demurred.

"I am Sir Nicholas Carew, the king's Master of the Horse."

She forced herself not to say that his reputation preceded him. "Lady Hastings told me everyone here despises innocence," she said instead.

"Lady Anne Hastings?" He smirked in surprise. "She *would* be forced to say that for the scandalous way she lives her own life."

It was clear he had some news of her that Jane did not. Lady Hastings, another of the queen's ladies-in-waiting, seemed perfectly gentle. Feminine. Certainly hewing closer to the ideal than Anne Boleyn did.

A tall, slim, and clean-shaven man, his hair in tight copper curls, came upon them then amid the music and scurrying for seats at the tables nearest the king.

"Must it be every girl here whose heart you steal before the rest of us have a chance?" the man asked with a clever smile as he slung his arm casually over Carew's velvet-clad shoulder in a friendly gesture.

"That would suppose any of you ever had a chance with them," Carew laughed. "And speaking of Lady Hastings, Mistress Seymour, may I present Sir William Compton, the king's Groom of the Stool. One cannot get much more influential than that," quipped Carew.

"You're only jealous you haven't the same access I do," said Compton.

"You know who I am, my lord?" Jane asked Carew in surprise as the two well-schooled courtiers, each glittering in gold braid and stones and looking a little drunk, stood before her in the glowing torchlight wearing competitive, boyish smiles.

"But of course. 'Tis part of the job and half the fun to know all of the ladies. Each of you is a prize in all our little games of courtly love."

"You play at love?" Jane asked as she was seated between them and great gleaming trays of food were placed on the long tables by stewards crisply garbed in the customary doublets of green Bruges satin.

"Pray, what else would you do with it?" Carew remarked with a laugh. "By my lord, you would not wish to truly be hit by Cupid's dart the way our sovereign says he is for Mistress Boleyn. Vulnerability is an unseemly business, to my way of thinking."

"Yet you are married to Sir Francis's sister."

"Not particularly vulnerably so."

Jane could see him watching his wife across the table as he said it. Elizabeth was stunningly pretty. She had pale skin but color enough in her cheeks to represent youth. Her hair was blond and her eyes were blue in the courtly ideal of beauty.

"But could true love not surprise you and should that not be the goal, as the poets say?" Jane asked, picking up a goblet, not of pewter or silver as she was accustomed to, but of fine Venetian glass that had been delicately stamped with the *H* and *K* emblem. The irony of the emblem hit Jane as she glanced at the king's table at the head of the room, where he sat boldly—and smugly, she thought—between the queen and Anne Boleyn.

"'Tis not the goal at *this* court, sweeting," quipped William Compton. "For it is not a place of love matches, rather one of power deals and brokered alliances. For example, poor Carew's exquisite wife over there, alas, was hoisted on him when the king grew weary of her himself."

"Tell the king's sister that all matches here are broken alliances, and she might have a different reply," Jane countered.

"You truly are an innocent, aren't you?" Carew laughed boldly and slammed down his goblet. A bit of ruby wine splashed out and stained the white tablecloth. "Do you not believe that my lord of Suffolk made himself essential to the lady for his own gain? You have only to look at his rather checkered past, followed by his swift and powerful rise here, to see that."

Jane had heard her parents make similar arguments over the years about Charles Brandon, Duke of Suffolk. Two previous marriages and a murder scandal dotted his life before his scandalous love affair with the king's sister, Mary Tudor. Jane, like the rest of the country, however, had been swept up by the romance of their story, not the likely underlying reality of it. But the longer she was here at court, the more reality there was to pull back the curtain on her girlish fantasy.

As they dined, Jane listened keenly to the repartee between the two rakishly handsome courtiers, and she watched their sly glances, trying at last to become more a student and less a victim of the world into which she had been so swiftly cast. She felt out of balance with it. True, these men had suddenly befriended her, making her feel less a wallflower and more a delicate lily, perhaps, but there was a risk in that, and she knew it.

Suddenly then, taking Jane away from her thoughts, the queen bolted to her feet on the dais, shooting a dagger glare at Anne Boleyn. The lively music from the gallery above ceased, and a deafening silence filled the hall as the two women glowered at each other. A heartbeat later, seeming to sense danger, a little man in bright orange and green jumped between them. The little man said something Jane could not hear from where she sat at a distance, and the king tipped back his head and filled the silence with his boisterous laughter. The moment was as fraught with awkward tension as anything Jane had ever experienced.

"Leave it to Will Somers to defuse any volatile situation with a jest," Compton murmured.

"I know not how he does it. But better his head at risk than mine. He has a certain power over our sovereign in the same league as Mistress Anne."

"He sounds quite malleable for a sovereign," Jane observed.

Carew laughed.

Compton cleared his throat and lifted his goblet in tribute to her.

"Why, Mistress Jane," said William Compton, "I would not have expected you to be clever. At least not so soon. Perhaps, little mouse, you may surprise us all yet."

Francis Bryan read the letter again as he stood at a long dark window later that night, his leather-booted foot propped on the casement. Such a plea from young William Dormer was the last thing he expected. Apparently, Dormer had only just uncovered a plot launched against him by an ardent village girl, one of no consequence to him, but one cleverly designed to keep him from his early interest in Jane. It was, the letter said, Dormer's greatest desire that Jane's influential cousin might intercede on their behalf to help him in some way right the grievous wrong of years ago. Despite the obvious futility now, still Dormer could not move on with his life without knowing for certain that Mistress Seymour had moved on with hers. Francis gazed out the window onto the pond below, across which two elegant white swans swam. The letter was solicitous to the point of being desperate, and even a hardened courtier like Francis was moved by the romance in it.

But timing was everything. He had just set about installing Jane in the queen's household, at great risk to his own standing with the rising power of Anne Boleyn, whom he was outwardly forced to support. Since Her Highness had lost so many ladies this past year to the lure of the royal concubine, Francis was trying to juggle both sides. He could not risk drawing attention to himself or his causes. Thus, it must wait, he determined, folding the missive and tucking it into his doublet until he could give a bit more thought to it. Sober thought, at least.

If it were true love, it would survive the test of time.

If not . . . well, perhaps there was some greater partner out there yet for Jane.

Although, by his life, Francis Bryan could not imagine who that might be.

Feeling strangely pleased with herself, Jane rose the next morning and dressed. Heartened by a feeling of growing confidence, she laced the front stays of her own long plastron and drew on fresh stockings without aid. The May Day joust would be her first at court. In spite of the air of quiet reserve the queen's attendants were instructed to adopt, the prospect was still enormously exciting. She was to sit with Lady Carew, whom Jane secretly admired in spite of how disparagingly her husband had spoken of her. Jane was learning that no one here was completely as they seemed, so she had no intention of judging Elizabeth Carew based on her husband's drunken rambling. At least not yet. She would also be with Margaret Shelton and Lady Hastings, the latter of whom was another of the king's apparent romantic castoffs. They were as plentiful as flies, Jane mused to herself in the rich honey sunlight streaming through the windows.

She had been spared attending the queen this morning at Matins, which for a change gave her a few additional moments with her own appearance. One of the young maids of honor then attached Jane's stylish new lavender velvet hood and hooked the long gold chain at her waist. It was not an opulent gown on par with some of the others here, but the velvet was rich and the gold braid was crisp. The growing loyalty she felt for the queen had allowed her, in a small way, to feel that she might actually fit somewhere into the complex fabric of court life. God certainly knew, there was nothing left for her in Wiltshire.

"Pray, is that my good cousin Mistress Seymour? You suddenly resemble a quite fashionable court lady," exclaimed Francis Bryan affably, coming upon her as she neared the lists across the gardens behind the palace. Grand blue, red, and green banners flew above them in the bright blue midday sun. Francis was wearing a partial suit of armor and an easy smile and carrying his gleaming plumed helmet.

"You do me the honor in saying so, sir."

"Ah, but 'tis true." His deep brown eyes twinkled in the sunlight against his pale skin and auburn hair, and Jane felt herself blush, feeling almost important as they walked together to the entrance to the lists—the place where the contests were to begin and where they would part.

"You joust today with whom, my lord?"

"Apparently I am to face the king."

He did not sound particularly daunted, Jane thought. "Shall you let him win?" she asked as the breeze ruffled her full sleeves and the hem of her dress.

"No one lets the King of England win. As you have seen, he is a great bear of a man who takes delight in being able to vanquish us all. Perhaps only Brandon's size would permit him to be a true challenge."

"Then I shall pray for you as soon as I see you ride out."

"By the Lord, I would be honored if you did." Then he touched the cuirass of his armor near his heart as if he had remembered something. "I have something I must give to you, but it warrants a proper explanation, the time for which I do not now have. But anon. It shall keep 'til then."

Jane smiled. "Would you like to offer me a hint?"

"'Twill be better if I present it, and the sentiment, fully."

He took her hand then and casually kissed the back of it in the French manner since he had spent much time this past year in France as one of the king's ambassadors. She had noticed it was one of his little endearing affectations. Each of the king's good friends had one. But Jane was enormously grateful to Francis for having brought her away from the embarrassment of spinsterhood at Wolf Hall, so there was little he could have done to displease her.

Certainly nothing he might tell her could endanger that.

"Ride well, good cousin," she said brightly, to which he then made a great bow.

It was not until she was seated in the stands in the very center of the queen's ladies, gowns touching like rose petals, that Jane saw the king in the stands in front of her. Once again he was flanked by the queen on one side and Anne Boleyn on the other. As a warm breeze blew, Jane turned to Elizabeth Carew beside her. "I thought your brother was to ride against the king," she dared to whisper as everyone else around her was chattering and gossiping excitedly. She knew no one would care enough to listen to her.

"That was true, until His Majesty danced the night away with Mistress Boleyn and turned his ankle rather sharply trying to impress her. My husband, who attends him each morning, said his foot is the color of a summer plum and as fat as a tree stump."

Elizabeth's tone was harsh, but it made sense if she had been disposed of by the king, as the gossip claimed. Jane's sense that Henry VIII was a shallow, selfish man redoubled inside her, and she resolved to keep as well out of his way as possible. Not that she was capable of catching his eye anyway, or that of any man, for that matter. William Dormer had certainly made that clear enough years ago.

"Who shall be Sir Francis's challenger, then?"

"My husband." Elizabeth smiled.

"Your husband versus your brother?"

"They are well matched in all things: whoring, drinking, *and* fighting."

Jane looked more closely at her then. Skin like ivory, a perfect chin, and a tiny nose, yet such jaded callousness. It changed her a bit in Jane's eyes. *Was that all the king's doing?* she wondered as she tried to imagine what Elizabeth must have been like before.

"Are you not supporting your brother, then?"

Elizabeth looked at her with a perplexed expression as the riders cantered proudly out onto the field to thunderous applause and trumpeted fanfare. "Of course I am. He is my brother. But this is court, little mouse. Is that not what he and my good husband so endearingly call you?"

Jane did not answer as her glance again caught on the king and Anne Boleyn. The spectacle they were making of themselves seemed particularly vulgar. Yet it was also difficult to turn away from. The king barely noticed the pageantry or contest before him as he laughed with Anne and slapped his knee like a young boy. The encounter reminded Jane of a spider casting its web around a big, colorful bug, the bug being entirely unaware it was about to be devoured.

How much better it was, Jane thought again, to be removed, to be merely part of the backdrop to such a spectacle and not a true piece of it.

Down on the field, Francis looked so dashing and lordly in his gleaming silver, the green plume of his helmet fluttering in the breeze, that Jane completely turned her attention to him. She felt a strange burst of familial pride knowing they were cousins, however distant. He was far more kind than her mother's cousin, the great Duke of Norfolk, who had yet even to acknowledge Jane.

Back in the stands, she noticed her brother Edward a few rows closer to the king. Like Norfolk, Edward acted as if he and Jane were virtual strangers, as if speaking to someone so ordinary would ruin his reputation. His fortunes and his status had increased greatly this past year, which seemed at the heart of the matter.

Jane was happy to spot her other brother, Thomas, standing on the corner of the field in the green and white uniform that marked him as Sir Francis Bryan's attendant. They had recently been in France together, and Jane could hardly wait to embrace him heartily and badger him for gossip and news from the French court.

She was so distracted by her thoughts and the lively group of courtiers that she did not see it happen. But she heard the great thud, then the snap of wood. A great collective gasp from the crowd and the clattering of armor brought Jane and the other ladies quickly to their feet. Francis was on the ground, writhing in agony, and Nicholas Carew was off his mount and at his side in a matter of moments. Both long jousting poles lay on the ground, and Thomas was sprinting toward the courtiers.

"God in his mercy!" Jane heard herself cry out as a hush fell upon the crowd, which had fallen swiftly into fearful silence.

"What has happened to him?"

"Sir Francis was flirting so boldly with Lady Hastings that he neglected to close his visor before he began," Elizabeth Carew murmured, both hands on her mouth in shock at the blood that now seemed to blanket everything.

"At least he is moving, so he is not dead," Margaret Shelton exclaimed with a hand to her lips.

"But look at all that blood," Anne Stanhope cried.

Grooms, guards, equerries, and physicians dashed onto the field then. *Yes, by the Lord, at least he was not dead!* Jane thought, stricken with fear for him and unable to stop trembling as they knelt around him, drew off his plumed helmet, and began to cover his blood-soaked face with cloths.

A litter was swiftly brought to carry him off the field.

"Should you not go to your brother?" Jane asked Elizabeth. Francis had no wife, and Jane knew that their mother was not at court, but attending Princess Mary at Ludlow Castle in Shropshire, where she had been consigned by the king.

"I am not at all good at these sorts of things," Elizabeth replied desperately and began to weep as Jane took her hand and gently squeezed it in support. Elizabeth Carew, whom she had not known long, held fast to her.

"Would you like me to go with you?" Jane asked.

"Would you do that?" Elizabeth sniffled.

Jane did not answer but in response led the way down the steps of the stands and back toward the palace, feeling suddenly that they could almost be friends. It was an odd thing to feel under the circumstances, Jane thought, but she still really had no idea what it felt like to have a true friend.

Then she thought of Lucy Hill and how they were very nearly friends. Yes, nearly.

"He's lost his eye, I'm afraid."

Thomas Seymour reluctantly made the announcement, then took his sister into a tender embrace. "Thank heavens you're here," she murmured to him in the shadow-drenched corridor outside of Sir Francis Bryan's apartments, where the king's physicians were still attending him. Hearing the news, Elizabeth collapsed against the lime-wash corridor wall and folded in on herself, her face blanched, as she pressed her hands over her mouth.

"His beautiful eyes . . . ," she wept. "He was always so proud of his eyes."

Jane went to Elizabeth then and sat on the floor against the wall beside her with an arm wrapped tightly around her shoulder in support. "An eye patch will make him terribly distinguished looking." She tried to offer up a smile for Elizabeth's sake, but it was a struggle when the situation seemed so grave, and when she loved him so dearly for how good and honest he had been with her.

"Could *you* ever care for a man with such a blighted visage, Jane?"

"By my troth, I could care for a man with a tender heart and devotion enough to overlook my own shortcomings," she replied truthfully.

Elizabeth looked at her through tear-brightened eyes. "I am grateful for your words, Jane." She then turned to Thomas, who stood over them. "How is his condition otherwise, Master Seymour?" Elizabeth asked as she glanced up at Jane's brother, who remained standing over them.

"Your husband is still with his friend, and he gave me leave, my lady, to tell you that the doctors do not fear for his life. Your brother is strong and healthy and he shall recover from this."

"Yet without an eye."

"Surely it is preferable to dying,"

"I am not so certain since, at this court, nothing is prized so highly as beauty."

"From what I have seen, my lady, wit and charm do beauty a fair battle, and there are few so witty or charming as your brother," said Thomas.

"Except perhaps the king." Elizabeth sniffled, trying to rein in her tears.

"I have not yet had the honor of being able to agree or disagree, since I have yet to actually meet His Majesty," Thomas replied, gazing down with a helpless expression at the two women still sitting on the cold tile floor.

"Pray, do not be too anxious for *that* experience, Master Seymour," Elizabeth countered in her trembling voice, which held a kind of warning. "Being impressed with our good sovereign can have a whole host of disadvantages and complications, the range of which, I fear, would quite surprise you."

That evening, Jane sat by firelight in the queen's company, along with Maria de Salinas; their friend the Spanish ambassador, Don Luis Caroz; the imperial ambassador, Eustase Chapuys; the queen's confessor, the Bishop of Rochester; and Cardinal Thomas Wolsey. They each took turns reading to the queen from the Book of Common Prayer, and the mood was somber.

"Mistress Seymour, tell us, how fares your good cousin?" the queen suddenly asked, her question full of true compassion.

Chapuys, a small man with a receding hairline and dark, hollow eyes, stopped reading midsentence and looked up at Jane with the others.

"I am told he shall recover, Your Highness. Praise be to God," Jane answered shyly. It was rare that she was called to speak aloud before so many assembled nobles, including the cardinal in his forbidding crimson. She heard her own voice break.

"Indeed a blessing. You take strength from your faith, Mistress Seymour," said the queen. "I like that."

"I do, Your Highness. You are a model for us all in that regard." Jane could hear her own voice quiver still, and she struggled in vain against it.

"Am I?" She arched her dark brows appraisingly, and her heavy chin doubled.

"Certainly."

"Well, as long as I stand in stark contrast to Mistress Boleyn, who follows another woman's husband about with open lust in those coal black eyes of hers, may God forgive me." Katherine made the sign of the cross piously then. "As you might suppose, I have little more patience for infidelity than I do faithlessness. I do pray daily for forbearance in all things. Should not we *all* do that?" The queen asked the question rhetorically and did so as she cast a censuring glance on lovely Lady Anne Stafford, who for some time had been having an affair with the king's married Groom of the Stool, Sir William Compton. And, as everyone knew, the king himself before that. But everyone at court was so intricately woven together, bound tightly by family, or loyalty, or lust—sometimes all three. Certainly much was tolerated or overlooked. It was like a strange, grand, flawed family, Jane had decided, and she continued to be glad she was only an observer of it all, since she had no earthly idea how she might cope if she were ever pulled into the midst of any of it.

"Mistress Seymour, would you be the one to next read to us for a while?" the queen then asked.

In response, the fat-faced Cardinal Wolsey glowered at her, his wet lower lip jutting out as his brows merged. Or perhaps she was imagining it. He did not seem to Jane a kind man. Rather he appeared a porcine opportunist who sat and laughed with Anne Boleyn with as much sincerity as he brought to his counseling of the queen.

Reading aloud before this important group now went well beyond Jane's area of comfort, since she had yet to learn what to do and what to avoid in their presence. She felt her stomach twist into a hard knot at the prospect. Her heart was racing and she knew what little color she had had certainly gone out of her face. *Speak, you must speak!*

"It would be an honor, Your Highness. Where shall I begin?" she forced herself to ask as she began to leaf through her own small volume of the book at hand.

"Ah, we've had enough of this for now. My Lord Bishop of Rochester here has spoken with your brother, and he tells me you are well versed in *The Imitation of Christ*."

"Verily, 'tis my favorite work, Your Highness, particularly the fourth book translated by the king's mother."

Katherine smiled and cast a glance at the black-and-white-garbed Rochester. The queen's approval was a rare thing these days, and Jane felt her racing heart slow by one small degree. "Most here have no use for such pious work. How lovely to see that I have company in my appreciation of it."

Jane lowered her eyes, suddenly feeling the weight from the envious stares around her. They apparently favored her position in the background as much as she did.

"I have only ever read silently, however, so I dare not vouch for how I would sound aloud to your learned royal ear."

There were muffled chuckles in response to her awkward flattery, and Jane felt her cheeks burn with embarrassment at their reaction.

"Oh nonsense, Mistress Seymour. Surely you were taught to recite aloud by your tutor. In Wiltshire, was it?"

"We had not a proper tutor, Your Highness, only our priest, who taught us our lessons."

The chuckles deepened then to rude outright laughter, and if Jane could have crawled beneath the covered table, she would have. The sensation of ridicule stirred old wounds, and she instantly felt thrown. Her throat had gone miserably dry and she knew her voice would crack if she spoke aloud again now.

It was the most curious thing in the world that she thought of William Dormer at that precise moment. He came into her mind almost like a phantom. But the ghost did not speak; it only shimmered there before her supportively, and after a moment, she felt an odd strength from it.

Jane's father used to tell her when she was a little girl that sometimes after people died an image of them came back to those who had loved them. She desperately hoped William had not died. In that moment, her anger and disappointment in him ceased completely. Right now, William and Wolf Hall felt very far away.

Chapter Eight

June 1526
Eltham Palace

*I*t was as much common knowledge in the royal galleries as in the servants' quarters below that the king meant not just to court Mistress Boleyn, but to win her completely. Yet competition loomed. The court poet, Thomas Wyatt, had begun a bold flirtation with the raven-haired beauty, whose skill at tying the king into romantic knots seemed unparalleled.

Jane knew about it mainly because the queen's friends delighted in seeing His Highness's pained fits of jealousy over such a handsome and talented young competitor. Since Wyatt had been commissioned to read one or two of his own poems during the last banquet, everyone was abuzz with the possibility of an impending clash between the rivals.

The banquet hall was decorated lavishly for the occasion and in a way to which Jane was certain she would never grow accustomed. The vast, vaulted chamber with its brightly painted beams was ablaze with torches and candles when she arrived in the queen's train. She was walking beside Elizabeth Carew in front of Margaret Shelton and Anne Stanhope and behind the queen and Ambassador Chapuys. In her dark dress, plain collar, and prominent crucifix, Queen Katherine made a poor comparison to the woman who emerged through the opposite archway, flanked by her uncle, the Duke of Norfolk, and Cardinal Wolsey, who had only just been in the queen's company the evening before. Anne strode regally, like a queen herself, brilliant in a dazzling gown of gold cloth that was ornamented with sparkling precious stones. As usual, courtiers and ladies began gossiping and whispering beneath the strains of music sung by Mark Smeaton, another handsome young courtier, who was standing in the gallery above.

Just then the familiar trumpet blare sounded the king's arrival as he entered the hall, along with his jester, Will Somers, and his entourage, Charles Brandon, Thomas Wyatt, William Compton, William Brereton, and Nicholas Carew. Francis Bryan was with them, now sporting a jaunty black eye patch bordered with tiny glittering jewels above a matching and luxurious velvet doublet encrusted with the same stones.

Jane smiled as she looked at him, her heart bursting with silent admiration. Ah, what a survivor he did seem! Adversity had not torn Francis down, only strengthened him, she thought, as the king draped an arm familiarly across his shoulder and leaned in as if they were sharing a great private joke. It was only a moment until she saw that they were both staring at Thomas Wyatt as they laughed. It was like three great factions coming together in one place. The king's, the queen's, and Anne's. The atmosphere was certainly charged. It made Jane shiver as she watched all three powers converge on the head table beneath a ceremonial drape stamped with the Tudor rose. Beside the two thrones, a third heavily carved chair had been placed. She watched Mistress Boleyn bob a careless little curtsy to the queen and then nod to the king himself before she sank into the out-of-place third chair.

While the court had steadily grown accustomed these past months to Anne's presence near the sovereign, her position and strength seemed to be increasing by the day. The king was obsessed with her. Fueling his passion was her open flirtation with Sir Thomas Wyatt. The king, after all, was married, Anne had blithely told Elizabeth Carew one afternoon at cards, so she had no intention of not proceeding with her own amours, unless, and until, those circumstances changed.

"This should be quite a performance," John Fischer, the Bishop of Rochester, remarked to Maria de Salinas, both near enough for Jane to hear.

"Sir Thomas *is* a brilliant poet, his flowery verse well captured in cogent couplets," Chapuys concurred.

"Oh, I meant not that. Only that Master Wyatt would do well to take care. As should Mistress Anne. The king is accustomed to winning what he desires, from the likes of Lady Hastings, Lady Carew, Mistress Blount—even Mistress Anne's own sister. This is a train of victory never interrupted by failure. And if I know our sovereign, he does not plan to begin now," the sage bishop observed.

After Will Somers dutifully brought the king to tears of laughter by ridiculing each of the men closest around them with pithy little barbs, the spindly court fool bowed to the king and made way for Thomas Wyatt to enter the center of the arranged banquet tables for his turn at the entertainment.

With the intensity of a student, Jane watched each of the players. She glanced at Anne, whose blithe expression had changed swiftly to one of coy flirtation with the handsome poet, who was now opening his book of verse. In the midst of this charged atmosphere, the poor queen sat like a quail on its nest, attempting to protect the fruits of her tenuous life.

The queen was to be pitied, Jane thought. She had thought that over and over, perhaps never so much as now. Quietly, her blood boiled like the contents of one of the great iron kettles bubbling in the hot royal kitchens directly beneath their feet—and this false amusement.

If it were Anne against me, Jane thought, *I would be more wise, more cunning. More quiet and clever like my brother Tom. Because no one ever suspects the plain-faced, quiet ones.* Even a little country mouse like Jane could see that well enough.

As Wyatt began to read with a boastful tenor full of flourishes, boldly directing his words and gaze upon Anne, Jane caught a glimpse of Mary Boleyn, newly returned to court from her new husband's family home in Hertfordshire in a show of family support for her sister. Mary was seated only a few chairs away at the same table. It was a surprise to see her here. She had grown stout in adulthood from childbirth. But on her face, as on her sister's, that graceful Boleyn essence was unchanged. Mary's discomfort as she watched her former lover and her own sister together on the dais was a palpable thing to Jane. It was obvious that it had not been her idea to return here.

There were crystal-bright tears in Mary's eyes to make the point clearer. Her appointed husband, William Carey, took her hand atop the table, but Jane saw that Mary's body went rigid at his touch. It seemed a move for show. As Wyatt and Anne gazed at each other and Wyatt droned on, Mary's and Jane's eyes met across the table and Mary's face brightened with recognition. Mary nodded to her and smiled grimly in acknowledgment. When the reading was at an end and the dancing began, Mary came and embraced her.

"What a long time it has been, Jane. I had heard you were at court now. 'Tis a good thing to see a friendly face here."

"I am heartened you remember me, Lady Carey. We were very young and our time together in France was so brief."

"You must still call me Mary, and I was not so young then as to not remember you," Mary replied.

Jane had heard the gossip from Thomas several years ago that Mary Boleyn had been pressured by her family to give herself not only to the King of France, but to two of his companions in hopes of advancing the family. She later heard about Mary and the English king, and that children had likely resulted from their union. Children he did not acknowledge, in spite of his acceptance of Bess Blount's son, Henry Fitzroy.

The music from the gallery changed suddenly to a more somber pavane, and the king led Anne past the tables to the center of the other dancers. Wyatt had been dismissed while Jane and Mary spoke, and the king was not smiling as he held Anne's hand through the dance steps.

"Ah, if only I had been as clever as my sister, I might still be there with him," Mary said with a sigh, watching them dance more stiffly with each other than usual.

"You still love the king?" Jane was surprised.

"He is the father of my children."

Jane's smile fell as Mary's husband excused himself from the table. She was shocked that Mary seemed so free to speak of such private matters. "But he does not acknowledge them as such, as he does the Duke of Richmond?"

Jane saw the flare of pain in Mary's eyes, and she regretted saying it immediately.

"Because I am married, he says acknowledging them would be a messy business and cruel to my husband, whom he fancies. That, of course, was all very convenient, I see now. Even that vapid little

Blount tart was smarter than I in her dealings with him. 'Tis a game to him, with honor and virtue the pins to be knocked down by one of his great royal balls," she said vulgarly.

"Pray, forgive me, but then is it not too painful to remain here for you now and equally distressing to speak of such things?" she asked as everyone watched the king dance and whispered privately about Mary's younger, prettier sister, Anne.

"Mayhap 'tis to be part of my punishment," Mary said philosophically, though her voice broke with the words. "That, and my father insists I remain here as a show of family support along with our brother, George. There are few around her my sister can trust . . . as if I am actually one of them." Mary caught the shocked expression on Jane's face. "Oh yes, once, I would not have dreamed of speaking such thoughts aloud, but the life I have lived since last we met has made me care far less now what others think of me. I fear it has all come tumbling out now to a friendly face."

As they conversed, suddenly from the corner of her eye, Jane could see that the king and Anne's exchange was becoming heated. They stopped dancing then and were simply standing in the center of the room, openly arguing, his arms outstretched in a pleading gesture, his huge rings glinting in the torchlight. Anne began gesticulating wildly, but the king only shrugged and looked sheepish.

"My sister does have him by the nose. No other can quite compare."

Jane suddenly thought of William Dormer again at the notion of being emotionally bound to someone. It was odd the way he still moved through her thoughts from time to time, the memory rekindling like a fire, then dying out into embers with a sudden distraction. The king had retreated to the dais, where the queen silently watched everything, and Anne stormed off in Mary and Jane's direction, her beautiful, flawless face red with rage, her lips twisted tightly into a pout.

"Come away with me this instant, Mary," Anne said impatiently, ignoring Jane, whom she clearly did not recognize.

"I should wait for my husband," Mary said in a surprisingly meek tone.

"Nonsense. Sir William waits on the king; you wait on me. You shall both serve the same master soon enough."

Jane glanced at the dais again, where the king sat now, ramrod straight, his chin up, holding the queen's hand and gazing out regally at the group of dancers who had assembled in his place, as if his open encounter with Anne had never even occurred. He was playing the game well and had clearly won the round.

"It seems you might be a bit too ambitious for your own good, sister," Mary dared to say amid the safety of the music and the crowd milling around them.

Jane held her breath. She could feel their flaring sibling rivalry.

"Do not underestimate me, Mary. I learned well by your mistakes. Bessie Blount's and the queen's as well," she said coldly. "Both of you were foolish. You know not how to actually love a man like that. There is no place in this game for surrender."

Then, as an afterthought, Anne paused and looked directly at Jane. She tightened her spine, and her small mouth lengthened into a hard line. "Who the devil are *you* to listen to a conversation between sisters?"

Jane had no idea what made her do it, but she bobbed a small curtsy then and lowered her head, as if it were completely out of her power to do anything else.

She despised herself a little for the submissive reaction.

"Oh, you must be the one they are calling the little mouse," Anne Boleyn said unkindly before she began to chuckle.

"I am Jane Seymour," she heard herself say.

" 'Little mouse' seems far more appropriate by the look of you. Come along, then, Mary. I need attending. You shall see to my packing tonight since I've a sudden desire to bathe."

"But where are you going?" Mary asked in surprise.

"Home to Hever of course, you fool. 'Tis time the king realizes he cannot live without me."

"You looked quite smitten with Master Wyatt. Is he not a more realistic alternative?"

Anne laughed harshly over the music, and the sound that came up from her throat was quite menacing, Jane thought. It certainly turned the skin beneath her heavy gown to gooseflesh.

"Wyatt is of no more consequence than that pup-eyed singer, Mark Smeaton. He is only meant to stir the king's jealousy."

Jane wanted to say that if tonight's little drama was any indication, that pot was well stirred indeed; Anne ought to tread carefully lest it boil over and scald her. But she held her tongue.

Mary leaned toward her sister. "By the look of it tonight, His Majesty would give you nearly anything you desire if you would give him that one thing which he desires."

"You truly are a dolt. I do wonder that we share a mother. No matter what *you* did, I am meant to be a queen, not a whore. Absence makes the heart grow fonder, so I need to be absent. For a time, at least. Just until I bring him to his knees."

Mary glanced back at the king, still sitting with the queen, laughing and conversing as though Anne did not even exist. Jane followed her gaze.

At that moment, bringing him to his knees seemed highly unlikely.

"He eventually grew tired of each of us who tried to challenge the queen. Perhaps, sister, you would do well to remember that."

"Like any of you had a chance of challenging her?" Anne declared. Her dark, almond-shaped eyes flared as she said it. "Now, follow me. I am weary and I wish to bathe. In the event His Majesty comes to his senses tonight, I should like to be clean. If not, my lavender perfume shall be a stirring reminder of what he has lost when he passes my empty rooms. Come along, then, Mary, and bring the little mouse with you. Whether she prefers the queen to me or not, she will do to dry my back when I am finished."

Lady Mary Carey left for Hever Castle with her sister early the next morning as a heavy fog and light rain swirled around the pathways and the low-lying neatly groomed plants of the king's knot garden. Jane was sorry to see her go. There was nothing of judgment in her eyes. Jane did not feel the same way about Anne, however.

Thankfully, with Anne gone, a lightness returned to the queen's apartments. There were still the constant prayers and the somber hours of quiet sewing, but the queen occasionally smiled, and so everyone in her retinue was allowed to breathe again. While Katherine did not entertain him often, everyone said how the king had changed in Anne's absence as well. He was calm now, less volatile. He spent most of his days alone, reading or hunting or writing letters and dispatches. He dined regularly with the queen, and only Maria de Salinas was called upon to attend her in case he might have a change of heart about remaining for the night.

Through the months, Jane only ever saw the king at a distance. The great copper-headed giant was more masculine and taller than anyone else except his friend Charles Brandon, and certainly more elegant. His array of jeweled Florentine velvets and embroidered

Burgundian silk doublets seemed as endless as his caps and square-toed shoes. Only the sound of his occasional burst of laughter, that most human of actions, made him seem anything close to a real person in Jane's mind.

No matter what, her loyalty was still to the queen, for whom Jane's pity trumped every other feeling.

After the court had begun the summer progress at Greenwich Palace, where the wild grass and flowers grew tall and fragrant in the open meadows behind the river, Anne Boleyn returned to their company and the lightness faded. Anne manipulatively drove the king to total distraction. In spite of the hours of counsel he kept with his friend Thomas More, or the holy advice he took from Cardinal Wolsey to ward off temptation, the whole court was made to pay for Henry's enduring frustrations with Anne. Twice he chased her to Hever Castle; twice she returned with him. Everyone agreed she played the game of courtly love better than anyone had before her. Far better than the king.

Then, as autumn rain soaked England with a heavy and endless downpour, things changed again. In October, when the court was installed back at Richmond Palace beneath the nose of the queen, Anne Boleyn began to assemble not just her allies but her own full court of ladies.

She boldly wooed them right from under Katherine.

Seeing the trend for herself, Jane slipped into the background as much as possible, but the king's emboldened paramour still made it treacherous for everyone. Courtiers lived in fear of angering one faction or the other, without knowing for certain who would be victorious.

Jane saw the king more often now. He spent nearly all of his time in the company of Anne or the queen, as if he were weighing the two. It was apparent to all that a decision was finally required of him.

There was one day when the rain was so relentless that Anne, her ladies, the king, and a few of his friends were forced to entertain themselves by strolling back and forth across the length of the long gallery.

For the first time, Jane was called upon formally to attend Anne. Jane had been sitting with Elizabeth Carew in the small alcove inside the queen's presence chamber. She glanced up with surprise at Mary Boleyn, who stood over her with the urgent request upon her lips.

"Oh pray, I would rather not. I would feel as if I had betrayed the queen, who has been kind to me," Jane tried her best to demure.

"Nice as that sentiment is," Mary whispered to her so as not to be overheard, "survival is the key. My sister's influence has grown and she knows it. You dare not reject her for what *he* might do! Believe me, I know well enough when he gets something into his mind; there shall be no stopping him."

Jane felt a mounting panic at the prospect of an impossible choice she could no longer avoid. She had no idea how she would defend herself if the increasingly sensitive queen discovered the betrayal. Still, she followed Mary dutifully and clasped the beaded rosary hanging from her waist to give her strength.

They came upon the king and Anne then, who were pausing in the center of the gallery, where three great maps of the world were hung above a row of terra-cotta busts on black-and-white marble pillars. The king was gesturing to a point on one of the maps but turned when he heard the ladies approach. For the first time, Jane's and the king's eyes met, and he smiled at her. She felt her reaction swiftly, as a fire of embarrassment raced to her cheeks, coloring them. She lowered her eyes quickly, but not before Anne rounded upon her sharply. As she did, Anne clutched a bright gold pendant hooked around her neck. She was smiling exactly like a Cheshire cat.

She leaned coyly then against the king's shoulder, making it clear that the locket had been a recent gift from the sovereign.

"Very well, then, sweetheart, shall we continue our stroll now that you have your reinforcements around you?" the king teased her as rain beat hard against the diamond-shaped windows along the opposite wall of the gallery.

The men who were gathered with the king were careful to control their reaction to the humor in the comment. Jane's brother Edward stood beside Francis Bryan, Francis's handsome face ornamented now by a new dove gray, pearl-studded eye patch. He nodded, acknowledging Jane, while Edward ignored her and said something about the monotony of the rain to William Compton and William Brereton.

Jane's indignation suddenly flared. Something was happening inside her, although she was not certain what. In all the months she had been at court, her own brother still treated her as all of the other men but Francis did—as if she were of no consequence at all.

"Your Majesty has a wife, so I keep my dignity among my companions," Anne said with insipid sweetness in answer to his little jab.

"Where do you keep your heart? For that is what I seek."

"My heart is around my neck for all to see, Your Majesty," she said, twirling the gold charm playfully.

"I suspect I shall pay dearly for the one as I have paid for the other," the king volleyed, clearly pleased with himself, and his paramour, today.

"Your pendant is stunning, if I may say, my lady," Jane heard herself say in a suddenly clear, committed voice, spurred on by her anger at Edward. If she were to be thrown into the mix against her will, at least she would do well with it.

Anne looked up at her in response. So did the king. *How very odd,* she thought, but Jane found that she liked his face up close. It was angular and strong, framed by a neat copper beard, his cheeks lightly dusted with the faint traces of adolescent freckles. His green eyes mirrored back something she could not define but still drew her. At first it looked like amusement, but then she saw a flicker of pain cross them before he cleverly concealed it with a wry smile.

"Indeed," Anne said, taking the occasion to hold up the pendant in front of everyone and flash the tiny miniature of the king painted at the center. "'Tis a good likeness, I think. Although the eyes are a bit less clever than they should be. Mistress Seymour, pray do not gawk, but have a closer look and tell us how you find it."

Jane did not want to be a part of this, but when the king arched his copper brows expectantly at her, she knew she had opened the door herself into a powerful world she had been trying for months to avoid.

"She is *your* sister, Edward?" Henry suddenly asked, hearing her name and turning toward Edward, who stood beside Francis Bryan leaning against the window, arms crossed over his chest.

"She is, sire." Edward nodded but did not say more.

"Ah. Well, then." The king paused as though he had been caught quite unaware of what to say next or how best to say it. "Indeed, then, Mistress Seymour, do tell us all how you find my likeness."

Brereton, Compton, and Wyatt all muffled snickers, delighted by the young maiden's discomfort as she stood in the presence of such a bold and powerful man. As the king looked at her, Jane saw Anne's gaze slip to Wyatt and the two of them exchange a private smile before Jane replied.

"Masterfully done, Your Majesty. 'Tis quite a flattering likeness, from what I can see."

"What you see is what there is, so be firm in your reply," he snapped with a sudden note of irritation at her vague flattery. "For example, do you find, as Mistress Boleyn posits, that my eyes are more clever than the portrait reveals?"

Anne Boleyn was sneering now at her predicament, still holding up the pendant, seeming to delight in the awkwardness of Jane's sudden moment in the light. Anne had grown only more haughty since they were girls in France, if such a thing were even possible, Jane thought, and she liked her even less. But she was glad Anne still did not seem to recall their encounter because there seemed even more danger and potential ridicule in that.

"I have not the occasion to know whether Your Majesty is, or is not, more clever than your image, as I have not been graced with an encounter before now."

"Well, image *is* everything, is it not?" As he glanced around, pleased with his own response, his companions chuckled, urging on the banter. "Keep that in mind when you are next in my presence, Mistress Seymour. Modesty quite bores me to tears, especially when I have such clever company beside me."

As the king took Anne's hand and they began to stroll the length of the gallery again, Jane saw her brother's angry glare before he drew Elizabeth Carew into conversation and strolled away. Francis Bryan came up to Jane a moment later and set out to stroll beside her.

"Worry not. They are only toying with you. They mustn't see your dismay or, like hounds to blood, they shall go after you even more next time."

"I am glad you are recovered. I have missed your encouragement," she said sincerely. It was then she remembered their brief conversation before the tournament. "Cousin, you never did tell me what you wanted to say that day before the joust. Think you now that it is a good time to reveal it?"

They fell into a slow strolling step behind the others. "I'm afraid I was hit so violently that I have quite forgotten anything that happened earlier that day." He looked quizzically at her, twisting his face into a frown, as if trying to remember. "Not to worry, though; if it had been anything important, I am quite certain someone will remind me of it in time."

"Quite right," Jane agreed, thinking it was all just as well, since it was probably a letter from her parents at Wolf Hall voicing their displeasure over the fact that she had been at court all of these months and had elicited no male interest that could further elevate the Seymour family standing. After all, what else could it possibly have been?

As he dressed for the banquet later that evening, Edward Seymour cringed and tried very hard not to think what a dreadful first impression his meek sister had made before the king. All these months, all the work, the flattery and manipulation, the exorbitant costumes and the subsequent debt accrued just to stay on the same footing as Carew, Bryan, Wyatt, Brereton, and Compton; none of it mattered, for in a single stroke, like the sharp slice of a rapier blade, she had cut her own brother off at the knees with her poor impression on the king.

Oh, that quiet way of hers, her voice thick like paste, her gaze never quite seizing on a person but drifting modestly down to her toes at the first breath of discomfort. If only she had been blessed with some modicum of beauty, her mousy ways could be overlooked.

Jane had never seemed to him a true Seymour. She certainly bore no markings of a Wentworth. His sister seemed to him a liability, which was the main reason he had long kept his distance. Her decision-making skills fared no better, especially when she showed an ill-timed loyalty to the queen, of all people, who was in the midst of an obvious downfall.

Edward had personally heard the king consulting Cardinal Wolsey about the viability of a divorce the last time Mistress Boleyn had run back to Hever Castle. So if it was to be divorce, by God, Edward would not be on the wrong side of *that* decree! He had worked too long and too hard for what he had.

He ran a hand down the front of his own velvet doublet admiringly. Still, had silly little Jane not at least carved out one unexpected niche? He had seen her strolling in the garden in the company of Elizabeth Carew and Anne Stanhope a number of times these past few days. For whatever inane reason, Mother wanted Jane to remain at court, so that was how it would be, and he must find some way to make use of her.

As they ambled along, Edward glanced ahead at the petite and alluring Anne Stanhope, her body poured so neatly into a tight blue velvet dress with a ribbon of lace at her breast to draw the eye. And it certainly did that. She could not be more different from his sister, Edward thought admiringly. Anne was a tart little thing, luscious enough to take the sting away from what his whore of a wife had done, if only he could get her to notice him.

It had been ages since he had been able to even think of a woman without wanting to murder his wife. That was the damage Catherine Filliol had done to him. She had stabbed him in the heart with his own father as the dagger. *Bastard.* Edward cleared his throat and shook his head to chase away the thought. He was not the most handsome man at this court, not by a fair distance, but unlike Jane, Edward knew how to utilize and enhance what assets he had been given, and he had risen here because of it. One of those assets was self-control.

Even if he did fancy Anne Stanhope, he would never allow himself to be reduced the way the king was, chasing after Anne Boleyn, nipping at her heels like one of her lapdogs for a bit of pleasure. His behavior was unseemly. If there was to be another romance for Edward Seymour, it would be calculated. He would have absolute dominance.

He found his younger brother, Thomas, in the library of his benefactor and Edward's companion, Sir Francis Bryan, finishing the last of a stack of letters. The two had just returned from France, and there were thank-you notes to be written. Edward was happy to have a trustworthy family face back at court, especially with things so swiftly moving forward with Anne Boleyn.

There was a tidal wave of change and Edward could see how easy it might be to be swept up in it, and swallowed, if one were not careful. And very clever. Fortunately for the Seymour family, Edward fancied himself both of those things. His younger brother, Thomas, though far more handsome, had always been in awe of that.

Thomas stood with an expression of surprise as Edward swept confidently into the room, velvet cape swirling at his trim waist. "Brother, I thought you were attending Sir Francis and the king," Thomas said as he looked up from his desk and the pale light played across his face in the small, stuffy mahogany library. It was furnished with only a chair, a shelf of books, and a desk littered with a pot of ink, a shaker of blotting sand, goose-quill pens, and stack of paper.

"That was then; this is now. We must discuss our sister."

"Jane?"

"Have we another worth discussing now that Elizabeth is married to a useless land baron?" Edward snapped.

"You need not be petulant. Better you get right to the point."

Edward glanced around the small room appraisingly, then

helped himself to the single leather chair, from which Thomas had just risen. He glanced down at the unfinished letter on the writing desk. Thomas had been writing to someone on Francis Bryan's behalf. The wording was full of flattery and the letter had been surprisingly well crafted. Edward's sense of rivalry only increased on seeing it, and he struggled to maintain his composure.

"The point is, Sir Thomas Boleyn and George, that irritatingly smug son of his, are moving fast with the king now that His Majesty has abandoned all reserve with Mistress Anne."

"That concerns us how, precisely?" Thomas asked with a tone of minimal interest.

"The Boleyns cannot be the only family who know how to utilize their daughter for gain."

"But, by my lord, who here would want Jane?"

"You are handsome, Thomas, I shall give you that." He shook his head disparagingly. "You have just never been clever enough to match that promise. Look not always to the likely path. Sometimes, brother, you must forge your own. Obviously Jane shall not do us any good in attracting a powerful husband. But our dutiful little sibling could help us to the king through his mistress."

"I fail to see your point, brother," Thomas said.

"If the whispers of divorce become a roar, and Jane is still seen in the queen's camp, we are all doomed. But if Jane could find a reason to abandon that sinking ship and ingratiate herself with Mistress Boleyn, the future for all of us would be limitless."

"Has our poor, dear sister the ability to ingratiate herself with anyone? She seems not to have much of a voice. Certainly she has no presence," Thomas observed.

"You might feel differently if you had earlier heard her with the king and Mistress Boleyn."

"Jane spoke to them?"

"She did, rather boldly, I might say, for our 'little mouse,' as they are calling her, which is what gave me the idea in the first place."

There was a small silence before Thomas spoke again. "So have you a plan in mind? Jane is such a loyal girl, I cannot imagine her abandoning the queen, especially for the rival."

"She can complain all she wants, but Jane will do what is right for this family in the end," said Edward. "We all will."

That night, wanting a bit of naughty fun, a few of the king's friends slipped away from the palace and rode into the village to find simpler women, a few more laughs, and a lot of ale. In the hot and smoky village inn, beneath the low-beamed ceiling and beside the huge, soot-stained fireplace, Edward waited for just the right moment. Through the candle smoke, the rousing music, and the raucous laughter, he could see that Francis Bryan was quite drunk.

"So will it be divorce for certain, or do you think it is just an idle threat?" Edward asked with a drunken smile, holding up a scratched pewter tankard as if he had asked the name of the tune rather than inquired pointedly about the future of the entire realm.

Edward watched his cousin take a thoughtful swallow of ale and gaze out across the crowded room, which was crowded with stout village women in simple dresses and white caps straddling men's laps and kissing them playfully to the tune of a fiddle and pipe.

"'Tis not for popular consumption as yet, my good cousin, but I am to accompany His Grace, Cardinal Wolsey, to France in two days' time to meet quietly with Pope Clement and the French sovereign, Francis I, about that very matter."

Edward leaned back in his chair. "So the fat is truly in the fire, then?"

"For the queen, 'twould seem so, yes. The Duke of Norfolk boasts quite forcefully, when he is among friends, that his niece Mistress Boleyn refers privately to herself as 'She Who Will Be Queen.' I grant you, she has a long road ahead, but by the look of things, if there *is* a way to divorce, I do not doubt she will be just that."

"Then I shall needs bite my tongue at George Boleyn's pathetic humor, and you shall needs aid our Jane in securing a firm place with Mistress Anne. If you are correct about a divorce, that small bit of planning might one day save us all."

"We are good by George Boleyn. He rather fancies me an elder statesman, or a kind of pleasant uncle since the Duke of Norfolk is such an insufferable cur. But I shall see to it that your brother, Thomas, accompanies me to France again, if 'twould soothe your worry about it."

"I see it as a great favor to the family, cousin." Edward nodded deferentially because he knew he was meant to. "And Jane, then?"

Francis adjusted the little strap for his eye patch, drained his tankard, and slapped it back onto the wet, rough-hewn tabletop covered in great plates of half-eaten food. Fat, unshaven village men in ragged work clothes, straight from the fields and stables, hunched over the table drunkenly.

"I shall put in a word for Jane as well with Mistress Boleyn's brother, but I must wait for the right moment. The more astute women in the queen's suite, as well as some of the more ambitious families, have already begun quietly to clamor in our direction since Mistress Boleyn last returned from Hever Castle. In the meantime, you would do well to advise your sister to stand out in any way she can, for there shall be a dozen others quite willing to press past her for a place in Mistress Boleyn's retinue, and I know Jane is not, shall we say, well acquainted with ambition," Francis said in a slightly drunken slur.

"I shall set my sister down the right path," Edward promised, "if you make certain there is a place for her at the end when she gets there."

"I favor Jane. I always have. I am not at all certain she is suited to tolerate Mistress Boleyn or her tirades, however. But for family, I shall do what I can."

"For family," Edward echoed as he raised his tankard again, this time in a toast to the Seymour family's one real ally, who he was determined would make them all famous.

Jane ascended a back flight of stairs up a rounded turret in the south wing of Richmond Palace. She was following a summons to attend Anne Boleyn at dressing. She had been given no choice by Edward, who, at last, had come to see her with the command. In spite of the momentary burst of anger she had felt against her indifferent brother in the king's presence, she still felt meek with Edward.

Once, long ago, her brother had represented everything mysterious and exciting in the world. But she liked the queen as much as pitied her, and her heart was heavy with regret as she followed her brother's orders to attend the queen's rival.

Suddenly, as she turned into the corridor, a man sprinted toward Jane from the shadows.

He was moving so quickly that she did not know who it was until he was nearly upon her. She recognized Thomas Wyatt's face, handsome in a feminine sort of way. He was smiling and chuckling to himself like an errant child. He was holding something gold suspended from a chain that flashed in the torchlight as they passed each other. For an instant, their eyes locked. Then, as always, Jane modestly dropped her gaze. Still, before she did, she saw that it was Anne Boleyn's pendant from the king that he held.

From the childish delight in his eyes, she gathered it was stolen. The moment ended quickly as Wyatt passed her, and Jane moved through the next corridor toward Anne Boleyn's small sitting room. She was surprised to see that the king's guards were now posted there, as if she were already queen. The sound of Anne's screeching, and the sight of her charging through the room, her face full of fury, took the moment over entirely. She was in a state of panic.

"I understand this not at all!" she bellowed. "I gave the pendant directly to you, Mary."

"And I took it with great care, sister," Mary Boleyn said, hands outstretched in a half-pleading gesture, her face white with panic.

Mary was standing with George Boleyn's wife, Jane Parker, and Thomas Wyatt's sister Margaret beneath a tapestry depicting the Annunciation as Anne charged at Mary. "I ask you to do one simple thing, only one, and you botch that! For all I know, you did it on purpose to make me look bad before the king! You would like that, would you not?"

"I have no wish at all to harm your position, sister."

"As if you ever truly could!" Anne brayed. "Make no mistake, Mary, I *will* be queen and anyone who would undermine me shall rue the day! Even you!"

It was a wide-eyed threat, but Anne's face was not mottled red now. Rather Jane saw that it was as white as alabaster and frighteningly cold with determination. The voice inside Jane's head was loud and insistent. *Speak out about Wyatt! Mary is your friend, or as close to one as you have ever had!* But her throat took control, closing over.

I cannot speak. I am no one. Who would believe me anyway in the shadow of a woman like her?

Jane despised Anne a little more with each incident, and as her gaze slid to Mary, who was a victim of a more powerful, dominant sibling, Jane thought how it was not so different from the way she felt about Edward. In that, she and Mary were kindred spirits, each a gentle cloud surviving in the shadow of a bold sun's bright rays.

"If I discover that you have betrayed me, sister, perhaps hidden my pendant to make me look a fool, I do swear—"

"By my troth, I have not. You must move through your own course with the king and find your own way in it. With that, I shall not interfere."

Sister versus sister. Different women in all ways, yet they had known the same goal. Then there was Bess Blount. Jane still marveled at how skillfully she had made her mark, then let him go when these two sisters had fought ardently for possession. One for his life, one for her memories of him. Skill seemed to Jane the key that had made the difference.

Hold not too tightly to that which you cannot truly possess.

The King of England seemed to Jane one of those things.

Later that day, she walked with Mary behind a group of Anne's declared new ladies past the water gate and down to the mossy bank to ride along the river in the king's grand, painted, banner-dotted barge. If it was possible, the king seemed to have dressed even more grandly today than the last time Jane had seen him. In magenta-colored satin with black velvet sashes, all of it jeweled, and wide fur-trimmed sleeves, he strode up to the rest of them, showing a slight limp. Still, Henry overshadowed everyone but Charles Brandon, who laughed with the king behind a raised hand.

Brandon was dressed in the same ornamented satin, which favored both himself and the king beneath the warm, gleaming sunshine. As little waves slapped gently at the stone pediment below their feet, Jane saw Thomas Wyatt casually approach Anne. He had timed it perfectly, waiting until the precise moment when Brandon and William Compton had the king in a jolly fit of laughter. When Wyatt turned to her, Jane saw, along with Anne, her pendant from the king around the poet's neck. The gold, a high contrast to his unadorned black silk doublet, glittered in the sunlight. Her haughty smile quickly fell, and a shocked flush took its place.

"Give it back!" Jane heard Anne say.

"I'll not," he replied flirtatiously. "I rather like it."

"'Twas a gift from the king," she whispered urgently. "He shall have your head!"

"His Majesty loves these little court games and admires a skilled challenger."

"Yes, but he *loves* me. I am no longer yours for the taking, nor are my gifts."

"Ah, what a different tune you did sing but a month ago."

"It might as well have been a lifetime! He cannot know about us. Those days are gone now. They must be!"

"I shall wager he will find amusement in the challenge. Especially since to do otherwise might incite the wrath of his wife and even his people," he said.

"That would suppose his people would ever know the means by which you suddenly met your death, or left England."

To Jane's surprise, Wyatt chuckled, undaunted by Anne's anger, seeing not danger but the game he was intentionally creating.

"Please, Thomas," Anne urged in a throaty whisper. "I have nearly got him where I want him. Can you not understand?"

Pleading did not at all suit her, Jane thought a little mischievously as she casually scanned the group. Then the boatman had arrived and they prepared to cross the crimson carpet that led the way onto the barge. She saw then that the king noticed Anne talking clandestinely with Wyatt. The predicament seemed sinfully delicious to Jane, who could not wait to see what would happen next.

In a swirl of his jeweled, open-sleeved black satin cloak, the king was at Anne's side. "Your pendant looks familiar, Wyatt," the king said with a smile.

"I am humbled Your Majesty would find it remarkable."

"It quite resembles one with which I am familiar."

Their eyes met. Combatants. The king seemed at the moment to find humor in the game rather than an outright challenge.

"If it brings Your Highness pleasure, I would be honored to share."

"There are some things, Wyatt, a man does not share," the king declared on a pompous note, but his tone had sharpened slightly.

All eyes turned upon the encounter then as the king's reply settled on everyone. It felt to Jane like some great staged drama where the character of the king might at any moment lash out with a prop dagger and slash the contender to death as the audience cried out in mock terror. Breaking the intensity of the moment, Brandon signaled with a nod to the king that the barge had been opened and that the line of livery-clad oarsmen awaited their embarkation.

"Ah yes, time to depart. Everyone should know when something is at an end," the king declared, leveling his incisive green-eyed gaze directly on Thomas Wyatt. He then wound Anne's arm through his own and led the way cheerfully onto his barge, with Charles Brandon at his heels.

Thomas Wyatt, Nicholas Carew, and Francis Bryan were left

standing beside Mary and Jane as the others began to follow Anne Boleyn and the king. They all heard William Compton's quick exchange with the poet next.

"Do not be a fool, Wyatt," Compton warned in a low voice. "You shall not win this one."

"Nor shall she. He has a wife."

"As do you."

"I am not a king."

"Precisely, my good man, precisely," said Compton, the all-important Groom of the Stool.

Jane sat beside Mary on one of the long benches that ran the length of the barge and was cushioned in rich, Tudor green velvet stamped in gold fleur-de-lis, watching the king and Anne as they sat closely together in front. The oars rhythmically slapped the water, propelling them smoothly down the river as Jane tried to make sense of what had just happened back on the shore.

"Forgive me, but I saw that Master Wyatt took the pendant," she quietly confessed to Mary Boleyn as Mary sat gazing straight ahead, seemingly a bit shaken. "I meant to defend you to her, but I simply could not find my voice."

"Not many can when faced with my sister. She is like a force of nature."

The breeze gently blew their richly decorated sleeves and the white gauze veils behind their French hoods.

"Yet still it makes me angry. I have so much boiling inside of me that never quite escapes."

"'Tis only because it has not been boiling long enough," Mary explained calmly.

"How can you remain here and watch them like that?"

"I was not given a choice in the matter, nor in any other matter.

I was told to attract the king, seduce him, and bear his son quietly. Then I was swiftly moved out of the way when he developed a fondness for Lady Carew. After that, I was told to say nothing when His Majesty acknowledged Mistress Blount's son and not mine, since my own sister was to be next in his bed. Compliance is a state to which one grows accustomed, I suppose, when duty is the thing."

Mary's expression went very sad then, although there were no tears in her eyes. "I have absolutely nowhere else to go, no money of my own if I make a fuss, no real hold over my own children if he should desire them. So I smile and blankly nod if his gaze happens to turn to me, as if I have no idea what it feels like to be touched by him, to caress his cheek, kiss his lips, or accept his passionate body over mine."

Anne and Henry were both laughing a little too loudly then, as if neither had a care in the world. What a bittersweet contrast to Mary, Jane thought, unable to imagine herself the object of the attentions of the self-absorbed sovereign, who cast women and their hearts away like playthings.

Jane felt awkward being in the queen's withdrawing chamber that evening, but it had become her custom to sit with the group of other ladies-in-waiting and join Katherine in sewing as they were entertained by a light, soulful chant sung by two angel-voiced children hired to entertain her. The duo stood beside the fireplace hearth in white robes as the warming blaze crackled and glowed.

How different were these two women's worlds in tone and character. Sober versus gay, elegant versus jolly. Jane still did not like being part of Anne Boleyn's circle, but as her family had taught her, loyalty first, last, and always. All the members of each household felt the strain. It was the same for the Seymours as it was for the Boleyns as they advanced in the tumultuous court of Henry VIII.

"So tell us, Mistress Seymour," the queen suddenly bid her as she held fast to a piece of lace in one hand and a sharp needle in the other. Jane's eyes were focused on the sewing, but her mind was not. "How did you find the river today? Was the weather fair and the water calm enough for a barge ride?"

Jane felt their eyes root upon her, then cut away. While the queen's tone was not accusatory, the implication of duplicity hung heavy in the grand room, where the queen was joined by the Spanish ambassador, Caroz, the imperial ambassador, Chapuys, Maria de Salinas, and a number of other women and girls who long had attended her. There were clearly spies among them.

"I have always been quite prone to seasickness, Your Highness. I rarely enjoy the water."

"A pity," she replied, still without looking up from her piece of lace. "I have always found the sea quite calming and the rest of the world tumultuous by comparison."

"Would that I found the sea calming for all of the incessant bobbing," Jane countered.

"Ah, *sí*. I am told Mistress Boleyn does not enjoy that sensation either, even on the river. I hear she was as green as Tudor livery earlier today."

At her own remark, the queen suddenly smiled. Her grin was slim lipped and reserved as she raised her dark eyes from her sewing.

"I am afraid I could not see her personally to offer an assessment, Your Highness. My seat was a fair distance from hers."

"Well, how did you find Mistress Boleyn's choice of entertainment compared to our own offerings provided here in these rooms? I am told His Majesty had the ensemble brought in from the French court to please her."

Unexpectedly then, the king appeared at the chamber door,

hands on his hips, as if her words had summoned him. As usual, he was a formidable presence, and everyone stiffened in fear, then rose swiftly only to fall into bows and curtsies.

"Perhaps your spies are not earning back your investment in them," he said with a jolly little sneer and then nodded to her. "Good evening, my dear."

The children had stopped singing as he moved toward Katherine. Women, ambassadors, and guardsmen shot to their feet, only to fall into deep bows and curtsies amid the sound of rustling silk, layered velvet, and the click of his shoe heels across the inlaid tile floor. The queen curtsied to him as well, albeit in a slight, more perfunctory way than the others. He then lifted her up by the arm and pressed a kiss lightly on her cheek.

There was the same carelessness in his movements as there was in hers.

"I do believe you would have enjoyed the music," he said to her in response to the question posed to Jane. As she sat again, a chair was swiftly brought so that he might sit beside her.

"I favor nothing from France these days," she replied icily.

"That is a shame since it produces such great culture and richness."

"Beauty is in the eye of the beholder," Katherine countered blandly as she picked up her lace and needle once again, then gazed down at it, but the unmistakable wound to her heart flashed in her eyes before she could look away.

"You cannot deny that France has great treasures to share with the world."

"Since even speaking the name of the place produces a rancid taste in my mouth, I find it impossible to respond to that," Katherine returned.

"Perhaps one day you shall see it as I do."

"There are some things, good husband, by God's grace, that I shall *never* see as you do."

Everyone in the room knew they were no longer speaking of music.

Angry at her daring, the king then sprang to his feet in a huff and a swirl of his cloak. His exasperation was clear. He had come to visit his wife out of duty. He was leaving so soon now out of spite.

He nodded to Katherine, and as he turned from her, his gaze suddenly slid to Jane, who stood in his path to the door. Their eyes settled on each other for only a heartbeat, but Jane thought his expression seemed to say, *I am trapped, unhappy. Can no one understand that?* But before she could be certain it was not only in her mind, he charged past her, his footsteps thundering down the hall, disrupting the awkward silence. When she looked back at the queen, Jane saw a mist of tears glistening in her dark Spanish eyes. Then Her Highness returned to her sewing as if nothing at all had happened.

In those next days, Jane began to exist fully between the two worlds that had been drawing her for some time—the one to which she was regularly summoned by Anne, and the queen's world, where the die seemed indelibly cast. Anne Boleyn had a way with the king that was almost mystical. Of course, no one dared speak such heresy, yet the change in the king's behavior as he moved between his queen and his paramour was remarkable, especially to Jane, who was witness to both.

Two days after the barge ride, Jane stood in a group of Anne's ladies out on the bowls field. The king and his friends were in the middle of a rousing game, the object of which was to pitch a small ball down a very long brick lane toward a nut. The victor was the one who rolled his ball closest to the nut. On Henry's embroidered costume, Jane could clearly see four French words sewn in gold thread. While her spoken French was only passable, Jane had studied enough to know that *Declarer, Je n'ose pas* meant "Declare, I dare not." For a married man, it was a great and obvious professing of his own inner turmoil over the two women in his life.

The sky was gray this early afternoon and slightly chilly. A gentle mist had begun to fall as they played. Jane slipped her hands into the velvet pockets of her dress and lowered her chin into her standing collar. The movement was as much protection from being noticed or drawn into something as it was a comfort against the weather.

Though she had seen them together on many occasions, this afternoon she sensed a new, palpable tension on the bowls court between the king and Thomas Wyatt. Jane was sure that the new embroidered declaration slashed across the king's chest was only one example of the royal response to it. The rivalry for Anne Boleyn had taken a bitter turn, and Anne played the king's declared refusal to choose her over the queen like a champion, openly flirting with both of them until the king's face was white with rage.

As the two men seemingly argued now over the score, the king began gesturing boldly, stabbing the air with his forefinger, which bore a large onyx ring stamped in gold with the letter *B*. It was obvious to everyone that it was worn in Anne's honor.

"Humbly, sire," Wyatt declared as the pendant around his neck glistened in a sudden pale ray of sunlight through the clouds. "'Twas my ball which struck the closest to the nut; therefore, I retain the victory."

"You are as blind as you are arrogant," Henry countered, clearly only half joking as the two men hovered over the two balls and the nut at the end of the court.

"We must find a way to decide the victory," Wyatt pronounced with a competitive little sneer that was common to the king and all of his friends when they were together. Jane held her breath, guessing then, as everyone else did, what was going to happen next.

Either Wyatt was very brave, she thought, or very stupid.

"This chain seems a perfect length by which to measure the distance," he said boastfully, as he drew the pendant from around his neck and held it up.

Jane's gaze slid cautiously to the king in the momentary silence that followed. His expression hardened and became very tense. His lips were tightly pursed, and there was a muscle moving in the back of his jaw that she was close enough to see. Yet his mouth was turned up in just the faintest hint of a competitive smile. Jane saw a strange and indulgent little smile pass between Anne and Wyatt then as she took notice of the pendant.

"Very well," the king at last agreed, to a collective, audible sigh. The pendant had escaped the king's notice. "But we must have someone fair to judge, someone wholly impartial."

He glanced through the assemblage, raised his onyx-ornamented finger, and let it land directly upon Jane.

"Mistress Seymour shall do to tell us who has won. Come forward, my girl."

"Oh, for heaven's sake, Hal," Anne droned as the king smiled at the plain and insufferably quiet girl who always seemed to be there.

If Jane could have melted into the brick pathway beneath her feet, she would have. Everyone, including the king and Anne, was suddenly looking at her. Henry's expression was one of smiling expectation. The others wore frowns of disbelief. No matter how they tried to hide their judgmental stares with small, polite smiles, their lifted brows and rolling eyes made the reality of their feelings clear.

She walked the few steps on trembling legs as one of the king's young liveried grooms laid the chain and pendant on the bricks between the two balls.

"Very well." The king smiled at her. "So, Mistress Seymour, as a valued member of our little party, you shall reveal to us all whose ball has landed closest to the nut."

The horror she felt, with their collective gazes heavy upon her, could be matched only by her sense of impending doom. It was clear that Wyatt's ball was closer. A deluge of thoughts pelted her like little stones. Eyes were daggers. Her heart slammed against her rib cage.

"I am no expert at bowls, sire," she forced herself to say, "yet I say that you are the victor."

"You can say it, but that does not make it so," Wyatt grunted angrily, snapping up the chain.

"Now, now. We've had our good bit of fun, Master Wyatt, but 'tis time to surrender all things that do not belong to you and give up the game."

"Surrender them all to Your Majesty, even if you are not at liberty to fully take them?"

"*You* can surrender them, or *I* can seize them. But either way, Wyatt, your time is at an end."

Jane thought the tone in his voice was frightening. The voice she heard now was the frosty one the king used with the queen, not the mirth-filled tenor with which he always greeted Anne. There were great murmurs through the group as the king and Wyatt faced each other like two great lions fighting for dominance. But of course, there was no question.

A moment later, Wyatt bowed deeply to the sovereign and took a step back in symbolic surrender. As he did, he handed the chain to Anne, whose flirtatious smile had dimmed as she gazed at the splashing fountain nearby with a statue of David and Goliath at its center. There was no longer an option. No real comparison between them.

Her choice had been made for her.

"My thanks, Mistress Seymour, for seeing the truth as the rest of us see it, and for being brave enough to declare it. I would not have expected that of you," the king said crisply, cutting through the tension.

"I serve Your Majesty first and foremost," she heard herself reply shyly, yet she was unable to force herself to look directly at him as she did.

It was still too much for Jane, as if she were looking at the sun. But as Anne swept past her, the fabric of their skirts touching, the two women exchanged a little glance. Jane was very certain that behind Anne's smile she saw a flash of something extraordinary. She did not realize it until later, but in that moment, Jane was envied by the most influential woman in all of England.

By January, Thomas Wyatt had been sent from court on a diplomatic mission bound for France. Everyone knew it was because he had lost the competition for Anne Boleyn. Jane could not quite fathom the hold that the strange dark-haired beauty maintained over the king for how malevolent it seemed.

After Wyatt's departure, Anne and the king became even more inseparable.

Along with George Boleyn; his wife, Jane Parker; Anne Stanhope; and Elizabeth Carew, Jane was regularly called upon now to accompany their newly formed little band. She still hated betraying the queen and did her best to avoid each summons. But in such matters, Edward was absolutely firm. Katherine of Aragon's star was swiftly fading as Anne Boleyn's was shining more brightly by the day. For the good of the family, they must acknowledge that and do what they could to stay near the center of power.

Jane tried not to think of how guilty she felt as she took a stroll with her brother Thomas early one afternoon when the court had settled in to rest and prepare for the evening of revelry ahead. It was that delicious hour of the day when the queen was at her desk or meeting with her Spanish attendants, the Spanish and Venetian ambassadors and the all-important imperial ambassador, Chapuys, who seemed always at her side these days. Anne and the king were likewise closeted, although their agenda on these lazy afternoons did not concern affairs of state. Or so the gossip went.

"I know not how much longer I can endure this," Jane unburdened herself, murmuring quietly to her brother as they walked along the cool, calming river's edge beneath another gray day of light English drizzle. "She is a dreadful and demanding harlot who sits pointing and doling out directions as though she were queen."

"I fear she soon shall be," Thomas said as they lingered at a little inlet where the grass was tall and a flock of geese passed overhead.

"Bite your tongue, brother. The king will *never* be able to gain an annulment from the queen. What on earth would be the grounds? They have had children together!"

"'Tis all quite complicated, but in listening to Sir Francis with Sir Nicholas Carew, apparently Cardinal Wolsey is nearing a conclusion to the secret negotiations he is carrying on with the pope over that very issue."

"How could that ever work when the queen's own nephew is the emperor, who has complete control over the pope?"

"Cardinal Wolsey is a master at negotiation. Carew says he has gone to closet with both of them clandestinely and will do so again.

Sir Francis has asked me to accompany him this time," he proudly revealed. Jane was stunned.

"A journey designed to run the poor queen through with the final blow? You cannot!"

"I cannot refuse them, Jane. Edward is the one who suggested me in the first place, and he would have my head if I refused now."

"Better you lose your head than your dignity."

"You sound awfully haughty for one who dines with the queen and hunts with the whore," he snapped uncharacteristically at her.

Thomas then stiffened his spine and shot her a defensive scowl. It was that same pursed-mouth expression their mother used when she felt cornered. Jane shuddered; mother and son did look so alike.

"I haven't any choice."

"Nor do I. Edward is right, Jane. She will be queen somehow. She is not giving herself up to him and she is driving him mad in the meantime, just to make certain she achieves her goal. Everyone here says they have never seen anything like it with his other mistresses. It is as if she is guided by some powerful dark art."

"Well, it certainly does not seem light and sunny to me. She has the most evil little extra finger, or at least some sort of growth at the end of her hand, and her voice is so low it sounds like a man's. But she is really more like a siren, tempting him with an illusion that only he can fully see," said Jane, unable to stop herself from talking for the first time.

"Well, I may never have seen anything like it either, but in this case I know the evil that it suggests," Thomas said.

"I just feel such pity for the queen. There is nothing worse, I fear, than loving someone you cannot have. I wish there was something I could do for her."

"There is nothing any of us can do for her but figure out how to saddle up and ride along on the journey without falling from the horse, or from grace. Fortunately for you, she is convinced of your favor," Thomas said.

"Yet I serve her greatest enemy, which makes me no better now than anyone else in this place."

"We all must do what we can to survive here. We have been taught to prepare for that all of our lives," he reminded her.

They smiled grimly at each other then, and Jane was glad her favorite sibling was here with her. She was not the same. This place had changed her. Thomas knew it because he knew her. And Jane knew it, too. But no one else but the two of them knew how different they were from those two naive little children at Wolf Hall.

"People assume what they will of the quiet ones," Thomas said, taking her hand as they began to stroll back toward the palace gate.

"Perhaps they should take better care with their illusions," Jane said, as a stray image of William whispered through her mind like a sudden Wiltshire fog. Then it dissolved, disappearing just as quickly as he had disappeared from her life.

Chapter Nine

June 1527
Windsor Castle

*T*he Sack of Rome in the summer of 1527 changed much for Henry VIII, the impatient king. With the pope imprisoned by angry, unpaid soldiers on the side of the emperor, the Holy Father's hands were tied in the ongoing matter of an annulment. No matter what diplomatic skills Cardinal Wolsey utilized at the moment, the issue was at a frustrating political standstill.

Anne Boleyn was not amused.

"Tell me that *not!*" the king raged. "By God Almighty, tell me she did not leave again!"

His guttural cry was loud enough that Jane and the queen's other ladies in the Royal Chapel could hear it. The crash of furniture and shattering glass from the king's private study next door followed, and the painted walls seemed to bow with the sound of his anger.

"She would not leave me! 'Twas promised between us!"

As they knelt at Lauds, Jane slid a cautious sideways glance to the queen, whose head remained lowered in prayer, but Jane could see the shudder that had taken over her shoulders, as if she were physically holding back her own grief at the pleading in her husband's voice for another woman.

Jane had known that Anne might leave court for Hever Castle again from what she had personally overheard these last days as the hope of an annulment slipped further from her fingers. But to see the repercussions of that meted out to the queen, who had shown Jane such kindness, felt physically painful to her.

Suddenly, the queen shot to her feet and charged with purpose across the open gallery. Jane and the queen's other ladies followed dutifully behind, barely matching her stride as they approached the open door of the king's study.

"Go away, woman!" Henry's growl was like that of a wounded dog as Katherine entered the chamber. Jane and the others paused at the threshold.

"Pray, my lord, let us go to Beaulieu to see Mary. 'Twould be good for us as a family to be away from all of this conflict for a while."

"Go if you wish, and then you may remain there," he said rudely.

"I shall not leave you for our daughter, nor for anyone else in all the world, Hal," Katherine returned so swiftly, and with such compassion, that Henry groaned with frustration.

"'Twould make it so much simpler if you would."

Jane saw the remark strike the queen—the weapon of words sharper than any dagger's thrust.

"Leave us!" he cried, realizing then that they had an audience just outside of the door.

"'Tis my wish that they remain," Katherine declared, but there was a slight tremor to her usually strong voice. "I do not trust myself when the conversation between us is about *her*."

"Her name is Anne," he shot back.

"I know perfectly well what her name is. Anne of the Curious Extra Finger," she countered stingingly.

"You dare to mock her so boldly before me, madam?"

"Is there anything to do but mock when the situation is so entirely absurd?"

They glared at each other then as rival combatants, not as two people who had known great love together and shared a life since they were very young.

"Katherine, we must speak privately," he said finally, cutting the awkward silence with a surprisingly gentle tone.

"Anything we have to say to each other can be said before these women. They are my companions and my friends."

"I am your husband and your king!" he said without seeming to think about the words or their implication.

"You *were* my husband. But, then, that is what this is really all about, is it not?"

He sighed deeply and then sank into a cushioned chair. "Would that I could still be the man you wish me to be."

"For that to happen, you would be required to try."

"Do you not believe I have tried, Katherine? All of these years, and with every fiber of my body I have tried! How I have tried to be a good and faithful partner to you!"

"One out of two, perhaps, can be claimed without sinning," she coolly replied.

The cutting way she said it was not lost on Jane.

The awkward silence fell hard again, and Jane felt herself squirm inside. She knew she should not be there in the doorway, nor should any of them, amid this private scene. While it felt as intense as one of the royal masques, complete with the players and the drama, this was someone's real life. She did not like the king, and she was no longer in awe of him after all she had seen.

"Please, let us speak privately . . . Katerina, I bid you," he said, calling her by her Spanish name in a tone that, to Jane, bore a lethal combination of sincerity and resolve.

His voice went softer then, as Jane and the others idled awkwardly beneath the massive curved, arched doorway dressed with drawn-back drapes and gold cords.

He pulled the queen forward, as if it were natural, and she fell to her knees before him. His voice went even lower then as he took up her hand, and from that distance, Jane thought they could be lovers for the gentle connection that brightened between them.

"We must separate," he said with the tenderness of a man who had just declared his love.

The queen stiffened again. "I understand you not."

"I mean to continue on in a life that does not include you as my wife."

"There is no such life, Hal, since we are legally wed until death should part us."

"Or the pope ends our marriage."

"He never shall."

Henry's tone began to rise again, and his face colored to a mottled shade of crimson. "Just because your nephew owns him does not mean he can ever purchase the favor of our sovereign God!"

"The truth shall be the victory, my lord, not the pope, not the emperor, and not your whore."

"I warn you, madam, not to call her that."

"I am Queen of England. I shall call a spade a spade."

"And I am king, by Almighty God!" He shot to his feet, a ran-corous ramrod of fury. The heavy gold baldric studded with jewels across his chest clanked with the movement. "Call anything what you will, entertain your fantasies as you please, but this will be the end of our union! We shall separate as man and wife for the error of it."

"It was that same Almighty God who joined us, my lord, and he alone can break our bond!"

"He made a faulty union based on a lie! You were not free to wed me since you had wed and bedded my brother first!"

Jane squirmed in her shoes, hurting for the queen's humiliation.

"Arthur and I did not ever consummate our vows! By all that is holy, we did not. You know that! *Dios mío*, would you stand here and call your wife a liar in front of these witnesses?"

"You shall be called my wife no longer, so the point is moot," he spat back at her cruelly, pivoting away in a swirl of amber-colored embroidery until once again his expression landed on Jane. His sea green eyes bore into hers, and she felt the oddly powerful con-nection.

It was only an instant, but it felt like an eternity.

"I must do this," he said brokenly.

"You lead with your heart, Hal, but it is your soul that shall take you into eternity."

"Neither matter to me if I do not have her."

"Then, by God, take her!"

"She will not have me like that!" he raged in frustration. "Not unless she is my queen!"

"Then God help you, my husband, because you make a deal with the devil for a bit of heaven in your bed!"

"She has only given me her promise, not yet her heart!"

"Well, I gave you my whole life!"

"I need more! *I need a son!*"

"You have Fitzroy."

"He is a bastard, Katherine!" he cried aloud, as if it were something she did not very well know.

"Well, your fantasy woman is a harridan."

He rolled his eyes and slapped his forehead, not as angry now as Jane might have expected, but his frustration was a palpable thing. "Och, I cannot talk to you!"

"And I cannot *reach* you. Your heart is lost to me."

"Then do not fight me. Let me go."

"Until my last breath, you will have a wife, and by God, it shall be me. I have never left you. And after all, Hal, where is she if she wants my place so desperately?"

Jane watched him shift on his elegantly slippered feet. There was an odd air of hesitation as the question dangled between them. She almost could not believe what she was seeing.

"The pope *will* give me the annulment because you were married to, and bedded with, my brother before me. I shall have my desire. But in the meantime, you know there is to be a banquet tonight to welcome our new Spanish ambassador. You will, I trust, attend with me for the sake of England's alliance with Spain."

"Diego Hurtado Mendoza is no one's fool, any more than Caroz was! You shall not use him to convert the emperor to your sinful desire, no matter how grand your banquet!"

She had gotten too angry and lost her advantage. Caroz had been one of her greatest supporters and companions. Katherine was still smarting from his return to Spain only the week before. Henry bit back a sudden smile. "I had no such thought in my mind, my dear. I only want to be certain your health is maintained with a proper meal and your heart is lightened by a bit of entertainment. That is what everyone shall believe as we welcome the new ambassador."

"I'll not change my mind in this, no matter who you turn against me with your outward false gentility," she warned.

"Nor shall I change *my* mind. But shall we away to prepare for dinner anyway, and make a show of it?"

"That is what the world will expect," she replied, clearly forcing up a tone of diplomacy. "There is much to tell you of our daughter, Mary, as I have just today had a letter from Ludlow about her progress, which in spite of our differences, I am excited to share with her father. For that reason alone, I shall make a show of it with you."

The shimmering pride of motherhood crossed Katherine's expression. Jane felt a shudder for the futility attached to such a nuance, since anyone could see it was too late for them. The king continued to seem not a lovable or tender man, but a vainglorious prig. It was difficult to imagine what such a parade of women saw in him beyond the crown. Perhaps that was *all* they saw, because there was nothing else there.

Jane would always feel sorry for the queen.

But Anne Boleyn, it seemed, was about to get exactly what, and whom, she deserved.

"Jane!"

Shocked by the sound of her name spoken with desperation, she stopped in her tracks outside in the vast corridor. "Forgive me, Mistress Seymour, for being too familiar. Urgency does have a way of bringing out the worst in me."

She had left the chamber with the others to prepare for the banquet, but as usual they moved ahead of her and she was left, like a calf to slaughter, alone. He loomed behind her now, alone as well. The vainglorious prig himself. *The king.*

Knowing it was he, certain of the voice, yet not wanting to look into those deep green eyes until the last possible moment, Jane pivoted back very slowly to face him.

"Forgive me if I startled you," he said.

"Your Majesty does only humble me," she lied, and quickly dropped into a curtsy, happy for a reason to lower her eyes against the bright light cast from his regal expression, which stood in stark contrast to the queen's misery.

"You are a discerning girl, Mistress Seymour. Your brother Edward speaks highly of your skills of discretion."

She was surprised to hear that Edward spoke of her at all, but she was certain if he had, it had somehow been to his own advantage.

"Thank you, sire," she replied awkwardly as he drew a sealed sheaf of paper from the folds of his great braided hunter green vest and held it out to her.

"I am told you were in France as a child, so I assume your French is sound?"

"My understanding of it is passable, Your Majesty, but I would not deign to declare my speaking skills anything but elementary."

"It only matters that you understand what you read."

"I do."

"Then take this missive and give me your opinion. You are respectful to Mistress Boleyn, your own cousin, and she favors your company, so I trust you. There are few women who keep company with both her and the queen about whom the same can be said. As a young woman yourself, you shall be able to advise me whether this letter I have written has an air of too much pleading, or if it might prompt Mistress Boleyn's return to court."

"Oh, sire, I know not whether—"

He cut her off as he awkwardly tucked the letter into the top of the long plastron of her dress, bidding her to swiftly secret it away.

"The queen must not know of this, you understand," he said, his eyes boring into her suddenly in a most unsettling way.

"Holding my tongue was my first learned skill," she said truthfully.

"Splendid. Read the letter anon; then I shall send a messenger to your chamber after the banquet. When he retrieves it, you shall tell him any misgivings or concerns you have with the sentiments enclosed so that I have enough time to alter it, if I so choose."

It was not a request. Jane heard that much in the clipped, slightly brittle tone of his voice. This was a royal command like any other, and as he began to scan the corridor nervously, she knew he intended her compliance to be swiftly confirmed.

"I shall do as I have been bid, Your Majesty," she replied, lowering her eyes again to his powerful stare.

It was then, for the first time, that Henry actually smiled at her.

"You really are a shy little thing, aren't you?"

"I haven't the skills to show great confidence the way the other women of Your Majesty's court do," she replied, feeling the heat rise in her cheeks, loathing the feel of his gaze upon her for the many lives and hearts that same look had destroyed.

"Better for you that you do not. With the exception of Mistress Anne, everyone around me is fundamentally the same, exchanging the same pleasantries, playing the same tedious games, issuing the same dreary compliments. The predictability of that can be loathsomely dull."

"I am sorry, sire."

"You mustn't be sorry, Jane. May I call you Jane without you blushing at every turn? Let us be more at ease together. Especially now that you hold my heart so very near to your own"

For a moment she did not know what he meant, and her own heart began to beat very fast until he indicated with his eyes the letter that she carried. "I am counting on you. Do not disappoint me, Jane."

After her awkward, impromptu meeting with the king, Jane secreted the letter to Anne Boleyn even more deeply within the bodice of her gown and returned to attend the queen. When Jane arrived in the privy chamber, she was later than the others and the entire room was in an uproar. Spanish words were flying like doves set free from a cage. Maria de Salinas held out dress after dress, brought to her in succession by a line of ladies' maids, for the queen's approval.

"Jane, do come here," the queen suddenly bid her, which was rarely her custom, as she gazed at her own reflection in the long gilt-framed looking glass and saw Jane hovering behind it. "Give us your opinion on the matter. I must wear a dress this evening alluring enough to remind the king why he married me, yet, at the same time, it must not be reminiscent of that whore."

Jane pressed the letter close to her chest and, along with the crinkle of paper, felt a little stab of guilt even though she was being forced into playing both sides against the middle.

She tried hard to examine the first two dresses. The one that Francis's mother, Lady Bryan, held out to the sunlight that streamed through the long windows was stiff black silk with a Belgian lace collar and cuffs. It was studded on the bodice with rows of small, costly black pearls. The second dress was velvet, the color of whey, studded on the bodice and the long, turned-back sleeves, with red, blue, and green gems. It was a beautiful dress, yet still it had nothing of the flair of one of Anne Boleyn's exquisite French designs that the other women of the court already secretly copied.

Behind her, Maria held a third gown of rich plum satin encrusted with shimmering coral beads and ornamented with gold braid. The design was simple, even if a bit old-fashioned, but the elegance of it was unmistakable, and in that it trumped anything her rival could have worn.

"Oh, Your Highness, I should not deign to give an opinion on such a personal matter," Jane demurred.

"You are correct, Mistress Seymour, you should not deign. But since it was asked of you, you are to offer your opinion enthusiastically."

Jane drew in a breath. She exhaled. The directive could not have felt more distressing, but it was a sensation she must push past.

"Very well. If it pleases Your Highness, since you wish to stand out this evening, I would think that would be most boldly effected in the purple. Is it not, after all, the one color no hopeful competitor might don?"

Katherine turned away from the mirror to the line of ladies. She gazed at the purple gown as if it were the first time she had seen it.

"That dress was refashioned for me a number of years ago. It once belonged to my mother," she said wistfully. "The jewels at the bodice, embedded in mounts of Spanish silver, are from a crown she once wore. I have not considered the dress often enough in all these years, as I have tried to be a good English wife."

Jane wanted so badly to say more, but the words caught like pebbles in her throat. She could not presume to know how a queen felt, and she certainly had too little experience with men to offer advice to her as a woman.

"In my opinion, the king will find that one a desperate attempt at competition," Maria de Salinas suddenly interjected. "And that is not a position in which Your Highness can afford to find yourself in the battle to save your marriage."

"However, Your Highness is here, and she is not," Jane said.

She felt a choking sensation beginning to close over her throat the moment the words left her lips. She had not meant to speak.

She certainly had not meant to say *that*!

Yet the presumptuous declaration had come anyway, and on a burst of confidence because she so respected the queen.

"Pray, do forgive me, Your Highness. Humbly, I bid you," Jane said meekly as tears of embarrassment pricked the back of her eyes, threatening to fall.

Katherine wrapped a motherly arm across Jane's shoulders. "There, there, my dear, what is this? Tears for honesty? Remember, you did not deign; I asked you. You are such a small, unassuming thing, but there is something bright behind those eyes of yours. You remind me of myself when I first came here all those years ago. Timid. Uncertain. But, oh, what was hidden beneath my own timid gaze! A gaze made compliant by my duenna back home, not by the fire in my soul!"

She chuckled at herself then, and Jane realized it was the first time she had ever heard the queen sound happy.

"It is an honor to have Your Highness understand a heart like mine."

As the words crawled haltingly from her lips, Jane heard the collective, condescending groan behind her. The women of King Henry's court did not like any form of competition, no matter how small. Jane now knew that well enough. Still, it had not stopped her from finally speaking out in a way only time and experience could have taught her to do. She had grown, and as awkward as it was, she liked how it felt.

"I am going to give you something," the queen said suddenly. "Come with me."

She moved with purpose out of the chamber into a small study, in which Jane had never been. The room was book lined and had a chair and writing table with heavily carved and painted legs at its center. On the wall was a portrait of the king. Jane lingered in the doorway as the queen went to a cabinet below an oak shelf filled with leather-bound books and drew something from it.

"Look at this coin. Do you see the face stamped on it?"

Jane saw that it was emblazoned with the image and name of Ferdinand II. "I do, Your Highness."

"My father was a bold yet patient man. He taught me many things about how to exist at a court like this one, how to have the courage of my convictions. Take the coin, Mistress Seymour, and carry it close to your heart. It shall give you strength, especially when you feel you can trust no one. That is something I have come to understand only too well."

The queen made a little motion then that Jane should put the coin next to her heart beneath the plastron of her dress. As she did so with a humble nod of thanks, Jane felt it settle in right beside the letter she had placed there from the king to Anne Boleyn.

. . .

My mistress and friend: I and my heart put ourselves
in your hands, begging you to have them as suitors for
your good favor, and that your affection for them should

*not grow less through absence. For it would be a great
pity to increase their sorrow since absence does it
sufficiently, and more than ever I could have thought
possible reminding us of a point in astronomy, which is
that the longer the days are, the farther off is the sun,
and yet the more fierce. So it is the same with our love,
for by absence we are parted, yet nevertheless it keeps its
fervor, at least on my side, and I hope on yours also. . . .*

Jane cringed, unwilling to read on as she folded the letter again, feeling a bit like a voyeur. She had been asked to intrude on a private scene and she felt gooseflesh from it. The king was unexpectedly poetic, she thought, as the words rang in her head after she hid it away once again.

He was clearly beyond besotted. No matter what gown she wore, poor Queen Katherine stood no chance against that. Jane wondered with the perspective of time now if she had ever actually stood a chance with William, when he clearly must have found someone else more appealing by now.

That he had never written to explain his change of heart still stung, even with time and distance, which should have brought her perspective.

When the messenger came, she used the French word *parfait* to describe the king's love letter because the impassioned words Henry had written truly were perfect.

Four days after receiving the king's missive, haughtier than ever and more demanding, Anne Boleyn returned to the court, which had moved back to Greenwich. She now boldly wore the king's pendant, with a miniature of his portrait, over the front of her dress.

"Would you like to see the likeness of His Majesty?" Anne asked

DIANE HAEGER

Lady Bryan yet again, doing it only because she knew the queen was nearby and would overhear her. The king had just bought two new rare monkeys for the Royal Zoo, and when the queen had asked him to show them to her, he had escorted his wife in the company of his friends Charles Brandon, Nicholas Carew, William Compton, William Brereton—and Anne Boleyn. She seemed always to turn up, like a bad penny, and Jane, along with everyone else, had to struggle not to roll her eyes.

Anne's new wardrobe of dresses were all designed to highlight the single piece of jewelry she wore—the pendant bearing the king's image. Conversely, while waiting for the pope's decision on what was now being called "the Great Matter," the queen wore her bold Spanish silver cross on a rope of sparkling white pearls. Its presence, to those who quietly gossiped, seemed to say that Anne might have the king's favor, but Katherine bore the will of Almighty God, and in that there could never be any real contest.

"'Tis an exquisite piece, my lady," Francis's silver-haired mother remarked evenly. Then she nodded deferentially to Anne because the king was present.

"But have you truly looked at the craftsmanship and noted the painter's skill, Lady Bryan?"

Jane, who stood directly between the queen and Anne, along with Lady Carew and Mary Boleyn, felt like a buffer for the queen's anger.

She saw Katherine stiffen and her lips go very flat and straight as she gazed into the monkey cage and tried her best not to appear as though she could hear the exchange. Jane watched her clutch the cross at her chest, draw in a breath, then exhale deeply as Anne chattered mercilessly.

212

"Do you not agree, Mistress Seymour? Mistress Seymour! *Mistress Seymour!* You have been spoken to!"

Anne's suddenly hostile tone drowned out Jane's thoughts and brought her abruptly back to the moment.

"Forgive me, mistress, I—," she stammered, having no idea what had been asked of her because her mind had wandered.

"Oh, never mind, little mouse. 'Tis not as if any man would ever give *you* something so exquisite anyway," she murmured cruelly as she clutched the pendant proudly. A disturbingly sincere smile brightened her expression as she turned toward the king and wrapped her other arm through his, clutching him tightly. "Amusing little creatures," she said of the monkeys who skittered up and down a tree branch at the center of the cage. "Not unlike Cardinal Wolsey about the ears, and with the positively hunted expression of our Mistress Seymour," Anne observed drily.

Everyone, including the king, laughed. The moment stunned her.

Jane had begun her life as the butt of cruel jokes, and today she was reminded, yet again, that no matter how long she was at court or how thick her skin became, nothing had changed in that regard. Nor had her secret, mounting anger toward those—toward one person in particular—who mocked her.

Chapter Ten

The year that had passed was another of great waiting and frustration for the king concerning the Great Matter, and everyone at court was made to feel the rumble of his discontent. Henry seemed particularly undone by the wait, and by the summer he began to suffer a series of odd ailments that tormented him. There were recurrent headaches and fevers that began after a particularly bad jousting accident, but the most troublesome ailment was a strange ulcer that had appeared on his leg and could not be healed. None of his doctors could fully diagnose or cure it. That, most of all, set him into an ill humor as he continued to try to seduce Mistress Boleyn.

As the years had worn on, the issue of the king's desired divorce fully polarized the court, and everyone was called upon to take sides. After a plague-riddled spring, when the sweating sickness had taken several of the king's most intimate companions, including William Compton and Mary Boleyn's husband, William Carey, the king's circle became much more defined.

The divided court spurred on Francis Bryan's and Edward

Seymour's ambitions, and both put their lot in fully with Anne Boleyn rather than the queen. There was a growing sense in the fly-infested corridors of the palace that siding with the king's paramour could exact fury from God, but Francis and Edward boasted that they were accomplished gamblers, and both were willing to take the risk.

Not only did the dissension create tension, but most days the palace corridors echoed with the uproar of the king and Anne's furious battles and their tumultuous reconciliations as well.

"I will not have it! I desire these rooms, and I mean to have them!" Anne screeched at Henry.

It was the day before the midsummer celebrations, and everyone had assembled at game tables set up in the great gallery that separated the king's apartments from the queen's rooms. They were installed at Greenwich, and in spite of her protestations against being separated from the king, Henry had left the queen in the early morning hours alone at Richmond and had come away with Anne and her ladies for the festivities.

"They are the queen's rooms, sweetheart; I cannot simply remove her."

"If you want me in your bed, you shall!"

"She is at Richmond now, and we have Greenwich here. Let us keep it as such. A swift cut is the cleanest; is that not what you always say when we go hunting?"

Thomas Seymour laid down his hand of cards. "I am telling you, no matter what our brother thinks, the marriage is at an end," he said quietly.

Thomas's glance met that of Anne Stanhope, who sat on the other side of the table. Then he returned his gaze to his own hand of cards. "By the sound of things, I would be a bit more careful if I were you with whom you cast your lot in this, Jane."

Along with Anne Stanhope; Thomas Wyatt's sister, Margaret; and Elizabeth Carew, Jane had been brought away to Greenwich. Anne, for some mysterious reason, continued to request Jane's presence. Most likely to flaunt her superiority over Jane.

"I still cannot abandon her, Thomas, no matter how the tide appears to be turning," Jane whispered, wanting to return as hastily as possible to the queen's somber rooms.

"You may soon have no other choice, or you could lose your place altogether. Is that what you want, simply to return to Wolf Hall? Lord knows there is nothing waiting for you there but Mother's disappointment," Thomas warned in the same whispered tone.

Jane knew that much to be true. To be sent home, unmarried, not even betrothed, was a failure in every sense. It was also a horrifying prospect. And still Jane could not quite wrap her mind, or her conscience, around betraying the beleaguered queen in the bold and sure way most of the rest of the court had.

The king came thundering down the adjoining corridor just then with tears in his eyes and Anne nipping at his heels like a lapdog. "Keep her at Richmond or bring her here, but I want her out of these rooms either way, or by my troth, Hal, you shall never see your way in!"

"God's blood, Nan, your vulgarity wounds me," he groaned and slapped his forehead as everyone bolted to their feet. There was a collective skittering and the screech of chairs scraping across the wood floor at his sudden entrance before they slipped into compulsory bows and curtsies.

Henry and Anne both ignored their courtiers.

"In truth, I think that if Katherine does not soon agree to end this travesty of waiting on the impotent pope for an annulment and simply agree to a divorce, then she ought to be made miserable enough to see the wisdom in it! The More in Hertfordshire seems the perfect place to do that."

Murmurs of surprise snaked through the vaulted gallery.

"You want me to imprison the queen in that remote and dreadful place?"

"Has she not done the very same thing to you, Hal, isolating me by indulging her fantasy of a union that never existed between you?"

Jane dared to glance up at the king just then, following the line up the thick bandage bulging on his calf, across his broad chest, to his tear-brightened eyes. To her surprise, for the first time, he did not seem to her a majestic, unreachable ruler at all, but rather a fallible, mortal man like any other. A cautious curiosity about this complex man had begun to blossom within her. She felt not the old antipathy, but more frequent bursts of compassion for him.

"What shall you give me if I keep her away?" Henry suddenly asked Anne, unconcerned with his audience, who silently hung on every word between them.

"What is the thing you desire most?"

She murmured the reply in a seductive mewl meant only for him, but Jane was near enough to hear it.

"Very well. The More it is. For now." The king's reply came tenderly as he stroked her small face with the back of his large hand.

"And Princess Mary, shall we not send her alone to Wales to better drive home the point to her mother?"

"If it brings this all to a close soon, then it is for the best," Henry grudgingly agreed.

Jane found Anne's dark-eyed victorious smile a little menacing.

"Splendid. Now I must attend to the refitting of my rooms to suit my taste, since it shall take an eternity to find the proper French designs to make me comfortable. If it pleases you, my lord, I shall assemble a little collection of these women to occupy and advise me as I embark on the task."

"As you wish." The king nodded and kissed her cheek, happy, it seemed to Jane, to be out of the fire for now.

"Lady Wyatt, Lady Carew, and Mistress Stanhope, you shall join me anon in the presence chamber. And Mistress Seymour, I shall have you as well. I should find favor with my cousin about me," Anne added perfunctorily as she spun on her heel and strode toward the door. She did not see Jane's grim nod as her own black mane of hair swung like a horse's tail.

And so to Jane the choice had come. Swiftly and surely.

Light versus dark. The end versus the beginning. She simply must do as her heart urged. She would go against her brothers and Francis Bryan in this. Jane would go into exile with the queen, if the great Katherine of Aragon would still have her. And she would face whatever fate awaited her there. Jane did not know a great deal, but she did know that she could not live a life in service to a she-devil like Anne Boleyn, reminded every day of all the things she was not and would never want to be. Even a desolate and windswept place with a reputation like the More must be better than that. It was also better than having to return to Wolf Hall, a failure and a spinster with no hope of a future.

There seemed to Jane no other choice but those two.

Thus, it was not really any choice at all.

PART III

Jane and Francis

Practice yourself, for heaven's sake, in little things;
and thence proceed to greater.
—EPICTETUS

Have no friends not equal to yourself.
—CONFUCIUS

*T*hree months' time passed at the More, a dank and shadowy prison set in the most desolate, windswept area imaginable. Against the fervent advice of both of her brothers, Jane and a few women elected to go with the banished queen. Once there, however, she quickly began to feel as if she were as much a prisoner of Anne Boleyn as the queen herself was.

The ladies collected at the More passed the time quietly sewing or praying and waiting, full of fear for news of the negotiations with Rome about the annulment. They knew what it would mean for their beloved queen. While Katherine's nephew, Emperor Charles V, assured her that he would make certain the pope did not surrender, part of Jane began secretly to hope that he would. An annulment would certainly put an end to what everyone privately believed was going to happen anyway. That way, perhaps the poor besieged queen and her daughter, Princess Mary, could retire to a more fitting palace and find some bit of peace.

But that did not happen.

In the end, Henry, her husband of twenty-two years, circumvented the pope. He gave up on annulment or divorce and simply broke with Rome altogether. He created his own church and his own rules.

Suddenly, Anne Boleyn was his wife—his pregnant wife.

And she was called Queen of England.

As Katherine's loyal staff stood somberly behind her, with tears in their eyes, Jane helplessly watched the proud, defiant Katherine brought to her knees. Anne's uncle, the powerful Duke of Norfolk, haughtily declared, "Since you are no longer queen, my lady, you shall no longer keep a queen's household at the king's expense or his pleasure."

"Et tu, Brute?" she said softly, not prepared for his betrayal.

"'Tis a matter of survival, my lady, only that," Norfolk replied icily.

The man beside Norfolk, Charles Brandon, had been her dear friend for decades. But like Norfolk, he, too, looked at her as if she were no longer of any consequence.

Brandon had always seemed arrogant to Jane, but never so bad as he had become after the death of his wife, Mary, the king's own sister. Some part of him seemed to have died with her, and now it was as if he was simply out to gain for himself what he could.

"Nothing the concubine does can ever make her queen in my place," Katherine declared, racked with trembling. Her body was fleshy now and worn with the trials of recent years. Her face had swiftly drained of its color from the shock of this cruel encounter.

"Forgive me, madam," Brandon interceded gloweringly. "But she already has."

The two men pummeled her with information then, back and forth, rapid, lethal, as if they were delivering blows. "You have until April to benefit from His Majesty's largesse. Then it is expected that you shall retire to some private house of your own," Norfolk explained in a dry monotone.

"I have no such dwelling," Katherine countered.

"You have until spring to find one."

"On what am I to live if I do?"

"As you are not queen, you no longer need a queen's household," Brandon said.

"No matter what he calls her, I *am* queen. My husband can place me where he likes, so long as I have a confessor, a physician, and Maria for comfort."

"You shall no longer be called queen, madam."

"While I live, I shall call myself so, as will those faithful few, no matter their number, who remain around me." Her tone, full of aching pride, bore only a slight tremor.

Jane longed to cry out that she would be honored to be among them, but this was not the time. Yet again her bitterness toward Anne Boleyn grew.

"Am I to know where I am to be moved, since my circumstances are to be so swiftly reduced?"

"If you refuse to make your own arrangements, my lady, there is a place called Buckden," Brandon coolly revealed, picking a piece of lint from his massive puffed velvet sleeve.

"Any further east and I would be in the sea," Katherine exaggerated drily of the twelfth-century Buckden Palace in Cambridgeshire.

Jane could hear Maria de Salinas begin to weep at the rapidly declining situation.

A fortnight later, the conversation continued to chill Jane as she and nearly all of the others were released from service to the queen and sent home.

The drawn litter in which she rode four months later, accompanied by Sir Francis Bryan, rattled and swayed along the twisted, rutted road back to Wolf Hall. A very different Jane Seymour from the one who had left clutched the Spanish coin once given to her by the queen as she watched her childhood home come slowly into view.

"It was good of you to accompany me, Sir Francis," Jane said shakily, feeling her heart beat more swiftly for the disappointed looks she knew lay ahead.

"'Twas on my way to my estates. I really should see my wife now that I have one before I depart for France," he said cavalierly.

The king was sending Francis again as an envoy to France in order to shore up relations with King Francis I, who had been caught unaware when Henry left the Church. Francis Bryan, considered an expert in diplomacy now, was to do damage control for Henry.

Jane had never met Francis's wife, Philippa, since she remained at their country home in Surrey and did not come to court, but she knew Francis had found happiness. Marriages, children, even dalliances were passing Jane by as she neared her twenty-sixth birthday.

"Yet you do, at least, have a partner, which is more than I can say for myself," Jane said.

He rubbed his bearded jaw thoughtfully as the stuffy litter continued to rattle and sway, the heavily laden trunks bouncing behind them.

"I am sorry there were no stellar options presented for you at court, Jane. I had hopes."

"Faith can be blind, but most men are not," she replied with a sigh. "There has only ever been one person in my life who has seen me differently, and that was a long time ago."

"Ah, yes, young Master Dormer."

"He must be well married now by his own ambitious mother."

"As it happens," Francis said nonchalantly when the litter was brought to a rest in the cobblestone courtyard of Wolf Hall, "Master Dormer is yet unmarried."

She glanced at him as a servant approached with a stepping stool. She tried to keep the tremor of surprise from her voice. "How do you know that?"

"We favored few have our ways," he said with a diplomatic smile. "People gossip about those who seek the sovereign's favor, and Lady Dormer has been prominent among that group through the years."

"I see."

"He is her only son, if memory serves."

"Yes," Jane confirmed. "One accustomed to being indulged as well as indulging himself, from a very early age. I was done with that, and with him, long ago."

"I remember that he might have taken some liberty with you, but at least he was interested enough to tell you he meant to marry you."

"How could you know that?" Jane shot back, feeling defensive suddenly. She did not want to open old wounds.

Francis scratched his beard awkwardly as he gazed out the window. "I would have you ask yourself, have you the luxury to be aloof with a man who once cared for you so deeply that he proposed marriage? Especially if you might, after all this time, still care for him a little?"

The question hit her as a servant opened the little door and a rush of fresh air swirled around them. How, she wondered, did he know any of that? But when she stepped onto the gravel drive, it was into her sister's waiting arms. Their conversation quickly ended in the surprise of seeing Elizabeth after so long.

"What are you doing here?" Jane wept, feeling the full press of her sister's sixth child between them.

"I came for a visit as soon as I heard you were returning from your exile. Was it awful there at the More?" she asked as Jane held her out at arm's length.

Her once stunningly pretty sister had aged with the years and the strain that repeated childbirth had placed upon her once small and delicate frame. Elizabeth's face was slim and drawn, and her beautiful blue eyes had dimmed. Jane had always envied Elizabeth. Until today. She now wore a dress of amber cloth ornamented with ivory lace, which paled in comparison to Jane's rich court-designed gown with its intricate plum-colored embroidery and fashionable slashed sleeves.

"Sir Francis," Elizabeth said, curtsying respectfully to their cousin. It occurred to Jane then that Elizabeth would never have the same kinship with Francis that she shared with him after years together at court. There was a strange, almost imperceptible little turn of the tide then, and she sensed that the balance of power had shifted between the two sisters. "Will you be staying with us?" Elizabeth asked him hopefully.

"I was planning on your mother's grace for only a night or two before I set off to Surrey."

"I know she will be honored. Especially if you bring us news from court," she said excitedly. "Everyone is wondering all about the new queen."

"Katherine shall ever be King Henry's only queen," Jane said defensively as her parents appeared at the half-timbered, gabled entrance to Wolf Hall.

The world tipped on its axis then.

She remembered their disappointment in her before she had left home and felt the sting still. That sensation would live within her always, no matter what glamour she had experienced at court.

Knowing not what else to do, Jane curtsied before them, but her knees were weak. It was her mother who brought her up with a surprisingly gentle hand.

"Welcome home, my dear."

Those unexpected words, filled with sincerity, hit her like a knife wound. For a moment, she could not think. She could never have expected what happened next.

"Dear girl," her mother said as she reached out to Jane, who had telltale tears in her eyes. "You are looking fit after your ordeal in the More. Was it too dreadful?" she asked.

"'Twas not dreadful at all. At least not until the last days," she amended, not wanting to think of the kindhearted queen, noble to the end, though she was intentionally separated by the vindictive king from her only child. Jane might have seen fleeting sparks of humanity in King Henry over the years—and softened toward him in those moments—but she still could not relate to him. Perhaps he deserved Anne Boleyn and the tumultuous existence he had created for himself. "By God's grace, I learned a great deal in my time with the queen."

"You can see our Jane has matured," said her father appraisingly as he reached out and drew her into an embrace that was as unexpected as her mother's kind and thoughtful words.

Jane tried very hard not to go rigid in his arms, but it was difficult. "Thomas wrote to us that the new Queen Anne causes quite a stir when she rides out in public. The loyalty of the people seems to have remained with Queen Katherine, whether she gave him a son or not," said her mother.

"Which, no doubt, is why she has been exiled even farther, to Buckden," Jane added. "If the king could see her sent back to Spain, I am quite certain he would."

"Well, Anne Boleyn is queen now," Francis said philosophically, almost as if someone influential might be listening. "And we all must needs honor her if we intend to remain in the king's good favor."

Francis Bryan had known a remarkable rise under Henry VIII, and, by extension, so had the entire Seymour family. They let the matter of loyalty drop.

They dined early that night in honor of Sir Francis, Jane's mother laying a splendid table complete with delectable roast lark and herbed pheasant. But the house seemed empty without Edward and Thomas, as she so fondly remembered them at Wolf Hall. They sat by glowing lamplight, often in silence now, interrupted only by the sound of silver hitting china, or her father's loud chewing and occasional extended belches. There was no music, which Jane had grown accustomed to at the king's palaces, and there were far fewer servants to attend them. Tonight, away from the elegance of the royal court, the soup was cold, and the lark sauce bitter. Her former fear and awe of Margery and John Seymour faded with each swallow.

After the meal was over, Jane and Francis took a stroll beneath the rich, golden orb of moonlight glowing on the meadow, bordered by cultivated yews and sweet-scented, newly blooming viburnums.

"I have a confession to make," he suddenly said. "'Tis quite a dreadful thing, too."

Jane could see by his strained expression that this was not a jest and that he was troubled by whatever he had withheld. "I could say it was not truly my fault, as it was forgotten in the melee of the accident." He pointed to his eye patch, as if that were necessary. "I have not worn the armor since then. But the bitter and slightly ironic truth of the matter is that when my man took the cuirass out last month for polishing, something I had stashed inside dropped from it. 'Twas a letter, Jane." He held it out to her now. "William Dormer had bid me to give it to you."

"He gave you a letter for me all those years ago?" She nearly choked on the question. This seemed so incredibly impossible and cruel.

"Pray, forgive me, but it is the truth. I swear to you by all that is holy, for the severity of my head injury that day, and the loss of my eye, I did not even remember it until the letter was brought to me a few days ago. Then, slowly, the pieces of my memory began to fit together. I tried to tell you earlier today, but I found I needed some liquid courage in the form of your father's Dutch wine before I could speak of it."

She was afraid to take the letter from him. Afraid to see the written words. She had spent so many years trying to heal from her single adolescent fantasy of love—to mature beyond the loss of it. Instinctively, Jane crumpled it up and shoved it into the fabric of her deep bell sleeve.

"Will you not read it?" Francis cautiously asked.

"I know not," she said truthfully. "What would be the point?"

"Love?"

"We were children."

"Is there an age requirement with matters of the heart?"

"Good sense would strongly suggest there should be," Jane countered drily.

"'Tis true you were both young, Jane, but his words of explanation ring true, and, if I may say, living at court most of my life, I am something of an expert on courtly plays at love. This does not qualify."

"Well, it matters not now anyway," she decided. "'Twas too long ago, and I am quite certain he has known the affection of many women since his few fleeting moments with me."

Her voice, like her knees, trembled as she sank onto a painted wooden bench beneath a pergola smothered in violet wisteria blooms, feeling as if the very life had just been knocked out of her, no matter how stoic she had trained herself to be.

"You must understand, my dear, that lust is not love."

"Tell that to the queen. The *true* queen."

His brows merged above the black eye patch, and he let out a heavy sigh. "Oh, now you have gone and berated my niece. You know I have long been a champion of Queen Anne."

"So has anyone who wished to remain a recipient of the king's largesse. I personally found it all distasteful, and I am glad to be away from it."

There was a long silence as the first strains of the night music, headed by a chorus of crickets, began slowly to rise to a crescendo. "Yet the question does thus become, what will you do without a court appointment or a proper suitor if you refuse to listen to him?"

"William Dormer did not press a suit with my family, or with me," she countered defensively, rising again on unsteady legs.

"'Twas not for want of trying, or lack of desire, sweetheart."

The voice, richer than Francis Bryan's, yet still familiar, came suddenly, and Jane felt as if she had been hit yet again, a blow from which she could not easily recover. Her gaze darted swiftly in the deepening darkness. When it finally landed on a tall form drawing forth from the shadows, she could see by his eyes that the trim and elegantly dressed man, after all these years, was William Dormer.

"You have not changed at all, Jane," William said calmly as he approached.

There was just the slightest hint of a smile dimpling his cheeks, tanned and healthy looking from frequent riding and hunting. Jane tried to step back as he stood before her, but Francis was there like a steadying brace. In the last pale burst of mellow sunlight, William's face shimmered. It was chiseled now, the well-defined face of an adult, with an air of grace that neither money nor a title, but only goodness, could provide. He wore no beard, and his clean-shaven face only added to his elegant beauty.

So like a Roman statue, Jane thought, envious of how magnificent his face was compared to her own plain visage.

"Would that I had been changed enough to match *your* transformation," she replied haltingly, unable to take her eyes from him for the complex memories that seeing him conjured. These last years apart were like an eternity.

She was certain he had no idea what a force he had already been in her life.

"You know perfectly well your beauty suited me."

She wanted desperately then to quip something about his lack of resolve in convincing her, but she managed to hold her tongue.

"I hope you will forgive this small deception conjured by Sir Francis and me, but when he told me that, through circumstance, you never received my letter, I knew no other course to take but this one."

"You might have let sleeping dogs lie," she replied, not meaning it.

"I could sooner have cut out my own tongue, once I learned fate had not allowed me a proper hearing with you."

"If you will both forgive me," Francis awkwardly interrupted their exchange.

Jane and William looked at him as if they had totally forgotten he was there. She knew that she certainly had.

". . . but I find I fancy a draught of ale, and then 'tis early to bed for me. Youth does not live quite so close to my bones as it once did."

After he had gone, Jane turned back, still uncertain whether she was angry or happy to see William after all this time. In spite of what she had once felt for him, there was so much water under the bridge. Yet the memory of them together in that field would never quite leave her mind.

"I was sorry to hear about the queen. Last time he was home, your brother Edward said she had grown very fond of you."

"And I, her." Jane looked away.

It was simply not natural to be so drawn to a man one barely knew.

"Did you read it?"

"No."

"Will you?" he asked.

"And what would be the point, Master Dormer?"

"Ah, so formal are we now, when once we were nearly lovers?" He reached out to touch the huge bell of her sleeve. The connection had power behind it. "The point, to my way of thinking, at least, is that I have never forgotten about you, never stopped wishing it had ended differently between us."

"Oh, William, pray do not speak of such things."

She turned away, but he brought her face back with a gentle, cupped hand.

"I'll not make any excuses for what happened. I won't say that I was young, or vulnerable to the power of my awkward body that day."

"I would not wish to hear it." Jane cringed, vanquishing the image yet again.

"Then I shall speak of it no more. But I cannot be silenced in the same way about my heart, since that part of me which you captured so long ago has never, nor shall ever, belong to anyone else."

"It has been years since we have even seen each other, William. How can you utter such words? Time has changed me. You do not know me any longer." Jane felt desperate and frightened at the prospect of what he was saying. There was an impossibility swirling around the two of them like bees to a rose as they gazed at each other, remembering some things and trying to forget others.

"Jane, please, listen to me. These past years, I have been trotted out to as many young ladies as there are likely at court, and all of them have come up short in comparison to you."

She chuckled, but it was a bitter sound. "Clearly you needed your memory examined along with your eyes. Do you not see what a plain, quiet woman I am? That will never change. If one has no beauty, at least she must have a fortune, and I have neither."

"I am told I have enough of both to negate the issue." He smiled wryly, hoping only to make her laugh.

"I speak seriously, William," she countered, trying to remain aloof.

"I know," he said, smiling at her indulgently. "Did you not ever hear that beauty is in the eye of the beholder?"

"Plato clearly had not seen me when he said that."

To her surprise, William laughed. "You see, that is what I have always been drawn to about you. Yours is not just wit for wit's sake. 'Tis fire inside you waiting to burst forth like a great volcano, and I have long hoped to be there when it does." He took a step nearer, until their chests were touching. Then, without asking, William pressed a kiss gently onto her cheek as if the years apart had been no more than a day. He dared to hold the connection between them as his arms encircled her and he drew her fully into an embrace. Jane could neither think nor breathe for the foreign, desirable sensations it conjured.

"We've lost so much time due to my stupidity and fate's intervention," he said with a sigh. She could feel his warm, slightly honeyed breath on her face. "Your cousin, Sir Francis, has said he would speak to your parents about us now to see if there is approval for our courtship. Tell me, Jane, that he can act as intermediary as well with my family."

"You wish to *marry* me?"

"I have wished it for over ten years, if memory serves," he replied, smiling a bit grimly this time.

Jane pulled away from him and wrapped her arms around her waist in self-defense. "This is too much too soon, William."

"Until your cousin came to me this afternoon telling me you did not reject me outright, that you never even read my letter, I believed there was no hope, Jane. Still, no matter how many willing candidates my mother has found since then, I have had no interest in marriage with anyone else. Can you not see that this is our time, finally? That we are meant to be? Read my letter, I bid you, please," he desperately urged her.

Jane hesitated, then pulled the crumpled letter from her bell sleeve. She smoothed it out and read:

> *My dearest heart,*
>   *It is said in the work of Thomas à Kempis, which you so love, that, so long as we live in the world, we cannot escape suffering and temptation. The truth in those words has brought me much solace, since I know how dear you hold them to your heart. I did wrongly by you*

that afternoon long ago, and "every vice will have its
own proper punishment." You were young and I was
tempted. For that, I believe I have paid a price. We both
have. But the fact remains as it was then. I do love you,
my heart. I do wish to marry you, as I do no other. If
you will but send word telling me I have at least a
chance, I will come away to you this very night. I love
you, Jane.

    Then. Now. Forever.
    William

"Apparently, I am not very good at choosing my messengers," William said as Jane lowered the letter to her side. She was surprised by how much it sounded like the king's missive to Anne. Those words had so struck her as having been from an open and desperate heart. Only when she looked up at him did she realize that there were tears blurring her eyes.

"Do you not still love me, Jane, even just a small bit?"

A second time, he filled the space between them by drawing her into his arms. And this time she let herself surrender to the power beneath a darkening night sky that was quickly filling with stars. For all of the clandestine embraces and drunken romantic encounters she had stumbled upon at court, Jane knew how different this was, because it was not only lust between them, but love. Yes, she loved William with her whole heart. She always had. She just could not quite believe he still loved her, too.

"More than a little," she finally admitted, and though her admission was softly spoken, she knew he took it, and its powerful meaning, as fully as she had meant it.

In response, William swept her up then and kissed her so

powerfully that she could not breathe, nor did she want to. Her mouth melted beneath his, and she parted her lips as he pressed his tongue sensually between them. Jane reached up and twined her slim arms, like a new vine, tightly around his neck, and William pressed himself fully, tightly, indecently, against her. They were not children, her mind said, calming her. They had waited many years for this. No matter what ardent liberties they took with each other now, they would marry soon anyway. And, besides, nothing in her life had ever felt this good. His powerful hands snaked down her spine as they kissed, and he pulled her so tightly against his groin that she thought for a moment he was trying to make them one person. A low growl escaped his lips, and she tasted it.

Abruptly then, and just as powerfully, William pulled back and skillfully drew her arms from his neck with forceful hands. His breathing was ragged and his face was flushed.

"We dare not do more until our wedding bed is beneath us, sweetheart. But then, I warn you, we shall bridge these years we have lost, and swiftly!"

Jane smiled as her mouth burned from his kisses. "May that well be a promise."

"Then Sir Francis has your leave to speak to my parents as well, since they are sure to be our biggest challenge?"

"Of course," she answered as he kissed her again, but not before she asked him, "Think you they shall find cause against it?"

But his answer was lost to the moment, the deepening chirp of the crickets, and another powerful kiss that convinced Jane to hope they might have a happy ending after all.

The next afternoon, Francis Bryan stood, gloves in hand, in the archway of the heavily paneled library, his arrival having just been announced to Lord and Lady Dormer by a servant. It had gone smoothly with John and Margery, who were relieved to hear that their daughter had managed to ensnare anyone's heart, much less that of an impressively wealthy heir like William. Due to Margery's royal connection, albeit somewhat weak and distant, as well as the family's current court ties, Francis expected mere formalities today with the Dormers, and he had not allotted much time or attention to what he would say. After all, did not the king himself trust Francis Bryan at skillful diplomatic negotiations with entire countries? Unless he missed his guess completely, this should be child's play.

"Sir Robert," he said, approaching the compact little man with the ring of hair and small dark eyes. He stopped to bow, then turned to William's mother. "Lady Dormer," he said with a nod.

"To what do we owe the honor of your visit, Sir Francis?" Robert Dormer asked, rising as his wife remained seated, gazing up with an oddly suspicious expression from her book and afternoon sherry.

"I pray you find the cause as charming as I do," he said, taking the seat Sir Robert indicated on an empty bench near their two upholstered chairs.

The musty old room was warm and full of flies. Out of good breeding, he tried not to wave them away. He longed for an open window but reminded himself that this was only a summer home for the Dormers. They had just taken up residence for the season and most likely had not had the chance to air the house properly.

"As you may know, there has been affection of some duration between your son, William, and my own cousin Mistress Jane. I am told by both that the affection has endured their separation while she was at the court of our king and I am assured by both parties, as well as by my own relations, that a betrothal between them would be looked upon favorably. Neither of them have the full bloom of youth about them any longer, as you know," he added with a hint of his most charming and successful court smile. "So I am assuming your side will see the move with equal favor."

"You should assume nothing, Sir Francis," Lady Dormer quickly interjected, and he could see her hands tighten and go bloodless as they curled around the carved mahogany arms of her chair. "While it may be true that the bloom of youth has left *your* relation, my son—an unmarried man of means—is not under the pressures of time. I shall not have our good name, or his future, burdened by such a marriage because of some residual youthful fondness."

Francis stiffened on the hard bench, having been caught entirely off guard by her fervent response. "Sir Robert, might I trouble you for your opinion on the matter in the event that it is aligned with my own? After all, the Seymours are a venerable family of strong standing in court circles, as you know."

"Their sons are hangers-on, clinging to the fringes of society. If my information is correct, it would be a humiliation to a family of means such as ours if we were aligned together, particularly by the indelible tie of marriage," Lady Dormer snidely interjected, cutting off her husband's reply without releasing her death grip on the chair arms.

Francis arched a dark brow, the one above his ebony silk eye patch, and kept his calm demeanor. He had certainly met sharper opposition at the court of France than in this old crone, he thought, but he dare not show it. "What you mean, I assume, my lady, is that Mistress Seymour is beneath your son."

"Well beneath."

"And yet your only son remains an unmarried man and has offered no heirs to your . . . good family name?"

"Sir Francis, you are welcome in this house, but pray, do mind your tone with my wife," Sir Robert finally spoke up as he lifted a warm cup of ale from a carved side table. He made no attempt to offer one to his guest.

"I meant no offense, only clarity, sir," Francis returned, his calm now beginning to turn to ice.

"You may be clear that there is no hope of a match between your cousin and our son," Lady Dormer again interrupted. "Besides, we have been in the midst of negotiations for some time with another family on our son's behalf. So the point is all rather moot."

Francis struggled not to appear surprised. William had told him personally that there was no one else. There never had been. "I had no idea," he managed coolly to say. "Might I ask if your son is aware of these negotiations?"

"Our son is aware of the overtures we have made to the family of Mistress Sidney," Sir Robert replied before his wife could stop him.

"Mistress Mary Sidney, daughter of Sir William Sidney?" Francis asked in surprise.

"I see you know of the girl," she remarked, shooting her husband a censorious stare. "Not altogether a surprise, however, since her family, like ours, is well-placed and financially beyond reproach."

She would be their entry into higher society, Francis thought. Sir William Sidney's position as a courtier was higher than his own because his reputation was above reproach and Francis had certainly had his difficulties in that regard. It was understandable, if a bit sad, considering the obstacles William and Jane had faced, and the years of estrangement they had endured, to have it all end here.

"Is there nothing I might do to convince you to consider an alternate alliance for your son? I am not without a certain connection in royal circles myself," Francis offered.

Lady Dormer barked out a very unfeminine laugh in response.

"You are a rake and a libertine, Sir Francis! You may well have powerful friends willing to humor you and your particular brand of
lechery, but William will have no part in that. He will be on sound
footing when he goes to court."

Francis arched the same brow and steepled his fingers in an attempt to maintain control. "Do you not mean *respectable* footing, my
lady?"

"Take it as you will. The Seymours are a low family with only
faint connections to the king, which that dreadful Margery Seymour
trots out vulgarly like a prize to anyone who will listen. I am afraid
an alliance with them is quite simply out of the question."

Francis could not quite wrap his mind around this woman sitting
before him now with the arrogance to lecture him on connections at
court when he had sat less than a week ago at a banquet in the
company of the king himself at Richmond Palace. Francis rose to his
feet in the strained silence and began to don his riding gloves. "Just
to be clear, neither of you make any allowance here for love?"

He watched the couple exchange a glance before Lady Dormer
finally rose from her chair to face him. "Love, Sir Francis, is highly
overrated. By your own enduring behavior, the stories of which
precede you, I can well guess you take my meaning. They shall both
recover from it, and William shall marry someone suited for him. As
to poor Mistress Seymour's fate, I cannot speak."

"Life is full of surprises, my lady," he shot back as he turned to
leave. "I pray you are prepared for those awaiting *you*."

"A veiled threat seems beneath one who claims to walk with our
noble king."

"I claim it not, my lady. I shall be next month in the party at
Greenwich for Queen Anne's coronation. And where, I wonder, will
you and your family be?"

Francis tipped his head, seizing her with a menacing stare, his black eye patch making him a far more formidable foe than the easygoing courtier he usually appeared to be. "No reply? I thought not. I am a tenderhearted enough libertine to know a great romance when I see one. A pity that your only son shall not be able to say the same. Jane may not know it now, but she is better off without the lot of you. Your son sees greatness inside of her, in spite of you. One day, perhaps she shall surprise us all."

Lady Dormer scoffed as her husband rose to his feet along with them. "I cannot imagine how."

"I suppose we shall see, won't we?" said Francis, wondering if there really could be some miracle in the offing.

When William returned to the manor that night, his parents were waiting for him like two sentinel dogs. The light from the fire brought the bony angles of his mother's face into harsh relief.

"Did you honestly believe we would ever approve of that Seymour girl, William?"

He walked cautiously toward them, guessing what had happened. "That is cruel, my lady mother, even for you. But I gather you have spoken to Sir Francis about our plan."

He moved to the fire as calmly as his trepidation would allow and extended both of his hands toward the flames to warm them. He heard them whisper to each other behind his back, but he refused to look at them. Better to let his mother rant, since he who struck first generally lost.

"A dashed hope is not a plan, William," she clarified icily.

"Is there a point in your distinction?"

"Since it will never happen between you, I suspect you should say that the point is imminently salient."

His body went rigid with resolve as he finally turned around. "I have only ever wanted to marry Jane, Mother, and no matter how many impediments you place before me, my wife Jane shall be."

"A pity youthful zeal contains so little practicality," she acidly returned, showing colors he had always known were there but had rarely seen.

"I cannot contradict you, Mother, except to say that my zeal is not a product of youthful fancy. I am a man, and my affections and my intentions toward Jane are true. You have known that since I was a boy."

Lady Dormer turned her mouth down into a mocking pout. "I did so hope you would grow beyond such folly, William. 'Twould have made everything so much simpler."

He could not help it. In spite of his intention not to give way to panic, he glanced at his father for support. But Sir Robert was as impotent then as he had been with Sir Francis. Lady Dormer had long ruled her husband. And as much as William had tried to distance himself from her, living on whatever family property she did not inhabit at the moment, Lady Dormer had long ruled him, too. This one time, however, was going to be different.

"I will marry Jane, and that is final," he declared defiantly.

"As it happens, my boy, you will not," said his father, speaking up for the first time. The sting of his rejection was a painful thing to William.

"You know that your mother has been in talks for some years with the family of Mistress Mary Sidney."

"Do you not mean she has been in the process of *bribery* for some years, Father?"

Sir Robert ignored the cutting remark. "We are close to completing the negotiations with Sir William, son. You know that."

"So they have finally decided the size of our family's holdings is worth surrendering their vain and silly daughter to us. Is that what you are trying to say?"

"Something like that," he confirmed, unable even to look at his son. They were caught in the trap of a woman whose relentless ambition knew no equal.

"Well, I told you 'no' then, and I declare it even more boldly now."

"Do not indulge the boy, Robert," Lady Dormer countered, calmly ignoring her son's declaration. "Our two families have simply come to terms. 'Tis cause for celebration since, along with her dowry, you shall receive a position in the household of Master Thomas Cromwell, His Majesty's own senior financial adviser. You shall be going to court at last, William, and you will attend the most wonderful banquets and masques with all of the dignity that we have always desired for you!"

"Do you not mean that *you* have always desired, Mother?"

She rolled her eyes in frustration and sank into a padded chair. "'Tis truly for the good of the family, William. You shall see that in time when you are mingling with the King and Queen of England and writing home to tell us of it."

"So that a mother may bask in the glory of her son's success? Is that how it is in your fantasy?"

"William, do mind your tone," his father interjected tepidly as he sank with a little thump into the chair beside hers.

"Well, 'tis *your* fantasy, not mine, that shall be dashed, Mother. I am going to marry John Seymour's daughter Jane, and there is nothing you can do to stop that."

"And on what shall you live?" she calmly asked.

His mother had always played to win, and he knew it. William struggled to keep himself in the game, out of love for Jane. "I have

Gainsbury and the surrounding lands that net a goodly enough profit, which is my inheritance from father's father."

"Or do you?"

William was stunned. "You would take away that which I have earned, in addition to all that I stand to inherit?"

"In a heartbeat. We would do whatever is required to see your marriage to Sir William Sidney's daughter come to pass."

"I understand this not, Mother. By your leave, pray, explain how the daughter of one knight so surpasses the daughter of another in your good opinion?"

"Mistress Sidney comes with the key to great riches and fame. Mistress Seymour comes with an embarrassing connection to that lothario Sir Francis Bryan. Our good name and our standing would be instantly reduced."

"Well, if I must be reduced to asking that same lothario for a posting in order to care for my wife, I shall."

"Do you know there is an outstanding debt on Wolf Hall, William?" Lady Dormer suddenly asked, cornering and caging her own son like prey.

This threw him entirely off his game. "I did not."

"It seems it is a rather large sum, or so your father tells me. Is that not correct, Robert?"

His father only nodded glumly, his chin doubling as it sank to his chest.

"'Tis quite extraordinary how much debt one can accrue in an attempt to clothe three offspring who play about the fringes of royalty. I am given to understand that the silver braid and beadwork on the last two doublets made for Edward Seymour's summer turn quite surpassed the cost of Jane's entire wardrobe for last year, and Sir John has been in quite a tangle about it."

"You bribed them to withdraw their support of our marriage? But that cannot be, as Sir Francis reassured me earlier today that they had given their support . . ." William's words faltered, and he almost could not breathe.

"Much can be accomplished in an afternoon. I'll not have my only son, the total of my life's work and worry, aligned with *country people* whose paltry connection to the aristocracy is only surpassed by their unimportant family name!"

William could see the vein in his mother's temple began to pulse with restrained fury. The Dormers may be wealthy, but they were no better than gentry, William knew. He had waited so long for Jane, and yet like a predator, his own mother, who had controlled his entire life, now led him irrevocably to his own slaughter.

"I shall reason with her father myself," William defiantly countered, hearing the desperation mount in his own voice.

"'Twill do you no good, my boy. He has already taken the money," his father revealed in a tone of calm persuasion. "I spoke to Sir John the moment Sir Francis left our home. In return, they have promised to withdraw their support for your marriage to their daughter. Sir John gave me his gentleman's word."

William wanted to cry out. To object further. He had always been a good and obedient son, doing everything that he was called upon to do. He had never asked for anything, never wanted anything. Until now.

Cornered. Struck. Killed.

With one lethal blow, it was over. He would go to court on the largesse of Thomas Cromwell, and Jane would remain at Wolf Hall; they were destined never to see each other again. Perhaps that was better than having to see the pain and disappointment in those gentle eyes of hers again.

. . .

Jane knew it was bad before her mother spoke a word. They were alone in the sunlit gallery lined with Seymour family portraits. There was compassion on her face, not her usual censure.

"Oh, my dear, I beseech you, do have a seat."

Also bad, Jane thought, since terms of endearment between them were as rare as jewels.

"Best to be quick about it," Margery said stoically, yet still her face held her true feelings.

Jane's heart began to race. Was it Edward or Thomas? Had something happened to her brothers? Father, perhaps, since he was not here with them at the moment? This could not be good.

"I would prefer it if you were quick," Jane said.

"'Tis Master Dormer," Margery said.

Pray God, no! Jane shot back to her feet, visions of the sweating sickness seizing him, or an accident, like what had befallen Sir Francis, flashing in her mind. She could not speak at the mere thought of it.

"He is engaged to be married."

Jane nearly laughed out loud, thinking for an instant that, of course, it was she to whom he was engaged. But then her mother reached out in an uncharacteristically maternal gesture and Jane's heart nearly stopped.

"There is someone else," she said gently, but Jane felt a huge, thunderous roaring in her ears.

Had she not just been with William, bound up in his embrace? Love between them promised? But none of it was real. William's promise was as empty as her heart felt now. Swiftly, her shock became anger, beating at her to react. But she did not. Jane even held back the tears that threatened to undo her. She was stronger than that. Oh, how court had changed her! Disappointment. Experience. Heartache. She was scarred. Embittered. But she was emboldened as well. Jane would find a way to persevere, and she would survive this latest heartbreak.

After all, it was true what they said: appearances really could be deceiving.

Chapter Twelve

January 1535
Wolf Hall

The tune had changed with the passage of time, but not the players.

Anne Boleyn had been queen for only two years following Katherine's exile, first to the More, then to Bucken and to Ampthill Castle. But after the disappointing birth of a daughter, a stillborn son followed in 1534. Each chipped away at her influence as well as her hauteur. Easily bored, with no new challenge at hand, Henry for his part had endured Queen Anne's second pregnancy by indulging in a discreet affair. No one, even the great gossips, seemed to know the woman's identity.

Over the years, Jane's parents received a steady stream of news from Thomas and Edward, both of whom remained in positions of increasing prominence at court. While the details fascinated her, Jane was glad to be away from anyplace where she might be reminded of William—and all she had lost.

She knew he had been swiftly married off to Mary Sidney and that he had gone to work for the increasingly powerful Thomas Cromwell in London, but that was all. She could not bear to know or hear more. The designs of her life were once more at Wolf Hall as a helpmate to her aging parents. And so she believed she would remain.

Then one gray and wet winter's day, as melting snow lay in patches on the ground, all of that changed when the king and a small group of companions stopped unexpectedly at Wolf Hall on their way back to Greenwich from a hunting trip.

"How fare you, good cousin?" Francis Bryan asked Jane as they embraced, his smile brightened by genuine affection.

"Apparently better than our sovereign," she answered in a low voice as she glanced over his shoulder at the pale and limping king, who was being tended to near his horse.

The scout had explained to Jane's father that His Majesty had taken ill with one of his now regular and debilitating headaches as they rode. Sir Francis, who was among the group, had volunteered Wolf Hall, which was nearby, as a place to repair.

It had been a year since Jane had seen Francis, who hunted with the king regularly now as Henry searched for any reason to avoid his wife. Jane and Francis stood on the threshold as the king hobbled slowly toward them then, surrounded by Nicholas Carew, Charles Brandon, Jane's brother Edward, George Boleyn, and Henry's personal physician.

The years had taken a remarkably heavy toll on Henry, she thought, particularly owing to Anne Boleyn. There were tales that swept across England of Anne's increasingly outlandish demands, their battles, and his resulting infidelities. It was well-known that the King of England never wanted anything for long once he had acquired it, and even the arrogant queen was apparently falling victim to his tendencies.

Before Francis could explain anything more, the king was before them with the others, and everyone in the Seymour household fell into deep bows and curtsies. To her surprise, he swept past them without acknowledgment, his face distorted by a pained frown. Jane could see that his once trim and athletic form was rapidly deteriorating. The king had gained a noticeable amount of weight. His handsome face was bloated, especially his cheeks, his hairline had receded further, and his face now bore the rosy patches of a heavy drinker. The added girth accentuated everything.

He wore his age and the stress of conflict on his face.

Jane had already noticed that his once elegant stride had been replaced by a pronounced limp. From her curtsy, she could see that his calf was even more heavily bandaged than she remembered. He looked to be a slightly pitiable creature now, and she even felt a spark of empathy.

While the royal physician attended to him upstairs, the others gathered in the library as great tankards of ale for the thirsty riders were hastily brought in. Once it was determined that the king and his companions would be required to pass the night at Wolf Hall, the house was sent into an uproar of clattering dishes, exhilarated shouts, and directives beyond the library walls, which the elegantly dressed men courteously ignored as they downed their ale. Jane was thankful that her mother had gone to oversee the preparation of a meal, which left her alone to indulge in the company of the few courtiers of whom she had actually grown fond during her time at court.

Jane's brother Edward, newly remarried to the court beauty Anne Stanhope, seemed softened to the idea of being home. He approached Jane, gathering her into an awkward yet sincere embrace as the others talked among themselves.

"You are looking well, sister," he said with the first genuine smile she could remember. "Francis told me what happened with that Dormer fellow. I am sorry I never quite found a chance to write to you of my regret."

"You are busy with your own new circumstances, my lord, 'tis understandable."

She could see that she had made her point deftly enough that he cringed slightly as he took up her hand.

Jane saw how much Edward, now in his thirties, was growing to resemble their father, and how much that fact must bother him after what had happened with Edward's first wife. Edward's once dark crop of hair had begun to recede from his forehead, like their father's, and his trimmed beard was peppered with a shock of gray. Like the king, Edward was no longer the trim, athletic youth she had so admired, but a thicker, more staid, middle-aged man.

"I'm sorry you were not able to attend the wedding," he said of the time when she had gone into exile with Queen Katherine.

"I was needed elsewhere at the time, as you know," she replied sweetly.

Edward smiled at his sister in response. She knew perfectly well that, like Francis and Nicholas Carew, Edward had advanced his position these past years by siding with Anne Boleyn over the queen. In that, brother and sister had followed separate paths.

Rarely had a day gone by since she had been forced to leave the More that she did not think of Queen Katherine, stripped of her title, her income, her daughter, and her dignity. Jane secretly despised the Boleyn witch a little more each day, as well as those who followed her. If there had been something Jane could have done to avenge her queen, sweet, gentle, plain Jane, as people still thought of her, would have done it in a heartbeat.

"Anne says you were always kind to her," Edward said of his

wife, breaking into Jane's thoughts then. "Yet you are always kind to everyone."

"So they tell me," Jane replied, pressing back her inner scorn with a gentle, yet cultivated, smile.

She found, as time went on, that she liked controlling what people thought of her. It was the only bit of power she had ever had, and she guarded it now ruthlessly.

When the king was not well enough to come down later that afternoon, it was decided that Jane should attend the servants who took him a tray of light fish broth and a small goblet of warm ale.

"Go on, girl," her father prompted, adding with his own impatience that the king was not to be kept waiting. Edward and Nicholas Carew escorted her behind the servants, liking nothing so much as a reason to be in the king's presence, whatever the circumstances.

She found him lying in the pitch-darkness with the heavy tapestry draperies drawn. "What troubles him?" Jane softly asked of the royal physician, a toady little man in black velvet who met them at the door.

"Only one of his headaches, mistress. He shall be fine, but just now he cannot do with the light, the scent of food, or even voices. I have given him the usual physic, so we should see it pass by morning's light."

Jane glanced over the physician's shoulder at the recumbent king, who looked further weakened from the sovereign they had all greeted at the door an hour earlier. He was egocentric, pompous, vain . . . yet, now, undeniably pitiable as well.

"Who is it, John?" Henry called out weakly. His eyes and forehead were covered with a moist cloth, so Jane guessed he could not see her.

"Mistress Seymour, Your Majesty," he answered softly. "She has brought you some broth and ale."

"Mistress Jane?"

"Aye, sire."

"Bring her near."

"But Your Majesty must—"

Henry held up a hand. "Now," he commanded.

The physician nudged her forward with a shoulder, but not before she saw him roll his eyes at her brother and Nicholas Carew.

"Sit with me, Jane, will you? I've had enough of the company of the lads. Besides, 'tis soothing to hear a woman's voice when one is in ill humor."

Having heard the king, Edward moved forward deftly to place a chair closer to the bedside for his sister.

"Are you there?"

"I am, Your Majesty."

"Ah, there is that sweet voice. I wager you did not think I would remember."

"Indeed I did not think it, sire."

"Well, speaking from experience now, the song of the lark is more soothing than the sharp cry of the blackbird. That is a sound that still fills my head a bit too often lately."

One glance exchanged with Edward and Jane knew that the king meant Queen Anne. She thought again of all the gossip about their outrageous battles and what she herself had seen. There were even whispers of divorce again.

"I wish I could look upon your gentle face, but just now the light sends my stomach into a terror that I should not wish you to witness."

"'Tis better to stay as you are, then," she said as softly as she could manage and still be heard.

She glanced again back at Edward, and to her surprise, he nodded his silent approval at the exchange.

"So tell me, Mistress Jane, have you quite forgiven me for how things ended with my brother's widow? I know you were forced to take a side."

"'Tis only the Lord's place to forgive, sire," she tried to demure, as she had years ago when she actually was the innocent girl she had become so good at portraying.

"Indeed. But if it *were* yours to forgive?"

"I loved Queen Katherine, sire."

"As did I, once," he said with a sigh, sounding more sincere than his usual jovial, seemingly carefree self.

She glanced back at Edward, and he motioned for her to continue, although she had no earthly idea what was proper to say next.

"'Tis only when I follow not my God, but my heart, that I find myself in trouble," she said meaningfully, pressing back memories of William. "So I try to avoid that."

"Do you now?" She saw him smile. "Find you no room in your life for love?"

"'Tis more that it has not found me, sire."

"You might not have the feathers of a peacock, sweet Jane, but believe me, if there is one thing I have learned, there is a certain alluring beauty in simplicity."

In the next moment, he was asleep, and Jane was ushered out of the room as swiftly as she had been ushered in. But not before an impression was made on everyone else who had lingered near the door, witnessing the exchange. Particularly Edward, Sir Francis Bryan, and the queen's own brother, George Boleyn.

In the wet and cold weeks of winter that followed, letters to Wolf Hall detailed the king's return to the queen—and to a new mistress as well, although neither Edward nor Thomas revealed who she was. Apparently the only requisite was that she be anyone but Anne Boleyn. Anne's ceaseless demands and jealous rages had driven her husband from her bed and from her arms and threatened to drive her from his future.

Francis Bryan and Nicholas Carew, who had supported her against the first queen, pulled cautiously away from her now, yet they walked a fine line in doing so. Henry's heart was a fickle, restless thing, and they knew it. They had witnessed the parade of women, including Bess Blount and Mary Boleyn, and even Carew's own wife, Elizabeth, so they knew to take care until it was not merely over, but dead and buried.

As spring came and the May Day celebrations were once again in full swing, the king and his closest friends watched the queen and her ladies dance around the Maypole in the cool and breezy sunshine at Richmond Palace. By bribing Charles Brandon with a case of rare French wine, Edward and Francis had secured the seats closest to the king for the event, which he normally gave over to George and his father, Thomas Boleyn.

But many things again were changing.

Anne's court during the May Day celebrations was a very different place from Katherine's. It now was as entertaining as it was elegant, and the women surrounding the queen were young, beautiful, and full of daring. They were dressed in gowns with plunging necklines designed in the French style, and their hair was worn long down their backs beneath small French hoods, mirroring the queen. The king and his friends sat laughing and pointing like boys at the seductive dance.

"William Brereton tells me that the queen is in need of another lady-in-waiting since Lady Zouche is with child," Francis carefully remarked to Henry as they watched the women twirl and dance.

"The queen is always in need of something, it seems," the king responded brusquely, and they could see his gaze clearly following Margaret Shelton in the little production as she flitted blithely around the Maypole near Anne.

"I was thinking of proposing Edward Seymour's sister for the post," Francis casually said. "She is experienced with court ways, and so would need a minimum of training."

"The queen has her chamberlain for that sort of thing. Let him sort it out," Henry said with a swat of his hand. He smiled at the girl he called Madge, and she smiled back.

"Might I have Your Majesty's leave, then, to speak to him on the matter?" Francis dared to press.

"Aye, that Seymour lark is a demure enough little thing not to ruffle the feathers of the raven nesting in the queen's rooms. It might be a good match. Heaven knows I have trouble enough keeping her temper down over dear little Madge," he said with a chuckle, nodding and smiling again at Margaret Shelton, who flounced her dress at the king.

In response, Francis, Edward, and Nicholas all joined him in a ribald laugh. George Boleyn alone shot Francis an evil glare.

William Dormer sat with his new wife, Mary, her father, Sir William, and his new benefactor, Thomas Cromwell, just behind the king at the May Day celebrations. Cromwell was an influential man. He exuded power from every part of his tall, slightly hunched frame, which was always swathed in velvet robes. Since Wolsey's death after falling ill on a journey, Master Cromwell was entrenched as the king's key adviser, and he needed a smart, ambitious aide.

William had willingly accepted the post in order to put his past heartbreak with Jane finally behind him. Yet hearing her name suggested by Francis Bryan as a possible courtier jarred him. It was of no help that Mary clung so tightly to his arm that it had begun to go numb.

He was stunned, and he tried to take the notion in fully, but his skin smarted under the pinch of his wife's desperate fingers. Desperation had always been unappealing to him.

Jane had never been like that. He had marveled at her independent streak, even on that first day in Savernake Forest. His mind had retained every moment of that first encounter, certainly glamorizing it through the prism of passing years. Ah, how he longed for the bittersweet innocence of childhood, when he had not understood what would be expected of him or of Jane.

Jane . . .

He squeezed his eyes to press away the thoughts, since they always came back to how he had hurt her. William had wanted to be different for her, and with her. Yet in the end he knew he, like the rest of the world, had played a part in hardening her once achingly gentle heart.

That Jane might now return to court, where he would be forced to see her, filled William with almost as much dread as excitement, and a battery of questions assaulted his mind.

Did she hate him for marrying Mary Sidney when it was he who had pursued her in the first place, then failed not once but twice to win her? He shook his head, knowing the answer. He was a wretched man who deserved the heartache he felt.

"My dear, are you unwell?"

William's wife studied him with a face full of concern. For a moment he was uncertain what to say since he knew he would never be truly *well* again.

Mary was not without appeal. Like Jane, she was small, demure, and obedient. Her eyes were large and brown, her lips full, and her heart open. As a man, he could be tempted by the novelty he saw in her. Mary's hair was also fair enough that in the dark of night, beneath the tapestry canopy of their bed, he could almost convince himself that it was Jane with him beneath the covers. God help him and his fantasies, but he wanted to see her again. He hoped to see her; he longed for it. Even in all of their years of separation, it was she who was his last prayer every night and his every fantasy after that. But what would happen when she saw him again, William could not even begin to imagine.

PART IV

Jane and William

Where desire doth bear the sway,
the heart must rule, the head obey.

—ANONYMOUS

Chapter Thirteen

$\mathcal{I}$t was another endlessly wet and gray day when the Seymours' drawn litter pulled up the wide pathway through the massive
golden gateway of Richmond Palace. Jane could see the golden-
domed turrets, brightly painted brickwork, and colorful flying
pinions. Though nothing had changed about the palace, she was
changed from the girl who had left. She was a woman of no illusions
this time, and only a sense of family duty to lead her.

With the sad announcement of the death of Katherine of
Aragon, the past had been fully left behind them at last. Feeling
magnanimous, Queen Anne had agreed, through her chamberlain,
to put aside any bad feelings and accept Jane as a lady-in-waiting due
to the high placement not only of her brothers, but of Sir Francis
Bryan as well. Jane ruefully remembered her father's pronouncement
in the Wolf Hall dining hall that she was to return to court. There
was no choice in the matter. She would help her brothers gauge how
the wind was blowing as they navigated the increasingly choppy
waters of the swiftly failing royal marriage.

Jane liked Richmond Palace precisely because Queen Katherine had favored it and Queen Anne did not. It was too provincial for Anne, lacking elegance, yet sporting all of the wonderful details of an Arthurian castle straight from the pages of Sir Thomas Malory.

In a gown of amber velvet, she stepped from the closed litter and into a swirl of activity. Horses were taken by grooms to and from the stables, and ox-drawn carts brimming with vegetables rolled past. Another cart, laden with dead geese, drew toward the kitchens as the daily task of feeding a mammoth-sized court began once again. There was so much going on that Jane's arrival was barely an event, but the two opulently dressed Seymour brothers were there to greet her nonetheless.

"You are looking elegant." Thomas beamed as he kissed her cheek.

"Father did not hesitate to remind me of the cost of this elegance," Jane said, remembering her father's words before she had left.

"This style of living takes money, and plenty of it," Edward put in as both brothers appraised her.

Since they had last seen each other, Thomas had grown into his looks. Now he was tall and trim. Any traces of boyhood in his face had given way to a perfectly elegant nose, square jaw ornamented by a neat, light mustache and beard, and azure eyes that could only be described as piercing. He and Edward both carried their mother's features, but Thomas had clearly inherited better versions of them.

As the trio made their way toward a wide, carved entrance door to the east wing of the palace, Thomas linked his arm through Jane's. Edward did so with the other arm in a futile attempt to keep up with their sibling bond.

"Now that you see her again, do you suppose there is any hope of it at all?" Thomas asked Edward as they passed the threshold and entered the first long, tiled gallery.

"There is always hope," Edward countered sagely. "The king grows more restless by the day, and I told you how softened to her he was at Wolf Hall."

"Was that not only the vulnerability of his ill health?"

"We shall put it to the test these next days, shan't we? When the queen is pregnant and his duty is done, the king feels perfectly free to indulge himself. It has been the same song since the earliest days with the last queen. Our timing in this is impeccable."

Jane stopped dead in her tracks at the base of a wide wooden staircase and reached out to clutch the wooden banister. "You two could not possibly be talking about me, could you?" she asked.

Edward began to lead her by the elbow up the flight of stairs. "We are indeed."

"Edward, Sir Francis, and I think the king may well be ready for someone new; someone patient and kind, rather than the tempestuous partner he has done battle with these last years."

"Impossible," Jane scoffed as they briskly walked together. "I have been in His Majesty's presence dozens of times, and he has never shown the slightest interest in me!"

"Much has changed since you have been away, sister. His Majesty's health has continued to decline and he has been made vulnerable by it. At first, Queen Anne took advantage of that weakness, raging her demands and pressing her power. But now, like a wounded bear, he has begun to resist, and even lashed back at her boldly. It has made for some interesting encounters to witness," Edward said.

"As you know," added Thomas, "upon the death of Sir William Carey, Francis took over his position in the privy chamber, which has brought him quite close to the royal center of things. And in those most private hours, a man talks to his gentleman servant."

"I thought our cousin was loyal to his more prominent relation, the queen."

"Francis may be a profligate, but he is a wise one. If the queen does not give Henry a son, the marriage will come to an end," Edward put in.

"Is that what he speaks of?" Jane asked skeptically as they made their way down a second, tapestry-lined gallery depicting scenes from Ovid's *Metamorphoses*.

"That, and of uncomplicated days with gentle, loyal friends like Wolsey, though he speaks guardedly of the dead cardinal."

"A bit late for nostalgia, as poor Queen Katherine grows cold upon her bier and the cardinal is six feet under at Leicester Abbey!" she exclaimed angrily.

Her sister-in-law, Anne Stanhope, had written to her that in the queen's final hours, her most faithful, lifelong friend, Maria de Salinas, had broken all protocol and risked everything to be at her bedside.

The poor queen had died three days before in the arms of her dearest Spanish friend.

"Yet he believed he loved Queen Anne," Thomas put in. "Surely you understand how blinding love can be."

Jane shot her brother a sharp look, feeling the sting of the reference to William. She could not help herself. The next words crossed her lips even as she tried to stop them.

"Have you met William's wife?" she asked.

The brothers exchanged a glance. "She is a pleasant enough sort. So is her father. The Sidneys know nothing of your history with her husband, Jane. I bid you to keep that in mind as you begin here."

Her heart squeezed and she felt the old pain as if it were new. This was not a beginning. It was the same performance with a predictable cast of players. Only she had been changed by the years. "I have seen with my own eyes the sort of beauty the king chooses," Jane said defensively. "You two are whistling in the wind with this," she warned callously as they reached the queen's apartments. It was a very different place from that over which Katherine of Aragon had presided. Jane saw that the first moment she stepped beneath the gilded arched doorway and into richly redecorated rooms dripping with gold cloth, heavy silver tassels, and large tapestries woven with seductive images. The one that first caught Jane's eye depicted Bathsheba with King David. Above the fireplace hearth was Anne's own emblem—a white falcon sitting atop a bare tree stump. In its claw were red and white roses. Jane knew that the tree stump was a symbol of domination over the king's previous failure to sire a male heir. Clearly the emblem had been constructed well before her less-than-successful attempts to bear a son, Jane thought as they advanced. It was strange to be back. She had changed. Nothing else had.

George Boleyn, now Lord Rochford, clothed in a sweep of silver-studded velvet, met Jane and her brothers at the door to the queen's privy chamber. His dark hair was more oiled than she remembered, and bore a streak of silver.

"Welcome back, Mistress Seymour," he said with his customary note of arrogance. Jane had not known him well before, but even from a distance he had always frightened her. Along with their father, Thomas Boleyn, and Mary, they were a tightly knit family obsessed with having complete control over their standing. "Sir Francis has done commendably well for you with this placement, considering his own growing distance from the queen," Boleyn coolly remarked.

"I am grateful to Her Majesty," Jane said as softly and sweetly as she could manage as she curtsied.

"See that you remember that, and your place. Your brothers and your cousin may be pressing their way forward with our good king, but none of you has done so admirably with me, or with the queen."

"So noted," Edward interceded, sparing Jane a reply.

When she was at last shown into the queen's privy chamber, Jane found Anne standing before a full-length mirror, half gone with a new pregnancy and looking like a garish bird in a shimmering gown of bright yellow silk with long, fur-lined bell sleeves. Her sister-in-law, Lady Rochford, was placing a gold-and-diamond-studded circlet on her head and arranging her long black hair beneath it. As Jane advanced, Anne looked her over, sniffed at her, then turned back to her own reflection without acknowledging her for several awkward minutes. Finally, without looking back, Anne coolly spoke.

"There is only one reason you are returned to court, despite what anyone may tell you, Mistress Seymour. My husband, the king, spoke up for you, obviously at Sir Francis Bryan's prompting. Personally, I would not have someone about me who had once chosen allegiance to my rival, but His Majesty seems to have a short memory these days, and an even shorter fuse. I'll not risk challenging him on something so trivial as attendants."

Jane was surprised by her acid tone, but with the king's record of amours, and her own inability to produce a male heir, it seemed likely that Anne was suspicious of everyone now.

It was at that moment that something very grand shifted inside of Jane.

The girl who had intentionally tripped her all those years ago in the presence of the French queen was vulnerable now. Her powerful hold over Jane was diminished, and she no longer had the upper hand. Jane had never forgotten that moment, like so many others in her life that had come to define her, even though the incident was long forgotten by Anne. Realizing that, she straightened her back and tipped up her chin. Anne did not even notice.

"It is an honor to be in Your Majesty's service," Jane finally said, feigning sincerity so well that she almost believed her own lie.

"I would work on your tone of voice, Mistress Seymour," said George Boleyn. "My sister will not abide simpering."

She curtsied deeply then so that neither would see the wild rebellion newly kindled in her eyes. She was here for only one reason: to help Thomas and Edward. Only family was worth suffering a jade like Anne. *Yield not to every impulse, but consider things carefully and patiently in the light of God's will.* She believed entirely in the tenets of *The Imitation of Christ*, the book that had defined her girlhood.

That night, Jane stood on the fringes of the banquet hall for her first true state occasion. The evening was in honor of Anne de Montmorency, Admiral of France, and no expense had been spared. The ceiling beams had been freshly painted in bright colors, and the molding was painted a shimmering gold, which the light of the candles and lamps cast in a flattering glow. After her audience with the garishly dressed queen, Jane herself had gone to change into a new gown of stamped blue velvet with gold-embroidered sleeves, provided on her departure from Wolf Hall by her parents. It was a costly creation, intricately beaded, and she felt almost pretty in it as she watched the rest of the court make their showy entrances. There were neatly plumed caps and diamond-studded headdresses bobbing everywhere as the guests began to mingle and everyone waited for the entrance of the king and queen.

It was beyond Jane to be impressed by any of it. Queen Katherine's funeral Mass had been said earlier that day. Frivolity like this seemed vulgar in light of that. But to Jane, nothing could be more vulgar than Anne Boleyn. Especially now, as she strode into the hall with her noticeable belly protruding to the peal of trumpets beside the king, who wore the same garish, bright yellow silk fabric as the queen. It was the color of treachery, Jane thought, as he nodded and smiled to the assembled masses as if neither he nor his wife had a care in the world.

Poor Queen Katherine. It is better that you are no longer of this world to witness any of this . . .

As they were shown to their tables by a large assemblage of liv-eried pages, Charles Brandon approached her. He, like the others, had aged in her absence from court. But by his steady gaze, she would know him anywhere, and she disliked him even more.

"If it isn't the little mouse returned to our big, happy family," he said pleasantly, taking up Jane's hand after she had curtsied to him. He led her away from the queen's other ladies and to a table quite close to the king.

The queen was already seated and speaking to the French am-bassador, who was with the guest of honor. She could hear their rapid Gallic conversation even over the music and laughter.

"His Majesty is correct; you are quite a different creature, are you not? Grown into someone quite pleasing," Brandon remarked flirtatiously.

"My thanks, Your Grace." Jane nodded to him as he glanced at the sea of far more elegant and beautiful ladies.

"If I may say, Mistress Seymour, I found what you did regarding the queen—or, rather, the *other* queen—to have been quite noble. I was always fond of Katherine because she was dear to my departed wife," Charles declared sadly, yet his voice lacked real sincerity as he continued to appraise the queen's most attractive new ladies, Mary Scrope, Elizabeth Browne, and Nan Cobham.

Jane did not know, under the circumstances, whether to believe Brandon. Like so many others, he had publicly thrown his lot in with Anne Boleyn early on. Now that the tide was slowly turning again, it seemed an odd opportunity for revelation to the contrary.

"Your Grace's words are high praise," Jane skillfully replied with a ladylike smile.

"Who have we here?" the king asked with a wide and welcoming smile as he came upon them suddenly, looking like a stout, red-faced canary in his yellow finery amid the happy tune his musicians played from the gallery above.

They were both still like boys, she thought, grown men with their adolescent smiles and competitive nudges.

"Ah, but, Mistress Jane," the king said affably. "How do you fare now that you have returned to our little court? It must be something of a change from the last time you were here."

"I fare well indeed, sire, thank you," she softly replied, lowering her eyes shyly. It felt like the polar opposite in tone of any response Anne Boleyn would have given, which brought her greater confidence.

At the precise moment that she looked up again, she saw him. *Him.*

Everything shifted as it always did, as it always would.

William, newly knighted, was standing with Master Cromwell and a pretty young woman in a pink dress. The new Lady Dormer. She knew it. Her heart seized at the sight of them together. Just seeing William touched her so deeply that she could not move, but now the emotions it brought were rejection and pain.

"The last time we saw each other, I was not at my best. Pray, tell me I appear a bit different on this occasion," the king said, ignorant of her distraction. Jane's gaze returned to the king's garishly bright, yellow, jewel-studded costume.

"I could find my king nothing short of magnificent, sire," Jane said.

"Indeed," he preened. "My, but you have a clever tongue. Have I not always said that, Brandon?"

"Indeed you have, sire," Brandon said with a slight sneer. Jane doubted that the king had ever said anything of the sort, and Brandon knew it as well.

"Do come and sit with us, Jane, and we shall speak of your family's beautiful estate, Wolf Hall, and the merry times I've had hunting in Savernake Forest there."

Since there was no empty chair, he hooked a powerful arm around Jane's waist and drew her onto his lap with a carefree chuckle. "Ah, here is the best seat in the house!"

At that strangely fortuitous moment, Jane's eyes met William's amid all the noise, laughter, and music, but his gaze silenced everything in her mind. She watched his eyes slide to the king, then back to her. She knew he could see that the king's and duke's attentions were trained on her as if she actually mattered in this world. At first she did not feel vengeful, though she did feel greatly empowered.

She liked thinking she could make William jealous. Suddenly, because she knew he was married and all hope was gone, she wanted him to hurt as much as she was hurting inside, as awful as that was. Jane turned away from William and offered a small, wan smile to the king. "'Twould be my honor, Your Majesty, to sit anywhere you would have me," she said sweetly, knowing that William was still watching her and that it would bother him.

As the king held fast to her on his lap, he and Brandon took turns regaling her with tales of their many hunting adventures through the years, especially around Jane's Wiltshire home. Fortunately, Anne was entirely unaware of the new focus of attention in her own midst. Jane tried not to settle back too far on Henry's wide thigh as a silver plate of steaming stewed sparrow was laid before them and a fresh goblet of wine was brought. She tried only to sip at the crimson liquid, not wanting to lose her wits at such a critical moment for her brothers. Both Thomas and Edward were seated across from her with George Boleyn and his father, Sir Thomas. Each of the four of them, for his own reason, had fixed his critical stare upon her.

"So tell us, Jane, what instrument do you most favor?" the king asked with a broad smile of true interest.

She was uncertain how to answer the question, knowing the king's reputation as a clever and intelligent man—even as he balanced her on his knee like a Bankside whore in full view of everyone.

"The lute, assuredly, but only if Your Majesty plays. I am rather clumsy with the strings," she said softly enough that he and Brandon strained to hear her over the din of chatter and rousing music.

"Well, I must give you a lesson, then. 'Twas clearly your teacher who was inferior, since you seem to do everything else with perfection."

She blushed at the compliment but was further empowered by it as well. She could see how drawn in he was by the demure front she was projecting.

Then, for the second time, William caught her eye.

Why did the world tilt so when he looked at her?

He was seated on the opposite side of the room, quite far from the royal dais. He and his wife were no longer beside Cromwell, who had taken a more prominent place beside the queen's uncle, the

Duke of Norfolk. A tapestry of Zeus rippled on its iron rod overhead as the servants moved quickly back and forth past it. It seemed he had not lost sight of Jane even for an instant, as she had him. Once, those eyes, now full of sadness and disappointment, would have completely controlled her every thought and action. Tonight, she would take away their power. William belonged to someone else. She said it over and over again, but she would have to keep reminding herself. Her survival depended upon it.

"If Your Majesty would not find it too much of an imposition, 'twould be a great honor," she replied sweetly.

"Does tomorrow afternoon suit you?" he asked.

"You have your poetry reading with the queen then," Brandon chimed in. "I could acquaint Mistress Seymour with the musical fundamentals in your stead."

"You know perfectly well you cannot play a proper tune to save your life, Charles," the king reminded him. "Besides, are you not to contend with your own new, young wife? I did warn you that marrying someone so young as Kat Willoughby would take all of your energy and focus."

"The only one ever worth all of my energy and focus was your sister, my beloved Mary," Brandon said solemnly. "Now that she has departed this earth, the rest is all just pale entertainment until God calls me to join her."

Jane thought it was a slightly forced pronouncement, particularly for a man who had married for the fourth time less than a year after the death of his best friend's cherished sister—the royal beauty who had supposedly been the love of his life for eighteen years.

"I would welcome help from either of you," Jane said graciously as a troupe of Venetian dancers, costumed in flowing silk, began a light entertainment in the cleared area in front of the dais.

William's pretty wife was chattering in her husband's ear. Jane watched the incessant moving of her lips, even as William stared straight ahead, not acknowledging her. It was a frenetic scene to Jane: the king and Brandon joking back and forth over her shoulder, the dancers, the fluttering silk, the loud music from the gallery above, the chatter and laughter, the milling servants. The queen's squawking laughter. The rich French wine was suddenly having an effect on Jane's head. There was a dreamlike haze to everything now.

"Splendid. Then it is settled. Tomorrow, 'twill be up to your king to teach you how to play the lute. And who knows what else!"

She smiled demurely at the sovereign's jaunty tone, even though she entirely understood the implication. "Pray, do not expect too much of me, sire. I fear I may not be as swift a learner as you are accustomed to."

"What I have been accustomed to is of no importance, as I find myself increasingly ready for a new experience, not a replay of the old," he responded with a sly smile.

It was difficult not to think that he was referring to Anne Boleyn. It was curious, Jane thought, as she glanced at her place a few seats away, that the queen did not seem to notice, or care, that Jane was sitting on the king's lap. She seemed utterly taken with the poet Thomas Wyatt, who sat beside her. If she bore the king a son, she would have earned the luxury not to notice or to care, Jane thought.

After all, what sort of threat could little Jane Seymour pose?

But a son had yet to be born.

When the banquet concluded and the call was sounded for the guests to adjourn to the Great Hall for dancing, Jane heard a page whisper to the king that the queen had grown tired and wished to retire. The news received, Henry waved the servant away with a nod, then turned back to Jane.

"I find I am rather weary of all of this myself. Would you care to join me for a breath of fresh air?" he asked her casually.

She knew it was not an actual question but a royal edict. Yet a part of her actually did want to go outside with him, away from all this noise, abandoning the perfume and the pointed stares. Just being with the king after all these years, certainly since his illness at Wolf Hall, was easier than she dared believe. She felt girlishly hopeful for her future when he was near, although she would never admit that to anyone. It was something she had given up hope of ever feeling the day she had heard that William was married. When Jane looked one last time for William, she saw that he and his wife had already gone from the hall. *Just as well,* she thought, bitterness masking the pain of rejection for the one she truly loved.

Henry led her then, undetected, through a small rounded side door into the biting winter air as the last rays of the sun dipped, pale pink, below the horizon. Feeling the shock of the cold on her face, Jane clasped her hands and lifted them to her lips, intending the white puffs of her breath to warm her fingers as she began to shiver.

"Would that I were those hands," he said as he gazed down at her, so much smaller and more fragile than the huge bear of a man before her.

His expression was deep and sensual, and it drew her, even in this cold.

"I want to show you something," he declared a little drunkenly.

Henry drew off his velvet cloak then to sheath her, and she felt relief instantly. His hand, as he drew her own into his, was still warm, and the firmness of his grasp calmed her shivering. They strolled past the duck pond, where ice clung to the edges of the water, which gently lapped the shore in the winter wind. He did not speak as they crossed over the bridge, but she could hear the trusses give a little creak with their joined weight. She felt him watch her, and she liked it.

A few steps more, and they were inside a round little building with a glass dome roof that let in the moonlight, and with it, the light from the deepening canvas of stars. Stoked by coal braziers and lit by candles tucked into wall sconces hidden by pretty screens, the place was a cozy little paradise, alive with plants, exotic trees, and the musical trill of dozens of birds. Jane chuckled in surprise as the king helped her off with his cloak.

"What is this place?"

"Do you like it?" he asked with a pleased tone.

"'Tis magical."

He was gazing at her with a grand smile. "I have had these birds brought from all over the world. Only the rarest, most exotic, have found a home here with me."

"I have been to Richmond many times, but I never knew this existed," she said delightedly, gazing up at the branches and vines, where little dots of color nested and chirped.

"That is because there are few with whom I share it. I alone possess the key."

To this, and the hearts of how many? Jane thought.

"Your Majesty is a surprising man."

"Verily, 'tis the reaction for which I most often aim," he said, biting back a wry smile. There was a fair bit of mystery hidden behind his bold green eyes, Jane thought. "Keeps people on their toes."

"I can imagine."

"You remind me, Jane, of someone who was once very dear to me. Her name was Bess."

He said it as if she had never heard the legendary tale of Bess

Blount, mother of the king's son, who had been part of his life for more than twenty years. They said she remained a confidante, even now. She had never met Bess, but Jane knew the sacrifices she had made, as her friend Mary Boleyn had, and Jane had always felt certain she would like her.

"Bess was like that goldfinch over there, delicate, a bit flighty at times—if you will pardon the pun," he said, clearly pleased with his own clever tongue.

Chuckling at himself, Henry picked up a bit of seed, and a small white bird landed in his palm as if it had been trained to do so.

"Do all the women you have known remind you of birds, and do they come when you call?" she asked, daring in that moment to try to sound as clever as he.

"Not all. But most. *You* do."

Jane reddened beneath his gaze, which he held for a disconcertingly long time. "You see over there on that branch by itself? The one with the patch of yellow on its chest, the lark?"

Yellow, like the queen's gown. Had she not seen Queen Anne tonight, Jane might have been flattered. Instead, she cringed at the connection.

"She is small and delicate, by no means the most striking bird, but her song is as sweet as it is gentle, and that draws me greatly."

"Your Majesty." Jane lowered her eyes with embarrassment. In spite of his reputation, she had not expected so bold a declaration.

He took a step nearer to her, closing the gap between them, and all Jane could think was, *I am nothing like the women you have loved and won. You are toying with me. You must be. What other earthly choice could there be?* He grazed her forehead then with a tender kiss, and Jane could no longer think for the foreign sensation it aroused. He had a musky scent, rich and masculine, tempered slightly with sweat. The glitter of so many jewels on his broad doublet shone in the lamplight as the little collection of birds fluttered above them with sudden bursts of movement.

He touched the bit of hair peeking out from under her hood. "'Tis the very color of wheat, your hair," he observed, as if that were a good thing. The admiration in his voice stunned her.

"You are unique, Jane," he murmured then, and she could feel his warm, wine-scented breath on her face.

She felt a thrill so deep down inside of her that she forgot to breathe. It had been so long since a man had made her feel anything close to desirable. Out of habit, she cast her eyes downward again. He inched closer. She felt her knees go weak as he drew her chin up with a single finger. The power behind the movement blotted out the reality of his growing girth or the thick bandage on his calf.

"Jane . . ."

"Your Majesty." But it was not Jane who had answered. The tone was deep and reedy, a man's timbre with a slight edge. "Forgive me, sire. But the matter is urgent. It concerns the queen." Both turned then to see the portly, dough-faced Thomas Cromwell before them in his black cloak and hat.

Jane thought him an odd-looking man, slightly cadaverous, with cinder gray hair and a pronounced Adam's apple that bobbed so visibly when he spoke that she could not look directly at him. His hands were like talons.

"What is it now, Cromwell?" Henry asked with an irritated sigh.

Cromwell cast a glance at Jane. His raised eyebrows were bushy and unkempt, not unlike his hair. "Should we not speak privately, sire?"

"Damn that woman and her infernal complaining! Out with it, Cromwell! I care not what Jane hears!"

Again Cromwell glanced at Jane, his irritation rising. "Your Majesty, I truly do not think—"

"As your sovereign king, Thomas, I command you to obey me! I do not suffer you to *think* as you do it! What trouble plagues the queen this time?"

"It is the child, sire. She has miscarried the child."

"Impossible. I was only just with her at the banquet!"

"It was over an hour ago that she took her leave." Cromwell's tone was tentative. He paused before he continued. Jane could see him gauging whether or not he should continue. "Her sister-in-law, Lady Rochford, just sent word to be delivered to you."

Jane watched the bold king, so tall and confident the moment before, fold in on himself, wilting in the echo of the news as his head dipped low against his chest.

"She promised me a son this time," he said haltingly, though the words were not directed at anyone.

"'Tis truly a tragedy."

"'Tis a *curse*! That woman is like a great plague upon the kingdom, and upon my life! Her raven hair and tender lies have blinded me!" He slammed both palms against his forehead as though he were holding a great rage back. "I have been so deceived! Tell me, was it a boy, Cromwell?"

"Oh, sire, I—"

"Was it my heir?" he raged.

"I am told the child was a male, Your Majesty. Shall I tell her you will come with haste?"

"I cannot look upon her right now. Tell her that, or any lie you wish," he responded bitterly. Cromwell bowed to the king, then silently left them.

"Perhaps some good will come of it. Thomas à Kempis speaks

of the value of adversity so that we might not hope so much for worldly things," Jane offered.

"You have read *The Imitation of Christ?*" His surprise seemed to calm him.

"The words within that volume brought me many hours of peace when I was growing up, Your Majesty, and since."

"'Twas my own grandmother who personally translated book four, you know."

"Aye, from the French. You and I spoke of it many years ago, but it would be easy to forget our conversation."

The hint of a smile lengthened his lips. "I am unaware of a woman since my mother who has ever read it." Astonishment highlighted his expression.

Jane smiled softly, trying to hide her delight. "I am surprised by that since the work is so grand."

"I am surprised by *you*."

Again she lowered her eyes, finding his gaze too powerful. Once again, he lifted her chin. "You are a gentle girl, Jane. I suppose I had forgotten what it was like to be in that sort of company."

"Bess?" she gently asked, knowing she was pushing the boundaries.

"She was the last, but yes, gentle to the core, like you."

He drew nearer to her again, and Jane felt with everything inside of her that he meant to kiss her. As much as that prospect filled her with excitement, there was also dread. "Should you not go to the queen?" she murmured as he tipped his head, leaned in, and grazed the column of her neck seductively with his moist lips.

His warm breath on her skin was like a balm for the wounds of her past. He reached up and anchored her jaw very gently with both of his hands, never breaking the seductive nearness between them as he brought her face to meet his own and settled his gaze on hers so powerfully that she felt weak.

"I want to kiss you, Jane, not chastely nor tenderly, but as a man kisses a woman when he is full of carnal passion." His lips grazed the apple of her cheek, first one, and then the other, with taunting restraint. "I am not a casual man when there is something worth truly possessing. But I believe with all of my heart in the value of resisting temptation. Just as Thomas à Kempis reminds us."

Jane's thoughts were fluttering randomly, desperately now, like moths to a flame. *Why the parade of mistresses if you truly mean that?* she wondered. But he still had command of her body; he was still holding her face, still murmuring seductively against her neck so that she could gather neither her thoughts nor her resistance against him.

Then suddenly, she felt tears blurring her eyes as she whispered, "Pray, what does Your Majesty want with me?"

"What I want with you, Jane, is everything. All that we both long for and deserve."

"Does Your Majesty seek a mistress, then?"

"I have never sought that, Jane. But I am a man of bold passion. A man who craves giving love nearly more than receiving it."

Again he kissed her cheek, but he barely brushed his lips against her skin this time. She could feel his desire beneath the restraint.

"Then what is it Your Majesty will have of me?"

Suddenly, he smiled and drew back. "Patience, my lark, is a great virtue. There is a plan for the two of us in God's eyes. You must only wait for it to be fully revealed."

"And you, sire, know of the Maker's plan?" she asked, her eyes wide and her voice rich with sincerity as he brushed away her tears, clearly pleased by the humility behind them.

"The Lord has surely led me to you, Jane. That much I know

without doubt. So I trust that His plan for us is as pure and true as what I see in your eyes."

She did not say that he already had a wife. Two daughters and a son as well in the Duke of Richmond. She did not say that he barely knew her. It seemed to Jane that God had long ago decided on a plan for King Henry's heart, and that could not possibly include Jane. Still, Katherine was dead and Anne had miscarried a son.

The world, her world, was changing again. Where long ago it had been closed by William Dormer, it seemed open again suddenly, and she was curious to see what was ahead.

That much she could not deny.

Mary sat at her dressing table rubbing milk of roses onto her hands and along her fingers as he watched her. It was a nightly ritual. Her golden hair fell long down her back over her ivory and lace dressing gown. William watched her, hoping to feel something—at least enough to make a child with her. *A child.* A Dormer heir. It was the one thing that would heal the wounds of the many disappointments life had cast upon him. In that, he did not feel so separate from the king or his lifelong, elusive goal. God knew leaving Wiltshire to come to court had not accomplished that.

The king . . . William's blood ran cold at the memory of the way the monarch had looked at Jane earlier that evening. Hungry eyes, not appreciative ones, had taken her in as something to be possessed, then devoured. He had seen that for himself and felt sick. He still did.

Mary turned around on the fringed stool, an ivory-handled hair-brush in her hand and an open invitation in her eyes. He buried his gaze quickly in the pages of the volume on his lap. He could feel his young wife's expectation, trying to call him so that she would not have to plead again for the affection she had every right to desire. But after catching a glimpse of Jane tonight, he knew true intimacy with his wife was impossible.

God, how he ached for Jane, body and soul, because it would never be fully over between them. She was imprinted on his very soul from boyhood and would never leave him. He would always want her no matter what he had personally done to make that fantasy impossible.

Her indifferent gaze when she had looked at him had cut straight through to his heart. Yet William knew he deserved that and more for not having fought harder for Jane. He could make a million excuses about loyalty and duty, but at the end of the day, he was the man who had the unique distinction of disappointing her, and for that William would pay for the rest of his life.

After passion with his wife had overtaken him and he had allowed himself the degrading fantasy of pretending she was Jane, William sat propped in bed, watching Mary sleep beside him. He tried very hard not to feel disgust at how he used her, but that was always impossible afterward.

William should have been pleased with his life. On the surface, he had everything a man could want. He was sleeping with his pretty wife in an elegant chamber near the apartments of Thomas Cromwell, one of the most powerful men in all of England. He had everything . . . but the one thing he truly desired. He was still not ready to give her up entirely. Not yet. Even though the King of England seemed to have set his sights on her now as well. But was it too late for him and Jane?

Edward and Thomas Seymour showed no surprise when, near midnight that night, Jane entered Thomas's small receiving room, with a view of the shadowy cobbled lane between the west wing and the royal kitchens. The brothers were playing a hand of cards by lamplight when she pushed open the door, whirled around in her blue velvet gown, then closed the door quietly behind her.

"Perhaps I was wrong," she announced, leaning against the curved, heavy, mahogany doorframe and letting out a dramatic sigh.

Edward tossed down a card. "About what issue?" he asked nonchalantly.

"The king's interest in me." She could feel her smile broadening at the confession, but she could not help herself. The prospect was as exciting as it was dangerous, and Jane had never entertained anything truly dangerous in her life. Perhaps if she felt even a modicum of respect for Anne Boleyn, she would feel regret, but years of watching that concubine torment the poor queen had leached that possibility from her heart.

"'Tis about time you opened your eyes," Thomas said with a conspiratorial smile. He was still elegantly dressed from the banquet in an embroidered doublet with thick padded sleeves and a crisp Venetian collar.

Jane took an empty chair at their carved maple-wood card table.

"We must be extremely cautious if we mean to make something lasting of His Majesty's momentary interest in you. There is no room for even the slightest mishap," Edward warned, laying down his cards and leveling his eyes on his sister with intensity. "In this game, you must be the complete antithesis of the queen, or there shall be no reason for him to leave her for you."

Jane could not control her gasp, even as she pressed her fingers to her lips. "Do you truly believe he would do that? That *I* might actually become—"

"Queen? Indeed I do. His Majesty is far more traditional a man than you might think—he wants only sons and a bit of peace as he grows older. These years with the concubine have worn him down. All of us have seen that," Edward confirmed as Thomas beamed at the prospect. "But she will not go without a fight, so our plan must be flawless. We have Sir Nicholas and Sir Francis on our side, of course. They have both left her camp of supporters, as she has worn them down with her belittling remarks and rages. But we need Cromwell. He is the king's most trusted adviser now, and without him it may all fall to nothing."

Jane thought of his expression earlier when he found them in the aviary. She had always known Thomas Cromwell as a supporter of Anne Boleyn based on their mutual commitment toward religious reform. Everyone knew the Seymour family to be traditional in their beliefs. But the world with Queen Anne was a very different place than it had been with Queen Katherine, and faith seemed secondary, Jane reminded herself.

"Leave Master Cromwell to me. I have an idea," she said confidently.

The brothers exchanged a skeptical glance. It was not the sort of thing Jane ever said.

"But, sister, you must focus all of your attention on the attacks you will need to fend off from the queen and Lady Rochford once your relationship becomes more widely known," said Thomas. "The viciousness of women cannot be underestimated."

Suddenly, Jane felt a smile bubbling up. A little chuckle followed as her gaze slipped from one brother to the other. Back and forth it went until they all were looking at one another slyly. Her smile was so contagious that, finally, all three of the Seymour siblings—these children of the humble Wiltshire countryside—were laughing in disbelief at the utter fantasy of how far they had come . . . and how much further they might go if they played their cards right.

"Nor should I be underestimated," Jane said.

Jane was exhausted from all that had happened that day when she slipped alone down the shadow-drenched gallery outside the queen's apartments and up a flight of stairs to her own bedchamber. She ached for sleep, and yet she knew she would get little. Her excitement was too great for sleep. *Could this actually be happening?* she still wondered, pondering that same thing over and over again since the moment the king had taken her away from the banquet earlier that evening and openly declared his interest. With a heavy hand, she twisted the iron handle on her paneled door, but it was another hand, strong and male, that reached behind her to push it open. Jane turned with a start in the forbidding darkness, gazing up into William's tormented expression. Yet it was not a surprise. Somehow she had known he would come to her and they would meet like this. It had always been meant to happen.

"How long have you been waiting here for me?"

"Hours . . . Days. A lifetime. Truly, I know not time," he said, and by his slurred tone it was clear to Jane that he had been drinking.

"You must go, William, back to your wife. I am certain she is waiting for you." Jane could not keep the bitterness from her voice, altered now by fatigue and anger as she pushed past him and into the small, dark bedchamber.

She went to a table and lit a lamp, then kicked off her soft-soled shoes. William closed the door behind them, then followed her so closely that she could still feel his breath on the nape of her neck. Her heart was racing. Her private room was small, and it was difficult to get away from him—if that was something she even wanted. But Jane was not certain that she did.

So much of her life was tied up in her love of this man.

Finally, when there was nothing else to busy her movements, she leaned against the side of the bed and faced him fully. The torment in his expression was so raw and so real that she shuddered with compassion in spite of everything else she felt. "What do you want, William?" she asked brokenly as tears clouded her eyes.

He ran a hand behind his neck as the tears in his own eyes splashed onto his smooth cheeks, and he sank brokenly onto the edge of her bed, hunching over and pressing his face into his hands. "I know only that I love you, that I will always love you. In spite of what I did to destroy it, we have been meant for each other since we were children. The fact that I cannot ever have you is a wound from which I know I shall never recover."

Jane sank onto the edge of the bed beside him. She was so close she could feel his warm thigh, which was pressed against her own through her dress. William reached over and tightly clutched her hand in his as if it—and this moment—were some sort of lifeline. She was surprised that he did not mention the king. But, then, what had always been between them had never included anyone else. William lifted her hand to his lips and kissed the back of her palm with such emotion then that she felt herself begin to tremble. Jane reached up and ran a hand through the thick hair above his ear, knowing what the intimate touch would lead to and not caring. She was wounded, too.

He turned his head slowly to face her, tears staining his cheeks and brightening his eyes. He kissed her hand again, then leaned in slowly to kiss her slightly parted lips. Jane did not refuse his advance; she craved it. God help her, the king's kiss felt nothing like this, nor did his touch, in spite of how majestic she thought he was only hours earlier.

Forcefully, yet with an aching gentleness, William pushed her back onto the bed and came down on his side, pressing against her and reaching up with a hand to touch her cheek. It was not unlike the seductive dance they had done together all those years ago in a field filled with red poppies behind Wolf Hall. He wiped away her tears with the backs of two fingers. Deftly, he moved in to kiss her again, this time far more passionately, opening her mouth with his own and pressing the full length of his body against hers. He pressed a hand onto one of her breasts and moved over her. Jane ran her hand through his hair again, craving the softness, craving him. But then, as they kissed and touched, Jane knew they could do no more than this. There was too much at stake for both of them.

As if sensing her resolve, William sat back on his elbow without argument and gazed at her beneath him. There seemed some comfort for him in her tears as he let just a fraction of a smile lengthen his lips. "You are not going to become my mistress, are you?" he asked sadly, already knowing the answer. "Far too complicated to become the lover of two men, I suppose."

He sat up fully then, and Jane sat up beside him. "I'll not become his mistress either, William."

"Then what are you doing with him, precisely, besides endangering your very life by challenging the queen?"

"I am being myself. That is all that I *can* do. Pray it shall be enough."

"Enough for what?"

Jane looked away from him as she smoothed out the skirt of her gown.

"You do not honestly believe that he will divorce her and marry you, do you?"

Jane shot him an angry glare. "Apparently, you do not have as much faith in me as my brothers do. But then that is really no surprise, considering how little fight you seemed to think I was worth in the end."

"I was told there was no hope."

"And you believed everyone else without even asking me?" She bolted to her feet, straightening her sleeves. "You asked for my hand twice, but never even asked me how I would feel if you married someone else! You never gave me a chance to fight for you, fight for *us*! And I would have done that; I would have fought for you, William. Just as I have fought for every single thing I have," she declared brokenly, feeling the anger and frustration rise within her. She loved William more than anything in the world, but he had hardened her in a way nothing else possibly could.

"You don't know everything, Jane. The decision was not as simple as that. There were extenuating circumstances."

"Love is simple, William. One either feels it or not. If you do, you fight for it. That is what I believe."

"That is a sentiment for fairy tales!" he declared, shooting back to his feet and towering over her.

"I want a fairy tale!"

"What you shall get with the King of England is a nightmare, not a fairy tale!" he raged, clamping his arms around her again and drawing her against his chest furiously. Jane could tell there was something he was not telling her, something about what had happened before he married Mary Sidney, yet whatever it was, it did not matter now. It would never matter again. William was another woman's husband. And if she had her way, and she was very skillful, she would soon become another man's wife.

William kissed her again, but this time she did not kiss him back. She merely waited for him to taste the broken heart that would never heal and that would never belong to him again. When he did, he released her and stepped back.

"I want you to do something for me, William."

"Anything," he replied softly.

"More than that, I need you to speak well of me to Master Cromwell."

"I have never spoken of you in any other way."

"I need the loyalty that belongs to Anne Boleyn. In spite of her decline in power, she is still a ruthless and influential woman."

He looked at her with a spark of incredulity for a time before he said, "You want me to help you become Queen of England?"

"Yes."

"I owe you that much," he finally replied, but not without a grudging note in the words.

"You owe me nothing, William. I ask it of you only as a friend."

"You should be my wife, not my friend."

"We all make choices," she said, trying hard not to sound bitter.

"This is not what I wished for us. Please know that."

She waited, but he said nothing else before he took her into his arms and pulled her close against his chest, holding her there chastely for a long time, as if somehow he could undo the years they had lost. So much had brought them to this point. So much had torn them apart. She hoped he would do this for her. But Jane would have to wait and see if the love of her life was up to the task of helping her become another man's queen.

Chapter Fourteen

January 1536
Richmond Palace

*J*ane came to her post as lady-in-waiting in the queen's apartments early the next morning. Anne was still in her bed beneath a swans'-feather counterpane of gold-fringed ermine. Her lap was filled with a collection of her favorite little yelping dogs. Her miscarriage the night before rested unspoken on the lips of everyone in the room.

The moment Jane entered the privy bedchamber, she knew something was wrong. The women around Anne's bed turned in unison to glare at her. She stopped halfway into the room near the grand fireplace hearth, which was blazing with a freshly stoked fire. It flared and crackled as she passed it, the sudden sounds setting her more on edge and causing the dogs to bark more furiously. Her instinct was to turn from the confrontation, but Jane had learned a great deal these past few years. Armed with the knowledge of the king's affection for her, she drew in a breath to steady herself, held up her head, and advanced. She wore a pretty gown of gray velvet with scalloped edges and trimmed with gold braid, which gave her even more confidence.

"Well, if it is not the little harlot herself," Anne remarked as she took a goblet offered by George Boleyn's wife.

Jane exchanged a little glance with Elizabeth Carew, whose expression was full of worry, but Jane knew she could not be undone by that. This was war. A war that had been brewing since their childhood voyage to France years ago.

As she came to the foot of the queen's bed, Jane curtsied deeply. "Your Highness. Please allow me to convey my regret over your loss," she said so sincerely that she almost believed it herself.

"Your regret? What do you regret precisely, Mistress Seymour? The loss of my child? Or the loss of your cover in the pursuit of my husband?"

From the corner of her eye she saw the other women exchanging glances, and she knew what gossip would ensue after she left. But this moment, and how she handled it, was critical. Out of habit, Jane lowered her eyes. What she felt, however, was anything but contrition. This was an evil woman who had been an evil girl, and there was little chance she would ever change. Jane could hear the whispers around her as she drew nearer the bedside.

"I am here to serve Your Highness in all things, now and always."

"Serve me up on a pike at Tower Bridge, more likely," Anne grumbled in her white satin and lace chemise with a luxurious miniver collar as two of her favorite chestnut-colored lapdogs lounged beside her on her coverlet. Her onyx hair had been brushed out, long and luxurious and in sharp contrast to the white bedding. "Did you think I did not see you last night, like the tart that you are, sitting astride the king's lap?"

"Mayhap you should retire for the moment, Mistress Seymour," offered Lady Rochford, Anne Boleyn's sister-in-law. "We want nothing to upset the queen."

A bit late for that, Jane thought uncharitably, but again she displayed her reverence with another deep curtsy. At that very moment, when she would have taken her leave, the double doors to the queen's bedchamber slammed back on their hinges, and the king himself strutted toward them in black velvet mourning clothes.

"I shall be the judge of who shall retire!" he bellowed as he advanced toward the grand canopied bed, followed by Nicholas Carew, Francis Bryan, Charles Brandon, and William Brereton. Thomas Cromwell entered with them in his own dark swirl of black velvet, but he wisely lingered near the door.

"How are you, my dear?" Henry asked his wife perfunctorily, and it was obvious that he cared little what her answer might be.

"You imagine I would be *how* precisely after last evening? And now I am forced to face your whore as well by morning's light!"

Jane stood motionless as Henry's face filled with crimson fury. "You need not blame someone else for what you brought upon yourself, woman!"

"Are you suggesting that it is my fault that our son is lost to us?"

"The blame certainly does not belong to Mistress Seymour, or any of your other ladies. You alone were the vessel for that boy!"

Jane could not quite believe it when she saw Anne's eyes fill with tears, even though her expression was still dark with anger. "Your neglect these past weeks has taken a toll, Hal. You must accept your part of the blame. Even though we shall have another son soon enough, we both must learn from our mistakes."

"I see, madam, that God does not mean to give me a male heir through you, no matter whom we choose to blame," he said more coolly, entirely disregarding her entreaty as he turned to leave the room. He paused for just a moment when his glance met Jane's. She knew it was wrong to delight in hearing his angry tone with Anne, but she could not quite help herself after everything.

"When you are out of bed, I will speak to you. Have someone call for me then," Henry grumbled. Then, having done his duty to see her, as he had once done for Katherine after her own miscarriages, he unceremoniously left the room. It was to the dismay of some, and the fear of others, who had been left to watch the exchange and wonder who would be victorious in this newest wrinkle in the tumultuous royal marriage.

It was Lady Margaret Douglas who approached Jane after the king had gone. The queen's most important ladies had gathered around her bedside, but not this influential woman. The expression on her face was stony. They had been cordial once, but Lady Douglas's loyalty was most definitely to Queen Anne.

"'Twould be best, Mistress Seymour, if you took your leave from the queen's sight for now," she said coolly.

Thinking then only of her brothers' positions and power base, Jane said, "Has my service displeased Her Highness?"

"'Tis not your service, Mistress Seymour, but rather your insolence that has displeased the queen."

"Mistress Seymour is the least arrogant person at this court," Lady Rochford suddenly defended, and Jane could not contain her surprise. George Boleyn's wife rarely spoke to her. "She cannot be blamed for her friendship with the king."

"If it were only friendship that she was after, perhaps you would be correct, but I have seen enough royal mistresses come and go in my time to know the difference."

Perhaps you were one of them once? Jane thought, surprised herself at her own growing callousness toward Anne Boleyn and her defenders, and the scandal she would be starting if she allowed things with the king to continue.

It was surprising to Jane how little fear she felt at that prospect.

It was no more than a few minutes later, as she lingered absently at a task designed to keep her nearby but out of sight, that Edward and Thomas approached her.

"Come away with us, sister, at least for now," Edward said smoothly. "There is a family matter with which we must contend." Both brothers were gazing at her casually, as if this had nothing whatsoever to do with the queen's displeasure. But there was no mistaking that they had meant to pluck her from the volatile scene.

Jane was angry by the time they reached the first corridor beyond the queen's presence chamber. "What in blazes were the two of you thinking?" she snapped as they walked swiftly, flanking her, passing guards and servants, tapestries, and blazing wall sconces. "I cannot concede my place to her now!"

"Nor can you miss an opportunity to closet with the king when he is alone and vulnerable, in need of a good friend's private counsel," said Thomas.

"Where is he?" Jane asked as they descended the first flight of stairs along another vast, window-lined corridor.

"At prayer in the Royal Chapel, not to be disturbed by anyone just now," said Edward. "We took the liberty of following him after he left the queen."

"Then what would make you think he would wish me to disturb him?"

"It is not a disturbance you will offer him but chaste female support, just as you have before. His Majesty is a vulnerable soul just now. Ambassador Chapuys's spies said they thought they heard soft weeping, which was when we came to collect you."

Eustace Chapuys, the imperial ambassador to England, and Katherine of Aragon's great and loyal friend, had been invited to return to court by Anne herself, who was still desperate to secure the emperor's acknowledgment of her as queen. With his niece now deceased, the emperor, for his part, wanted an alliance with Henry badly enough to send Chapuys back into the fray. But the reality of the matter was that Chapuys did not like Anne, nor would he ever, and her camp realized that the ambassador would likely be working toward her downfall now that he was here. Jane's brothers thus trusted Chapuys's account of the king's mood.

When they came to the private door at the side of the chapel, Thomas carefully opened it. Then he turned back to his sister. "All that you have witnessed and endured has led you to this moment," he said with quiet intensity. "We trust that you understand the vital importance of becoming indispensable to His Majesty, though not necessarily through your virtue."

Knowing her duty, she pressed rising questions from her mind and entered the small candlelit chapel. She saw Henry at the altar on his knees, his head lowered to his steepled, meaty hands. Filtered light poured over him in a kaleidoscope of color through the stained-glass oriel windows decorated with images of the saints. Jane was afraid to advance on him like this, but Edward nudged her forward, then closed the door on her. She stood motionless for a moment, listening to the king murmur. His words echoed through the small nave.

"Forgive me. You were a good woman who deserved better than I gave you . . . I am still uncertain what came over me, or that I ever will know . . . By God's grace, may you rest in peace, Katerina."

He sank back onto his heels as Jane approached him, and he looked up in surprise with tears brightening his moss green eyes.

"Forgive me, Your Majesty."

"You must call me Henry. And there is nothing to forgive. I am glad you are here, Jane, though I know not how you passed beyond the guards."

"I took it upon myself to enter by the private door," she lied because she did not want to implicate her brothers when she knew how much she would need their help in the coming days.

"Resourceful as well." He bit back the ghost of a smile and brushed his tears with the palms of his hands.

"Are you all right?" she asked gently, almost caring.

"Not at all, actually." He took her hand and stood, then led her to the first pew behind them. The wood smelled strongly of beeswax, and the air was filled with incense and the prayers of ages. He sank back against the pew seat, still holding her hand. "I know not what happened to me, to my life, and the only thing that makes any sense to me now is that she is a witch who cast a spell upon me." Jane knew he meant Anne. "Yet I cannot go back. I cannot change what I have done."

"'Tis true none of us can go back," she said calmly, surprising herself with her tone, one that made her sound far more wise than she knew herself to be. "But we can all change the path we are on if we realize it is the wrong one."

"No one, it seems, but me has ever believed she was the true queen, which means with Katherine dead now, I am a widower. More appropriately, a never-married man. That is what I believe. But what do *you* believe, Jane?" His gaze was intense upon her and yet weary at the same time.

"Oh, Your Majesty, surely I am not qualified to contemplate such things," she demurred, lowering her eyes only slightly before she returned her gaze to his.

"And yet I do very much want to know your thoughts, even so."

"You know well I was devoted to Queen Katherine, so perhaps I am not the most impartial voice on the matter."

He leaned nearer. His breath was warm and slightly spiced. "Please, Jane."

She paused for a moment, considering whether or not to be truthful. "I do believe Queen Katherine was Your Majesty's true and lawful wife until her final breath."

"Which would make me a sinner and a widower, yet now a free man, able to remarry."

"My judgment is not the one that matters."

"In my eyes, it has become so."

"I would not think England would tolerate you denying a second wife in order to take a third. That is what I think."

"I have spoken intensively of divorce with Master Cromwell and Master Carew, and my lord Norfolk as well," he pondered. "All had long supported Anne and her brother, Lord Rochford, staunchly, but now, suddenly, they seem willing to counsel me in it."

So that was why she had seen less of them all in the queen's apartments since her return to court. She was surprised to feel a small burst of sympathy for those seeking to find their way to safety, like rats fleeing a sinking ship. She knew how that felt and did not envy anyone close to the queen in these critical days. Jane alone believed herself to be safe for how carefully and patiently she had played the game.

Henry extended his leg and grimaced. It was then that she noticed once again the thick bandage beneath his ecru-colored stocking. "Does it hurt?" she cautiously asked.

"Mostly when I stand. Although I would deny that to Carew or Brandon with my dying breath because they would never let me hear the end of it."

"It sounds like a competition between my own brothers."

"Oh, yes. Edward. And the other?"

"His name is Thomas."

"Oh, Thomas, yes, right, of course. I miss my own brother." He sighed. "Speaking of *The Imitation of Christ* reminds me of him, as much as it does the rest of my family, so I thank you for that."

He tipped his head back and exhaled deeply. She could hear how troubled he was. Even so, he still had not let go of her hand. "I need to be away from her, away from here, find the uncomplicated life again. I need to ride, to hunt, to go hawking as I did when I was a youth. Not to feel so tethered as I do by her . . . by this leg, or by these infernal headaches that torment me."

He let go of her hand then and began to massage his temples with both hands. His moods changed so swiftly, Jane saw, and it was a little frightening, although she did not let it show on her face. She had become quite expert at never showing her emotions.

"I am leaving for London by the morrow," he told her as he dropped his hands into his lap. "There are the Shrovetide celebrations there to which I am committed, and a final session of Parliament I must attend. 'Twill be good, I think, for me to be apart from the queen for a while. But not so good on my heart that I shall be parted from you."

"Your Majesty," Jane again demurred as he turned his eyes heavily upon her.

He touched the back of her wrist seductively with his fingertips.

"You mustn't act as if you do not know I have feelings for you,

Jane. Nor should you play too heartily that you feel nothing for me in response."

"You are a married man. I am afraid I must."

"You did not kiss me yesterday with the chaste heart you now profess." He smiled devilishly.

"'Tis virtuous to seek purity even if we fall short."

"Allow me to guess—Thomas à Kempis?"

Jane colored at his amused tone and cast her eyes downward yet again, expert now at displaying the humility her mother had so long desired her to cultivate. It was a signature move that seemed to work to her benefit, as her mother had promised it would long ago.

"I am only teasing you. I actually find your attempt at virtue incredibly seductive."

He drew closer then and very gently kissed her neck just below her earlobe, and Jane felt the heat from his touch race through her body as he moved his lips nearer her mouth. Then, as the last time, he stopped to kiss her cheek with the same tender, smoldering sensuality to which her body reacted. She did not love him as she did William. Too much of their lives and memories were still bound up in each other. But at least to herself, Jane could not deny that Henry had a seductive power that intrigued her, and she could see now how so many women had compromised themselves for him. Secretly, Jane had every intention of being one of them. Although more smartly and more carefully than they had. Life had shown her that there was really nothing else, nor any reason not to become one of his women, come what may. It was a good thing he did not suspect the experience her heart had gained. She would be too much like all the others if he did.

Henry pulled back then to collect himself. Jane reveled in the power she felt at seeing him excited. That she had done that to a man, much less the king, was like a potent drug, and already she wanted more of it. But she must remain patient. There was a role for her to play, and to win the prize she must continue to play it flawlessly.

Henry gently lifted her chin again, as she knew he would. "Do not be embarrassed, my little love, by what we do when we are alone."

She heard the word but assumed it was a mistake. He could not be in love already.

"Yet we are never truly alone. Our God is with us, always judging our every move."

"I shall not ever make you do anything you feel goes against God, Jane." He kissed her lips this time and held it, but she could feel he did not mean to push her in the shadow of the powerful God they shared and were both bound to. "Ah, but how you do stir my soul! I cannot promise I will not try to convince you that the act of love between us would not be right someday."

"It never shall be so long as Anne is your queen," she said so haltingly that he stopped, gazing at her deeply then, the green of his eyes completely mesmerizing her.

"That is one of the reasons I must leave here for a few days. I must have time to think, Jane, to be certain how to proceed. When I return, we will speak again."

"Unfortunately, I do not believe I shall be here when you return," she revealed.

"How can that be?"

"The queen does not like me and I am certain she will have me sent away in Your Majesty's absence."

She watched him stiffen. "That shall not happen. I will not allow it."

"It might be difficult to prevent what you are not here to see."

"Yet to be forewarned is to be forearmed. Your relation Francis Bryan is to go to France, and Brandon has gone to see to his estates, or I would have him look after you. Anne would never dare to go against Charles. But in his absence, Carew will be a sufficient protector. No one would cavil with him."

"'Tis true enough," Jane conceded. She did not want to feel the sudden fear she felt at the prospect of his departure, no matter who was left behind to keep her safe.

"I have something for you I have wanted to give you for a time now," he said. He reached up to his own neck then and unclasped something on a heavy gold chain that had been hidden beneath the collar of his broad black silk doublet.

He did not hand it to her but rather removed it from his own neck and placed it around hers. He leaned in as he hooked the chain beneath the fall of her headdress, and the musky scent of him—along with the power of who he was—became intoxicating. To Jane's surprise, she felt that private part of her beneath her gown stir hotly when he touched her. She shifted against it, then held up the pendant at the end of the chain. When she saw that it bore a small painted image of the king himself, she was stunned to see that it was eerily similar to the one he had once given Anne when he was married to Katherine. Jane shivered at the memory, but that only made the stirring inside of her that much more powerful.

"This is so you shall never be able to forget he who loves you. Although now it seems even more essential that you wear it so that you are reminded that no harm can come to you, so long as you hold me next to your heart," he declared, pressing the image against her chest with his own fingers, then meeting her gaze again. "Can you not say that you love me just a little in return, Jane?"

"If Your Majesty is free to love one day, it shall be you who will have my heart."

He clasped a hand to his own chest and gasped as though he had been struck. "Ah, she doth wound me, and yet I love best what I work for most heartily."

Jane knew her brothers would be proud of how well she was playing the game. Yet a part of her truly had begun to hope that one day Henry might wrest himself free of Anne Boleyn. No matter how unlikely that seemed for how many times Anne had drawn him back into her web, Jane was beginning to think she might actually want him even more than Anne Boleyn ever had.

The portion of the court that had stayed behind at Richmond after the king left for London had their own Shrovetide celebrations. Anne, who had recovered from her miscarriage, presided over a banquet the size and grandeur of which rivaled anything the king himself would have designed. Jane, Edward, Thomas, and Nicholas Carew sat across from the queen as the handsome young musician Mark Smeaton serenaded Anne with a tune called "By My Heart." Even those who favored the queen whispered how the mice did play when the cat was away. As her insufferably haughty brother, Lord Rochford, preened beside her on the dais, as though he, not Henry, were king, Anne batted her eyes and smiled girlishly at Smeaton. As she did, Carew whispered to Jane behind his hand.

"Now, you see, *that* is precisely what you do not want to do when dealing with our sovereign. 'Tis the hunt he favors, and in this case the queen is the one who is hunting Smeaton," he joked. "She and her brother are so close that Rochford is jealous of the attention she gives to other men, and Rochford's wife is jealous of him caring more about his sister. It really is all quite comically incendiary."

"Do you truly think so? I assumed she was only playing at one of those infamous games of courtly love of which everyone speaks."

"Perhaps it is so. And yet timing is everything, they say, and a husband who seeks a reason to be rid of a beautiful wife usually does not have far to look. Apparently, that is not a lesson this queen has ever learned."

"You believe the queen is with Master Smeaton?" Jane asked with a little gasp of genuine surprise.

"He would not be the first, and I doubt he will be the last, *if* she actually manages to keep her crown."

"You do not believe she will?"

"Is that very question not where *you* come in?" Carew smiled and turned his attention back to Smeaton, a slim, dark-haired youth with penetrating aqua-colored eyes. His attractiveness was obvious, even to Jane. "The king has asked me to keep an eye on you in his absence, and your brothers have asked me to counsel you in behavior to win the sovereign without the use of outright seduction."

Edward nodded in agreement. "I believe he will try to bed our sister upon his return from London," he interjected, leaning forward to stay out of earshot of the queen.

"His Majesty vowed he would not press me," Jane defended a little tepidly.

"Yes, that would be the likely course of events," Carew agreed with Edward.

"Some women have done well by it," Thomas observed, also leaning in to join the conversation. "Mistress Blount is now a countess, after all."

"And my own charming wife lives in the lap of luxury," Carew said with self-effacing humor.

"But for every one of those, there are a dozen Mary Boleyns who believed the way to his heart was between his legs," Edward observed.

Vulgar but true, thought Jane.

As a lively tune was struck, Anne joined Smeaton to sing a duet. George Boleyn appeared at their table then, and Jane was not certain what he might have overheard.

"Enjoying yourselves, are you?" he asked rhetorically, and Jane felt her heart beat a little faster, his acid tone apparent to them all. "I am surprised at you, Carew. You know what happens when you lie down with dogs."

"I have known you long enough to realize the result is fleas," Nicholas countered without missing a beat.

"Forgive me." Boleyn bowed dramatically. "I had forgotten what liberty the king's Gentleman of the Chamber feels he is afforded with the queen's brother."

Anger kindled brightly between the two former friends over the post that George Boleyn had wanted but Carew had won. George leaned nearer to make himself heard over the spirited music and Anne's off-key singing. "Are you certain you want to cast your lot in with *her?*" he asked rudely, glancing at Jane. "Nicholas, be reasonable. We were the best of friends. You were there from the beginning. You saw how it was with my sister and the king. He sacrificed everything for *her.*"

Carew leveled his eyes in a serious way that Jane had never seen from the usually carefree courtier. "It appears to be a decision His Majesty regrets more with each passing day."

"This little mouse will *not* supplant my sister!" Boleyn declared angrily. "No matter what the trio of you do to put *her* forward!" Boleyn's eyes swiftly darkened in the silence. He steadied himself, then added, "Well, then. I see that our friendship has indeed come to an end. I am sorry about that, Nicholas. And believe me, I am a much more agreeable friend than I am an enemy."

Anne was flirting even more boldly now with Mark Smeaton, not seeming to care who saw them. Her wounded pride was making her careless, Jane thought. That would never be her. Every single step she took from here forward would be planned and plotted. The best part was that no one expected anything like ambition or skill of the little mouse, and Jane found that she quite liked it that way.

Jane returned to her room late after the banquet. She was exhausted, since it took a great deal more energy to maintain the image of demure innocence now that it did not come naturally to her. Edward's wife, Anne, had come with her, and she sank onto the bed as Jane drew off her own hood. She went then and opened the carved chest at the foot of the bed where she kept all of her ornamented headdresses. She was preparing to toss it aside with the others when she caught sight of William's blue kerchief from long ago, hidden beneath the layers of fabric.

Her heart surged in bittersweet remembrance, as it always did when she thought of him or anything that had happened between them. Anne followed her gaze to the chest, and her expression became sympathetic.

"If you are planning to master the art of being unreadable, sister, you have much more to learn."

Jane tossed her hood on top of everything, burying the kerchief, along with the memories. "Just missing home a little, I suppose," she lied. "It has been a long day."

"Edward told me about the boy from Wiltshire. I hear he is at court in the employ of Master Cromwell now, is he not? That must be awkward for you since you were engaged to him for a brief time."

"My brother would do well to keep quiet about things he does not understand," she said more harshly than she meant to.

"Forgive me," Anne replied. "I should not have pried like that. We do not know each other that well yet, after all. I only thought perhaps, because our two families—"

"'Tis you who must forgive *me*," Jane said with a sigh. "I am unaccustomed to much of what has happened to me these past few days, and even though I believed I was handling it well, I clearly am not."

"'Tis that Dormer fellow, isn't it? The one married to Sir William Sidney's daughter." Jane sank wearily onto the floor in front of the open chest without responding. "I have seen more than once the way he looks at you."

Jane wanted to tell her. She ached to tell someone, especially another woman who might understand the journey her heart had been on with William all these years. Slowly she drew out the kerchief, pressing it to her breast as if she could take in the memories that the touch of that fabric alone brought to her. Then she looked back at Anne. She was pretty, Jane thought, in an elegant, aristocratic way that made true empathy unlikely for someone like her. Yet, still, Jane felt she must tell someone.

"I have never spoken aloud of him to any woman."

"There is a first time for everything," Anne said with soft encouragement.

"I am going to need a stout bit of ale to even attempt it. But things have become so complicated here lately." Jane pressed the kerchief back into the carved chest.

"We've got a flagon here of the king's best wine. Will that do?"

Jane cringed a little at that thought, considering she was about to share the history of her great love for another man while not only drinking the king's finest, but wearing his image across her heart as well. And yet, no matter what Henry had awakened in her, how she did long for William still! Jane doubted that would ever change, no matter what the future held.

"I cannot find a way to speak about it just now," she finally said when she knew that the words and the full depth of their meaning would not come to her. "But perhaps one day."

"I would welcome that, Jane," said her sister-in-law, the only woman in Anne's retinue she could even partially trust. "And I will be there if you do. For now we must make certain that the king does not see the exchange of glances between the two of you that I have. The last man who was caught—the poet Thomas Wyatt—was banished from court and has not been back since. I do not suppose things will bode any better for Master Smeaton once word of tonight's behavior becomes more widely known. We should all be well warned by that."

Two days later, Thomas Cromwell sat motionless, the royal proclamation hanging from his veined hand. So it had begun in earnest, William thought, as he watched his employer. Both tried to make sense of the king's order that Cromwell and his staff vacate his hard-won rooms down the all-important connecting corridor from the king's official apartments. He knew that Cromwell must handle his public reaction with dignity and aplomb, for there would be no changing the command since it involved a woman. He had told William that he had learned this lesson well from his old tutor, Cardinal Wolsey, and feared doing otherwise.

"I have had these rooms as royal secretary for many years," Cromwell said flatly, turning his haggard expression from William and gazing out the window down onto the king's knot garden.

"Does it say who is to take them, sir?" William asked cautiously.

"His Majesty's Chief Gentleman of the Chamber and his wife, apparently."

"Edward Seymour?"

Cromwell's tired eyes were full of disappointment. "That surprises you when everyone at court whispers of the king's growing attraction to Seymour's plain-faced sister?"

William betrayed nothing of his feelings for Jane. Though he was well apprised of the Seymours' ambitions, he was shocked that their plans were coming to fruition so rapidly. Suddenly, he was not so certain that he could go along with them.

"The queen shall not be amused by this turn of events," Cromwell blandly warned.

The consequences of the king's newest obsession seemed to William like a gathering storm from which none of them could escape.

"Would you excuse me, sir?" William asked suddenly, cutting off the encounter. He knew where he must go, and he must go there now. Before Cromwell could respond, William bowed to him, then turned and very quickly went out of the room.

Jane opened the door and stepped back. His was the last face she expected to see in her private rooms in the daylight hours, and she reacted to his appearance with a little gasp.

"I must speak to you," William said urgently, threatening to burst through the doorway without invitation. His expression was filled with panic.

"I have company," Jane managed to respond, backing away so he could see Edward's wife, Anne, perched on Jane's bed. She regarded William with a curious smile.

"Well, now, this is awkward," Anne remarked.

William looked at Anne; then his gaze slid back to Jane.

"I would not come here if it were not important," he said.

"I can keep a secret." Anne smiled.

"I trust her," Jane confirmed. "Have we any other choice?"

He came into the room then, and Jane quickly closed the door. He loomed before her, tall and powerful, full of unspoken desire. Jane blushed at his nearness for what it always awakened inside of her.

"Master Cromwell is being moved from his apartments, and they are doing it this evening in the dead of night to avoid a scandal. Your brother Edward and you, Lady Anne, will be moved in directly afterward."

Jane felt a jolt of surprise. Henry had told her many things in the times they had spent together, and yet still she had not expected this. At least, not so soon. Jane was not certain she was ready to play on such a grand field, feeling after so much work that this could become her undoing.

"Oh, dear." Anne covered her mouth to hold back a smile. "A scandal seems unavoidable."

"He wants you, Jane," William said desperately.

"And I want him. If it comes to that," she shot back too quickly. "There is really nothing else for me anyway," she amended, feeling guilty even as the words left her lips.

William burst forward then and gripped her arms tightly as they hung at her sides. "'Tis not too late. You can stop this!"

"Why would I? You have a wife already."

He hung his head, obviously stung by her clipped tone and the harsh truth in it. Jane looked at him in silence, wishing he would say something to argue that point, yet knowing there were no words that would make any difference.

"Might we speak privately for a moment?" he asked futilely as Anne arched her brows at him.

"I cannot see how any good would come of *that*," she said flatly.

William shot a quick glance at the door; then he looked desperately back at Jane. She could feel the way his heart was torn in two. "What do you want, Jane? Tell me that."

He was pleading with her. Pleading for something that could never be.

"What I want does not matter. It never has."

"It *always* has," he corrected her sadly. "It always will."

The energy between them was a charged thing, and Jane felt her heart beating very fast. William reached up tentatively and lightly brushed Jane's cheek with the back of his hand, in full view of Jane's sister-in-law. "You have always had the most extraordinary skin. The first time I touched you, I remember thinking it was like gossamer," he said, his voice tinged with sadness. "Be careful, won't you?"

"I have my brothers and Master Carew to watch out for me," she replied haltingly, trying to be optimistic. Yet both of them knew what danger lay in wait for her in the coming days.

"Then be happy. You so richly deserve that."

"I do intend to try."

"I will be around as much as I can if you need me."

"I wish you would not. Seeing you only makes it more difficult." She had not expected it, but her eyes filled with tears as the words left her lips.

William paused for another moment. "Then I shall do what I can to contribute to your happiness."

As he left her in the doorway, Jane found herself anxious for the king's return to Richmond. She certainly felt safer when he was near.

Or was it love?

Early one afternoon, Jane sat in the queen's presence chamber at a card table of carved oak, along with Edward; his wife, Anne; Thomas; and Nicholas and Elizabeth Carew. As bright winter light streamed in through the diamond-shaped windowpanes, casting jewels against the tapestry-covered walls, they played another game of primero. While Jane was required to be present as a lady-in-waiting, she did her best these days until the king's return from London to make herself scarce in her duties, particularly as the queen was often in a foul humor, unless Mark Smeaton or her brother, George, was with her.

The king's most recent mistress, Margaret Shelton, was scheduled to marry Sir Henry Norris in the spring, and Anne seemed to delight in flirting with him right in front of her own attendant as a way to pass the time. She was in an adjoining room now with the two courtiers.

Turnabout, in Anne Boleyn's world, had always been fair play.

As Carew dealt the next hand of cards, they could hear Anne's throaty yet girlish giggle through the walls.

"Smeaton and Norris would do well to take care when the king returns," Thomas observed. "Do neither of them see how the winds of change have been stirred?"

"Do keep your voice down. You sound like a silly child," Edward snapped in a condescending tone.

"I would prefer childish to arrogant," Thomas retorted.

"Gentlemen, enough!" Carew intervened. "This is not a game we play against each other."

There had never been an outright display of sibling rivalry between them before, and it surprised Jane. After all, did they not have the same goal in mind?

"I only meant these are uncertain times, even for the queen," Thomas explained.

"We know what you meant," Edward pushed.

"Edward, please," Anne said, stilling her husband with a gentle hand on his arm. "There is no need for us to fight among ourselves."

Jane sensed someone enter the room behind her, and she turned to see Cromwell with William Dormer, having come to play cards with the others. Cromwell wore an unadorned black coat over his growing girth; William presented a stark contrast to his mentor in a puff-sleeved doublet and trunk hose of blue and gold-striped satin. When Anne glanced at her, Jane quickly lowered her gaze, as was her custom. Edward, however, saw the exchange.

"What is it?"

"It is nothing, my dear, truly," Anne said.

"Do not tell me that! The greatest care must be taken by all of us now. One false move could spell disaster," he whispered furiously just as the king's private page, Francis Weston, who always traveled with Henry, approached the table. Wearing the royal livery of green velvet with a Tudor rose emblazoned on his doublet, Weston bowed to Jane. As he did, the double doors were opened by two guards, and the queen stormed in. Margaret Wyatt and Lady Rochford were with her. Biting back a little smile as she curtsied along with the others, Jane wondered what drama was about to unfold.

Her smile fell quickly when Weston offered to Jane his gloved hand, which contained a letter. The folded vellum was stamped with the king's seal. In his other hand was a velvet pouch clinking with coins. From the corner of her eye, Jane could see Anne's approach. She heard Elizabeth Carew's little intake of breath, and she could sense her brothers' trepidation.

Jane was at a loss. If she accepted these items, she was making a public statement about her intentions with another woman's husband. The minute she did, Anne would become the scorned woman, and Jane would become the aggressor. Without Henry here to protect her, the danger was great, especially with Anne's contingent of supporters surrounding her.

This was about to be the performance of Jane's life.

"His Gracious Majesty bids me to give you these, mistress, with his compliments, and instructs you to respond to his words after you have read them so that I may return to him at York Place with something to warm his heart," Weston explained.

Anne and her retinue were only steps away. Neither William nor Cromwell moved. Jane's heart thumped with dread. It felt as if she were diving off a cliff as she fell dramatically to her knees before Weston.

"Kind sir, I pray you remind the king on my behalf that I am a gentlewoman from a good and honorable family. My own brother here has been much loved and rewarded by him. Yet for me, personally, sir, there are no greater riches than my honor, and I would not harm that for anything."

Weston looked embarrassed, realizing then that they had an ever-growing audience for what he had expected to be a simple exchange. "Mistress Seymour, please understand I cannot return these to His Majesty. It is, after all, only money, which he prays you shall put to some good use for your own pleasure while the two of you are parted. I am given to understand the letter fully explains his wishes," he said, lowering his voice, though everyone in the chamber—including the queen—could hear what they were saying.

"Pray, tell our most gracious sovereign that if he still wishes to make me some gift, let it be on the occasion when God sees fit to make for me some honorable match."

Jane knew she had said the word "honorable" a little too boldly because she could hear Carew groan beneath his breath. The line she walked at that moment could not have been more dangerous.

In the silence that ensued, Jane took the sealed letter. The stares upon her were weighty. With the greatest sincerity, she pressed the vellum to her lips, then gave it back to Weston, unopened.

"But, mistress, I simply cannot—," Weston began, but his words fell away beneath Anne Boleyn's cold stare. It appeared that Weston knew he had fallen into an unenviable situation. "Mistress Seymour," he said, bowing to her before he turned and left the chamber to the echo of gasps and whispers.

The queen clapped in a harsh, discordant manner, interrupting the chatter.

"How very noble of you, Mistress Seymour," she said bitingly. "My husband has always had an eye for the ladies. Although, in your case, I cannot imagine how *you* suit his tastes."

Jane cast her glance downward. She was buying herself time. There was no sincerity in the action.

"Have you nothing to say, Mistress Seymour?"

"I believe my sister's response to the king speaks for itself, does it not?" Edward intervened then, all of them knowing that his important post in the king's privy chamber carried enough weight to protect him.

Anne arched an ebony brow. For a moment no one in the room

knew where she might next cast her anger, but her posture was as stiff as a bare winter tree. Then her gaze seized on Jane's pendant.

"What do you wear so boldly around your neck, Mistress Seymour? Pray, do show me, as it looks quite beyond your financial means."

"It looks *just* like the one His Majesty gave to you," George Boleyn observed drily.

Jane reached up and grasped the pendant, but it was too late to conceal it. She watched Anne's gaze narrow into something quite menacing, and her posture grew more tense, like that of a cat about to strike. Jane struggled to hide her fear, since fear was something seized upon by seasoned courtiers. Right now, she thought, Francis Bryan, her longtime protector, could not return swiftly enough for her liking from his post in France, since she could not be entirely certain yet where the king's loyalty would end up. His marriage to Anne had been too tumultuous and too lengthy to yet completely trust that.

"'Tis nothing, Your Highness, but a trinket," Jane tried to say as Anne approached. Steady catlike steps narrowed the charged chasm between them. She could smell Anne's noxious lilac-water scent as she drew closer.

"Then you will not mind showing it to me," Anne said as Jane clutched the king's image more protectively. "The workmanship is too familiar for it to be only a trinket, Mistress Seymour."

"If you please, Your Highness, it can be of no significance," Nicholas Carew tried to intercede, but the queen cut him off sharply.

"Silence, traitor! You have nothing of value to say any longer. The company you currently keep has surely poisoned you."

Jane saw William cross the room toward them then, ready to insert himself into the dangerous mix. She longed to warn him that he must not implicate himself, but she knew she had no more control over William now than she ever had before.

Suddenly, Anne lunged at Jane, snatching the pendant from her chest. Jane gasped and stumbled backward, instinctively pulling the pendant out of harm's way. In one swift movement, Thomas also lunged into the scuffle. But it was Jane's own hand that fiercely batted the queen's fingertips away.

"Why, you brutal little she-devil!" She recoiled and cried out with a wail of pain, then lurched forward again, pulling Jane downward as they tumbled to the wood-plank floor.

The collection of ladies shrieked in horror as skirts flew and arms flailed. One of the queen's shoes came off as Edward, Nicholas, Thomas, and George Boleyn all dove into the mix in an attempt to stop the skirmish.

"Let me see it!" Anne screeched as her hands and arms batted about, her legs kicking every which way against those who were more powerful and trying to restrain them both.

"Your Highness knows well what it is!" Jane finally blurted out.

Anne disentangled herself from Jane, and George caught his sister by the arms as she rose to her feet. The irony of how history was repeating itself with this pendant had not been lost on any of those present. One star rose while another fell. Just as it had been for Katherine of Aragon before her, so now it was with Anne Boleyn. From the corner of her eye, Jane saw her sister-in-law restrain William, whispering words of caution to him; Thomas, Edward, and Nicholas hunched against the wall, catching their breaths from being kicked in the chests by the furious queen. Jane cautiously stood, alone yet defiant. There was blood on the back of her hand where Anne had scratched her. A deeper scratch wound along the milky white column of her neck.

It seemed as though hours passed before Anne shook off George's grasp, walked calmly toward Jane, and took the pendant, which bore the image she already knew she would see, in her hand.

"A tolerably favorable likeness, considering His Majesty has grown more fat since the portrait he had painted for me," Anne said icily. "You were right not to accept his latest gift, since you shall never keep him. You are just like the others. In the door, out the door. Is that not right, Lady Carew?" she shot venomously.

Elizabeth lowered eyes in embarrassment as they quickly filled with tears. Jane noticed Nicholas grimace beside her at the mention of the royal affair, which had been cruelly brought back to light with Anne's remark.

"Be careful, sister. Perhaps you should take a moment," George cautioned.

Anne's desperate expression made her look like a feral animal as she continued to clutch the king's painted image glittering around another woman's neck.

"While His Majesty is away, I want you and your jewelry out of my sight," she said evenly, boring daggers into Jane with her bottomless dark eyes. "Is that clear, Mistress Seymour?"

Jane only nodded, afraid, not of Anne Boleyn, but of what contemptuous slight might issue from her own mouth if she spoke.

"And mark my words, mistress," Anne further warned as Jane backed away from her properly, as she knew to do, "there shall be *no* divorce between myself and the king, so you are wasting your time."

Later that same day, as the sun began to set behind a row of bare-branched lilac trees, poised liked sentinels outside of Cromwell's tall leaded windows, William could feel himself begin to breathe again. He was relieved that his wife had gone home to their estate in

Kent for a few days with her father, because he was not at all certain he could have kept the heartbreak from his eyes.

He did not love Mary, but he had no wish to hurt her.

Across from him, at a large desk littered with papers and folios, an inkwell, and a dish of blotting sand, Cromwell sat frowning, his deep-set eyes casting over some endless communications that he must reply to in His Majesty's absence. As he silently watched his benefactor, William's mind wandered back to the events of the day. He had shocked himself at how closely he had come to restraining the queen in order to defend Jane. William did not truly know what lengths he might have gone to out of love for her . . . until today.

Cromwell pressed the king's seal into the soft wax on the folded vellum. He blew on it, then handed it to William across the desk. "See this goes to Ambassador Chapuys. 'Tis for the emperor's eyes alone," Cromwell grumbled just as the door opened so suddenly that both of them jumped. William's back had been to the door, so he did not see her until she was halfway across the room. The queen was about to confront them.

"You knew about this all along, did you not? You could have stopped it! You are as much a traitor to me as Carew and my own uncle Norfolk!" Anne was raging so boldly that her face was mottled crimson, making her seem ugly and old.

"I have no idea what Your Highness is referring to," Cromwell said with masterful calm as he and William rose, then bowed.

"Pray, look me boldly in the eye, sir, and tell your queen you did not know in advance that you were moving out of your suite to make way for that Seymour clod and his wife! Now there shall be a clear path for the harlot to maintain her precious honor as she dances blithely into her mésalliance, and thus into the king's bed!"

Cromwell cast down the stamp of the royal seal that was still in his hand, jowls shaking. "My opinion on the matter was not asked nor given, Your Highness."

"Oh, bollocks!" she swore with most unfeminine verve. "You have cast in your lot with the Seymour girl just like everyone else! Lie to me *not*!"

"I have cast my lot nowhere, Your Highness," he calmly defended, knowing, as they all did, that a measured tone was the thing that angered her most of all.

"I thought we had an understanding, Master Cromwell, you and I. How many hours did we closet together and speak of the new religion and of reform?"

"Not so many hours, Your Highness, as I did closet with the king on matters of divorce."

"You are an imbecile and a fool!" she raged, and William saw hauteur replaced by desperation. "I am Anne Boleyn, Queen of England!"

"Queen Katherine wielded the same power, and where is she now? Where is my mentor, Thomas Wolsey?" he asked with such calm precision that she froze for a moment.

Even William was afraid to breathe in the echo of the question.

"You go too far, sir," Anne warned. "Perhaps you should take a lesson from your precious mentor on what happens to those who betray the Crown!"

"That is a lesson we *all* might do well to take, *Your Highness*," Cromwell intoned, trying his best to defend himself, but what would happen next was anyone's guess.

After she had gone, they could still hear the echo of the collective footsteps of the queen and her guards. Cromwell sank heavily back into his chair, letting out a groan as he rubbed his face with one large hand. William lowered himself into his own chair a moment later, seeing his employer's troubled expression.

"Do you believe she meant to threaten you, my lord?" William asked as Cromwell took a stack of papers and absently straightened them.

"I do not suppose the queen ever says anything she does not mean to."

"Have you any recourse to protect yourself?"

Cromwell arched a single beetle brow as he straightened another stack of papers in that same passively self-soothing way that had become his custom. "You need not worry about your livelihood, Dormer, if that is what you are after. Your post with me is secure—wherever my rooms shall be."

"'Tis not my post about which I am concerned, my lord Cromwell, for I am a loyal servant to you for granting me an opportunity at court when no one else did."

Cromwell studied William discerningly then. "Why, William, I did not know you cared," he returned with a clever smirk and a slight lift of his brows. "Yet I shall admit to being concerned about Her Highness lately."

"While I was not at court then, stories of what happened to Wolsey are horrifying to this day. One can hardly imagine the heights from which he fell so swiftly."

"I suppose all of us are less safe with this new talk of divorce. A cat strikes out most viciously once it is wounded, and Anne is certainly that," Cromwell observed.

"Might I ask if you believe the rumors could be true that he will divorce her?" William pressed.

"Henry found his way round marriage once. I suppose that somewhere in her heart, assuming she has one, Anne Boleyn knows he might do it again. Thus, the drama."

"And you, as his most-learned counsel, would be just the man to bring it about, which she knows full well?"

Cromwell's expression bore no traces of pride in his power but grew more troubled. His brows knit together as he considered the question. "Very well, young Sir William, if you would like to engage me in a bit of folly, what would you have me do about the threat the queen poses to me?"

William felt entirely out of his league with such a weighty question. Even finessing Cromwell into this much of a conversation on the subject seemed just short of miraculous to him, as he was still largely inexperienced in court matters. But he must do this for Jane; he must plant the seed because she had asked him to. Because he loved her, and he owed her that much.

"Well, Master Cromwell, I can say only what my father used to say: in war, a target cannot strike back if it has already been soundly hit. I was never quite certain what that meant until I met our queen."

Cromwell's frown lengthened into a cautious smile. "Such a ruthless streak you have. But I fear His Majesty could not put England through the scandal of another divorce without sound cause."

"Would England not find infidelity sound enough?"

Cromwell fell silent and William felt he had overstepped his bounds. White-hot dread snaked through him as the silence lengthened into what seemed an eternity. Then, to his complete surprise, he realized that Cromwell was actually considering the notion he had cautiously proposed.

"Well, in a purely speculative way, of course, there would need to be an evildoer upon whom one might assign the crime. Have you someone in mind, Dormer?"

The joking tone between them had changed swiftly. Their conversation had shifted, and William knew in that instant that the next words he uttered might have the power to change history.

"I can only ask if you have not seen Her Highness in the company of Master Smeaton. There seems not a reason to falsify something if there is evidence of misconduct before us." William felt himself choke as he spoke the indictment. But it was not a lie. He had seen for himself these past months the queen's open flirtation with the handsome young musician. He had also witnessed her hatred toward Jane, which inflamed him. Anne Boleyn was a brazenly selfish, spiteful woman who must be stopped. Even if that meant the end of any hope for a future with Jane.

To William's complete surprise, Cromwell's clever smirk returned.

"Well, now. I would have guessed your sights would be set on Sir Henry Norris," he said with a grin.

The court was rife with rumors that Norris was dragging his heels about marrying Margaret Shelton, to whom he was betrothed, because of his wild and inappropriate obsession with the queen. William had seen it, as well as her flirtation with Mark Smeaton, now that he thought about it. And the queen always seemed most closely attentive to her own brother, Lord Rochford. It was all rather unseemly, the way she appeared to make excuses to whisper to George Boleyn, to take his hand in public and kiss the knuckles slowly, which even by country standards seemed to him slightly incestuous.

"I shall certainly watch for that in these next days and go from there," Cromwell finally declared, growing suddenly more serious again. "But if His Majesty does seek a divorce, and then finds a way to marry Jane Seymour afterward, mark me, my boy, you will have the satisfaction of knowing that our king has you alone to thank for it."

Chapter Fifteen

February 1536
Hampton Court

*I*t was another evening of revels and music performed by a troupe of minstrels from Venice—and dodging the queen's angry stares and muttered comments to her loyal retinue of ladies. Jane was defensive, weary of the daily stress of waiting upon the very woman she meant to depose. But this evening promised one difference.

Thanks be to God, the court had moved to Greenwich and the king had returned from London.

Jane actually found herself excited to see him and to feel that spark between them once again. It was a spark that might well become a flame . . . if not for a heart so full of William, in spite of how they had quarreled.

It always seemed so hopeless. It could lead only to someone's unhappiness. Or worse yet, their doom. Like Cardinal Wolsey. Or Sir Thomas More, both of whom Henry believed had betrayed him. What would he think if he knew of Jane's abiding love for William?

Henry VIII seemed a very unpredictable character when it came to those for whom he greatly cared. For those unfortunate few who had experienced the extremes of his emotions.

Jane felt a chill even as her heart strangely stirred at the thought of him.

She moved elegantly now, still largely unnoticed by the others, in a gown of amber velvet with a long beaded plastron. It was far different from the one in which she had first been received at court so many years ago. She felt like an entirely different person in it. What set it apart was the traditional gabled English hood, rather than the far more fashionable French hood that most of the court women—the smart younger ones, particularly—donned in deference to the queen.

Anne still preferred all things French, which Jane disliked for her memories of her time there.

And she must do everything she could to set herself apart.

Jane had taken to heart her brothers' and Nicholas Carew's counsel, and she had every intention now of carrying through with their instructions. She could not be more beautiful than Anne Boleyn, but she could make certain that she was a great deal more wise.

As was her custom, Jane stood in the background of the collection of brightly clad women, hidden mainly from view by the hoods of Margaret Shelton, Lady Margaret Douglas, and Lady Jane Rochford. She was watching Anne's open flirtation now with Francis Weston and Henry Norris, and Jane was unable to believe how brazen she was in it. As Henry had spent the afternoon hawking with Charles Brandon, his other courtiers were free to attend to the queen while they waited for the king to grace them with his presence. Anne reveled, as usual, in the attention. Mark Smeaton sat nearby, quietly strumming his lute to entertain them. And, it seemed, to keep a watchful eye on her.

"Oh, now, my lord Weston," Anne said, laughing as playfully as a young girl, which was unseemly to Jane for how little of the girl there was left in this queen. "You would do well to take care of such playful overtures for how many spies surround us. Courtly games can be seen as much more by some."

"When the cat's away, we all do play the more," Norris added flirtatiously.

"I fear Sir Norris needs not such an excuse, as he attends Your Highness far more than he does poor Mistress Shelton, even in the presence of the Great Cat," Francis Weston quipped, seeing how Norris was ignoring his betrothed, who stood nearby.

Jane watched Anne's expression sour. She could almost see the thoughts churning around behind her dark eyes. Jane's sympathies for Henry increased with his wife's every giggle. Anne was unparalleled in her self-absorption, Jane thought.

"Poor, dear Weston, I fear you indict Norris only because you want our dear Madge for yourself."

The silence that followed was broken by muffled snickers. Weston nodded to Anne with a flourish, then said, "'Tis true that I *do* love only one in your household."

"And who might that be?" Anne asked with a playful little smile, clearly toying with him.

"Why, Your Highness, of course," he replied with a bashful smile and a wink.

To her credit, Anne knew the danger in such a revelation. She bolted to her feet, her smile evaporating instantly, since everyone present could hear the exchange. Silence fell like a powerful, heavy thing as she swiftly left the room, the swish of her skirts the only sound in the vast, beamed gallery.

"Well, now, *that* was awkward," her brother's wife, Anne, remarked in Jane's ear, as it was her custom to say.

"Indeed it was."

"At first I thought Her Highness was entertaining Master Smeaton, but did you see the look between the queen and Weston just now?"

"'Twould have been difficult to miss," said Jane.

"The queen plays with fire, I fear."

"She seems to fear the heat very little," Jane remarked coolly.

She did not see Cromwell behind her near the door with the powerful Duke of Norfolk, who was newly returned to court from the diplomatic mission to France. She missed the conspiratorial glance between them as well, one that acknowledged their mutual feeling that the queen was destined for a great fall.

It was not until the banquet that evening that Jane finally saw the king herself.

As a statement against what she had witnessed earlier between the queen and Weston, Jane wore the king's pendant more prominently over a bodice designed to show it off. Part of her was surprised at her own hubris in doing so. She had also chosen not to hide a scar on her neck that she had received during her fight with Anne.

Yet for all of her daring, Jane felt sheltered on the arm of her brother Thomas and her protector, Nicholas Carew. Edward and Anne Seymour followed closely behind. As they walked into the swirling mix of music, candles, and laughter, her sister-in-law had a new, haughty air about her as the family rose to prominence, but at least she was pleasant enough to Jane—her new confidante—and at the end of the day, that was really all that mattered to a girl who needed the reassurance of female support now more than ever.

Lord, but he looked magnificent. That was her first thought as the king strode regally into the room amid trumpet fanfare and cheers hailing his return. Charles Brandon and Francis Bryan, newly returned from France, flanked him, all three elegantly dressed and bejeweled, their velvet caps plumed, laughing and joking as if they had not a care in the world.

In spite of everything against them, Jane felt her heart race as she caught Henry's eye from the center of the crowd. She felt herself flush with as much excitement as embarrassment to be singled out with a prominent nod. Perhaps it truly was not a dream that she was meant to be someone meaningful to England's king.

He approached Jane openly then, pulling her toward him through the crowd. He was smiling broadly as he drew her against his wide, slashed-velvet sleeve, then greeted each of her brothers and kissed the back of Anne Seymour's hand.

"I trust, my lady, that you are enjoying your new accommodations?" he asked Edward's wife, a woman to whom he had never publicly paid the slightest attention before now.

Jane had been in her company many times and had no idea he even knew Anne Seymour. Clearly, it was not just Jane's own status that was rapidly changing. Still, driven by self-preservation, Jane surveyed the room for signs of the queen while Henry spoke to Anne. She was relieved for the moment not to see her.

"Your Majesty's generosity is humbling. We have yet to fully take it all in," Anne said with appropriate flattery and a deep curtsy.

"Since our accommodations are so near to each other now, I am certain we shall all become the very best of friends," Henry said magnanimously. "Edward, you shall keep us on our toes in that regard?" he said, chuckling affably.

And then he saw the scar on Jane's neck and his smile swiftly fell. "Jane?"

She curtsied clumsily. "Your Majesty."

"You have been injured. Pray, tell us how."

"'Twas only a scratch, sire."

"It may well be a lance blow to your exquisitely gentle flesh for how it wounds me to gaze upon it."

Jane lifted her hand to cover her neck in mock embarrassment. He saw the pendant then, and she could see him putting the two elements together as his copper brows lifted in sudden surprise. "Lady Seymour, my new friend, I trust *you* shall speak the truth of this to me? Know you how this wound occurred to our dear Jane?"

Brandon and Carew exchanged a worried glance. Jane could feel the conflict thrust upon Anne, and she suddenly regretted the calculated move not to hide the evidence of her encounter with the queen.

"Speak up, girl, when your king commands!" Brandon prodded in the silence that fell.

"It came by the queen, Your Majesty," Anne finally replied and lowered her eyes.

"The queen?" the king asked incredulously.

"She was not pleased by my good sister's choice of jewelry, apparently, Your Majesty."

Again Henry glanced at the pendant bearing his own image. "'Twas I, then, who caused this wound?"

No one dared at first to answer as the musicians in the gallery above played on with a lively tune. Over the music, the king said, "Jane, is this true?"

"She is the queen, sire. As her humble servant, I did not think to question her displeasure at me."

"So I have scarred your exquisite flesh in this way by not protecting you properly." He seemed truly to care, and that struck her. His face blanched and the genial smile was gone from his expression.

"Perhaps I should not have worn it," Jane weakly offered, hoping he could not tell that she did not mean it.

Suddenly, Cromwell was upon them, listening intently. Then William, like a shadow, was behind him as well. God's blood! Why was he always there, looking at her with those eyes? Silently reminding her of who she used to be when she was trying so hard to move on and become someone else?

"Would Your Majesty like me to call your physician for the lady?"

"At once, Cromwell."

William frowned, and Jane could not bear to look at him any longer. What she felt for the king was as complex as what she felt for William. It was not an easy road any of them trod.

"This must be dealt with immediately," the king decreed, still frowning as he nodded to Jane. "Forgive me, but I must speak with the queen. Pray, stay and enjoy your evening. I shall call upon you anon."

Jane knew there would be no stopping him. He was angry. As Henry turned to leave, Jane's gaze went from Henry to William. Their eyes met. His expression held jealousy; she knew hers held disappointment.

"Do you think you might actually have brought about the end of them?" Anne Seymour quietly asked Jane as they stood stock-still amid the music and revelry after the king had gone.

"Anything that happens to Anne Boleyn has been brought about entirely by herself," Nicholas Carew said.

An hour later, a page bent over Jane's shoulder as everyone dined and informed her that the king desired to closet privately with her. She was to go directly to the Seymours' new apartments, which she knew connected with His Majesty's own. Just before her summons, the queen entered the great hall and sat beside her brother, Lord

Rochford, without much fanfare, and certainly not with her customary merriment.

As Jane rose, so did Edward. "You cannot go alone in this tense new atmosphere. It would not be safe. I shall accompany you. No one will think anything of a brother and sister departing together for their accommodations."

"Unless those people are wise enough to remember the location of those accommodations, or to notice that the king and Jane are conspicuously absent together," Anne remarked.

Jane could feel the snap and crackle of change in the air as she and Edward followed the silent page down one long gallery after another until they came to Edward's new apartments. At the closed door, illuminated by a flaming torch, Edward turned to his sister, took her hands up, and held them tightly. Jane could not remember a greater moment of intimacy between them in all her life. But she was important to him now. She was critical to *all* of the Seymours.

"I know this is a difficult time for you, sister. Much is expected of you from all of us without a great deal of assurance from any one, least of all the king. But we have all changed much since our naive childhood days in the Wiltshire countryside, and I think with a little sly work, we Seymours can all give the Boleyns a proper challenge."

"It is your desire that I become queen?" Jane asked tentatively, still wanting his approval.

"With every fiber of my being. Do you wish it for yourself?"

A smiling image of William danced across her mind then, rich and full enough to be real, but Jane pushed it back stubbornly. *You cannot do that to me any longer. You made your choice; now I am making mine...* "Unlikely as I am for the role, I am beginning to want it anyway. But you and Thomas must not forsake me in this. It is all rather daunting to go up against her."

"We are here for you, sister. So is Anne, Carew, his wife, Elizabeth, and a silently growing faction who disapprove of that Boleyn woman pretending to be queen."

A faction? Little Jane Seymour had her own faction? She felt herself tremble at the prospect as the page pulled back the tall, carved door, ushering in a cold gust of air.

"I assume His Majesty would prefer I leave you now and return to the banquet," Edward joked. "You can do this, Jane," he encouraged.

"I do care for him a little."

"Make him believe it is more than a little, and you shall have the world at your feet," he said.

Henry was slumped over in a tall padded chair, head in his hands in a very unroyal fashion as she approached him in the Seymours' drawing room.

"Thank you for coming, Jane. I simply could not bear all of the merriment around me this evening."

"Had I really any choice but to come when you commanded?"

He glanced up at her, his face in this light more lined, more aged and full of worry than she had ever seen it. "Everyone has choices. Take the queen, for example. I have just been informed that some of her decisions in my absence have been, shall we say, less than wise." He drew her down onto his lap just then, and she allowed it. The air was charged between them. "You attend her daily. What do you know of what has been occurring?"

"My access to Her Majesty has been diminished of late," Jane demurred, suddenly not wanting to be the one to hurt him by telling him what she and everyone else already knew. "I know very little other than that she is not fond of me."

Henry gently touched the long cinnamon-colored scar on her neck. For a moment, his jaw slackened and she saw the pain in his expression increase. "I am so terribly sorry. Anne can be a dangerous woman when she feels threatened."

"I was told as much by the former queen."

Henry tipped his head to one side, and she saw a grim smile break through the serious expression. "You really are not going to say things only to try to impress me, are you?"

"Never, sire."

"How you do so remind me of Mistress Blount and a simpler time of my life," he said wistfully. "But I have told you as much before."

"I was mightily proud to be compared to the mother of the Duke of Richmond, sire."

"Were you?"

"Who would not be?"

"I think not the current queen—my less than loyal wife."

"Think you, sire, that she has actually been unfaithful?" Jane dared to ask.

"I am told to prepare myself for evidence to that effect. Men who have free access to her might well have enjoyed that liberty." He ran a hand up the column of her neck and along her cheekbone tenderly then. The more she let go of her youthful fantasy of William, the more she liked the feel of Henry's rough, masculine fingertips against her smooth skin, and she felt it ignite something within her again.

"There was more than one?" Jane asked with a convincing tone of innocence, thinking of how Anne had behaved publicly with both Smeaton and Norris, even Weston.

"So Cromwell reports. But he pleaded for time to find evidence before he takes part in destroying anyone's life."

"That seems just."

"Oh, Jane," he sighed, his hand falling away from her face as he laid his head wearily against the back of the chair like a man who had just fought in some great battle. "So few people around me seem to know what is just, much less how to act upon it. But you do, don't you?"

"I like to believe that I do, sire."

"Then what would you advise me to do?"

She was taken aback. "About the queen?"

"And about you. I love you, Jane. I know that I do. I feel it every time I look at you. But legally, for now, I am a married man, one who has struggled valiantly for years to tie myself to the one woman who might be bent on making me a laughingstock and a cuckold. God knows, she has not done her duty of making me a father. At least not one of a proper heir." He drew in a calming breath, then exhaled.

"And here you are, so precious to me, with your honesty and innocence so tantalizingly near. And I am like a boy with a plate of warm, fresh, sweetly fragrant gingerbread before him, of which I am not allowed to partake."

"Still, are you not a man who must lead his country first rather than follow his heart?"

He touched her throat again, but this time his hand slipped down to her cleavage and the place where the strip of lace met her warm, bare skin. His hand stilled there for a moment as he leaned over and very tenderly kissed her.

"I am a man of many loyalties and passions, Jane. 'Tis difficult for someone such as myself to give up one for the other."

"You desire it all?"

His answer came as he kissed her again, more roughly this time, and his fingers pressed their way beneath the lace and velvet onto the swell of her breasts, then found her warm, wide nipple. "Oh, yes, God help me, that I do. What do *you* desire, Jane? For I do believe I would give you the world if you asked me for it."

She could feel him grow hard as he pressed his manhood against her, and she softly said, "To maintain my honor, so long as I am an unmarried woman, sire. That is *my* utmost desire."

She knew she had hit the mark perfectly, which her brothers wanted of her, when his hand stilled, then fell away from her breast. There was compassion, not anger, in his tired green eyes.

"Oh, Jane. Forgive me. You have been such good counsel, and such comfort. You deserve only respect from me and the rest of my court. I want to lift you up . . . I want to *marry* you."

"That is not a wish for Your Majesty rightly to have," she said in a tone schooled by years of watching Anne Boleyn.

"Not now, perhaps," he conceded on a weary sigh. "But there is nothing so constant in this world as change."

She let a slim smile lengthen her lips, feeling for the first time in her life in control of something—even if it was only the art of seeming innocent.

"I am honored you wear my image still. It gives me hope," he said and pressed a tender, more chaste kiss lightly onto her cheek. "Change *is* constant. But without hope there is nothing."

"I suppose that is true," she carefully conceded.

"Perhaps I should not tell you this, but Cromwell is working even now on a possible case for divorce."

"With infidelity as the grounds?" she asked, now understanding how and why their conversation had begun as it had.

When he nodded his head affirmatively, she added, "Do you believe England would tolerate another marital fissure?"

"I am not fool enough to believe my people ever developed any sort of fondness for Anne. I would imagine most would be well-pleased to be rid of her."

Jane only lowered her eyes. She did not dare to respond to that, because if she did, she knew he would hear pleasure in her voice, not compassion.

"Tell me only that if this divorce were to come to pass, you would look favorably upon my official overtures toward you."

Jane felt the heat in her cheeks rise again at the mere thought of herself as Queen of England. When she lowered her gaze, Henry lifted her chin with a single steady finger—one that bore his onyx signet ring.

"Would you, then?" he pressed.

"'Twould be my great honor, sire."

"Hal. Certainly my future wife must call me what my family always has." He smiled at her. "I do believe we shall make a splendid match, Jane, and in it, pray God, I shall find a bit of peace, as well as a son or two."

"I would hope to give you an army of them." She felt herself smile in the radiant glow of his joy, if not yet quite her own.

He kissed her deeply then, pressing his tongue between her lips as only William had ever done and pushing his hardened manhood against her like a declaration. Then he wrapped his arms around her so tightly that she almost could not breathe. "If only we could set to work on that task right now," he murmured hotly against her mouth and pressed her dress sensually against the place between her legs that already was stirring for him. For a moment he moved his fingers in a rhythm that mirrored what would one day happen between them, and Jane felt a rush of excitement as their rough kiss deepened.

"I fear I should not be the maiden you desire as your queen if we did," she replied, pulling away just enough to speak, and keeping in mind the map to success Anne Boleyn had left her.

"I suppose you're right. For now at least," he conceded with a sigh, straightening his codpiece. "But once the world knows of my intentions, you shall be mine, body and soul."

"You speak as a warning that which to me shall be an honor," she wisely said.

She saw by his pleased expression that she was playing the game exceedingly well.

An entire lifetime had led her here, and at this moment, Jane Seymour felt positively masterful.

Thomas and Edward were waiting together for her beside the fireplace hearth in one of the grand apartment's other rooms. Edward's wife, Anne, had retired for the evening, which Jane regretted when she saw how Thomas anxiously paced the room. Edward pounced on her the moment she closed the door behind her.

"Did he propose?" Edward asked excitedly.

"Not in so many words."

"Did he say he was going through with the divorce, at least?"

"He said he was exploring the option."

Edward slammed his fist against the stone hearth. "'Tis not good enough! That will only give the Boleyns a chance to redouble their efforts!"

"He did declare his love," Jane announced meekly, hoping to placate them.

"As I am certain he has done to a multitude of ladies whom he hoped to bed!" Edward said hotly.

Jane felt instantly reduced by the boundlessness of her brother's ambition, which rose far beyond her own.

"Now, let us not be too hasty, brother," Thomas offered in a more measured tone. "'Tis at least a step, and our Jane has gotten further than many."

"What do *you* know!" Edward spat. "This court is littered with the footprints of other women who believed they were taking steps toward a crown!"

"Well, what have *you* gotten us?" Thomas countered.

"Whatever has been achieved so far was due to *my* standing at this court, *not yours!*" Edward countered.

"Always you, eldest brother, greatest son," Thomas grumbled.

"When you see Anne Boleyn a divorced woman and our own sister Queen of England, then you may boast, Thomas, and not before!"

"Are you challenging me?" Thomas growled.

"Stop it, both of you!" Jane finally put in angrily. "You speak as though I were not even here. This is *my* life!"

"Where on earth would you have gotten that idea?" Edward asked snidely. "You are a marketable commodity in this family, the way Anne Boleyn was for hers. You shall do as you are bid, and you shall gracefully share the spoils, since without my connections to this court, you would not even be here, nor would you remain!"

"Edward, that is quite enough," Anne Seymour interceded from the doorway. She was in her nightdress in her bare feet, her hair tousled and loose down her back. "If I can hear you down the corridor, so can the king. Keep that in mind." She drew near and put her arm around Jane, who could feel herself trembling now from the weight of all that had happened to her that day.

"Are you all right?" Anne asked with sincere concern that touched Jane the more for how her brothers were fighting as if she did not matter at all. But Jane could only nod for the enormity of it all.

She let Anne lead her to her own new bedchamber in the apartments then, too weary to argue. Besides, there was always that slight chance that the king might want to call upon her in the morning now that they had reached an understanding, so she must not come too fully undone and mar her face with the telltale stain of tears from continued arguments.

Jane slept a deep, dreamless sleep that night, and when she awoke, it was to the sound of horses' hooves and the shouts of grooms from the cobblestones below her window. Jane stood at the stone window embrasure, unable, in some oddly perverse way, to tear her eyes from the scene below. The king and queen entered the courtyard together. They were dressed for riding, both in hunter green velvet, and they were holding hands as they neared two grand, sleek black horses, both caparisoned in tooled silver and held for them by liveried grooms.

It was neither disappointment nor even betrayal that seized Jane's throat just then, making it almost impossible for her to catch her breath. Anne Boleyn was Henry's wife, after all, or at least in the eyes of England, if not God. It was in that moment that Jane realized that she actually loved Henry—truly loved him, even if it was a love based on rivalry and duty. It was certainly not the same love she felt for William, yet there was physical pain now in watching him leave with another woman that confirmed it for her. No matter the promises, he was not to be hers. Anne Boleyn was still the victor.

She held that moment in her mind and cradled it against the pain of having lost William. She should not have let Henry touch her. She should not have allowed him to awaken her body the way she had allowed William to do all those years ago. Jane felt wanton. Used. Not because she had done anything herself that crossed the line of virtue, but because she had refused to turn away from the temptations of a married man. No, Jane surely was not the girl people believed her to be. In the game of courtly love, she had played one hand too many, and now it seemed she had lost the contest altogether.

"It is said the queen told His Majesty last night that she is with child again. Naturally, that changes everything," Anne Seymour somberly revealed.

"Yes," Jane agreed. "Everything will be different now."

"I am told since the queen never liked Princess Mary, the king wished her to visit his daughter as a condition of their renewed closeness, so they have gone together to Windsor to see her."

Jane thought of Katherine's sweet, shy child with a bittersweet mix of nostalgia and sadness. Poor Mary, stripped of her mother, her title, and her place in the succession, all to accommodate Anne Boleyn's voracious ambition. It seemed fitting that, to keep her place, if she could, Anne must pay court to that same child whom she had rejected.

In that, Jane was almost happy to see them go together. *Almost.*

"Will you be all right?" Anne asked. "I know you had hopes for a very different outcome." They were both gazing out the window down at the king.

"I have had many hopes dashed through the years," Jane replied stoically. "This is for the best. Particularly for little Princess Elizabeth, who shall benefit from her family remaining together."

"I saw William Dormer at the banquet last evening. Curiously, he was not in the company of his wife. And I am told he is to remain here at Greenwich with my lord Cromwell while his wife attends the queen at Windsor."

"It seems you are told a great many things, sister," Jane replied with little inflection.

"My family has been at court a long time, as you know. If one is privy to good fortune, one makes connections."

"Good fortune, indeed," Jane said blankly.

She had danced around the edges of good fortune herself for years now, never quite allowed to dive into the pool that might have brought her total fulfillment. Perhaps, Jane thought, as she continued to gaze upon the king and queen as they led their horses into the forest beyond the palace, it was time to take what small bit of comfort she could find with the man who had always held her heart. If, perhaps, he still wanted her.

PART V

Jane and Henry

A woman of the utmost charm.

—POLYDORE VERGIL ON JANE SEYMOUR

Everything that deceives may be said to enchant.

—PLATO

Chapter Sixteen

April 1536
Greenwich Palace

"*Y*ou win again!"

Jane laughed at Francis Bryan, slapping her final card on the table as she sat across from him, William Dormer, and Anne Seymour, with whom she played a rousing hand of primero.

"She *is* suspiciously good at this game," Francis noted with a wink, dashing as ever in a charcoal-colored doublet and matching eye patch. "If I didn't know better, I would think our Jane had learned how to cheat."

"I have learned a great many things these past years, cousin."

William sent her a sudden glance full of meaning, and she looked guiltily at her cards.

Jane was so glad to have Francis returned these last months from France, and glad that he felt at ease in the company she had kept with William these past few days during the king's absence. It helped, perhaps, that Francis had been the one to try to arrange their marriage long ago. Thus, he seemed enough of a romantic not to begrudge the star-crossed lovers a simple friendship now. If friendship was what it was between Jane and William. In spite of everything they had endured, the battles and the anger, it was unspoken between them that they both wanted to spend time with each other. With the king and queen away, she and William played admirably around the edges of courtesy, and both did their best to be cordial, but there was always a charged energy when they were in the same room like this. As they played or strolled through the gardens, dined or danced, Jane could not help but feel there was unfinished business between them. She knew that he felt it, too.

When she lifted her cards for the next hand and saw the words *Arbor at sunset* scrawled in ink across the queen of hearts card, Jane was not entirely surprised. William's expression bore absolutely no evidence of the invitation when their eyes met again, but she knew it had come from him. She also knew what meeting him alone would mean for them both. Still, in spite of the risk, Jane knew already that she would go. She would go anywhere, do anything, to be in William's arms once more. Everyone was married, it seemed anyway, or betrothed or committed. Even the king and queen had apparently reconciled.

"I understand Minister Cromwell has gone back to London," Francis remarked to William as he played his hand and Jane folded the card in, secreting it among the others she held.

"He has indeed, my lord."

"And yet he did not take you with him?"

"My lord Cromwell said it was a private matter that did not require my attendance upon him."

"It is rumored that he continues to seek justifiable avenues for annulment, if not divorce, in case the queen is not brought to bed with a son this time either. I suspect Master Cromwell does not wish news of that spreading until the time is right," Francis said.

"Think you all that the only reason the king has gone off with her now is to mark time?" Anne Seymour asked.

Jane felt herself stiffen. She did not want to think of Henry just now.

"What other reason might there be? The queen is a selfish harridan who has brought the king nothing but disappointment; she has dissipated and aged him before his time. He would do well to be rid of her," said Francis.

"Those seem treasonous words from one who once supported her, cousin," Jane meekly put in.

"Not so treasonous as her behavior with a veritable bevy of courtiers," Francis countered with a sneer. "She could well lose her head for it."

"If it were proven," added Jane.

"They say Master Cromwell has learned well from Cardinal Wolsey's mistakes," Francis said. "If it happened, he *will* prove it."

"Pray God that our good queen is delivered of a son," Anne Seymour said bitingly. "That does seem her only hope."

The April sunset was alive, filled with shimmering crimson and gold, and splashed across the broad horizon as Jane slipped alone out the side door of the east wing, hurried down the stone steps, raised the hood of her cloak, and dashed behind the row of plane trees. Most ladies who regularly attended the queen were taking advantage of the peace and freedom in her absence and did not watch too closely for one another. They were resting at this hour and would later dine with a few of the men who had been left behind as well. Still, Jane made her way carefully down the pathway, bordered by colorful vines and blooming shrub roses and concealed by the trees.

William was waiting for her on a painted white lattice-wood bench beneath an arbor spilling with lush pink roses, as she knew he would be. Her heart raced when she saw him, and he rose to his feet the moment he caught a glimpse of her. He reached out his hands and drew her tightly against his chest.

"How I have missed this," he murmured deeply. "How I have missed *you*."

Jane smiled. "As fate would have it, you see me nearly every day."

"Not like this," he said, smiling back at her and reaching up to very gently touch her cheek.

She thought how this was just how Henry had touched her before they kissed last time, but she banished the thought. They were such very different men.

"I know I always say this to you like some besotted boy, but I am convinced there is not another woman in all the world with as beautiful skin as yours. It is exactly like alabaster."

"You are far too partial for your own good."

"A man in love is always partial."

"A man with a wife can afford no such bias."

"What of the man who seeks a divorce?"

She tipped her head, feeling the weight of his question. "Who are we speaking of here, William?" she asked cautiously.

"I called you away to speak privately like this because my mother has died, Jane."

"Oh, William, I am sorry!" she exclaimed, hiding the conflicting feelings of sympathy and hope behind her words.

"It was she alone who sought my marriage to Mary, she alone who withheld my sinecure, who tied my hands in my bid to marry you."

She looked away from him, but William brought her face back

around and cradled her jaw like a delicate thing in both of his masculine hands.

"My heart is yours; it has always been yours, Jane."

She felt the desperation in his kiss and let him pull her more deeply into his arms, let him part her lips and explore her mouth with his tongue. She let him press his hardened maleness tightly against her own center, let him sweep his hands down her back to her bottom and anchor her to him intimately, arousing her with every part of himself.

Never . . . She would never love anyone else like this!

"I cannot let you ruin your life for my sake," she struggled desperately to say as he kissed her again and again until she felt drunk with desire. She stroked his hair back from his temples, then ran her hands down the broad width of his back, taking pleasure in the fit maleness of him, so different from Henry.

"We have no children, or the promise of any. I will pay what she asks and confirm any story she tells," William said huskily. "She can say I am an evil lothario, or that I neglected her, whatever will help keep her dignity. I am fully prepared to leave court and make a life with you in Buckinghamshire, or anywhere you wish."

Unable to process what had been laid before her, Jane tried to gather her thoughts and calm her heart. What she had wanted all of her life was before her now, at last, yet the decision was not the easy one she had always expected it would be if a miracle like this ever happened.

"Do you not love me, Jane?" he asked desperately against her ear in a way that made her shiver as he drew her ever closer to his heart.

"Eternally," she admitted, laying her head back for a moment against his chest and taking in the unique scent of him that would be with her forever.

"Forgive me for not asking sooner. When it seemed that you and the king might . . ." His words fell away as she turned to gaze into his eyes, which held such history for her.

How like him, she thought, *to have a sense of propriety, even at this wild court.* It was the very thing that had kept them apart all these years, and while it had disappointed—nay, infuriated—her in the past, she saw the honor in it now, and could not love him more for that.

This was a true crossroads, a choice that only she could make. Not her brothers. Not William and not the king.

"I must have time to think," she finally said. Her hesitation did not involve her feelings for him, but she was not eager to do to another woman what Anne Boleyn so cruelly had done to Queen Katherine. She must reflect. "This has all happened so quickly."

She knew by the way his shoulders fell and he cast his glance at the ground that he understood. His next kiss was achingly gentle, a fragile thing. As fragile as the two of them were together.

"It feels like an eternity," William said.

She walked slowly back to the new apartments after that, deeply in thought, hearing nothing but the sweep of her own gown across the stone floor. Jane's sense of guilt flared as she even contemplated a life with William. Mary was Lady Dormer, no matter how much she wished it to be otherwise. Anne was still Queen of England.

Jane was glad to be alone when she entered the elegant suite of rooms to which she had been moved; she was quite sure everyone would see the truth of her decision written into every part of her expression. She needed a few minutes to collect herself.

Then she saw it. It was a large ivory sheet of vellum, folded and stamped with the king's personal seal. It seemed to bulge from an object tucked within its folds. On the front of it, one word, simply written. *Jane.*

And so her world mightily shifted yet again.

Thomas had fallen victim to his brother's foul humor all morning, and he had grown tired of it. With every accolade and gift bestowed upon him recently by the king in order to impress Jane, Edward was becoming more pompous and more insufferable than ever. He was the classic older brother, always certain to remind the younger one of the difference not only in their ages, but also in their standing. Today had been one of the worst. He walked a pace behind Edward, who had been told that Jane had returned to the apartments, and Edward was fully prepared to scold her yet again for not having kept a better hold over the king when she had the chance. Thomas had thought to argue, but there really was no point in that.

The folds of Edward's velvet cape fluttered against Thomas's knees as they walked at a clip that was near a run. Edward cast open the door with great force, and Jane whirled around, startled enough that the paper in her hand fluttered onto the Turkish carpet beneath her slippered feet.

"Here to enjoy one last moment in these rooms, are you, before we are all cast from court?" Edward petulantly asked.

"Edward," Thomas cautioned.

"You have had one task all your life, only one, and you could not fulfill even that, Jane."

"I really think that is enough, Edward," Thomas tried again, facing fraternal ire that was decades old and deep.

"You had it all in your mousy little fingers: a new life, riches, and the king at your feet, and you handed him back to his wife on a platter!"

"I cannot keep that which belongs to another, and I did not intend to be a plaything," Jane replied defensively.

"And where would the queen be if she had adopted that passive stance? She fought for him!" Edward raged.

"I am nothing like Anne Boleyn," Jane countered in a tone that was firm enough to surprise both of her elder brothers. Thomas could tell Edward was taken aback because he went silent for a moment, which was not at all his custom when he was angry.

"You well could have used what you had a bit more boldly," he finally said angrily. "Certainly better than you did. Now we are all at a loss. We Seymours made a strong stand against the Boleyns, and now they will want to completely vanquish us!"

"Not if we vanquish them first," Jane returned, which shocked Thomas. He had never heard that confident tone in Jane's normally meek voice. But there was something more, something in her eyes, as she motioned with her gaze to the letter lying at her feet. Thomas bent down to pick it up as Edward went to a table set with crystal and silver wine decanters and a collection of goblets. He filled one with ruby liquid for himself and took a sip, steeling himself.

"We shall need to make a plan. Salvage what we can of our dignity, at least. Humility will be the key. Especially with that woman, the queen . . . ," Edward muttered.

As Thomas scanned the letter, he felt the blood drain from his face. It was the last thing he expected to read.

"Edward, perhaps you should have a look at this," Thomas offered, extending the letter between them.

"We cannot be bothered with our sister's drivel just now, with our family's welfare on the line."

Jane and Thomas remained silent until Edward finally took the missive from his brother's hand. After a cursory glance at the words, Edward's expression turned incredulous.

"Is this . . . recent?" Edward asked her in a breathless tone.

"'Twas waiting for me today." She held out the signet ring, wrought of Spanish silver and enamel work, then. There could be no clearer signal of Henry's intentions. A king's signet ring was his most personal effect.

"Is this the token of which he speaks in the letter?" Edward asked, taking the jewel from her to examine it.

"It is."

"This changes everything."

Thomas watched a flame of ambition reignite in Edward's blue eyes. "Thomas, you retain your connection with that gentleman from home who now serves Master Cromwell, do you not?" Thomas knew Edward meant William Dormer, and he exchanged a little glance with Jane. "Cromwell must know of this, and of the king's renewed intentions with our dear sister."

Dear sister. Thomas could not stop himself from rolling his eyes.

"That lad is certain to help our Jane become queen, since you shall remind him of the reward attached for him if he does, do you not think?" Edward asked.

His face was bright now, his expression entirely changed. "Dearest Jane, I do heartily commend you," he said, making a light, somewhat comic bow of contrition to her. "I entirely underestimated you, it seems."

"Indeed you did," Thomas agreed.

"I would prefer we not involve Dormer," Jane suddenly said, breaking the jovial atmosphere.

"Why on earth not? You have known each other since you were

children. I recall there was once talk of an engagement, but is that not ancient history, particularly now that he has a wife?"

Thomas watched Jane's face carefully, and Edward caught a quick glance between the two. "Dormer has a wife and you have the king's signet ring. You *will* be Queen Jane, and Dormer will help you. Is that clear?" Edward's obstinate tone, so much like their mother's, sent a snaking chill down Thomas's spine. Edward was ambitious and self-serving. It infuriated Thomas. Someday Edward would regret the disregard with which he treated his younger brother. He may say little and argue even less for now, but Thomas Seymour took everything in and learned from it all. In that way, he was just like Jane. For the unassuming younger Seymour siblings, the future was becoming limitless.

In the end, the decision of whether to marry William was made for her. If the king still wanted her, she would push away any remnants of fantasy and go to him with her head held high—and her love for another man hidden deeply beneath years of self-denial. She thought about writing William a letter of explanation, but Jane knew she would only weaken by pointing out to herself, and to him, all that he meant to her. Whatever Thomas said when he went to William seeking Cromwell's support would be enough, at least to clarify, she prayed.

Jane looked down at the king's heavy signet ring on her left hand, feeling the importance of it and its weight. She knew what lay ahead for her. The ring divided her life. One path led to the love of her life, one that she knew she could never take. The other led her far from that love directly toward the queen's crown.

Chapter Seventeen

$\mathcal{I}$t was a very different Anne Boleyn who returned a few days later, as she clearly no longer carried the support of the court or the king. The day before her arrival, Chapuys himself had come to Edward's apartments, deferring to Jane with a gracious bow as if she were already queen, once he saw the signet ring on her finger.

The imperial ambassador informed her that not only did Jane possess the full support of Katherine's daughter, Mary, but now the powerful Master Cromwell supported her as well.

Chapuys was matter-of-fact as he explained to Edward, Anne, Thomas, and Jane that while the queen and Cromwell had once enjoyed a friendship, something had tipped the scales regarding his loyalty recently. He had pulled away from the Boleyns, and he was now firmly entrenched in the growing Seymour faction, which also included the influential duo Nicholas Carew and Francis Bryan.

"But what of the child she carries?" Anne dared to ask in a low, cautious tone.

"*If* she carries a child," Edward responded without looking at his wife.

"I thought we were all to take it as fact when they went away together," said Thomas.

"I do not suppose we can take anything as pure fact when it involves such a conniving and heartless woman," Chapuys put in. "The king has, at last, discovered what the rest of us have long known. I know I was partial to the true queen, Katerina, but I say, as the emperor himself does, that a divorce and a sound royal marriage are long overdue and highly desirable for the king." Chapuys looked directly at Jane then. "Now that you have Princess Mary's blessing, it seems there is nothing left to stop you."

"Our dear little sister, Queen of England." Edward boastfully twirled the tip of his beard with two fingers.

"Will he fully pursue a divorce now?" Jane dared ask. "And what if she *is* with child?"

"Dear sister, you worry too much," Edward said.

"Trust me," Chapuys put in. "Cromwell is, as we speak, preparing to present his evidence against the queen to the king, so it shall not matter either way."

Jane felt an odd sense of foreboding begin to rise, not fully grasping what it meant and yet afraid to consider it further. "But the child, especially a son, would still be his heir."

"If it were *his* son. I have it on rather sound authority that her ladies are giving evidence to the contrary at this very moment," Chapuys said smoothly, with a slightly menacing smile. "Just to lower her resistance to the notion of divorce, you understand."

As long as no real harm came to her, Jane reasoned, Anne Boleyn had earned the same fate that had befallen poor Katherine of Aragon. She twirled the loose and heavy signet ring around on her index finger, realizing that she had gotten to this place only because her own heart had hardened. She did not care about Anne Boleyn's fate, and she completely understood Henry's calculated plan to divorce her. It was whispered that Anne had begun to understand it as well.

That evening, as Jane walked along the courtyard path to the banquet hall with Elizabeth Carew and Anne Seymour, she spotted Queen Anne at the large picture window above them, which faced the lush courtyard. To Jane's surprise, Anne was clearly sobbing as she held her squirming three-year-old daughter, Elizabeth, in her arms. Henry stood behind her, like a great auburn shadow. His hands were out in a pleading gesture, and it was clear that husband and wife were arguing. *So it is done,* thought Jane, as she looked away. He had informed Anne of the divorce. *I, Jane, Queen of England . . .* The thought floated across her conscious mind so suddenly that it shocked her.

To Jane's surprise, she liked the feel of the thought. *Yes . . . I, Jane, Queen.*

In that moment—in that bold realization of things to come—the hurts and disappointments, the anger and embarrassments of the past, gave way to all the possibilities that lay before her. She stifled a victorious smile as they passed beneath the window. Elizabeth and Anne continued to gossip without pause.

It seemed an ominous sign that the commencement of the May Day celebrations, culminating tomorrow in a joust, was not to be attended by the queen's uncle, the Duke of Norfork, or by Thomas Cromwell. Such a thing would have been unthinkable even a month ago, with everyone in such bold support of the second queen. Yet Jane was relieved that William would not be there, since she was certain she would weaken at the mere sight of him. She had been avoiding him for the last month.

"Divorce is a sticky business, particularly after the last time," Edward Seymour intoned. "I am certain Master Cromwell, with his great legal mind and years of experience, simply wishes to make certain there is no room for error."

When the three Seymour siblings entered the crowded banquet hall, enlivened by rousing music, they could see George Boleyn already seated in an elegant costume of velvet with great puffed sleeves, ornamented by jewels. But his normal hauteur seemed diminished.

Jane smoothed down the rich brocade fabric of her own gown as she sank securely into an armchair. She sat between her two brothers and directly opposite Lord Rochford and his father, the Earl of Wiltshire, whose glum expression was as marked as his son's. Jane realized that his wife's chair was empty. The May Day banquet was an annual event, and like Cromwell and Norfolk, Lady Rochford never missed it. Jane tried to shake the foreboding feeling creeping like a cloud over the festivities. Something dark and powerful was stirring.

She took a swallow of rich Spanish wine, remembering proud Queen Katherine. When she was sent away, Anne Boleyn would be provided with better accommodations than the poor Spanish queen after she was toppled. Knowing Henry's soft spot, he might even give her Greenwich, the cozy palace she favored the most.

When Anne entered the hall a few moments later, the queen quite literally looked like a different woman from the one Jane had known and feared since childhood. Dressed in dove gray, her hair swept back severely and covered by a matching gray hood, she was accompanied by a group of younger ladies who rarely attended the queen. Her principal ladies, Lady Rochford and Lady Margaret Douglas, were nowhere to be seen. Anne's normally confident expression was gone, and there were dark circles beneath her eyes, which matched the sober look of her gown. Jane was struck by the change, but still, she was hard-pressed to conjure real sympathy.

Anne Boleyn was a ruthless woman who surely would land on her feet and live a quiet, luxurious life, probably in her beloved France, once this was all over.

Jane's brothers leaned together in conference behind her back and whispered to each other as the queen took her seat on the dais.

"No Master Smeaton this evening?" Thomas sniped.

"Perhaps the king has grown weary of his tune," Edward said with a slight smile.

"Ah, but the king is not here either," Francis Bryan remarked as he sat down beside Thomas and entered the debate. None of them wanted to guess just what that actually signaled.

Before the end of the banquet, Jane received a message through the king's page, Sir Francis Weston, instructing her not to return to her own bedchamber but to accompany Edward and Anne Seymour to their withdrawing room. She knew Henry meant to again use the private corridor between their two apartments to reunite with her, and for the first time she was excited by the daring prospect. A great many things excited her now that she knew the King of England meant to make little Jane Seymour from Wolf Hall his queen.

Her sister-in-law daubed fresh flowers of lavender scent on the column of Jane's neck and on her wrists, pinched her pale cheeks, and straightened the silk pearl-lined fall behind her hood as they waited. Everything must be perfect. *She* must be perfect. She had risked far too much these past months, and she could not afford to risk more.

Henry stalked broodingly into the room a moment later, and Anne Seymour dipped into a deep, slightly clumsy curtsy.

"Leave us," he barked at Anne, who backed out of the room as swiftly as she could without tripping on the hem of her gown.

The desperation with which he then drew Jane against his broad, slightly pillowy, medal-covered chest took away her sense of reason.

"No matter what you hear," he murmured hotly against her cheek, "know that I am not a bad man!"

"I *do* know that," Jane replied, trying to cheer him although she did not understand what was wrong. She pressed him back and gently cupped his copper-bearded face between her two hands. "What has happened?"

It was a moment before Henry replied. "I have only just found out some disturbing information tonight—a deed that changes everything—and I need to feel something good and kind to stop the madness from taking me over completely."

"How may I help?" Jane softly asked.

"Only by becoming my wife," he said as he drew from his doublet a large, glittering ruby ring set in gold. He held the jewel like a child offers up a trinket of his own creation, eager for approval.

"But you still have your wife," she gently reminded him as the gem sparkled in his hand between them.

"That is over, Jane. She has offended me for the final time. Cromwell is seeing to the last details as we speak."

The kisses that fell upon her lips then were rough and full of demand. He must have sensed her uncertainty, Jane thought, because in the next moment, Henry led her from the drawing room and to her bedchamber beyond a closed set of paneled doors, which he closed behind them as he continued to devour her mouth and neck with what felt more like desperation than passion. Jane could not have stopped this progression even if she had wanted to. He had made her the promise, given her the token of that promise, and now he meant to seal the pact that they were making.

As she lay on her canopy bed with Henry arched over her and a silvery beam of moonlight streaming through the long window, Jane was quickly overpowered by his passion. She felt a strange, unexpected sensation, knowing at this moment that she was beyond the point of objecting. She need not bother with protestations about her virtue or with waiting until he was a free man, because the King of England had made his intentions clear this very night. He was about to endure another cataclysmic scandal for her sake; thus, submission was her duty. So much of Jane's life had been about duty and rationalizing it that she felt no shame as Henry unlaced her gown and drew it over her head, moving them closer to something from which they could never turn back.

The king was naked a moment later, a burly mass of flesh, muscle, and thick copper coils of chest hair. He arched over her and entered her with an unrestrained grunt, not taking care to be gentle with her. There was something primal between them as he opened the door to forbidden pleasure, thrusting himself over and over forcefully into that most intimate place as he tangled his fingers in her hair. He came down hard on her mouth then and groaned as he moved. She tasted it, her mind reeling with the forbidden carnal sensations she was not supposed to enjoy. Thinking that only added to the building ecstasy as he drove into her small, pliant body, his own suddenly awash in perspiration. His rough, red beard scratched her mouth as he drove his tongue between her lips, mirroring the frantic pulsing movement of his body until, abruptly, she felt him tense, then slacken against her.

Afterward, he lay docile and smiling as he trailed a path from one bare nipple to the other. Only then, when it was over, did thoughts of William creep relentlessly back from the dark corners of her mind past the barrier of finality Jane had so cautiously erected. Almost as if he had known he needed to take possession of her body in order to win her mind and her heart, Henry had forced this intimacy between them. Any tiny glimmer of hope that William's pleading might lead the way to a happy ending between them was over now.

William Dormer belonged to Mary Sidney. Jane said it to herself over and over again now. And she was the possession of King Henry VIII, no matter how either of them wished it were different. Perhaps that was why Jane had not fought Henry harder. She had allowed the king to make the final decision she was simply unable to make for herself.

"They are so wonderfully small," he remarked of her breasts. "Perfect little things."

"I am glad they please you, my lord," she said shyly.

"Did I hurt you?" he asked, his own smile fading with the possibility. "I fear I did not take care to be gentle . . . It shall not always be like that, though. You shall grow accustomed to what will happen between us."

"If it were to be just like that for the rest of my days, I should call myself a blessed wife," she replied, knowing that saying so would please him.

Henry held up her hand that bore his signet ring. "It is time to replace this with something more official," he said, and reached down, drawing off the signet ring and replacing it with the huge, sparkling ruby surrounded by diamonds.

"You are my passion and my love. Soon you shall be my bride, Jane. You shall need to begin assembling your own household. I imagine there are many you do not wish to keep on as your own ladies," he said.

Jane had never considered that, but it was true. There were very few she trusted besides Anne Seymour and Elizabeth Carew.

"I have been giving some thought to calling your sister to court," Henry announced. "Would that please you?"

Jane had not seen Elizabeth for two years, since she was away at her own estate. The prospect excited her.

"It would please me greatly, sire."

"Lady Mary Dormer has also been proposed to me," he went on.

Jane felt herself go very cold. "By whom?"

Jane almost did not want to hear.

Henry thought for a moment. "Cromwell, I believe. Her husband is in his employ, and I have known her father for many years, since he is cousin to my friend Charles Brandon. They are good, trustworthy sorts, although I know the girl's husband not at all."

Her mind flew with things she might say. Her heart was reeling from the great blow. Of course Henry did not know William. Perhaps Mary's father was the unknowing instigator of this, for everyone sought advancement whenever a new change was upon the court.

"May I consider it?" she asked with believable sweetness, unable to imagine a circumstance, however, in which she would ever say yes.

Arrested and hauled away like a common criminal.

That was how it looked to Jane and the stunned crowd of ladies attending the queen two days later at the afternoon tennis match. Anne had put up a great struggle with the royal guards, calling out with a piercing cry for the king, but Henry was nowhere in sight. Even Jane had not seen him since the day before, when he had stormed out of the May Day jousting tournament. After Charles Brandon had whispered something to him privately, the king had left Jane alone in the stands without even an explanation. An hour later, Edward informed her that the king had left Greenwich for London with only his aide Henry Norris amid a great shouting match between the two men.

The gossip had run rampant in the suddenly somber palace. The flirtatious court musician, Mark Smeaton, had been arrested and taken to the Tower of London. The whispered offense was adultery with the queen.

"It is said he has confessed," Anne Seymour whispered to her as the tennis game was abruptly ended and the crowd began to disperse amid the fading sound of the queen's cries.

"That would make the grounds for divorce a bit more simple this time," Thomas drily observed, not seeming particularly moved by the scene. "The good Lord knows no one would have been able to accuse the last queen of adultery."

"The only thing left in our way now is that bastard son, Fitzroy," Edward interjected.

"'Tis enough!" Jane censured her brother and cast a scowl at him.

"I only mean to reassure you, sister. I am mightily pleased for you," Edward declared in a boastful tone.

Jane began to feel ill. Some things were better left unseen. She could not quite wrap her mind around what she witnessed and heard. Trumping up charges against innocent people would be as horrid as premeditated murder. But nothing seemed so important to her brothers as her becoming queen. Was it so for Henry and his supporters?

"Francis Bryan told me it was not only Smeaton. Norris was always fawning over the queen as well. That is probably why the king has taken him to London. He'll want to interrogate his old friend himself before letting the ax fall."

Jane thought back to the flirtatious encounter between Anne

and Henry Norris that afternoon in the queen's apartments. She only prayed that Henry was not involved in the calculated expedition of his divorce. She could not blame him for wanting to set himself apart from such a ruthless woman, but creating the means out of whole cloth would be an entirely different matter before God.

Mark Smeaton, Henry Norris, and even Anne Boleyn's own brother, George, Lord Rochford, were imprisoned in the Tower. The moment he returned, Henry made the announcement to Jane with tears in his eyes. Only the poet Thomas Wyatt, initially implicated, had managed to convince the king's henchmen that the rumors were untrue.

"'Tis one thing to suspect so great a crime in a marriage as adultery, but another thing altogether to see it so broadly confirmed," he said brokenly, pressing a hand against his forehead as if he were physically pained by the ordeal. "Even with her own . . . *brother.*"

Jane went to him, colored sunlight spilling in through the wall of stained-glass windows beside them.

"All of them?"

"There is evidence. The testimonies have been given. I have just closeted with Master Cromwell," he answered against her neck. He drew her hard against his broad chest as if his own life depended on their connection. Jane could feel his tears then, wet and warm on her throat.

"I tried with her, Jane, so help me God, I did."

"I know," she said softly. "I have been here to see much of it with my own eyes."

"So you have," he said, pulling back to give her a grim, watery smile that faded as quickly as it had come.

Only then did she notice the slim young man lingering behind him near the door. He was handsome, yet gaunt, as though he had recently been ill. His hair was a slightly darker shade than the king's, but the limpid color of his green eyes and the turn of his jaw were identical.

"I could not possibly endure this without the two most important people in my life together to give me courage," Henry said, pivoting back, but with an arm tightly anchored around Jane's corseted waist. "Harry, bid your father good night with a kiss." He motioned with his plump, jeweled fingers for the elegantly dressed youth to draw near.

"Sweetheart, I know this is sudden, but I present to you Henry Fitzroy, Duke of Richmond, my son. He came here to support me as soon as he heard what was happening," Henry proudly explained.

Of course. Bess Blount's son. Jane remembered seeing him here and there over the years, but only on great occasions, when the size of the crowd had always precluded their meeting.

"I hope to be a comfort to you, Father."

"You always are, my boy." Henry sniffed and wrapped his other arm around Fitzroy's slim shoulders, establishing an unlikely triumvirate: the king, the bastard son, and the future queen.

Henry's tears had dried, and Jane saw the pride that replaced them. She exchanged a little glance of complicity with Fitzroy, seeing in that moment that they both loved and understood the king.

"Family is *everything*," Henry declared, his voice catching on the last word. As he pulled them both closer, the tears again began to fall, and Jane could almost feel the pain of betrayal that weakened him.

To her mind, Anne Boleyn had only ever brought turmoil and unhappiness, and even Jane was growing anxious to be rid of her. When her trial was over and Henry had exiled her to France, as Jane assumed he would, their lives could truly begin.

"Ah, Harry," Henry wept, seeming to break down a bit more with each murmured word to his son. "You and your sister Mary have truly been gifted by God to have escaped that woman's venomous wrath. I am told she would have poisoned you both if she had not been imprisoned, such was her great ambition to see her own daughter on the throne of England to the exclusion of all others."

"I miss Mary," Fitzroy admitted.

"As do I. I am afraid she has been unfairly punished with this dark cloud upon my heart for so long, and for that I am to blame."

Jane wanted to ask then if he should not send for Katherine's child to bring him the same comfort as Fitzroy, but as the idea flared in her mind she thought better of it. As soon as it was within her power to do so, she would return Mary to court to reunite with her father. But for now, she would try to keep things simple, since she could see how much he needed that. The three of them sat by the fire together for a while before Fitzroy kissed his father, then bowed to bid him good night. As he turned to leave, he looked back at Jane.

"Does she not remind you of my mother?" Fitzroy asked Henry.

"I thought so as well. Jane certainly has her essence. I've told her that before," the king concurred.

"I must like you for that alone." Henry Fitzroy smiled boyishly at her.

Once he was gone, Henry folded her into his arms again and said, "He does not look well, does he, Jane?"

"That I cannot say, my lord, since he was unknown to me before this evening," she hedged, knowing that, even so, Henry Fitzroy had nothing of the glow of youth and burgeoning manhood that should have defined a seventeen-year-old young man.

Henry went again to his chair and laid his head against the stiff back, more weakened than she had ever seen him. His eyes were still clouded with tears. "That boy is the world to me. Nothing can happen to him. Especially not now, when the rest of my world is falling apart."

She pressed a hand supportively onto his velvet-covered shoulder. "I am sure you worry needlessly."

"In my world, there is no such thing as needless worry, sweetheart," he said with a sigh. "Let us to bed, then, where my mind will allow only thoughts of you," he added, and she saw that he was trying not to be too forceful. "If you wish it, that is."

"I do wish it," she replied with the skillfully demure tone that had won her family so much favor.

"I want you to know that I am leaving again by the morrow for London. I must keep a lower profile for a time, repairing to York Place. I will have you conveyed nearby. 'Twould be better, until all of this ugly business is over, if we were not seen together."

Jane had to say that she agreed, and tried not to feel too dispirited.

Seeing her hesitation, Henry chucked her gently beneath the chin. "I shall take my barge down the river often to see you. You shall not keep me away."

Jane smiled encouragingly, but still she could not shake the dark feeling that some great ominous cloud was nearing her, too, and no royal barge could outrun it.

Jane slept little that night. Instead, she lay awake watching Henry's own fitful slumber, wondering what places his dreams were taking him as he thrashed and perspired and called out to the darkness. Her gentle hand on his temple and the hushing maternal sound she made soothed him for a while so that he dozed again. Then she lay back and gazed up at the painted ceiling, the details of which were lit by the moonlight. Henry was fascinated by astronomy, so the ceiling was intricately painted with stars, planets, and distant galaxies. They had made love again, but not with passion so much as his need, and he had fallen asleep afterward, leaving her in a heightened state of her own awakening.

The next morning, three hours after Sir Francis Weston and William Brereton had followed the others to the Tower, feeding court gossip all the more, Jane received a visit from her arrogant cousin, the Duke of Norfolk. He was accompanied by Thomas Cromwell, and Jane was glad she had her sister-in-law beside her for support.

Jane's heart skipped a beat as she and Anne dipped into deep curtsies before the two powerful men. Her first thought, upon seeing their sour expressions, was that they had discovered her history with William. In this dark period, plagued with arrests and accusations of adultery, was she next?

Cromwell was in his usual robe of long, crisp black silk, his fat face shiny with perspiration. Norfolk cut an imposing figure in an intricately embroidered doublet, his weathered face full of craggy lines caused by a long history of war, conflict, and political maneuvering.

Anne took her hand and squeezed it, both full of fear.

"A visit is long overdue, my good cousin. I trust you will forgive me," Norfolk bid her. His seeming sincerity brought her as much surprise as it did confusion. They had never spoken before, and he had never acknowledged her presence.

"Your Grace is a busy man, far too busy for pleasantries with a distant relation," Jane acknowledged.

"A relation nonetheless," he countered effortlessly. "And blood really is the thing, after all."

It was an odd phrasing, with so many people recently imprisoned in the Tower of London for offenses punishable by death. For a moment, she could not think how to respond.

Thomas Cromwell padded forward, interrupting her ruminations. "We also thought it was time we offered you our formal support," he announced.

"Am I in need of your support?" she asked with a note of cautious surprise.

"A crown is a heavy burden, my lady."

Jane did not yet possess a crown. There was much more to endure before that became a reality. Yet these two powerful men paid court to her as if she were a queen—when there was still another on the throne.

"Is support *all* that you wish for me?" she dared to ask Cromwell, forcing her voice to remain steady.

"In truth, no."

Jane's heart fell at his response.

God save me, she thought. *God save William.*

"The real reason we are here is to escort you to Hampton Court, where you shall begin planning your wedding, as well as selecting your household staff."

For a moment, Jane misheard the words, and she thought he had meant the Tower instead. Everyone feared the Tower at the moment. If one of the king's dearest friends, Henry Norris, and the queen herself could be arrested and sent there, no one was safe. And it was Norfolk, after all, who had seen his own niece, Anne Boleyn, taken there. What might he do with Jane, his other relation, if she did not behave to their liking?

Jane wrapped her arms tightly around herself to ward off a

sudden shudder. "But how can I plan a wedding when there has yet been no divorce?"

Norfolk's craggy face remained expressionless. "The king's party has already gone. 'Tis by his command that we leave, just past midday."

"Whom do I take?" Jane asked, hearing the panic in her own voice, unaccustomed to the pressure of decision making.

"A queen does as she pleases, my lady," said Cromwell.

"So you are here to serve me, then?" she asked, feeling a spark of confidence.

"Indeed we are," answered Cromwell.

"Splendid. Then send for Princess Mary to be delivered to York Place. They will reunite there."

The two powerful men exchanged a glance, and Jane could see it was the last request either of them expected to hear. For a moment, both of them were pressed into silence.

"Oh, cousin, I am not certain that would be a good idea with everything that is about to—"

But Jane cut the duke off. "Your Grace declared yourselves here to serve me, and that is what I wish. His Majesty is in need of his children around him just now. He has told me so directly."

"It is only that the disgraced queen never wished to be reminded that there was another queen before her, or a child to compete with her own offspring," Cromwell explained.

"Well, if you did not know it before, be aware that I am nothing like this queen."

Again, the two men exchanged a glance, but she saw capitulation in both of their expressions, a tacit agreement that they would do as she asked. It was at that precise moment that Jane felt her first jolt of real power. It surged through her, unlike any other sensation she had experienced before.

"Now, who do you recommend to oversee the details of my wedding? I am certain he wishes us to marry directly after the divorce, since the matter of an heir is still paramount in his mind."

Jane knew that she sounded aloof, perhaps even slightly haughty. But if she was going to gain their respect and their compliance, she would need to make certain that she betrayed no fear.

The divorce would go through, and she would be queen, whatever that took.

"I do have someone in mind, Mistress Seymour, well vested and trustworthy. His name is Sir William Sidney. He has a lovely daughter, Lady Mary Dormer. Her husband is in my employ; thus, I can assure you that she shall fit seamlessly into your new household," Cromwell offered.

Jane wrung her hands as she paced the tiled drawing room floor, her heels pounding out the rhythm of her heart. Sir William Sidney and his daughter were downstairs in the courtyard ready to accompany Jane to Hampton Court, where she was to wait, protected, until after the divorce. Cromwell had informed her that the Sidney duo was most anxious to be a part of her train. Surely God was playing with her in this, for what other explanation could there be? Jane remembered only parts of the conversation with Cromwell after that, even though it had occurred only an hour earlier.

"You must take better care not to give yourself away," Anne warned her as she finished dressing Jane for the journey.

The costume was new, commissioned by the royal tailor. It was more elegant than any of her other traveling gowns, made of a rich amber silk with a tasseled yellow sash and prominent rosary hanging from the waist. There was also a slim line of rare miniver sewn into the bodice. Like her jewelry, the dress made a statement about Jane's growing influence. "These are dangerous times at court, and no one is safe. If the king gets wind of any more betrayal, there's no telling what he might do," Anne continued.

Jane lowered her eyes in agreement. She must do this. She must take on the unaware wife of the man she loved in order to protect herself and William.

"Now, this will be entertaining," Thomas murmured under his breath as they approached the young woman and her father, who wore such hopeful, naive expressions that Jane felt a rise of nausea flood her already guilty heart.

"I am sorry, Jane," Francis Bryan said quietly. "I tried to put him off the idea of including them as soon as I heard, but Cromwell and I have never been on the best of terms."

Sir William bowed to her, and his daughter Mary curtsied as though Jane were already queen. That seemed to be the new standard of things.

Mary was the first to speak. "I have been waiting a very long time for this moment." Her wide, buttery brown eyes met Jane's cautious gaze.

"Oh?" Jane managed, hearing how much the single word sounded like a croak. "And why is that?"

Now it was father and daughter who exchanged a glance.

"Forgive me, Mistress Seymour, for saying so, but I never fancied the former queen," Sir William revealed. He moved in closer and lowered his voice as if he were about to utter some great state secret. "It was not right the way she stole another woman's husband like that. She was shameless, and poor Queen Katherine was so unsuspecting."

"That *was* a shame," Jane concurred, trying not to look too closely at the balding, kind-faced man and his pretty daughter. "Queen Katherine was a wonderful, noble woman."

"After she was banished, I did not wish to attach my family to court," he explained. "But now with you by our king's side—"

"I am not there yet, my lord," she cut him off gently. "Much could yet happen."

"Oh no, mistress. He is as good as widowed already. Everyone is saying the case against Lady Anne is secure."

Jane felt an uneasy dread crawl up her spine. "Surely she shall be shamed in her divorce and banished from England, and nothing more."

William's wife looked at her with a sweet, soft smile, but her words were full of venom.

"If you will pardon me saying, my lady, banishment is not good enough for someone who takes another woman's husband, then makes a cuckold of him."

Though she spoke of Anne Boleyn, Jane was uneasy to hear such a sentiment from the wife of her own great love. Jane felt as if she might be ill right then and there.

"Where shall your husband be, Lady Dormer, if I were to take you permanently into my employ? Amid all this talk of infidelity and divorce, should you not pay heed to that question?"

Mary Dormer's smile was indecipherable. "Oh, my William? He is as faithful as a monk, and bound by Master Cromwell, who gave him his opportunity at court. One of the homes we own is in Wiltshire, very near where your family resides, in fact. Did you not know that? He favors that property the most of all our holdings."

"You might have been too young to remember," Thomas suddenly put in with a slight raise of his eyebrows. "But Master Dormer was with us as children when we were called to France to attend the late Princess Mary when she became Queen of France."

Jane cast her brother a confused little look, but his expression told her that he had spoken the words intentionally. "I remember," Jane said, managing those two words, though each tasted like rust on her tongue.

"As to my husband, since you so kindly asked," said Mary Dormer sweetly, "he shall work closely with Master Cromwell and the king at York Place until the end of this business with the queen; then he shall join us at Hampton Court. I am most proud of the advancements he has made, as you might imagine." She beamed in a way that pierced Jane deep in the heart. Her words remained there, twisting.

"Yes," said Jane, her stomach tightening with the thick sludge of guilt. "I can imagine."

They rode together to Nicholas Carew's elegant mansion in Beddington, which was secluded enough for the king to conceal her there during this growing tumult. They would progress to Hampton Court soon after. Beddington was only a mile by barge down the river from where Henry was installed in London at York Place, as Cromwell and the Archbishop of Canterbury, Cranmer, worked toward the trials of the accused men and an annulment of the royal marriage, which would be much speedier than a divorce. Jane was surprised to feel a slight kindling of empathy for the beleaguered queen.

For so many years Anne Boleyn had wanted nothing more than to be queen. Now Archbishop Cranmer was about to announce, with the stroke of a pen, that she had never been queen at all. And while Jane knew it would be unwise to protest, with decisions already made at the highest level, she was reasonably certain that the accusation of infidelity with five different men was unfounded. She did not have proof to aid the embattled queen, but she had spent enough time in Anne's company to know she likely had only ever indulged in such flirtations to incite the king's jealousy. She had never truly wanted anyone but Henry.

As it had been with Katherine, Jane knew it was Henry's ardent desire to be free of the marriage that was primarily driving this wild and slightly frightening course of events, and she was trying her best not to let it frighten her. To preoccupy her mind, Jane marveled at the sheer elegance of Nicholas and Elizabeth's home in Beddington Park—a stately redbrick structure with a clock tower, a brightly painted blue door, and a long driveway guarded by a great iron and golden gate. The mansion was surrounded by lush emerald lawns and flanked by heavy evergreen trees.

It was a cool and windy day for May, and Jane felt a chill as she walked before the Carew servants, who lined the walkway in order to be presented to her. As she passed them, they bowed and curtsied to her, as nearly everyone she met did now. It was overwhelming and distracted her—until she saw her sister, Elizabeth, waiting for her near the open door, radiant and smiling. They embraced deeply, and Jane felt unexpected nostalgic tears wet her cheeks.

"Hal mentioned you might come to court, but I had no idea he meant so soon." Jane wept with happiness. "I am heartily glad you are here. Your husband is at home with the children, then?"

"He is, but he sends his love. It was such a kind invitation from the king that Anthony could not deny me a chance to attend my own sister, the queen," she said with a genuine smile.

"I am not queen yet, remember."

"You shall be soon enough, once she is dead."

"The marriage is to be annulled," Jane quickly countered. "There is no reason to execute her."

"We shall see about that, shan't we?" said Thomas as he came up the steps to greet his youngest sister with a hearty embrace.

Jane shook her head to cast off the comment, glad to have the three of them reunited like this. As to anything else, she decided not to think about it. For now.

Dresses were strewn everywhere. There was an entirely new and elegant wardrobe assembled and prepared for her review in the grand, carpeted withdrawing room to which Jane was shown. Behind her, Elizabeth, Lady Ughtred, Elizabeth Carew, and Anne Seymour awaited her reaction with smiling faces. Jane was stunned by the yards and colors of luxurious silk, embroidered velvet, ermine, pearls, and beadwork laid like an offering at her feet.

"'Tis breathtaking," she murmured, pressing two fingers to her lips.

"'Tis a wardrobe fit for a queen," said her sister with a note of happiness further brightening her face.

"Commanded by a king for his lady," explained Elizabeth Carew.

"Hal saw to this?"

"Approved of each pearl and button," Lady Carew confirmed. "He confides to my husband that he is tired of being unhappy, and you make him happy."

"And now you really must decide what you shall wear for your wedding. There'll not be time to add the jewels if you do not, and His Majesty has ordered that your wedding dress be very grand," Elizabeth said.

Jane's wedding dress would be ornamented as her predecessor sat in the Tower of London. What, she wondered, must Anne be doing alone in her chamber, which was actually a prison cell, as Jane chose fabrics for her wedding gown? Perhaps if she had not seen Katherine's sad end, the bitter irony of Anne's situation would not come to mind now.

Jane had been witness to a great many things in her life. Now she was at the epicenter of it all. On her wedding day, Katherine had worn a dress of white embroidery and miniver; Anne had worn a gown of crimson velvet with rubies. She would wear emerald satin so that everyone could see how it matched her new husband's eyes. Her dedication to him would be reflected in every choice she made for the wedding.

Yet, even after everything, the image of Anne Boleyn, alone and frightened for her life, haunted Jane. But she pushed it aside. No one could outrun their destiny, and she felt that down to her soul.

Later that afternoon, as Jane sat wearily amid the pile of gowns, each of which she had tried on, she accepted a small goblet of claret from Lady Carew's maid. She lay against the back of an embroidered settee to catch her breath with her new ladies of honor. Mary Dormer's presence made the wine necessary for her.

"Is it to be a big wedding, then?" William's wife asked as the group idled for a while.

"I shouldn't think so," Jane replied. "His Majesty, after all, has already done this before."

"Twice," Elizabeth Carew put in with a slight smile before she took a sip of her own wine.

"Mine was a quiet event as well. My husband was adamant that it should be small and private. My father would have liked something more grand, and he fought for that, but William would not be put off his stance," Mary said with a wistful sigh.

Jane and Anne Seymour exchanged a little glance before Jane looked away. Any reference to William was a painful one, and Jane stubbornly pressed his image, and the memory of their passionate kisses, to the back of her mind yet again.

Jane did not realize how late it was getting until she noticed the slant of shadows on the floor. Suddenly, Francis Bryan stormed through the doorway, short of breath.

"'Tis done. The queen is condemned to die. They all are!"

Roused from a half sleep, Jane struggled to sit up and focus on her cousin, her brothers, and Nicholas Carew, who had followed Francis into the room. She was seized with terror at the announcement and could barely breathe. Was there truth after all in the whisperings she had heard earlier?

"All?" Jane murmured as she absently grabbed her neck.

"Smeaton, Norris, Brereton, Weston, and Rochford have already met their ends on the Tower lawn."

"When?" she croaked, unable to find her voice.

"Two days past. The king did not wish you to be disturbed by the details, but now with the queen herself condemned to die, His Majesty thought it was time you were informed. Anne Boleyn is to be executed next for the crime of infidelity. Cromwell has come to report to you, but I told him 'twould be better coming from me."

So that was why she had been spirited away from the rest of the court; not to protect her, but to keep her from voicing the objections Henry knew she would present. There was little she could say to spare the woman most loathed by all of England.

Francis sank beside her and gently drew her hand into his lap. "Are you all right, cousin?"

"He said the marriage would be annulled. There is no reason for her to die!"

"It was annulled. Cranmer made the pronouncement this morning, thus also declaring Princess Elizabeth a bastard."

A harsh word, gently delivered, did not make it any easier to hear. Yet Jane could not help but remember Princess Mary and how devastating the same pronouncement had been for her mother, Queen Katherine, long ago.

"Is that not enough? Must she die as well?" Jane asked in a dry whisper, yet already knowing the answer reflected on the faces of her companions, who were not nearly as stunned as she was.

"His Majesty is coming by barge to see you. He will arrive this evening."

"So he sent a team in advance to soften the blow?" Jane snapped bitterly.

"I believe he thought 'twould please you, knowing you are a step closer to becoming queen."

"A step nearer for me is a step nearer the grave for her," she said.

"Jane, have you forgotten how she treated you all these years?" Elizabeth Carew tried feebly to remind her. "I see that your throat still bears the scar of her wrath that day."

Instinctively, Jane reached up to press her fingers to her neck as she scanned the faces of her friends, deeply feeling the cataclysm that neared.

"And remember what happened in France all those years ago," Thomas put in with a note of support for the others' sentiments.

You remembered me not at all from when we were children in France, did you? she thought bitterly then of her rival. Jane had worn the scar since that time as one of the many things that had hardened her. But even now, was she hard enough for what lay ahead?

"You cannot lose your courage now," added Francis. "Not when you have come so far."

The crash of her conscience, the pressure and guilt, were almost too much to bear. And suddenly, out of the blue, she knew she must see William. The need called to her. He was here with Cromwell. She was certain of it.

As everyone whispered together, two liveried servants came to stoke a fresh fire. Jane went to Francis and drew him away to the window.

"He is here with Master Cromwell, is he not?" she asked softly, knowing he knew whom she meant. "I need to see him, cousin . . . privately."

"There'll not be much time," he warned in a tone so low only she could have heard.

"Then I shall take what I can gratefully," Jane said.

They could outrun the moment, but not the future.

Jane and William knew it as they embraced desperately inside the hidden grotto down a short, wooded trail that had been built by Nicholas's father. It was a place of which few knew, and where no one would disturb them. Their time would be brief. Francis had warned them. But like a drowning man grasping at straws, William clung to Jane desperately, kissing one cheek tenderly and then the other. Their lives had paralleled each other's for so long. Now, not only Jane but William could see that in the distance their paths were about to diverge forever.

"She is dead." Jane murmured the words painfully, sinking against him as if somehow he could shield her, take her into him, and keep her there, safe from harm, safe from the future.

"I know. But they say it was quick. He brought a swordsman from France."

"'Tis so violently horrid. He sent me here to have me out of the way until it was over. He did not need to do it that way." Jane began to weep. "Cromwell got the annulment from Archbishop Cranmer . . . She could have gone to France. She did not need to die!"

"The king is a man, though, Jane," William tenderly tried to explain in a soothing tone. "And you must know that his pride was wounded. How could a man not avenge that much flagrant infidelity?"

"If ever she was unfaithful . . . I was in her company often, William, and yes she bantered with them and smiled at them. God knows I did not like Anne Boleyn, but I do not believe her guilty of the crimes for which she has been executed. Now I am to take her place, two days hence! What if he finds fault with me next? What if he learns about *you*?"

"That would be impossible," William said, but his smile was a grim line in his impeccably handsome face. "He loves you, Jane. As do I. And I always will."

They sank onto the edge of the iron bench at the grotto's center, their arms still wrapped around each other. He touched her then in an intimate way, as if they had been the lovers both had always hoped to become. He ran a hand gently down her neck to the crease between her breasts, which the new fashion of her dress formed. His fingertips lingered there on her warm, smooth skin, and Jane did not move or object. She wanted this, and so much more. But there was no future for them, only a long, disappointing past of *almosts*.

"You know, I used to daydream about our children, and in my mind our daughter always looked fair and gentle, just like you," he said achingly.

"Poor dear," Jane tried to jest, though her heart was broken.

"Her name was always Jane. Jane Dormer," he whispered tenderly, and she saw his eyes glisten with tears as he leaned over and kissed her.

"You'll not be able to do that again after today, or we shall both end up like Anne and those men," she said, touching her lips.

"I know you are right, but my heart resists believing. As it has resisted for so many years. I would have married you, Jane," he murmured pleadingly. "I would marry you right now."

"I spent my life wanting to be your wife. That will never change."

This time, it was Jane who kissed him with all of the wild abandon she felt. She pressed William's hand into the bosom of her gown until she felt him arch with restrained passion. She moved her own fingers down to his codpiece and let them linger there, touching the part of him she would never fully have. She tasted his desire.

I, Jane, have known great love . . .

"Be happy, Jane," he said achingly as he drew her hand from his codpiece and pressed it to his lips for what she knew was the last time.

"I would settle for remaining alive, which may prove more difficult to achieve than I previously had thought," she tried to joke, but there was truth to her words that neither could deny.

"He'll not harm you, or he shall have Sir William Dormer to contend with," he declared on a boastful little smile, belying what she knew was true heartbreak at the end of something so enduring.

They were interrupted then by the trumpets' blare, the jangle of heavy silver harnesses, and the thunder of galloping horses fast approaching the manor along the trail outside of the grotto. The king had arrived.

So had the end of their story.

William kissed her again, and she tasted the salt of his tears, along with her own.

"Promise when you are Queen of England that you'll not forget the country lad who once saved you from drowning at the edge of a little pond."

"I could never forget the other half of me," she murmured as she softly wept.

Outside, just beyond their temporary little haven, a sentry called out the king's arrival. She could hear Henry's deep, throaty laughter and that of his companions who followed. They both could. It belonged to the man who had sealed their fate.

Epilogue

October 24, 1537
Hampton Court

*A*nne Seymour had tears in her eyes. The candle lamps made them glisten like jewels as they fell along her cheeks in ribbons. "Was that the last time you ever saw him?"

"Of course," Jane answered weakly from beneath the pile of satiny bedcovers, a defeated little thing with gray skin and hollow eyes. She barely resembled Jane, Queen of England, mother of the king's heir, their twelve-day-old son, Edward. "William is too much a gentleman to ever attempt to see me. I saw him and Lady Dormer together at a distance last Michaelmas, but he never approached me after that day in the grotto. You really are the only living soul who knows the entire story."

"I would've thought your brother Thomas—"

"He never knew the end of it. To be honest, I no longer trust Thomas or Edward, especially after the death of the king's son, poor Fitzroy. Thomas swore to me he was not involved, but I knew how afraid he was that Mistress Blount's son would end up as heir to the throne before I could produce a rival. We Seymours were raised to do our duty fully," she said bitterly. Fatigued from speaking, Jane closed her eyes for a moment. As she did, her mind filled with the colors and images she liked the most, those carefree early days at Wolf Hall before fate had yet to claim her . . .

Her sister would be here to care for her son. Edward and Anne as well. For Jane was dying; she knew that. She could feel the life draining out of her from the very moment she had given life to her son. She knew, somehow, that Edward was meant to live, and even as she faced her own final breath, she was glad. She had paid an enormous price for it, but Jane had done what neither Katherine of Aragon nor Anne Boleyn could do in more than twenty-eight years. She had given Henry VIII a legal son and heir.

"Read me that passage one more time from Thomas à Kempis, would you? It will comfort me, Anne."

Anne Seymour picked up the volume on the queen's bedside table and opened it to the page marked with a ribbon. "Love is swift, sincere, pious, joyful, generous, strong, patient, faithful, prudent, long-suffering, courageous and never seeking its own; for wherever a person seeks his own, there he falleth from love."

There was a calm smile on her face now. "I want you to keep this story I have told you, and lock it away for someday after Hal and I are both gone. After William and Mary have left this earth as well. 'Tis too beautiful to be lost to the ages." Jane drew in a shallow, labored breath. "Tell me, Anne, how does it begin again?"

Anne Seymour wiped the cloud of tears from her eyes with the back of her hand and drew in a deep breath. "It begins, *I, Jane* . . ."

Author's Note

Sixteen months after her marriage to Henry VIII, and the birth of Edward VI, Jane Seymour died on October 24, 1537, at Hampton Court Palace. The few details of her connection to William Dormer that exist today were told, not by Jane and William themselves, but by the daughter of William and Mary Dormer in a book called *Life of Jane Dormer*. William did serve Thomas Cromwell while Jane Seymour was at court, and his eldest daughter was indeed named Jane. Details beyond that of what truly happened between Jane and William shall remain a mystery locked to the ages.

Photo by Alexander C. Haeger

Diane Haeger is the author of several novels of historical and women's fiction. She has a degree in English literature and an advanced degree in clinical psychology, which she credits with helping her bring to life complicated characters and their relationships. She lives in Newport Beach, California, with her husband and children.

I, Jane

DIANE HAEGER

QUESTIONS
FOR DISCUSSION

1. Prior to reading *I, Jane*, what were your perceptions of Jane Seymour as an historical figure? Were those perceptions mostly formed by the many biographies of Henry VIII or by popular culture (i.e., miniseries, movies, or television)? How, if at all, were those perceptions changed or perhaps expanded by reading the novel?

2. Discuss how Jane's relationship with Sir Francis Bryan evolves throughout Jane's life. Why do you think he felt such a deep and lasting connection to her? Why did he elect to try to help her with William several times in spite of the odds against their romance?

3. History tells us that Jane Seymour was a meek and plain-faced woman. For William Dormer, what do you think were the characteristics that set Jane apart from the more beautiful and wealthy eligible women of his day? Why do you think he felt such an indelible connection to a woman he did not frequently see?

4. For many years, Jane found Henry VIII's behavior and personality largely repugnant, although she was bound to engage with him as a member of the court, which ultimately drew him

to her. Why do you think Jane eventually allowed herself to soften toward the king? Do you think she compromised her principles? Or do you believe she truly came to care for Henry VIII by the end of her life and saw it as a kind of giving in to fate?

5. Jane was witness to Henry VIII's first two tumultuous marriages, including his open cruelty to both women, as well as the tragic end to each union. Her loyalty was tied to Katherine of Aragon and she was deeply affected by the queen's fate. Do you think Jane believed she could be different for Henry or was she simply resigned to her destiny?

6. Since each woman managed to captivate the same man, discuss the ways in which Jane Seymour was like Katherine of Aragon and Anne Boleyn. In what ways were they different from one another? For example, do you believe each woman truly loved the king? Do you believe even Jane Seymour could be considered ambitious?

7. In the novel, Sir Francis Bryan is unable to get William's impassioned letter to Jane due to his jousting accident. Do you believe William and Jane should have fought harder to be together, or was the lack of a letter enough of an impediment?

8. In the novel, William Dormer marries Mary Sidney in order to save Wolf Hall for the Seymour family. Did you find that

act heroic? Do you believe there was some element of self-preservation in it? Do you think William should have fought for Jane by confronting the prospect of his own poverty and allowed the Seymours to face their own financial crisis?

9. Before their marriage, Jane knew that Henry had ordered five men executed for crimes which she doubted any of them had committed with Anne Boleyn. Jane had already seen the lengths to which he was willing to go to be rid of a queen with Katherine of Aragon. How do you think Jane rationalized marrying a man capable of such rage and violence? Do you believe she was in awe of his position? Or did she truly care for Henry, the man?

10. If Jane had not died in childbirth, do you think her marriage would have endured? If not, would it only have been Henry's wandering eye and general discontent in relationships that separated them? Do you believe Jane and William would have found their way back to each other later in life?